Annie felt the heat grow in her body and knew that she had to communicate its intensity to Vicky soon. Then Victoria's eyes closed and she lowered her head. They turned toward one another slowly. Annie waited for Victoria to lift her head and say something, but when she did look up, she said nothing, only looked with glazed eyes at Annie. "Do you want me to let go?" Annie asked hoarsely. Victoria bit her lower lip and shook her head, moving her long hair across her shoulders. The longer they stood, holding hands, the more the crowd seemed to recede. Electrical charges, Annie thought, going up and down our arms, across our hands. Melting, my arm is melting down into her hand, Victoria thought in sudden panic, but kept herself perfectly still, as if the welding were accomplished.

TOOTHPICK HOUSE

A NOVEL BY HOUSE

LEE LYNCH

THE NAIAD PRESS INC.

1986

Printed in the United States of America
First Edition
Second Printing March, 1986

Cover design by Tee A. Corinne

Typesetting by Sandi Stancil

Library of Congress Cataloging in Publication Data

Lynch, Lee, 1945–
    Toothpick House.

    I. Title.
PS3562.Y426T6 1983   813'.54   83-4093
ISBN 0-930044-45-2

For

Deborah Pascale

I thank Debbie Pascale for sharing her life with me as I wrote *Toothpick House*, and for the great patience and strength she offered me throughout.

I also thank Barbara Grier for believing in me these fifteen years; Caroline Overman for being my "stylistic conscience;" Tee Corinne for her enormous support and inspiration; Michele Cliff and Adrienne Rich for suggesting I could write this novel and giving me direction; Carol Feiden, Judy Sloan and Carol for their help with the first draft; and Linda Anderson for typing.

ABOUT THE AUTHOR

Lee Lynch has been writing wonderful short stories for fifteen years. They have appeared in a number of movement periodicals, *The Ladder, Sinister Wisdom*, and *Common Lives/Lesbian Lives* and in the anthology, *The Lesbians Home Journal*. *Toothpick House* is her first novel. A collection of her stories, tentatively titled *Old Dyke Tales* and a second novel, *The Swashbuckler*, will be published in the near future. The photograph of Lee Lynch on the back cover is by Tee Corinne. The ring in the photograph is the ring referred to in the letter below.

In the years since I've been out, I've worn many women's rings. Among others, I've kept the U.S. Navy ring that never fit, a twist of wire given me by an artist, and a signet pinky ring.

I still wear a pinky ring as a connection to my old gay past, a signal to other lesbians, a part of our language. My lover and I have worn the plain silver bands that signify our commitment to each other for eleven years now.

Last year I added Kady's ring. One she made, heavy with silver, its labyris like a shining stamp of courage resting on a background dark with soldering anger. I "traded up" to it from a smaller, less potent ring—as she predicted I would. The ring is so loud it took me months to wear all the time.

I call it my power ring and wear it on the index finger of my right hand. A finger I use in writing, pointing, making love, accusing, guiding tools, beckoning and admonishing. The finger I use now to display my ring so it stands out like a statement.

from a letter to "The Inciter"

CHAPTER ONE

Annie Heaphy walked along the beach, picking up flat stones. Fog horns sounded their hoarse, lonely cries while the morning haze began to lift under one of the last hot suns of fall. Annie, oh Annie, she hummed to herself, when you going to come to rest, when you going to lay down your nasty habits, your hassling, hustling job and feel good? She stooped to pick up a stone that caught her eye at the edge of the water, then skipped it across the surface only once before it fell in. Sighing, she looked back toward her tiny home, the battered beach-house that was her root as well as her fragile shelter from the world. Peeled and stripped by salt and wind, it looked from a distance to be no more than a bundle of delicate sticks propped tentatively against one another. It was as bare, as barren as the three lonely willows leaning into the curve of the beach road beside it.

Mornings on the beach, her clearest time of day, Annie Heaphy marched off the nightmare of the day before. All day she drove her heavy yellow cab, at night she met her friends in bars. Only in the mornings could she expel it all and take in new fresh air off Long Island Sound. Now she skipped another stone across the waves, wishing she, too, would be rewarded after centuries of smoothing by this graceful flight over the waters. "*And in me the wave rises,*" she chanted aloud as another pebble faltered, then skipped once. Taking careful aim, Annie squinted toward the little waves. "*It swells, it arches its back.*" The stone flew twice before it fell. "*I am aware once more of a new desire . . . ,*" she offered as she skimmed another stone three times across the surface of the rippling water.

Annie Heaphy glanced at her watch and threw one last

1

stone, her spirits lifting when it too skipped three times. She turned again toward her home, her short yellow hair standing up as the wind blew her cap off. Sweeping the cap up absently from the sand she began to run with a long, slow stride until she reached the Volkswagen in her front yard. The shack next door went alive with radios and kids slamming doors. It sounded like back home to her, and she missed momentarily the crowded Chelsea section of Boston. She turned the car key and swung backwards onto the beach road, her muffler shot, leaves settling in her wake. Her house stood alone against the will of the wind and the waves. The foghorns went on, as if they were the voice of the house itself, telling its story.

~ ~ ~ ~ ~

"Hiya, Annie."

"Hiya, hiya."

"Number forty-seven today, Annie. Get moving on that rush hour." The dispatcher put his cigar back in his mouth and chewed on it thoughtfully.

"Is it gassed, Mr. G.?"

Mr. G. scratched his stomach, shouted an order into his mike and grinned, "Sure beats the hell out of me, tomboy."

Annie aimed a series of punches at him. "When you going to get rid of that cigar, Mr. G.? It stinks."

"Soon's you take off that dirty old hat, kid."

"Never!" Annie shouted back as she ran down the stairs and into the yard. She went up and down the rows of cabs until she spotted number 47 and climbed in, relieved it was ready to go. She set her cap toward the back of her head and called in. "Ready and rolling, Mr. G. Thanks for giving me this crate again."

"Hey, forty-seven, you got no gratitude? Least you got brakes today."

"No thanks to you, buddy."

"For that you got to Branford, three-thirty Oakdale. For seven-thirty."

"That gives me minus two minutes."

"Better hurry, kid."

"Got you." Annie settled into her routine. After a young

mother with twins, a no-show in the ghetto, a businessman who tipped her well and two Yalies who angered her when they tipped her with all six cents of their spare change, Annie picked up an elderly woman. The midmorning sun was warm and she relaxed as the woman talked. Annie looked at her in her rearview mirror and remembered her own grandmother, Nana Heaphy, sitting in an easy chair in her mother's house, smiling and nodding at everything that went on. Like this woman, she wore dark, silky dresses. When she shopped for them with the aunts, there was a chattering and a nagging at the poor woman until you would think they were competing for a prize. It must have been even harder for her father than for the aunts. Never able to get a word in, he had become a taciturn, scowling man, unable to compete with his sisters. In contrast, Annie's mother was so blonde and quiet she must have seemed like an oasis to him. All the aunts had brown, crimped hair and were, like Nana Heaphy, short. As Annie grew up she saw them widen and grey. Her mother moved among them aloof and young-looking.

The aunts said her mother put on airs and warned Annie not to be like her, but to emulate Nana, her namesake. "It's good to be proud," Aunt Lily would say, "but remember your family is the salt of the earth, dear." Annie resented their intimations. She looked a cross between both her parents, with their blue eyes, her mother's straight, blonde hair and smooth, pale skin, and her father's playful Irish features, full of dimples and a hint of baby fat. Annie wasn't tall, but she was not as short as the aunts and would never let herself widen like them. Salt of the earth was all right, but it was not her ambition. If it was airs she had, then let them disapprove.

Annie Heaphy liked fine things and admired people of a slightly higher class. She didn't put the aunts down, or perhaps she had when she was younger, but now she was twenty-two. She saw them seldom, and no longer felt she was betraying them when she went to a museum or a concert. Still, the aunts walked in her and pulled her down. Else why had she quit college? Why was she driving a cab? Why did she hang around with low-life dykes in a bar? Something was holding her back. She wondered if it was a combination of her heritage and her gayness. Her family set limits on her ambitions, her sexuality made her socially unacceptable. Dykes weren't welcome anywhere unless they dressed in sheep's clothing; Annie was only comfortable in wolf's clothing. All the rest of the morning in the cab she pondered it, hardly noticing who she drove where. A hunger pang in her stomach made her pull over.

She counted her tips and decided to treat herself to a Chinese lunch at a nearby restaurant. Annie gave her order and headed for the bathroom. As she was washing, another woman came to the door and stopped, gasping audibly. Here we go again, Annie said to herself, shrinking inside.

"This is a ladies' room, sir," the woman said indignantly.

Annie turned to her and glared. "I know," she said.

The woman flushed when she heard Annie's obviously female voice. "I'm *so* sorry. I thought you were a, a . . . ," she faltered.

"I know what you thought," Annie replied scornfully and walked out shaking, not wanting to wait for her order, ready to cry. She ground her teeth in hatred as she looked around the restaurant and saw all the straight people comfortable in their world. The woman from the bathroom returned to her table and animatedly described what had happened to her, looking all the while for Annie. Her companion craned his neck to stare. Annie wanted to kill, to rip and tear the restaurant apart. Then she noticed a small, very old Chinese woman through the kitchen door. The grandmother, she knew from previous visits. She remembered again her own grandmother and felt calmer as she watched the little woman intently making the next day's wontons. Glad her eyes had rested on her, she turned back to find the straight couple had gone. Through the window she saw them entering a Yale building across the street. She hated Yalies. Like the two in her cab that morning, they were snobbish, self-centered and did not live in her world, the real world. She walked to her cab feeling vindicated that she had upset the smug life of a Yalie, but she wondered while she ate if she wasn't somehow jealous of them. She could have stayed in school and made something of herself as they were doing. Annie finished her lunch and drove off, wondering for the thousandth time what she would do with her life.

∿ ∿ ∿ ∿ ∿

A doorman opened the heavy, polished wooden doors to Victoria Locke's apartment building. "The last of their kind," he told Victoria once more. "Everyone's putting in those glass doors. Easier to keep up. Myself, I like to keep them small panes of glass sparkling like your eyes, Miss, when you was a little one. Of all the little tenants you was the best, the prettiest. Now I hear you're the smartest. You'll be graduating Yale this year won't you?"

"In the spring, Dennis. And you know it's not hard to be best when there aren't any left but me," Victoria smiled down to the bent old man.

"Well, then I'm glad it's you that's left, because you always was my favorite."

Victoria stepped through the door onto the worn red runner. She would have liked to sit in the lobby and listen to Dennis as she had when she was small. Once in a while she had been able to elude her mother long enough to hear about the tenants who had lived there during his reign as handyman and later when he worked his way up to doorman. She wondered if Dennis understood her appreciation of him or if her shy wordlessness made him think she was becoming as condescending as her mother. She tried to smile warmly at him, but knew it looked like a pained grimace.

"She's gone shopping, your ma," he told her. "Should be back any time now," he assured her. Victoria didn't want to hear another lecture from her mother on keeping up appearances, so she turned her back on the faded brown leather chairs in the lobby with their frayed patches and cracks, the bowl on the lace-covered table which had once held fresh flowers every day.

Victoria went toward the sixth floor in the elevator whose wooden walls and brass handrails shone under Dennis' polish. Amazing old man, she thought. I would be as loyal as he is if I had anything to which I could be loyal. She shifted her suitcase and smoothed the top of her long, wavy light brown hair. She left the elevator and faced a mirror hanging in the hall. There she was: two flat triangles of cheeks, a broad, rectangular forehead, a long nose almost sharply pointed at its tip. Her eyes were perfect almonds in the angles, the same light brown and shape. Prettiest I am not, she thought. But probably the most primped in the building. Her mother had brushed her hair a hundred strokes a night until she was old enough to do it herself and she had never been allowed to wear her glasses in public. Even today, the last Thanksgiving break she would have from Yale, she had her glasses well hidden in a case in the pocket of her camel's hair coat. Her mother said they would make her narrow nose more so and would emphasize her full lips. It took going away to Yale, where she transferred her junior year, before she learned to wear them.

Victoria turned toward her parents' apartment feeling a chill of anxiety. She had stopped wearing makeup this semester and her mother would not like that either, but without it Victoria felt much better. More like herself as a child, she thought as she turned the key, remembering how a maid used to open the door to her as she returned home each day from her private school across Central Park. The maid's name was Heidi and, as in the children's book, she had long blonde hair rolled on top of her head, pale skin, and clothes she had brought with her from France where she lived near Switzerland. She was hired for three reasons and thus, Mrs. Locke had rationalized, was a bargain. She cleaned and did some cooking, she spoke French so Victoria could practice, and the family could refer to its "help." Heidi left after several years to marry and Mrs. Locke thought her terribly ungrateful. Victoria was not allowed to show grief over the loss of a maid, but she still remembered the empty feeling.

All this nostalgia must be because graduation is so near, she thought. Still she wished she could see Heidi again as she opened the door to high ceilings, large windows and sunny rooms. She set down her suitcase and took a good look at the living room which opened from the foyer. The furniture had been there since the Lockes moved in. It was an inheritance from Mrs. Locke's family. Old-fashioned pieces, all in a style the name of which Victoria fought remembering because her mother boasted of it so often. Elegant, her mother called it. She sighed. Her poor mother, never able to replace it because they didn't have the money to buy the quality on which she insisted, almost never asked anyone to dinner anymore. It is an empty address, Victoria thought, a hollow, pretentious, fancy address.

She walked to the window, half-covered with heavy brocade draperies, and looked across the park. At least she still has this. She can still say, "My view."

"Ah," Mrs. Locke said coming in the front door and startling Victoria. "My Yale senior is home. I've just come from Bonwit's. They were having such a wonderful sale and I got so many Christmas presents. You'll be impressed with yours."

Victoria, bored with the prospect of another unwearable tea dress, accepted her mother's quick kiss on the cheek. "How are you, Mother?" She asked as she had been trained to do.

"Exhausted. We went to the theatre last night and saw something awful off-Broadway. I'll never be lured off Broadway again and would recommend that you beware too. No taste, Victoria, none," she clucked as Victoria hung her coat in the foyer closet. "I see those flannels are holding up. That's a good girl. Make them last."

"The zipper doesn't work well." Victoria showed her mother as she turned.

"And you wore them like that? Oh, my dear, what if someone had seen you? I'll take that to the tailor's in the morning. Meanwhile, freshen up and dress for dinner. I'll change and make the cocktails. Your father will be home very shortly."

Victoria took her suitcase to her room and unpacked the books. She carried few clothes as her wardrobe at school, though conservative, was still not one her mother would approve. She turned on the light at her desk and fingered the expensive desk set sent her at high school graduation by her aunt and uncle whom she saw once a year at Christmas. Already I feel hemmed in, she thought. If she weren't so frightened of her parents she would enjoy New York, but she might as well live on a desert island for all she knew of the city around her. The libraries, the museums, theatres, concert halls: they were her city. Not the expensive stores in which she could shop only when there were sales and the park she could visit only with a companion. She used to date not because she liked any of those preppy, well-scrubbed boys at high school, but because she might see something of the city with them. Well, it's only two days, she comforted herself, tripping on the skirt around her vanity. "Damned useless piece of furniture," she whispered when she heard it rip. "More moaning about how much it'll cost to get sewed or replaced." She looked through her desk for something to patch it, closed her door and lay on her back with a stapler to reach the tear. When she surveyed her handi-work she felt proud of herself and resourceful, though she knew she would be chastised if her mother found it. Glue might have been less obvious, she thought. Her discomfort increased as she changed into the clothing she was unused to wearing. She heard the clink of glasses down the hall and knew it was time to play at cocktail party with her parents. Not feeling able to invite guests to their home, they treated their family like guests.

Later, Victoria could not remember what they had talked about and she wondered if her father was drinking that much every night now. She climbed into bed weary with boredom and took up a book of fables by La Fontaine which she had been translating. She returned to a favorite and reread what she had underlined: " 'They chain you up?' the wolf said. 'Can't you run/ Just where you like?' 'Not always, what's it matter?' 'It matters this: with all your feasts I've done./ You have 'em. You grow fatter./ At such a price I value life as nil.'/ Thus said, the wolf ran off, is running still." Ah, to run off, Victoria thought, remembering her childhood when a favorite game was just that. Her mother would take her to Central Park and she would slip away from where she read on a bench and go to her favorite group of rocks. She vividly remembered running up and down the rocks and hiding behind them to play games with other children. Her mother despaired of curing her from playing with the "park youngsters" and Victoria bathed in the memories for days after each escapade. Eventually, her mother would not be able to resist a warm, sunny day in the park and would lead her there again for what she came to think of as her real, true adventures.

Victoria drew the covers over her chin and stretched her legs under the soft worn sheets. She turned off the lights and brought her pillow down to her arms where she hugged it. Someday, she hoped, she would be hugging more than a pillow. A real person would be there and they would go everywhere together. But not some straight-laced snob like her parents wanted her to marry. A free spirit. Someone unlike anyone she had ever known. And a good friend as well as a lover. Her depression settled over her again. Here I am dreaming like a little girl, she thought. By this time in my life I should know what I want. Rosemary wants to teach. Claudia wants to be a psychiatrist. All the seniors seem to know their futures. I want—something. A something and a someone. A wolf in a fable, a real life. She dropped deeper toward sleep, and woke from a half-dream along a path in Central Park with Heidi. I'd forgotten that, she thought. No wonder I loved to play in the park. I wonder how many times I went there with Heidi. Her hair shone like sunlight. Victoria hugged her pillow closer as she fell asleep with a bright light in her eyes.

$$\sim \ \sim \ \sim \ \sim \ \sim$$

By the end of the day Annie Heaphy was sinking, with the daylight, into darkness. Her depression grew with fatigue and the rush hour seemed too hectic to keep up with. She took her cab back to the garage and went to the bar where she accepted a beer as she would a savior. No one was there yet, but she knew Peg and Turkey would be watching out their window across the street for her car. The owner Marcy, sixty, bleached-blonde, bulging in a tight skirt, leaned her elbows backwards on the bar.

"How are you today, sweetheart?" Marcy asked in her hoarse, loud voice.

"Pretty good, Marcy."

Marcy began her daily complaints. "I blew close to a grand souping this place up. And you think you ungrateful kids bring me more money? No! Tabs," she said, fanning a stack of them at Annie.

"Not mine," Annie defended herself.

"No, you're a good kid. But some of these, I don't know."

Annie winked at Rudy behind the bar. "How's Ellie today after that barrelful she put away last night?"

"Still love-sick," Rudy whined in his camp voice. "Barfed all night long, then first thing this morning, *before* going to the restaurant, mind you, she's playing all these hot songs on the stereo. I can't stand it."

"After *that* brush-off she's still got her sights set on Dusty?"

Rudy nodded, then leaned across the bar to Annie. "It took me and George *both* to get her up the stairs."

"Thank goodness she lives with you two, not me."

"Don't do me any favors." Rudy flicked his bar rag at her.

"Who's Dusty?" Marcy asked from behind the bar where she poured herself a soda.

"A big hunk of diesel-dyke, honey," Rudy answered.

"Don't know what she sees in her," Annie said. "Except she's got a good job and plenty of money."

"Don't put your nose up, Mabel, she owns her own place."

"How'd you find that out, Rude?"

"One afternoon, none of you girls was here, she practically told me her life story. She's not so bad."

"Hey, here come two tabs," Marcy pointed out the window.

Rudy rolled his eyes at Annie.

"Ain't you spiffed," Annie called as she hurried to the figures coming through the door. She hugged them both at once, whispering, "Scrooge is on the warpath."

"Shit," Turkey exclaimed, stomping a heavy black boot on the linoleum. "I was hoping to put more on my tab."

"You were going to treat?" Peg and Annie teased her at the same time.

"Not me!" laughed Marieanne Concetta D'Alessio, smoothing the tight, wavy hair that rose to a thick crest like a turkey's at the top of her head, then grew almost flat down to her neck. She was broader at the hips than at the shoulders and wore white jeans, red suspenders and a large, short-sleeved men's white shirt. Peg, taller and narrow, in shape from teaching physical education, stood gracefully at Turkey's side in flannels and blazer, her hair thick and sculpted around her head.

Peg led them to a booth, sheltering them from Marcy, and brought them beer.

In the back door Eleanor posed, calling, "Hi, y'all!" until she was sure she had been seen. They laughed as she sashayed toward them, her short white waitress apron tied like a scarf around her long, thick brown hair, and her discount house white sneakers pointing their way across the floor. She threw herself at Annie Heaphy and kissed her on the lips. "My darlings, I've missed you so much."

"You didn't even know we were alive last night, miss," Peg scolded her.

"It's good for me, girl. A little drunk never hurt anyone."

"You should know," Turkey guffawed.

"So should you," countered Eleanor.

"So should we all," sighed Annie.

"Want a beer?" asked Turkey.

"Me?" Eleanor pointed to herself. "Why, I'll never drink again."

Annie looked at her speculatively. "Then how about a Southern Comfort on the rocks?"

"My hero!" Eleanor exclaimed, hugging Annie again.

"Ever notice she can't keep her hands off you, Heaphy?" Peg asked.

"Only when they're not on you."

"Cut it out, you butchy things, and tell me what I did last night. Did I carry on?"

Peg laid a hand on her arm. "Do you remember *why* you carried on?" she asked gently.

"Sure. That nasty old Dusty didn't want nothing to do with me last night. I thought it was the end of the world. But remember what they say," she raised her glass, "when at first you don't succeed . . . ."

"Now you just have to convince Dusty," Annie said.

"That'll just take time. I know she's the woman for me and what's more, I'm the woman for her. I haven't met anyone I like so much since I left Tennessee."

Turkey winked. "Seems to me I've heard that before."

"But this time I'm sure. She's real handsome, don't you all think?" The others looked around the table at one another. "Well?" Eleanor insisted.

"If you like that type," Annie replied diplomatically.

"She's down to earth," Turkey helped, then looked at Peg.

Peg started. "I like her d.a."

"Ah, you guys just don't appreciate a good woman when you see one. Look how you never appreciated me. No wonder

I'm turning to someone else's arms."

"Alright, southern belle, we get the message," Annie chuckled.

"Going to do something about it?" Eleanor asked teasingly. "No."

"Oh, you. You'll see, all of you. When I ever saw that full moon up there in the daytime sky I said, this is it, El, you ravishing femme. Tonight's the night. My mama always said you can get what you want at the full moon. We lived in the city, but she grew up in the country and knew the country ways. That's why she liked it when Pa was off in the truck at the full moon. She liked to get what she wanted, but she didn't want him to get what he wanted. And you know what he wanted."

"You saying it runs in the family, El?" Turkey asked coyly.

"What?" Peg laughed. "Getting what they want?"

Turkey shook her head. "Not liking men."

Eleanor responded with pride in her voice. "Sure does. My Mama's been warning me about bad men since I was a baby. Only trouble is, she never did mention where I could find me a *good* man. And I just never bothered looking for one."

"Mine was the same way," Peg said. "She was always telling me scare stories about men stealing little girls or about boys trying to 'get away with' things. It's like some mothers get the message across stronger to stay away from men than to love them. They can't seem to help warning us even though at the same time they're trying to teach us to devote our lives to men."

"And we're the lucky ones who listened," Annie concluded.

"Except," Turkey said sadly, "they can't face how good we listened to them."

Eleanor looked proud again. "Mine did, she took it real well," Eleanor said. "I just walked in the door with Butch . . . ," she broke off at the sounds of protesting laughter. "What's the matter with 'Butch?' That's what we called her, honest to God. She was my second steady girlfriend. This was when I got out of reform school and Mama was around for a while. Butch was twenty-five; I was still a lot younger. She was the tallest, skinniest, butchiest looking girl, wore a string tie and all when she could.

I brought her home one day and said, 'Ma, Butch is staying over with me tonight.' "

"Mama looked Butch up and down like she did the boys my big sister used to bring home and said, 'Just don't you be taken her downtown drinken and getten in trouble with the law.' "

" 'No, Ma'am,' Butch smirked, I can see her now, 'I aim to stay right here with El. Guess we'll find enough to do without goin' looken for trouble.' Butch was from the country like Mama and they took to each other good from the start. Butch and me would go in my room for hours and come out to get food Mama left hot on the stove for us. Sometimes Butch would come over when I was in school and sit and talk with Mama all afternoon. I swear if Pa wasn't in and out of there I might have lost Butch to Mama.

"But meantime, I've found my own true love, the first girl I'd even think about taking home to Mama since I came up here to find a better job. Least I found Dusty even if I couldn't find the job." She looked at the clock over the bar. "I've got to go home and change! Where will you all be?"

"On the fateful nght that Ellie made a fool of herself again," Peg pronounced, "the meeting was held: downtown at the Pub?"

"Do you think she'll be out two nights in a row, El?" Turkey asked.

"It's two-for-one night at the Pub," Annie remembered.

"Then that's where we'll all be whether Dusty is or not," Turkey predicted.

Peg kissed Eleanor's hand. "She'd better be saving her money if she's going to support this girl's tastes."

"You're so right," Eleanor beamed, getting up to leave. "See you all down there."

"Speaking of later, we'd better get something in our stomachs besides booze," Peg suggested. "Who's for pizza? I'm buying."

"Me, teacher!" Turkey shouted, waving her arm.

"How about you, Heaphy, want to come up for pizza?"

Annie thought of her empty house. "Sure, Peglet, thanks. It's easier than going home and coming back."

They waved to Rudy. "You just get our little girl home safe

tonight," he warned.

"If we don't she'll be safe in Dusty's clutches!"

"Heaven help us!" Rudy shouted out to them as the door slammed on their small and safe bar world. Peg went to get pizza while Turkey and Annie hurried to the apartment to set the table. A group of young boys moved toward them.

"Annie, let's cross the street now."

Annie looked at the group. "They're too young to bother us."

Turkey looked up at Annie, frowning. "Maybe you're right."

Looking at the group again, Annie noticed it had gone quiet. They were staring at Annie and Turkey. The two exchanged glances. "But then, I could be wrong." Annie conceded, guiding Turkey by the elbow to the street. As they crossed catcalls followed them. They looked at one another when they heard the word "lezzies." "But they're too young to think like that, Turkey."

Turkey slammed a fist against her other hand. "They're never too young, Annie. It's crowd behavior. Makes them feel even stronger to reinforce the identity of the crowd by oppressing those they see as weaker than themselves."

"Can the sociology, let's get inside," Annie said, moving them off the stoop of the building and through the front door. They ran to the third floor of the old house and Annie sat on the top step. "Doesn't it make you feel kind of cowardly to run like this?"

"No. It's their weakness which creates these situations, not ours." Turkey unlocked her door and turned to squat next to Annie, putting her short arms around her. "Annie, baby, you got to stop letting this get to you. Our lives are going to be hard enough without wasting energy on those little shits."

"Me? You're still red in the face."

"That's just from holding my breath waiting for you to calm down. See?" Turkey puffed out her cheeks and got redder.

Annie considered tickling her, but heard Peg at the front door. They hurried to find clean plates. "Don't you guys ever do dishes?" Annie asked.

Turkey answered with her usual joke, "Sure, once a month . . ."

". . . whether they need it or not," Peg finished, setting the pizza on the table.

"Smells good," Turkey breathed as she opened the box with a flourish. "Um, my favorite: everything. But what are you guys going to eat?" she laughed.

"Shut up and dish it out, lady," Annie ordered.

Settling down with a slice, Peg asked, "You guys pass those little creeps?"

"Yeah, why?" Turkey asked through a mouthful of pizza.

"Heard them saying, 'There goes another one.' I looked around and there wasn't anyone but me so I figured it out."

"I hate it," Annie said bitterly.

"I felt like going back and punching them out. Or dragging them home and telling their mothers what rude little pigs they are."

"Who do you think taught them?" Turkey asked.

"Wish I had a gun," Annie scowled, no longer eating.

"I'm telling you, Annie, they're not worth all this energy."

"I know. It's just that I get so angry. This one old man wouldn't stay in the cab with me when he realized I was a woman. Do you believe that?"

"Wow. Where's he been?" Peg asked, putting another slice of pizza on Annie's plate.

Annie began to eat absently. "I don't know, but he didn't get any further. He got out of the cab and started yelling that I should at least dress like a girl. And that I'd better tell the company to send someone who knows what he is." Annie set her pizza down and put her head in her hands.

"Heaphy, Heaphy, you going to cry?" Peg asked, full of sympathy, rising and moving to her. When Annie didn't answer she knelt beside her and put her arms around her. "Come on, Heaphy, we can't let them beat us down. I mean, we're the bulldykes! We're the strong ones. We're going to win because we play smart against their dirty pool."

Turkey reached over and grabbed Annie's cap. Annie reached blindly for it. "Nope," Turkey said. "You got to prove your stuff. Earn your cap. Besides, your pizza's getting cold."

Annie smiled up through her tears. "You guys," she said affectionately, shaking her head. "I think I feel this bad about it because I'm just not happy—period. This sure ain't the gay life I imagined. I've got to find a better way to be me. Give me the hat, Turkey, or I'll get my gym teacher to clobber you."

Peg stood and started toward Turkey who fell to her knees, pretending to tremble.

"No, no," Turkey pleaded. "Anything but that. Not a gay gym teacher. Oh, my worst nightmare: being attacked by a girls' gym teacher." She stopped and struggled to her feet. "On the other hand, maybe it was my *best* nightmare."

"Why do we take their shit?" Peg asked.

"What else are we going to do?" Turkey shrugged.

Peg was silent for a moment, brushing off her slacks and straightening their crease. "I've gone to a few women's liberation meetings at Yale."

Turkey stared at her with her mouth open.

"You'll catch flies," Annie said, tossing a piece of crust at Turkey.

"*My* roommate?" Turkey asked. "A libber meeting? Do they let dykes in? I thought they were too scared they'd be called queers."

"They let me in, but they were kind of distant. And it seemed like they wanted to ask all kinds of questions."

"Like what we do in bed?"

"No, Heaphy, it was more like they wanted to . . . ," she paused, embarrassed, "to sleep with me to find that out. Some of them anyway."

"Were they cute?" Turkey asked.

Peg ignored her. "They really believe in what they're doing. In starting daycare centers so women can work; in getting abortion legalized so women have more control of their lives."

Turkey grumbled, "All they got to do is stop sleeping with men."

"Maybe that's next, Turk. But anyway, there were no men at the meeting. And I couldn't help but like them."

Annie shook her head. "But what does that have to do with us?"

"I'm not sure yet, but there's going to be a meeting for gay women soon."

Turkey started clearing the table. "You mean you're not the only one crazy enough to get mixed up with libbers?"

"I guess not. They were saying that we're already feminists in a sense because we love women. They think they can learn something from us. So I was thinking of telling them what happens on the streets. How acting like we don't want men scares people. I don't understand it yet, but it's all sloshing around inside my head."

"Speaking of sloshing," Turkey said, slamming the refrigerator door, "who's for more beer?" She handed it around and proposed a toast. "To the Peg. Who's beginning to understand what I've been saying all along!"

"Oh, I know all your theories, Turkey, but this seems more real. This is about you and me and poor Heaphy who got emotionally beat up today."

Annie Heaphy scratched her head under its hat and mused aloud. "I don't know, Peg. I don't know if I want to think about it all. I'd rather build a little shack on an island and not let anybody but dykes live there." She straightened her cap and looked into her beer.

"I think that's what the libbers are talking about. Only they're saying we're already on an island and when a lot more women join us we can have the rest of the world too."

"I don't know," Annie repeated, shaking her head slowly. "Sounds very hard to me."

∿ ∿ ∿ ∿ ∿

The train rolled out of the Stamford station. An older woman bustled into the seat next to Victoria. As soon as she was settled, the woman peered into Victoria's face and asked her name. Victoria told her and put down the book which had been boring her.

"I'm Louise. Louise Barshov," the older woman said. "I'm

very pleased to meet you Victoria. Are you always called that?''

"Yes," Victoria smiled. "I prefer it. How far will you be travelling?"

"All the way to Providence, I'm afraid," the woman said, pulling knitting out of a bag and beginning to click her needles wth the sounds of the train. "Do you go to school in Boston?"

"No, New Haven. I was home for Thanksgiving. Am I that obviously a student?"

"My oldest daughter when she was in school," Louise offered after extracting a photo from one of the shopping bags at her feet.

"We could be sisters, couldn't we?" Victoria asked, shaken by the similarity of the daughter to herself.

"Then yes. Not now," Louise answered brusquely.

Victoria noticed the set of the woman's lips. They made her mouth look sharper, almost cruel. Louise shook her head. "Marriage was not good to her." She sighed and pulled at her white curled hair as if to straighten a patch of it. She picked up her knitting again. "That's her beast of a husband in the picture opposite her, and those are her kids."

"They're lovely."

"Not any more."

Again the woman's tone of voice had changed and her lips became a narrow slash in her face. Victoria began to get apprehensive about the fate of the daughter and the mother's changing manner. "What happened to them?" she asked. She felt a tie with this look-alike.

"*He* happened to her," she said cryptically, stabbing at the wool with her needles.

"Doesn't he treat her well?"

"Didn't he, you mean."

Victoria pulled back her hair and fingered her book, tempted to move away from this frightening woman. She noticed that the woman was dressed in shades of black and grey. "They're no longer together, then."

"Nor would you be, if he hit you like he did her."

"He hit his wife? Why?" This was something outside Victoria's experience. People made jokes about husbands beating their wives, but it didn't happen to anyone she knew. Louise seemed respectable enough, with her hair professionally set, her suit a nice cut and her daughter a college graduate.

"Why do men do anything? *I* certainly don't know. Now she's a skinny woman's rightser or whatever you call it in New York. New York! Providence is too small for her and Boston too close. *He* might find her. I say kill him. If he finds her take a gun and shoot him. I'd like to shoot mine."

Victoria watched, fascinated, as Louise became more fanatical. Like a Jeckyl-Hyde character she became increasingly sinister. Each time they went under a bridge more shadow seemed to have settled across her, making her look darker and smaller, as if she was shriveling before Victoria's eyes. She sounded as if she really meant what she said about her husband. "You want to shoot your husband?" Victoria asked in disbelief.

"Dirty thing. I've cooked and cleaned for him the best part of my life and there he sits, sweating into his undershirts. Hairy old man. I wish he'd die and leave me in peace. I *dare* him ever to lay a hand on me. I should have left him years ago." Then she asked, her hands moving even faster on her knitting, "Why should I?" her voice suddenly loud, her eyebrows raised. "Why should I let him off so easy and go scrub floors on my hands and knees?" She looked accusingly at Victoria. "He'd be sitting pretty, let me tell you, with his pension and without me to feed. No, I *earned* that and I'm keeping it. You'll see. I'll outlast him and then I'll live in comfort. Take a cruise somewhere. Go out on the town." She looked slyly at Victoria. "Maybe find a boyfriend. How about you? A pretty girl like you must have a boyfriend."

As terrified as she had become of the old woman, Victoria knew now that there was something wrong with her. How inconsistent to hate men one moment and want a boyfriend the next. Or is that real, she wondered. Is that how women really are: torn between wanting marriage and fearing to live with men. "No, Louise, I don't have a boyfriend," she answered quietly, afraid to upset her.

"Well, good for you, then. You're better off. Look at my poor daughter." Again Louise was calm and motherly. "She gave her two sons up to him just like that. Said they reminded her of him. Said she wants to be free. *I* can't understand her, can you? A lovely girl like that getting all skinny and sickly looking. Running around the streets in sandals in the middle of winter. All her friends have their hair chopped off and look like men. I suppose she'll cut all hers off one of these days. Imagine, a grown woman, a *mother*, in blue jeans, not eating meat. Have you ever heard of anything so ridiculous?'' Louise had become menacing again.

Victoria, frightened into silence, shook her head noncommittally and picked up her book. "Tsk, tsk," she heard Louise say, but did not look over again. She was as much afraid that the woman was not crazy as that she was. So much of what she had said made sense. Louise was simply looking at reality and talking about it. Most people found it too painful to do so. Was the frightening shadow that had settled over Louise simply something Victoria had cast over her so that she could call the woman crazy and stop listening to her?

After pretending to read for awhile, Victoria set her book down and went to find the water fountain. She looked for another place to sit, but the train was crowded. Louise looked up when she sat next to her. "And what about yourself, dear. Tell me why you don't have a boyfriend."

Oh, no, Victoria groaned to herself. But she answered politely, "I suppose I haven't found a boy I really like."

The old woman surveyed her and Victoria thought she looked like a witch or a fortune-teller. Then she demanded, "Who was the last man you liked?"

Victoria considered telling her to mind her own business. Instead she felt impelled to answer against her will, "Michael." When the woman lay down her needles and continued to look at her she went on. "He was a mechanic where my parents used to spend their vacations in New Hampshire. There weren't many children there and he used to take me fishing. He taught me to fish."

"Did he beat his wife?" Victoria was startled by Louise's non-sequitur. Still, she had to go on as Louise watched her unwaveringly, her eyes narrow.

"Not that I know of." She pictured Michael's house where he had taken her once when he had forgotten the bait. The small motorboat had skimmed across the lake and Michael eased it onto a beach, lifting Victoria free of it and onto the sand. She was ten and he took her little girl's hand and they ran across the narrow road to a long white house whose porch looked like a storage room, filled with old furniture and tools. A girl younger than herself ran around the corner of the house, but stopped suddenly when she saw Michael.

"Are you being a good girl?" he had asked.

She hung her head and whispered, "Yes, Daddy."

"Good, then I want you to meet Vicky." He knelt between the two girls and pushed them together. "Hello," they both said. While Michael went to get the bait they stared at each other. The little girl wore a grey dress and no shoes. Victoria was in white pedal pushers and a matching blouse. Feeling like a big city girl she had asked, "Do you like your school up here?" Michael's daughter ran off.

"Was he your boyfriend?" Louise asked.

"Oh, no, I was small. He worked for the place where we stayed. I suppose he was paid to amuse me."

"What in the world did you find in him to like?"

Victoria defended Michael. "He was different from anyone I'd ever met. He repaired boats and cars and had a farm. And he was wonderful to me." She would not tell Louise that she had not been allowed to play with the only children there, the staff children. Michael had come as a savior during her loneliness when her parents noticed that she was spending all of her time following them around. "This is a vacation!" her mother had chastised her. "Your father and I want to enjoy ourselves. Don't you have anything to do?" She had complained to the resort about their lack of programs for children and the next day Michael gave her a ride in a speedboat. He asked her what she would like to do for the summer.

"I want to catch a fish!"

"Then you will," said the stout, cigar-smoking man with short arms and a rolling walk. Her mother had been horrified. "I told them that they needed recreational facilities for children. Not that I wanted my daughter made into a tomboy!" After another day of trailing after her parents because she was so bored, Victoria was sent fishing with Michael.

"I caught a fish," she told Louise. "Several, as a matter of fact. One of them was a foot long."

"Ugh," said Louise, returning to her knitting.

"We threw them all back. Michael said if we didn't need them, there was no use killing them. After all, I remember him saying, if they didn't enjoy swimming around all day they wouldn't do it," Victoria reminisced, smiling.

"But did you like the man or did you like what you could do because you were with a man?"

Victoria looked at the old lady innocently knitting, head bowed. She shivered to think that the old woman was probably right, it was not the man but the privilege she remembered so fondly. "He was kind to me," she offered weakly.

"Was he kind to his kids?"

Victoria remembered his little girl's face again. She had stopped short at the sight of her father.

"Or his wife?"

"I'm sure he was," Victoria said firmly. "He was a kind man. I'm sure he was good to his wife and children."

Louise chuckled and was silent, leaving Victoria alone with new thoughts, staring at the gnarled old body busy with its needles. What did the old lady care if she held a warm feeling about Michael in her heart? Why did she want to ruin it? Why shouldn't she like men? Just because one old woman and her daughter had bad experiences with them? Yet it was true that Michael was the only man she really liked. How eerie that a stranger should bring this into focus for her.

Victoria realized suddenly that the landscape was more familiar and began to get ready. As she swung her suitcase down to her seat she noticed that Louise was looking less sinister and more respectable. Her white hair shone in the sunlight and her clothes seemed almost stylish. Victoria put her coat on, balancing in the aisle. Louise looked up at her. "I can tell you're a smart girl like my daughter," she smiled benignly. "I just think girls can be too smart sometimes and make mistakes."

"I'm not sure what you mean," Victoria said, swaying against the seat, suitcase still in hand.

"No, young people never hear what old people say. At least you were polite enough to listen." She set down her knitting and raised her hand. Victoria took it reluctantly, remembering the fairy tale where the palm of the princess's hand was pricked with a poisonous thorn. "It's been lovely talking with you, dear. Good luck to you," Louise said in a sweet, grandmotherly way.

"It's been nice talking to you, too, Louise," Victoria answered politely.

"Has it? Then I'm sorry." Louise's face darkened as she scowled at Victoria. "You mustn't have been listening after all," she said, dropping Victoria's hand as if it had burned her.

Victoria almost ran down the aisle in her haste to get away. At the door she was for once glad of the crowd of people. She felt safer. Her hand stung and she looked down at it, feeling as crazy as she thought Louise was. There was no stain; the barb had been verbal, the wound in her head. She could feel the woman's words take hold with such ease they might well have been in her own mind to begin with. She wondered if she had been dreaming the whole time. "Can I be the witch? Trying to tell myself something I already know?"

The train stopped and the people behind her pressed Victoria out the door.

"Victoria! Victoria!" she heard on the cold and busy platform. It was her friend Rosemary. "I didn't know you would be on this train. What is it? You look as if you had seen a ghost!"

Victoria stared at her. "Oh, it's good to see you," she sighed in relief, realizing she had never before been so glad to see the sharp-chinned, lank-haired woman.

"Would you like to share a cab?" Rosemary asked in her formal manner.

"That's the best idea I've heard all day. Let's go back to the real world, eh, Rosemary?" she laughed.

"I'd hardly call our ivory tower real, Victoria. You of all people should know how I feel about the enforced unreality of the environment with which the privileged classes surround themselves. . . ." And her voice droned on, as comforting to Victoria as the sun had been when she drifted in Michael's boat, her fishing rod poised to catch whatever came her way.

CHAPTER TWO

Annie Heaphy stumbled on the rug in Eleanor's doorway.

"Those fags I live with have to be so fancy with their furniture," Eleanor apologized. "I trip over that half the time myself."

"It's elegant, anyway," Annie said sarcastically as she pulled off the army jacket which would have fit in better at home in her own beloved shack.

Eleanor took it and hung it in a closet. "Everything has to be pretty for them, believe me. I mean, who ever heard of a white rug? My mom would have gone cuckoo with cleaning it. They're forever renting a rug shampooer. Sit down and take a load off your feet. What do you want to drink?"

"Wow! They have a bar!" said Annie admiringly, sliding onto a stool.

"Why, of course, of course. Nothing but the best."

"You know, you're really lucky to live here."

"Luxury has its price. I've told you guys what I put up with. The parties that go on all night—not that I don't enjoy them. And they're so bitchy sometimes—not that I'm not. They do take awfully good care of me, though, and the rent is cheap. Won't you join me in some Southern Comfort?"

"Don't you have any nice northern stuff?"

"Ain't no such thing. All the best whiskey's southern. Why, Jack Daniels comes from my home state," Eleanor boasted.

"I'll stick to beer."

"Suit yourself, Yankee," Eleanor said, handing Annie a beer as she walked to the couch. Annie watched her, knowing she was committed to making love now. "Come sit down over here, Annie." Eleanor patted a cushion next to her.

Annie twirled on her stool. "This is fun," she said to delay leaving the stool. She wanted desperately to revoke the course she set for herself when, balking at going back to her house alone, she accepted Eleanor's often repeated invitation after Turkey and Peg had left the bar. In addition, she felt badly when Dusty had not shown up again. Eleanor had been very let down. Now she hoped that she was not throwing away a friend for a night's companionship. Slowly, she walked to Eleanor on the couch, realizing how unattractive she found her lips, wishing she did not have to kiss them.

"You don't look happy, honey. What's the matter?"

"Nothing, El, nothing. Just tired. Thinking of getting up tomorrow." Annie felt guilty that her reluctance was obvious to Eleanor and sat close to her, facing her and laying a hand on her shoulder. She clung to her beer with the other hand, although her fingers were getting cold and the beer warm. She gritted her teeth in a smile.

Eleanor rubbed her cheek on Annie's hand. "What do you want for Christmas, Annie?"

"Oh, I don't know. How about a . . . ." Annie stopped herself from saying lover. That was a joke she, Peg and Turkey shared. It would only hurt Eleanor or lead to more than Annie wanted. "A six-pack."

"Is that all you ever think of?"

"Then how about a new muffler for my car?"

"How about ten dollars or under?" Eleanor laughed, lifting Annie's cap and smoothing her hair.

Annie knocked her hand away, more roughly than she had intended. "Don't mess with the hat."

A hurt look flashed across Eleanor's eyes, but she laughed again. "Do you wear that thing to bed?"

Remorseful, Annie smiled. "No. Just in the shower."

"Silly." Eleanor moved closer to Annie and snuggled into her shoulder. Sighing, Annie put one arm around her, chugging at her beer with the other. "Put that down, Annie."

"Didn't finish it," Annie complained into the can.

Eleanor took a turn at sighing and sat up. "Well, at least I got you here, away from your precious house. I suppose that's a big step."

"I'm sorry." Annie hung her head. "I'm real tired, El." She put her arm back around Eleanor's thin shoulders. "I'm not sure I have the energy to do you justice."

"What will be, will be. Will you stay over anyway, even if we don't do anything? You know, 'Help me make it through the night?' "

Annie smiled to hear Eleanor sing the song she played endlessly on Marcy's jukebox and to hear her own thoughts in the other woman's mouth. Feeling unsure of herself, she looked up at Eleanor. "Maybe I shouldn't."

"Why the hell not?"

"I'd feel I was here under false pretenses."

"I'm *asking* you to stay, Annie. That nasty old Dusty didn't even show up at all tonight. How's that for a brushoff? I keep thinking about how hard it is waitressing all day when I can't depend on Dusty being there at night. All I got is the bar to keep me from going nuts."

Annie was humming Eleanor's song inside her head. It had weighed on Annie at the bar and increased her own sense of desolation at the thought of going home. When her roommates lived there she had loved the long drive back. Now, remembering the deserted beach, she weakened again. "As long as it's okay with you."

"Oh, it's real okay with me. You'll have to sleep in my bed because Rudy and George usually come home with company and stay out here for awhile. But I promise I won't touch you."

Annie nodded gratefully and went to get into bed while Eleanor fixed them a bedtime snack in the kitchen. She felt like a kid sick in bed in a pair of Rudy's pajamas rolled up on her arms and legs. Eleanor came in with two glasses of milk and chunks of chocolate cake.

"Well, it's nice to know I can make you smile," Eleanor said when she saw Annie eying the cake. "Here, hold this while I get undressed." She changed into a black shortie nightgown while Annie averted her eyes. "Like my negligee?" Eleanor asked as she climbed in next to Annie.

"It's real sexy," Annie giggled. "I feel like we're having a sleepover party," she said as she gave Eleanor her cake and milk.

"Me too. This is kind of fun. I never thought of you as *fun* to sleep with."

Annie pretended to look hurt.

"Just exciting," Eleanor grinned lasciviously. "Now, you all take off that hat and eat so we can get up in the morning. Long as we're not going to do anything worthwhile we might as well get some rest.''

They finished their snacks and pulled the blankets over themselves, turning off the light. Annie lay in the dark stiff with self-consciousness. It would be hard to fall asleep, not having made love. "You know, this is new for me, El.''

"What?''

"Platonic sleeping together.''

"Me too. Don't really seem natural, does it? It'll ruin our images. Some butch you are,'' she teased Annie, pushing lightly at her in the dark.

"Can you see us telling Peg and Turkey we slept together and them not believing it was innocent?'' Annie laughed to cover the warmth that stole over her from Eleanor's light touch.

"Never! We'd have to prove it. Some night let's ask them to come to bed with us and we'll have a sexless orgy.'' Eleanor began to laugh too.

"We wouldn't even need beds. Four sleeping bags on the floor.''

"We'd never all fit in a bed,'' Eleanor added.

"We'd go through the mattress!''

"Rudy and George would come in when they heard the noise and find all those tangled up arms and legs and hair . . . !'' Eleanor couldn't finish from laughing.

Annie was doubled up on the bed from laughter, her cap finally falling off. "Oh, stop, that's enough!''

"This is almost as good as sex!''

As they calmed down Eleanor moved closer to Annie who jumped. "Your feet are so cold!'' Annie said, reaching under the covers to warm them as she would a lover's. "You do need someone warm in your bed.''

"Um, that feels good, Annie. We should have thought of this months ago. Do you think Turkey and Peg ever sleep together? Like this?''

"I don't know, but they ought to.'' Eleanor settled her head on Annie's shoulder.

Annie sighed deeply and leaned her face against Eleanor's hair.

"Tell me a bedtime story, Annie.''

"Goldilocks?"

"No, silly, something real."

"How about *Gone With the Wind*?"

"Don't make fun of a defenseless Southern belle. Something about lesbians."

"Oh, you mean a dirty story."

"You're awful. Not a dirty story, a real romantic one."

"Once upon a time Miss Scarlett realized that it was Topsy she loved all along . . ."

"Oh, Annie," Eleanor pulled away from her, pretending to be disgusted.

Annie held her back. "Dorothy fell in love with Toto?"

"Was Toto a girl?" Eleanor giggled. "Tell me your come out story. I never heard that."

"Do I have to?"

"Either that or make love to me. I'm not ready to sleep."

Annie hesitated, feeling again a stirring glow from Eleanor's words, enjoying holding her slight body.

"Besides," Eleanor interrupted her wavering will, "I've told you mine."

"Yeah, poor kid. What an awful way to come out. In jail."

"Reform school. They didn't call them jails. And it was nice. She made me feel like I had a real home for the first time ever. I would've stayed at the school forever if she hadn't been sprung. I loved our little cottage. At least until they put two more girls in there. But even then it wasn't so bad, because their girlfriends were in other cottages and they were out all the time."

"I feel overprivileged."

"Why?"

"I came out with a Cliffey."

"What in hell is that?" Eleanor asked, rolling over to face Annie. Annie kissed her, their bodies barely touching, her lips finding a spark in Eleanor's. "Oh, no," Eleanor sighed. "You're not getting out of it that easy. Now I want to hear. Tell me." She pushed Annie back into the pillows and laid her head on her chest.

"Natalie went to Radcliffe. That's the woman's school at Harvard."

"How'd you meet her?"

"At the library. The Boston Public. It's kind of corny."

"Love stories always are, aren't they?"

"I guess so. Stop me if it's too silly for you."

"Oh, Annie," Eleanor chided her, slipping a hand across Annie's chest and under her ribcage.

"I used to go there every Saturday. To the library. Mostly to get away from my family. My house was always full of old ladies, cousins, aunts, neighbors. It felt like bingo night at St. Ann's. I'd go to study. I was in high school. Junior year. I didn't have any friends except neighborhood kids. We'd go to the football games together. Or shopping downtown, walking to school, but I had nothing in common with them. I didn't know I was gay, but I read a lot and they called me The Intellectual. So me and my shadow would go to the library."

"Sounds dull, honey," Eleanor said, running her hand along Annie's side.

"Actually, I didn't study much, so it wasn't. I'd go into a room and pull out a book and get lost for a few hours. At lunchtime, though, I always went to this courtyard in the middle of the place and I'd eat my sandwich there. One day I noticed this girl looking at me. I'd noticed her before, so I smiled at her. Well, that's as far as it went for a few weeks. We'd smile. I was shy and it turned out she was too, back then."

Annie shifted on the bed. "You still awake?" she asked when Eleanor didn't move.

"Oh, yeah. Just too comfy to move."

Annie stroked her hair. "So one day, of course, the only place to sit was next to her. You sat on these low cement benches. We smiled and finally she asked me what I was reading. She was reading *The Well of Loneliness*. I found out later that she'd been carrying it every Saturday in hopes that I'd talk to her." Annie laughed. "She was gay, but she was only a freshman at Radcliffe and scared to death she'd be kicked out if anyone found out. She's a big shot on the campus now, a senior. But then she was just a scared little queer and she thought I was, too. You know, I wore jeans and sneakers and a hat."

"Not the same one!" Eleanor interrupted, pretending horror.

"No, no. Usually a Red Sox cap, then. Anyway, we went for coffee. She was majoring in literature and I'd read a lot so we had plenty in common. I'd never heard of *The Well* and she lent it to me. All she said was it was the life of an English woman writer. We didn't talk about meeting the next week, but she knew the book would bring me back. Luckily, it was spring and we could leave the shelter of the library for the Common and the public Gardens, the Charles River and the docks.

"It was a sweet kind of relationship. She said we budded, then blossomed together, first holding hands, then walking arm in arm and so on. We didn't sleep together until that summer. She was a counselor at some camp in Vermont and I worked at the Chelsea library shelving and stuff. I missed her like we were blossoming plants the blossoms had been torn off. I'd finally started fantasizing about her. When she got her first weekend off I met her. I was scared to death because we stayed at a country inn and it was so respectable looking and I was far from home and, of course, I knew what would happen if I wanted it to.

"We went on being lovers till I graduated from high school. But I remember the courting best, if you'll forgive the expression. The weather growing warmer, colors being born, everything expanding and filling with life, like me. Toying with love. Before we had to face the daily realities like where can we sleep together and where do we go from here."

Eleanor raised herself to look into Annie's eyes. "That is a sweet story, girl. And just like you. A quiet kind of first love, that took a long time to happen. What happened to her?"

"The summer I graduated high school she started some kind of study program in Spain. She didn't come back until the end of the winter. She was so different. So—sophisticated, I guess. I mean, she'd always been a lot more with it in terms of getting along with society and fitting in at Radcliffe. She could pass easily for straight. But before she went away she was like a kid a lot, especially alone with me. Like a kid who's been pushed into the adult world and puts on a good show when she wants to. I didn't stop loving her because she finally became part of that world, but I didn't feel I could keep up. And she didn't want to give it up. You know, she'll always be one of those lesbians who goes to cocktail parties and people say, 'Oh, that's so and so the lesbian,' and go back to their drinks because she looks just like them and acts just like them and keeps her love life totally separate from her social and professional life. I think it's a new kind of closet that's been invented for women who love women but also love the straight world."

"And Annie Heaphy doesn't."

"You're damn straight I don't love their world. Shit," she sneered, putting her hands on Eleanor's shoulders and gripping them. *"This* is my world and if I've got to be a cab driver then I will be before I take my hat off for anybody. I may have a lot of faults, but I'm no hypocrite."

Their eyes were locked and Eleanor was smiling at Annie's angry pride. "You lowclass dyke," she hissed.

"You poor white Southern queer," Annie countered and suddenly they were kissing hard and holding each other very tightly. They had found something in each other to which they responded. Rolling on top of Eleanor, Annie, with short, firm caresses, made love to her, but it was all an outward flow of energy. When Eleanor tried to touch Annie, the touch was parried. Annie was masterful, everything she thought Eleanor wanted her to be, until Eleanor began to fight her, caressing her back, moving until she was no longer underneath Annie, but next to her and finally finding an opening to make love to Annie, too. They went on for awhile roughly touching each other, Eleanor as if to purge the straight world from Annie's body, Annie ridding Eleanor of the night's hurt and disappointment. Then, their passions met and they retreated from their fight as if to admire and appreciate each other. I'm making love with a friend I respect, thought Annie, and she smiled in the dark, still for a moment.

"What's the matter?" Eleanor asked.

"Whether we do this again or not, I like you."

"I like you too, Annie." And then their caresses were gentle until they slept.

∿ ∿ ∿ ∿ ∿

Victoria was ready to knock, but the door to Rosemary and Claudia's room was wide open. Claudia was dancing inside, arms wide, eyes closed, dipping and spinning in unrhythmic abandon.

Victoria knocked anyway, once lightly and again more heavily when Claudia did not hear.

Claudia's whole body started and her eyes jumped open. Balanced in a backward step she swayed side to side, then thrust her round body forward and to the door to grab Victoria and pull her into the dark room which faced an alley. "Want to dance?" she yelled over the cha-cha.

"No!" Victoria shouted back. "Why don't you turn that thing down? Aren't people trying to study?"

"I was indulging myself," Claudia admitted, turning the stereo down, still lightly dancing in her long flannel nightgown.

Victoria watched the girl's joy in dancing and her unself-consciousness in her body with its heavy breasts and protruding belly. Small bare feet poked out from under the nightgown. Claudia began to unroll curlers from her hair. "What did you do last night?" she asked Victoria.

"I read, listened to music." Victoria remembered dancing by herself to Debussy. "What did you do?"

"Went to a film. *David and Lisa.* Have you ever seen it?"

"No."

"It's about two kids with emotional problems. I must have seen it six times. Fascinating."

"For a psychology major."

"Rosemary liked it too. I want her to understand my interest in psychology. She sees it as a 'male tool to further enhance male strength by rationalizing it.' I believe we can use it to understand their strength and our own." She cleared books off a chair. "Want to sit down? What are you doing here anyway? We usually have to drag you out of your room."

Victoria looked at her feet and took a deep breath. She was lonely, restless, excited by the coming winter holiday when her parents would be away and she would be free in the apartment in New York. There was finally not even the money for a live-in maid. She also felt at a loss about what to do with herself those two weeks, when she could do anything she wanted without having to report her activities to anyone. "I suppose I was bored."

"Want to come to the women's poetry group?"

"Is that all you're doing today?"

"Yes. Rosemary's going to read."

Victoria tried not to sound negative. "I've heard her read before."

"There'll be a discussion afterwards. Come on. You're a poet. You'll like it. There won't be any bearded men showing off there. Just us."

"I really don't care for poetry readings," Victoria protested, wringing her hands in frustration. "I suppose I'm looking for something more exciting to do."

Claudia looked surprised. "Exciting? *You*, Victoria Locke, looking for something exciting to do?" She slipped her curlers into a flowered cosmetic bag. "Like what?"

"I don't know. I suppose nothing." Victoria slumped dejectedly into the armchair Claudia had cleared, unsure whether to change the subject or not. "Oh, Claudia, I want to plunge into something. To get lost in it, do you understand what I mean?"

"Sure I do. I just never expected you to feel like that. I do a lot," Claudia said, slipping onto the arm of the chair and looking into Victoria's eyes. "What sort of things do you get lost in?"

Before Victoria could answer, Rosemary's bedroom door opened and she appeared in a long skirt and peasant blouse. Her lank brown hair was rolled on the top of her head, strings of it falling out already. "Good morning," she said in surprise to the tableau of Victoria and Rosemary. She walked to the stereo turntable and stopped the cha-cha.

Victoria looked up at the girl's thin, pointed face. "Hello," she answered.

Claudia lifted herself away from Victoria and attached herself to Rosemary's arm. "Victoria wants something exciting to do, but doesn't want to come to the group," she said, leaning her head against Rosemary's shoulder as they both looked toward their friend. Rosemary awkwardly took her arm from Claudia's and rested it across her shoulder.

"What *do* you find exciting, Victoria?" Rosemary asked solemnly.

"I'm not sure anymore. Nothing seems to satisfy me. I have this vague, restless feeling."

Rosemary looked at Claudia. "Surely we can think of something. Why don't you go and wash up, Claudie, so we can go," she said gently. Claudia let go of her arm slowly and, with a lingering smile at Rosemary, left them. "How long have you felt like this, Victoria?"

Silently, Victoria cursed herself for confiding in Claudia. I don't need a therapist because I want to have some fun, she thought. "Weeks now," she said, giving in because she did not see how she could avoid answering, without being rude.

"What do you usually do?"

"I've never felt quite like this."

"Oh, come now," Rosemary admonished her.

Victoria had to admit that Rosemary was right. "I usually throw myself into studying or a book."

"And that's not working?" Rosemary sat down across from her.

Victoria shook her head sadly. "No."

"You probably need a lover."

"Rosemary!" Victoria exclaimed, shocked.

"Well, it's true."

"I don't want some man suddenly controlling my life. I've tried that. The minute they touch you they think you're their property."

"You're a true feminist, Victoria. You can see relationships in a political light."

"Politics my eye. I don't like the way they treat me. Even the least obtrusive man, once he's certain of you, gets possessive. I don't want that, Rosemary, and I certainly don't find it exciting."

"No, I see that. And for that reason I'm going to tell you something I've been wanting to tell you for a while, but there hasn't been the right opportunity. I've spoken with Claudia about it and she agrees that since you are our best friend you should know. I hope that it won't hurt our friendship."

Victoria was bored by Rosemary's speech and barely interested in what confession she had to make. She yawned, picking some lint off her chair. The room, devoid of sunlight, was dark and depressing. It was filled with Claudia's clutter.

"Are you prepared for me to say something quite startling?"

"Yes," Victoria sighed irritably.

"This is not easy to say, but, I suppose I may as well get used to saying it." Rosemary swallowed so hard Victoria could hear the gulp and looked at her. "Claudia and I are thinking of becoming lovers."

I hadn't even thought of a woman lover, Victoria thought to herself, not at all surprised that her immediate reaction was to consider taking a woman lover as a choice for herself. "I'm glad," she said simply.

"You think we should?"

"Well, I don't know much about this sort of thing. I always assumed it just happened—taking a lover or falling in love."

"Perhaps it does for some people. But we don't entirely believe in love," Rosemary proclaimed, pursing her lips.

Victoria was shocked again. "Then why be lovers?"

Rosemary spoke as if giving a prepared lecture. "Both of us want to give our whole selves to feminism. As sex is a physical need and companionship is very important," she said in a rush, blushing, "we feel that we should provide for both. If we married, we would have to divert our attention away from the movement to men." Composed now, Rosemary sat straighter. "If we can meet each other's needs, we'll have a solution to our problems."

"Are you sure Claudia feels this way too?"

"It was Claudia who brought it up. Of course, her political thinking lags behind her instinctual search for a solution and a psychologist *would* worry about her basic human needs. One night she became," Rosemary looked uncomfortable, "affectionate, and I found it not unpleasant. However, I stopped her so that I could evaluate the implications a physical relationship would have for us."

Victoria surprised herself by saying very low, "You mean you had to rationalize getting what you wanted."

"I'm not sure what you mean."

Victoria tried to imagine the two in bed. She was certain that Claudia was as passionate and uninhibited in her affections as she was in everything else she did. Rosemary would be a bore, asking how everything felt and what she should do next. But the idea of women loving women, though a frightening option she had never before considered for herself, was exciting. Sarcastic still, she asked, "When will you decide?"

"We're going to talk about it again this evening. First we're going to see what the poetry group has to say. I've written several poems in the last week based on Sappho's fragments. I hope that will make a discussion of lesbianism seem natural."

"Instead of asking her father for her hand, you're asking her poetry group?" Victoria laughed. She wondered once more why she remained friends with Rosemary. They did have the same interests. And Rosemary, like herself, had never been part of the Yale social world. She lived in the same dormitory and was easy to see and they shared many of the same classes. Yet Victoria could not stand the woman and had avoided her for weeks at a time since they started school. "What do they do?"

"Who?"

"Women lovers," Victoria answered, shy to say lesbian.

"I've been reading up on that, though there's not much to read. Claudia says it will come naturally, but I've picked up a few techniques. First, and terribly unappealing, there is tribadism . . ."

"That's all right, Rosemary. I didn't mean a detailed description. Never mind." Victoria wondered if Rosemary knew how she sounded: studying how to make love! "Listen, I wish you luck with your reading, your discussion and your decision, but I've got to go for a walk or something. Perhaps I'll see you later."

Claudia rejoined them as Victoria stood to go. She was wearing denim cover-alls with no top under the bib and she stood with her thumbs hooked in the straps. "This is how the farmers where I come from dress, you guys. What do you think?" Victoria noticed the soft curve of Claudia's breasts flattened behind the bib of the overalls and thought, how lovely. Claudia was looking curiously toward Victoria as if to determine whether Rosemary had told her what she suspected she told her.

"I think you'd better go cover yourself, Claudia," Rosemary said in a high-pitched voice.

Victoria laughed. "You look wonderful! I can finally picture you growing up on a farm, a spunky little tomboy."

"I haven't been allowed to dress like this since I was about five," Claudia giggled as she ducked back into her bedroom.

"Sometimes she's such a child," Rosemary apologized.

"But you love her," Victoria teased, then corrected herself. "That is, you don't love her."

"It's not that I don't love Claudia. I respect her and care for her in a sisterly way, not romantically."

Victoria wanted to shake this stiff, mistaken woman who was so afraid of the power of her own emotions. If it were me who loved, she thought, I'd do the proverbial shouting from the rooftops. "It sounds to me as if you've politicized love to death."

"As usual, we don't agree, Victoria. We'll see who leads a fulfilled life. You're at the mercy of your emotions. Why, if you wanted to come out, which of course I feel you should, you would have an incredible amount of trouble dealing with it because you would go about it all wrong. You would probably never succeed in coming out at all. You'd fix on a person and then have to adjust to her being a woman, rather than choosing the way you wish to live and rationally finding the appropriate person with whom to share that life."

"Come out?"

"It's lesbian terminology. It means becoming a lesbian. It implies that all of us have homosexuality in us just waiting to 'come out.' "

"I see. And why do you think I should come out? Have you caught me ogling women?"

"Be serious, Victoria. First of all, lesbians don't 'ogle' women."

"Why not? I'm beginning to think women are beautiful."

"Secondly I, of course, feel that all women should come out. The more we support each other, the stronger we will be. The less we give to men the weaker they will be. It's said that behind every great man there stands a woman. Well, it's time to take the props out from under the supposedly great men, expose them for the weaklings they really are and free ourselves to realize our full potential."

Rosemary has good ideas, Victoria thought. Very good ideas. If only she would let them live, express them without politics. "Your heart is in the right place, Rosemary, but you really shouldn't reject its power."

"The Power of the Heart. A good title for a poem. Will you write it or shall I?"

"Let's both and compare."

"By Thursday?"

"Midnight deadline. I'll meet you in the laundry room and we'll have a private reading." Victoria's eyes twinkled. "Unless you're busy."

Rosemary blushed. "I'll thank you not to take my relationship lightly."

"But Rosemary, don't you think having a lover can be fun?"

"Sure she does," said Claudia, emerging from her room with a full-sleeved silky blouse, which looked part of a cocktail outfit, under her overalls. "She won't admit it to you, though, will you Rosie?" Rosemary blushed again. For once she was without words. "It will be, Rose, believe me," Claudia winked and giggled, glancing quickly at Victoria who laughed back.

"Calm down, Rosemary, we mean well. Let's drop it, all right? We'll have it out in the duel."

Claudia's mouth opened and she arched her eyebrows. "What duel? Over who?"

"Thursday midnight in the laundry room," Victoria said, swaggering as if there were pistols on her hips.

"A poetry duel, Claudia. The subject is the Power of the Heart."

"That sounds romantic," Claudia smiled seductively toward Rosemary.

Rosemary frowned. "Romance was not my intent," she told Claudia.

Claudia looked mischeivously toward Rosemary.

"Mine will be full of romance, Claudia," Victoria assured her, amused by their interplay. "I knew I'd find something exciting to do."

"Are you going to write now? You'll have a head start," Rosemary complained.

"No. Don't worry, Rosemary. I'm going for a walk around

campus. For a fall day it feels an awful lot like spring. I need to be outside."

"Are you sure you wouldn't like to come with us to hear some women poets?"

"No, thank you," Victoria replied as she rose, thinking that she couldn't stand more than one Rosemary at a time.

"Then we'll stop by later."

"All right. Let me know the result of your discussion." Victoria stole an amused look at Claudia who shrugged before Rosemary had time to turn.

"We will, won't we, Claudia?" Rosemary asked gravely.

Victoria closed the door as her two friends looked into one another's eyes. Even more strangely excited than before she had visited them, she returned to her room for her camel's hair coat, fastened her hair back from the last fall breezes, and strode briskly out of the dormitory.

∿ ∿ ∿ ∿ ∿

Annie Heaphy woke before dawn and was seized with panic. Never could she stay beside the woman with whom she had slept. Always she had to flee before the other stirred unless she had been pinned down to a day's plans. Even then she would find an excuse to escape temporarily: she would get the newspaper, or milk for breakfast. This morning, with Eleanor next to her still in her black shortie nightgown which looked sordid against the stark whiteness of her skin, Annie could think of nothing but how to get out. Eleanor had described herself as a light sleeper. Annie rolled slowly to the side of the bed. She stopped and held her breath, waiting to see if Eleanor had noticed. The woman did not move. As Annie looked at her she tried to recapture the stirrings of real affection she had felt for her last night. She felt only horror. The liquor they had drunk rose in her system and she tasted it. Her hands tingled as they did always after drinking. Her head was full of a dull ache. She needed something to get rid of the feeling. Sleep would do it, but no, she thought, the panic settling even deeper. No, no, no. I've got to get out. She reached one arm slowly to the pile of clothing she had discarded next to the bed. All of it but her underpants were within reach and she put them in one pile she could grab. Her shoes she remembered she had left in the living room. If only Rudy or George didn't put them away somewhere out of sight. Could she go home in socks? What would she wear to work? What would Eleanor think when she found them or when Annie showed up at her door asking for them? Worse still, what if George or Rudy answered the door and she had to explain it to them?

She had to get hold of herself. She took a slow deep breath and slid out from underneath the covers to drop onto the floor. I should have gone in for guerrilla warfare, she told herself, slipping the brim of her cap between her teeth. In one movement, she took the pile of clothes in one hand and grabbed her underpants with the other, rising slowly, clownlike in her awkward stealth, toward the living room.

"Annie, where you all going?"

Annie jumped. She dropped her hat from her mouth and caught it between the two handfuls of clothing. "To the john, Ellie. Go back to sleep." Hoping Eleanor had not opened her eyes enough to see that she was carrying her clothes Annie stood still, waiting.

"Mmmm. Come back quick, it's cold."

Annie did not want to lie and stood there in silence, hoping that Eleanor would just drop back to sleep. When there was no further sign of life, she moved slowly and softly out to the living room, dressed and did not stop until she sat at the counter of a twenty-four hour diner. "Tea," she ordered, her back to the slowly lightening sky. "And two eggs over with home fries."

"Bacon, honey?" the middle-aged, tired waitress asked.

"No. Thank you," Annie smiled, feeling more herself from this contact with the waitress. "You look beat."

"And ain't I. This'll be right out," she said, handing it to the elderly cook.

Annie Heaphy ran her hand across the yellow fringe of hair that felt dirty under her cap. After this she would go home and shower. She looked at her watch. It had stopped and she set it by the diner clock, a small plastic alarm clock next to the iced tea dispenser. "Can I have a Coke?" she asked the waitress who moved swiftly for all her exhaustion. Annie fed the cold carbonation to her hangover and felt fresher for it. With some of her discomfort gone she hung her head into her hands to wait for the food and found herself drifting, half asleep, into a comfortable fantasy of a faceless woman. She swayed over her Coke, relishing the imagined feeling of being in love again. It disgusted her to think that she had slept with someone she didn't love. "Crap," she said very low. "Why do I do it?" The thought of Eleanor still repulsed her and she resolved not to think of her sexually anymore or she wouldn't be able to face her later. "I should have gone home and read," she whispered into her bubbling Coke. Again she closed her eyes and hummed silently to herself. Someone was playing Johnny Mathis songs on the jukebox and she lifted her head to glance at the only other customer in the diner. He was rail-thin, his unwashed hair hung into his eyes beneath a stained watch cap. Was he a homeless drifter? A local city creep, finished hustling for the night? Whoever he was, he snapped his fingers to the music, sharing whatever it meant to him with Annie. She shuddered in distaste, and asked herself, "Is this the kind of life I'm part of?"

Back in her car, she found a rock station on the radio, turned it up loud and roared off toward her shower. She drove fast along the street, its houses alternating, toward the end, between shack and summer home. Annie wished that she could afford one of the larger ornate homes. She sped toward the rising sun, and rolled down the window, hoping the still chill dawn air would help to clear her head. Passing the last house, she stopped beating time to the music on her steering wheel and enjoyed the austere beauty of the newly-stripped willows lining the curve. On the left she saw the beach, sand just touched with the light of the sun which sat at the edge of the horizon on the water, as if waiting for instructions. Annie Heaphy, feeling momentarily better, yelled through the wind her car made, "Come on up sun, I'm ready for you!"

High on this early disappearance of her hangover, she cut the engine and coasted into the dried mud driveway. She whistled as she jumped onto the small porch which would get screens only if summer people came. The inner door was still locked, not gaping as she had once found it, all her things ran-sacked before the would-be thieves were convinced there really wasn't anything there. She locked it behind her and hooked it, tossing her hat onto the old school desk under the front window and sitting down in a sagging wooden-armed porch chair to take off her shoes. It was good to be home, but the house was so empty this morning it seemed to echo. Not even the foghorns sounded. She thought of the fear she had about coming home barefoot and was lost to depression again. How, she wondered, would she ever face Eleanor now that she had run away from her? Would she understand? Maybe I'll stop by the restaurant sometime today, she thought. Apologize. Explain why I have to leave in the mornings. But I don't know why. Could it be guilt of some sort? Am I afraid of getting entangled? Of getting hurt? She knew all the easy explanations, but she did not believe them.

Annie dropped her shoe and walked toward the tall tin box shoved into a corner of the bathroom that served as a shower, bunching her twice-worn clothing and stuffing it into the milk crate that was her hamper. It was overflowing. Have to get to the laundromat, she thought. Maybe I'll do that tonight and skip the bars. Then she would not have to see Eleanor, or feel embarrassed in front of Turkey and Peg. As she adjusted the temperature of the shower she decided to clean the house, too. And to start reading the latest edition of *The Ladder* which she had not been home long enough to sit down and read since it came. Full of resolve, and clean, she shivered her way into her bedroom and fought with the knobless chest of drawers until the underwear drawer opened and she could dress.

A day in the life of a queer, she thought later, standing by her small kitchen window with a cup of tea. Is this what it's going to be like the rest of my life? A night here and there with a woman I don't really want to touch? Getting high to forget the purposelessness of my job, my life? Driving a cab for lack of anything better to do? Then she wondered why she was dis-satisfied with driving the cab. It's a perfectly respectable oc-cupation, she thought as she always did when having this argu-ment with herself. Helping people, in a way; performing a service. And I'm pretty free, except that I have to be there every day. And what would I do with myself if I didn't have to drive? Go back to college? They don't teach me anything I want to learn. Who cares what wars men wage against each other? Who cares about Shakespeare? Then she chuckled aloud, remembering the lines from *The Tempest* she had tacked up before dropping out of school. She reread them: "Let me not,/ Since I have my dukedom got,/ And pardoned the deceiver, dwell/ In this bare island by your spell,/ But release me from my bands/ With the help of your good hands." These lines had meant much to her when Natalie returned from Spain so changed that Annie decided to transfer to a school in Connecticut where two neighborhood friends had gone. She found them living in the shack across from the beach. When they both moved back to Boston she quit school to add cabdriving to the bartending job she already had. The house had got a hold on her. Its isolation and closeness to the shore were something she had never experienced before. But since her roommates left, it was too empty, only reminding her of her own emptiness.

So, she continued the argument with herself as she broke up a piece of stale bread for the birds, I got something out of Shakespeare. What I got wasn't anything I couldn't have gotten reading it at home. The birds had begun to sing for their breakfast outside her window. She watched them hop, withholding the bread because she knew they would scatter when she opened the window. She leaned her head against its pane and a few of them jumped and flapped their wings. She would have gone back to school at night if she had thought it worthwhile. To what end? she had asked herself. I don't want to be a doctor, a lawyer, a stockbroker, a teacher. Of course, I don't want to be a cabdriver either, she sighed, back at the beginning of her circular argument. She raised the window quietly and threw the bread to the birds. They fled, but swooped back one by one to peck at the ground and fly away with their prizes. She watched two grackles dance. One held an oversized crumb and stared while the other approached. Then it would back away and eat a bit of the crumb. The other would approach. Finally the first dropped what was left of the bread, and flew away. The other bird watched it depart as if the crumb were an empty victory.

When Natalie changed, that's when it all fell apart. If ever it was together, she thought. They were to finish school, get jobs and live happily ever after. "Hah," Annie said aloud, frightening a sparrow bold enough to sit on her sill. She remembered to close the window to cut off the draft that had been chilling her. And now she was looking for a new lover. Was that only because she wanted to shape her life? Couldn't she give her own life shape? But she had, and this was it: an endless circle. Annie Heaphy circled the city in her cab, driving, in the daytime, in and out of it bearing passengers like gifts that came to her and gifts she gave away. At night she made circles in and out of the bars and apartments of her friends. Dove in and swooped away as she found a lover and became drawn into someone else's idea of the shape her life should take. She circled in and out of her days: waking, working, wallowing in subterranean places, then waking again. I'm getting dizzy, she thought, I may fall down if I haven't already. The flight she was on only mellowed with alcohol. When she drank she forgot she was in flight or just enjoyed the purposeless drifts in the winds. Yet the next day she suffered this overwhelming depression. She could stop drinking, but then she wouldn't even have the bars.

She turned to the refrigerator to get a beer. The idea of it was pleasant. She would walk to the beach with it cold in her hand, feeling its promised release. Her eyes stopped at the clock on her refrigerator. She had planned to go to work early as long as she was up and make extra money in the commuter hour if there was a cab turned in from the night shift. Now she hesitated, lured by her ambitions of cleaning. She could stay home and clean the house, the yard, drink some beer, do a lot of reading and maybe call Eleanor to come over after she got off work. She rinsed out her mug and set it on the chipped porcelain of the sink so hard it almost broke. "You stupid loser," she cursed herself. "You can't stand the sight of her, the touch of her except with some very hard prodding and now you're ready to set up housekeeping with her just because she's available. That's really rotten. It's better she knows you don't really want her. Don't go confusing the issue. Dusty's what she wants and Eleanor's not what you want."

Mad at herself, Annie grabbed her cap from the desk and pulled it on her head snugly. She went looking for her shoes.

Or am I taking the easy way out by going to work, she asked herself, suddenly not at all purposeful, but filled with self-doubt. Ah, I don't know and I don't care. She surrendered to the routine of the day and pulled on her workshoes. Walking to the kitchen window she silently said goodbye to the birds who seemed so busy and carefree. Why can't I live like them, she wondered. Always I look for more. She watched them gather their food and wondered if all of them stayed through the winter. Would she, too, have to build a new home in the summer? Last summer she had been lucky, but now the landlord was talking about fixing the place up for summer rentals. She couldn't stand the thought of some beachboy and his wife honeymooning in her home. She would not come back to it after the summer, although Peg and Turkey had offered their apartment if she needed a temporary place to stay. No, she thought. This either is my place or it isn't. I don't share with men. If only I could save enough to buy it, but on what I earn that could take forever.

"Coo-ah, coo, coo, coo," she heard and realized she had been hearing the call for a few moments. Her anger subsided and she craned her neck to see which bird was crying. A beautiful pink and grey pigeon-like bird with a long tail sat on the ground, its neck swelling with each soft, somber note. "A mourning dove," Annie Heaphy thought. She listened, calmed, for a while, then found another piece of bread to reward it for its song. Touched by the bird's beauty and sad sound, she stayed a moment longer listening to it, wondering if it was a sign that it had chosen her home to mourn.

∿ ∿ ∿ ∿ ∿

Victoria escaped from the iron gate of her college court-yard into the New Haven street. All she could see were other Yale students. The heavy grey Yale buildings dwarfed her and she felt chilly between their cold stone walls, though the sun was bright. She walked quickly away from them wondering if she would ever think affectionately of her alma mater. She scorned the old men who came teetering to their reunions every year, boasting in their self-congratulatory speeches of their school, their class, their careers. Victoria was in the first class which had allowed women to enter the hallowed halls and she had not been ready for the highly competitive atmosphere of an all-male school. She had watched the other women become hardened by it. Victoria had wanted badly to stay at Hunter where the student body was still primarily female and the years of tradition had not yet been spoiled by the greediness of men. Her father, however, did not have a son to graduate from Yale as he had done. He was determined to carry on the family tradition by keeping his daughter imprisoned there. It was not that Victoria could not handle it, for she could best any man, she felt, but that she feared for her inner softness, a quality Yale taught her to scorn, but which survived, a cherished part of herself, the part that yearned for excitement now.

As she walked along the shop-lined street, Victoria looked at the other women and wondered if this was not, as she had assumed, a personal trait, this softness, but if it had something to do with being a woman. Since she came to Yale she had been denying a difference between men and women, keeping her grades up at all costs to prove that she could. She had never felt a kinship with the other women because they, like the men, covered up whatever was inside them to achieve by Yale standards, success. Now she had seen an underside, a softness to one of the most competitive women she knew, Rosemary. And who had found it but another woman, one who, in her own childish way, had refused to join in the competitive game. Claudia was generally thought rather stupid and suspected of being passed in courses due more to the midwestern money the college wanted to unearth than her own ability. Victoria had found her to be fun. Now she wondered if Claudia was simply a woman who was able to act out her desires. Instead of covering her feelings over with layers of intellectualism, she expressed them. Victoria realized it would be impossible to know who she herself was and what she wanted from life if she continued to add layers. She would have to scratch through them someday to find herself unless she stopped now and let them out.

Perhaps Claudia has saved Rosemary—and me, while she was at it—a lot of work later in life, Victoria thought. We won't need expensive psychoanalysis if we find out who we are and what we want right now. Victoria drifted into one of those boutiques that had sprung up everywhere to sell postcards, woven pillows, pottery and generally useless paraphernalia on which the middle class could spend its excess income. She wished for the bookstalls of Paris or the shops on King's Road in London. She left and wandered into a shop which sold Indian clothing. The proprietor was pushy and Victoria not interested in buying so she moved on, feeling a little bouncy, a little free. Today, for almost the first time in her life, she felt that something had changed, that she had been given a glimmer of lightness, a hint that her path would not be totally circumscribed.

She stood outside the store watching the people pass. Women from Yale, women from the town went by, their hair flowing, their movements graceful. Victoria found herself watching and enjoying them. She went into an ice cream store and bought a soft ice cream. Licking it made her want to giggle. She crossed the street to the Green smiling. Now, she thought, if men are good at this academic business and women aren't really, or at least, haven't acquired the skills to as high degree as yet, isn't this because men invented academia? We are playing by their rules. We are playing with a handicap. They already have the hard crust, or are more inclined by their previous socialization to develop it, and we must make do with the equipment that we have. Then we're taught to use feminine pretenses: cosmetics to cover the physical evidence of, for example, staying up all night preparing for an exam; and we're closer to our emotions so that, although we may be more easily drained, we can very quickly draw on our reserves. Those of us who survive, that is.

As she ignored the comments made by male loiterers who were sitting on the benches she was passing, she remembered two classmates who had dropped out of sight. One had attempted suicide after her failure to pass a required pre-med course. Another had been expelled for sleeping with one too many professors to get good grades. Victoria wondered how many other dropouts had been a result of the pressure to succeed in a game designed for men. In survival of the fittest, who defined the fittest? She sat on a bench, crunching the last of her cone as she thought. Does brute strength really make one most fit? No, supposedly intelligence helped. Perhaps with women doing some of the planning, humans could evolve in a way that they could resolve conflict without war. She began to see what the feminists went on and on about. Women, the natural protectors of home and growing humans, would find a way to fight without killing, to succeed without risking extinction, to achieve gracefully, without stepping on other people to do so. She rose and walked again to escape a teenage boy who had sat on her bench and was inching toward her.

Victoria realized that Rosemary's confession had stirred up a lot of things in her mind which must have been formulating for quite a while. She never thought like this. She had thought she wanted to be a recluse, a cloistered unworldly being, and most of her fantasies were of the life she would lead when she did not have to be bothered with the world as it was. The fact that her parents did not have much money did not bother her as she could always teach at a university. Her grandparents had what she thought of as "comfort" money in trust for her. It would be so easy to hide forever, but suddenly, today, she wanted to be part of the real world and to keep being stirred by women. Two women passed her in blue jeans and pea jackets. Their faces were excited and they moved fast, almost breathless as they interrupted each other talking and laughing. One skipped suddenly in happiness and the other clapped her hands at her friend's pleasure. Beautiful, Victoria said in wonder, feeling herself melt even more. If only I could reach out to a woman. An older woman passed, hair gray under a flat-topped, round hat, purse clasped in front of her, hands pulling her coat shut against the wind that swept through the open space of the Lower Green. Why do we wear all this stuff, Victoria asked herself. Why is she wearing nylons that make her legs cold and a stylish coat that's so thin she can't protect the top of her body? She felt revelations peeling blinder after blinder off her eyes until she grew tired with everything new.

She crossed a street and sat on the library steps, looking down at her own thin slacks. What I need is a pair of blue jeans, she thought, excited by the idea. Mother would never approve, but she doesn't approve of much I do. She remembered her two weeks alone in New York. Am I about to have an affair with a pair of blue jeans? Me and them alone in New York? She laughed and jumped up to stride toward an army–navy store on Elm Street. She was anxious about size, but decided not to worry about a thing with which thousands of people dealt every day without falling apart. As she passed the campus' small brick buildings and more massive stone walls, she tried not to be intimidated, but walked swiftly and assertively. It seemed as if she normally walked like a ghost, trying to float above it all. Would she be able to keep this new spirit close enough to her to feel it all the time? Or was it only something to let out on special occasions, like when you learned that your only friends might become lesbians.

Unsure if it would last, she hugged her excitement to herself and savored it. I feel like carrying a flag proclaiming that *I've* come out, she thought. I've come out of my shell a bit. I've let out a lot of festering thoughts. I've emerged from some confused thinking about who I am to take a peek at who I want to be. Around her people, mostly young, went in and out of stores that catered to their tastes. They all looked excited and fresh and as if they were buying clothing to go out on a Saturday night. Victoria had not done that since her last attempt at dating Yale men when she was a sophomore. She shuddered at the memory of the cheering, drunken crowd at the Yale football game to which her last date had taken her. She had supposed at the time that her aversion to the game came from the pointlessness of chasing a ball over a field. Now she wondered whether it wasn't instead the way the crowd shouted things like, "Kill them!" and "Murder them!" as if they were in a Roman colisseum.

She smiled at the long-haired woman on the corner leafletting against the war, then went into the army–navy store and gazed around her. There was a great pile of blue jeans stacked along the walls. Undaunted, she walked up to a salesman and asked what brand he recommended. When he explained that different brands fit people differently, Victoria refused to be confused and took one of each in sizes she guessed. Another man stopped her as she went into a fitting booth.

"Three at a time, lady."

"Oh," she said, suddenly deflated, weak, afraid. "Can I

leave the rest right out here?" she asked, indicating a corner.
"No."

"Oh." She walked back with the jeans, incredulous that the man should suspect her of trying to steal. She felt anger rise in her at the atmosphere of paranoid oppressiveness in the store. Abandoning all the jeans on a wrong counter, she walked out. Afraid the man would follow and chastise her, she went quickly down the street. Before her courage dissipated, she turned into another shop, bought the first pair of reasonably fitting jeans she tried on, a pea jacket and a workshirt. Almost out of the door she turned back and bought a pair of laced work shoes.

Bearing her packages like victory spoils, Victoria marched back to her dormitory and laid them on her narrow bed. Just their presence in the tall-ceilinged, perfectly neat room changed it. She was afraid, though, that someone would walk in and did not put them on. "That's enough for one day," she thought. "I'm me, no matter what I'm wearing." She would wear the new clothes when she needed to say who she was to someone else.

Though tired now, she did not want to stay in her room on a Saturday night. She walked restlessly through the dormitory, then wandered on to the dining room with a book. She read Sappho with her franks and beans, imagining herself in Sappho's school on Lesbos. Now there's an idea, she thought. If I'd gone to a school like Sappho's, how different I would have been. She stared dreamily over her book at the students who laughed and talked among themselves, almost human outside the Yale class-rooms.

Lingering after her dinner she read: "Whom shall I make love you, Sappho,/ who is turning her back on you?/ Let her run away, soon she'll chase you;/ refuse your gifts, soon she'll give them./ She will love you, though unwillingly./ Then come to me now and free me from fearful agony. Labor/ for my mad heart, and be my ally." Victoria put her head on her hand and stared at nothing, wondering if she had fallen in love with an idea. Am I a lesbian, she wondered? Is that what I felt for Heidi and, in high school, for Etta? I may never know, she told herself sadly.

Later, in bed, gazing toward the streetlamp-lighted sky outside her window, Victoria smiled again. Rosemary had swung open her door about 10:00. "You asked me to let you know our decision," she said, eyes on the floor.

Victoria smiled from under the pool of light her study lamp made. She was relaxed in her long, elegant blue robe as she fingered a carved letter opener her parents had brought back from North Africa. When Rosemary didn't continue she asked, "Do you want to come in? Is there something wrong?"

Rosemary stepped through the door and Victoria saw that her face was pink right back to where her tightly pulled hair started. "We've decided to go ahead with it," she said, her voice quavering slightly, her hand playing with the end of her braid.

"Oh, I'm so glad," Victoria said calmly, wanting to rush to Rosemary and hug her.

"You still think that it *is* the right thing to do, then?" Rosemary asked, her eyes seeking approval.

Victoria was surprised that Rosemary should ask. "Of course. If it's what you want."

"*I* know it's right," Rosemary said firmly.

"Well, I hope you'll both be very happy," Victoria said, smiling again. She felt as if she had just been invited to a wedding.

Her face solemn, Rosemary thanked Victoria and left, walking like a child dragging her feet as she goes to bed. Victoria wanted to run after her and tell her that it was all right, Claudia would not hurt her.

Now, in bed, Victoria felt again the excitement she had experienced when Rosemary first told her. As if I'd caught the bouquet at her wedding, she thought as she snuggled further under the covers, settling for the night with her arms around herself.

CHAPTER THREE

Annie Heaphy, Turkey, Eleanor and Peg sat over their fourth pitcher of beer at Marcy's. A neon advertisement blinked in the rain-wet window.

"Jeeze, you guys are depressing tonight," Turkey complained. "I should have stayed home and studied for my sociology tests. Three big ones in my own major in one day."

"What's to be happy about?" Peg asked morosely. "The other girls' gym teacher's laid up with a broken shoulder and I've got to be on the gym floor six periods now. Plus two hygiene classes. I love my job, but acting straight all day gets to me."

"Yeah, and we looked in every bar in town," Eleanor agreed, her chin on her hands. "Dusty must be with some chick tonight. She won't be needing me. Just when I need her most."

"What else went wrong?" Turkey groaned.

"Like Peg says, I like my job," Eleanor explained. "But the boss made another pass at me today, then wouldn't give me my share of the tips when I wasn't interested in him. We had a real yelling match. I don't want to leave this job."

Annie was still avoiding Eleanor's eyes. They had not been alone together since the night they spent at Eleanor's apartment. "You didn't miss much. Tips stank today. It's the rain. Besides, at least you've got Dusty to look for," she accused.

"I'm personally beginning to think love is more pain than pleasure."

"You sound like my ethics teacher," Turkey complained. "Who are you quoting now?"

Peg slumped in her uncharacteristically disheveled black vest and pants. "Me."

"You're damn right," Eleanor began, "love is a pain in the butt. Right, Annie?"

"I've forgotten," Annie gibed back. They exchanged a secret, wary grin. Eleanor leaned across the table to kiss Annie's cheek in forgiveness.

"What's with you two?" Turkey asked, groggy with beer.

"Nothing," Eleanor shrugged innocently.

Annie pulled her cap down, hiding her eyes. "What's wrong with love, Peglet?"

"It hurts."

"But ain't it worth it, Peg? Don't you think it is?" Eleanor said, looking for reassurance.

"Maybe. I don't know. I guess I feel like Heaphy here. I've forgotten the pleasure. Gloria walked out on me a year ago."

"You're forgetting your new women's libber friends. Or are they all too ugly to love?" Turkey asked, making a horrible face to imitate the "libbers" of her imagination.

"No, Turk," Peg laughed. "That isn't true. They're every bit as good looking as you." Turkey looked threateningly at her. " 'Women Are Beautiful.' That's what one of their posters says."

"Intrinsically?"

"Cool it, Annie, with your big words," Turkey said. "As a budding sociologist," and she preened, puffing out her chest in pride, "it seems to me these dames could use a looking glass theory lecture. They ought to see themselves as *I* see them." She made an even worse face.

"Us women *are* born beautiful, you Turkey," Eleanor boasted. "We can't help it. Maybe you ain't looked hard enough." She patted her flat hair and went off to the bathroom.

When Eleanor was out of hearing, Peg asked, "You stayed with her the other night, didn't you, Heaphy?"

"Yeah," Annie said, embarrassed.

"You and Ellie?" Turkey asked, shocked.

"It wasn't anything. Just the one night." Peg and Turkey were quiet. "She's uptight because I snuck out before she woke the next morning."

Peg nodded. "Figures. The old Heaphy syndrome."

"I can't help it. I *have* to."

"Boy, wow, if it was me finding a woman who wanted to sleep with me, I'd hang around. Probably for a lifetime," Turkey laughed. "Definitely till she was tired of me."

Peg looked concerned. "I'd feel as if I'd left things unfinished."

"Maybe I want to leave them then. Maybe I'll stay when it's time."

"Here comes Ellie, you two," Turkey whispered.

"That's what I like about this dump," Eleanor half-complained as she slid past Peg. "There's never a line at the bathroom."

"Now, I *like* this place," Annie said. "Don't put it down. It's got a nice homey atmosphere."

Eleanor teased her. "Just your style. Fried cockroach at the grill, alcohol with that rich old taste of wood at the bar."

"A bar's a bar, if you ask me," Peg concluded.

"Very astute," Annie raised her glass to Peg.

"There goes big-word Annie, the English major. You read too much, Heaphy, that's your trouble," Turkey said.

"And you don't read?" Annie countered.

"I don't carry a book to read between customers."

"Neither do I anymore. I'm too damn tired all the time."

"But remember when we first met you? You were carrying *three* books by Willa Cather, for pete's sake," Peg marvelled.

"Hey, I was about to finish one and I wasn't sure which one I would read next, you guys."

"But Brains," Turkey teased, "you were in a *bar*!"

"Did I know I was going to meet you guys?"

"You don't go to a bar to *read*."

"You sure don't when *you're* around," Annie laughed at Turkey.

"You should have seen these two," Peg said to Eleanor. "There was Heaphy, a beer on one side of her, a book in front of her, and two *more* books on her other side. She was sitting in the old back booth by the kitchen with Marcy's cat on her lap. Turkey spotted her and talked about the weirdo in the back booth for over an hour. Next thing, I knew, Turkey's sneaking up on Heaphy, who looks perfectly content, purring into her beer with the cat. Clutzy Turkey, stepping along on her tiptoes, is almost ready to scare the life out of poor Heaphy, when she gets one of her dainty little feet," Turkey held up a large booted foot with both her hands to show Eleanor, "caught around the leg of a chair. The chair tips, catches the tablecloth just right and pulls it. Marcy's been piling dirty ashtrays and glasses on this table all day to wash all at once, and the whole thing topples around Turkey who's taken the path of least resistance and plopped on the floor while it all lands around her."

Annie took up the often told story. "When I heard the noise I looked over and saw this big dyke flat on her ass in the dirtiest, wettest mess you can imagine, looking at me like it's all my fault. She lifts her hands from under an upside-down ashtray, wipes the ashes on her pants, and holds her grey hand out for me to shake. 'Hi, I'm Turkey,' she says. 'So I gathered,' I answer and she hauls herself up to her feet on my hand, upsetting the cat and laughing her wild Turkey laugh."

They all broke into laughter to picture the meeting once more. "So here we all are," Turkey said, "still guzzling two years later in the very same library."

"Marcy might have redecorated, but I still wish we had a nicer bar to go to," Annie said.

"Come on, Heaphy," Peg urged. "They're all the same, 'nice' or not. You get the same old hangovers. Drink the same amount of money. I wish we could have a coffee house or a place where we could sit and talk."

"What about your women's center?" asked Eleanor.

"Oh, it serves its purpose. But it's very organized. I mean, you can't go there to hang out."

"Especially if you're a dyke, right?"

Peg looked at Annie worriedly. "Nobody *says* anything. But sometimes I do sense they're afraid women won't come back if they walk in when someone who looks like me is sitting there. I'd like to have a place just for us."

"Till we have someplace better, can't we have a good time here? Don't anybody want to dance just once with me tonight?" Eleanor whined, looking at Peg and Annie. They shook their heads no.

"If it'll perk you up any, Miss Scarlett, ah will," Turkey offered.

"Don't you ever get tired of slopping around out there?" Eleanor laughed as Peg rose to let her out of the booth.

Annie and Peg sat in silence as the couples jiggled across

the small floor. Rain drove against the plate glass window. A few older gay men at the bar joked back and forth about the same old things, watching every move the younger bartender made. A neighborhood woman, her long hair a shoe polish black, played up to the men. Two women used the bowling machine. A biracial straight couple sat in a back booth under a gold-flecked mirror which reflected everything that went on.

"So you coming to the women's dance at the Yale Law School next month, Heaphy?"

"With those faggy women's libbers? You kidding, Peg? I thought we were going to New York."

"We'll go to New York too. But Heaphy, there are good vibrations at the Women's Center."

"You're just trying to convert me," Annie accused Peg.

"No, really I'm not," Peg answered with the uninhibited conviction of intoxication. "We'll have a good time. You don't know what a high it is. All these *women*, a lot of them just out, not scared of anybody, not even *with* anybody. All dancing together because they want to. And more straight women coming out every day."

"Every night, you mean," Annie laughed. "Then where do the bad vibes come from?"

"I'm not sure, but I have a theory. I think lesbians go through a phase before they come out. It's called petrified." They laughed. "When they see a dyke they project their own wish to *be* a dyke onto her and end up expecting her to attack them sexually since they can't attack the dyke yet. Make sense?"

"I've always thought the ones who talk the loudest are closest to coming out."

"And the shame of it, Heaphy, is that some of them talk so loud they talk themselves right out of coming out."

"And it's not like we're addictive or dangerous."

"We're not addictive?" Peg asked innocently.

"Shh," Annie warned, grinning and winking. "Don't let on or all your libbers will run away!"

"So what do you think, Heaphy? Will you come with me this time to protect me from all those ravenous women?"

"Peglet, you just about got me convinced," Annie said. "But it's bothering me a little, talking about them like this, like men would."

"You mean like sex objects?"

"Maybe. Like we're hunters. But I'm not thinking about sex really. Just looking for a woman. And if the libbers don't know about us dykes, how will they know what they want?"

"The old irresistible routine, Heaphy? Once they see us they won't be able to think of anything else?"

"Sounds good. Maybe I will go this time. Just to meet some. What do I have to lose? Where else have I got to go except in circles? Drive the cab around the city all day, go to the bars at night, get up the next morning swearing I won't do it all again, but here we are. At least you're teaching, doing something worthwhile, even if you do have to come here to unwind from acting straight all day. Yeah, what the hell. I'll go."

Peg grinned tiredly at Annie. "If you were femme I'd kiss you. Now we just have to persuade Eleanor and Turkey. I talked to some women downtown who want to go with us."

"Turk and El will go if we do."

"Great. And I think you'll like it. I really do."

"You're probably wrong. Maybe you'll meet the love of your life there, though. And I can say I was there when it happened. But meanwhile I have to get home if I'm going to get up in the morning."

"If you're talking about leaving," Eleanor said as she and Turkey returned, "I got to get my beauty sleep too. Let's polish off the pitcher like good little girls," she said, unsteadily filling their mugs.

"Beauty sleep for the beautiful," Turkey teased, borrowing Peg's comb to scrape through her tight hair.

"I don't know why you bother to comb that stuff," Eleanor teased back. "It never goes nowhere."

Turkey returned the comb. "Old habit, I guess." She adopted the straight-faced look that meant she was going to tell a story. "I took this good-grooming badge in Girl Scouts where I learned to comb my brillo regularly, mutilate my cuticles and wipe myself in the right direction."

Eleanor giggled. "You'll have to tell me which way is right sometime. My Mama being a country girl I guess I never learned like sophisticated city folks."

"I learned. I learned like good grooming was a biblical command," Turkey went on. "My Girl Scout leader taught the badge and I had a cast iron crush on the woman. As a matter of fact the whole troop worshipped her. She was married and had about seven kids, but I know it was just because she was Catholic. Otherwise she would have been a raging diesel dyke. You should have seen her. I think I got to like sociology because of her. I got comfortable with groups. We had a group crush on her and because of it we did everything in groups. Where Mrs. Attle went, there went our little band. We babysat for her in a group—even when she was home. We did a dozen badges at once—if she taught them. We went to the dusty old Peabody Museum every Saturday to do volunteer work—because she loved it there. We were all going to have seven kids—just like her. The whole group I'm sure wiped itself right—'cause it knew she did. And got a thrill thinking of her every time we did. Poor Mrs. Attle. If she knew now that's about the only time I think of her . . . ," Turkey guffawed. "Group behavior sure did turn me on." She lifted her beer. "A toast to Mrs. Attle, the little-old-sociology-major-maker!" Beer sloshed out of the mug and down Turkey's sleeve.

Peg and Annie laughed, but Ellie threw up her arms in exasperation. "Turkey, I have never in all my life seen such a slob."

"It's thinking of Mrs. Attle that does it to me. Can I walk you to the door?" she asked, offering her arm. "Anybody got an umbrella?"

"Dykes don't use umbrellas," Annie grumbled.

"Won't do you any good," Eleanor reminded Turkey. "You're sopped already. Smell like a brewery. Thanks anyway, but I'll get a ride home with Rudy," Eleanor said. "You are coming home tonight, ain't you, roomie?" she called to him.

"Ain't nothing to hang around here for, is there?" he answered jokingly as the older men protested.

They went into the rain while the bar made the last of its late night noises. Turkey and Peg ran toward their apartment.

They waved when Annie finally urged her wet car to life and chugged past them, coasting through red lights to avoid stalling.

Safely home later, Annie stepped through the last puddle and sat suddenly on the steps to her porch. It was so good to be home, she thought, affectionately patting a step. She had her home, lonely as it was. She had gone to the bars seldom when her roommates were still around. They'd hang out on the porch playing cards. The old house leaned silently over her and Annie leaned trustingly against its porch rail. She looked up through the trees flanking the broken walk.

It had cleared as she drove home and the stars burned in the cold, dark sky. Shit, she said aloud, as the stars began to turn above her. She looked down and breathed deeply several times. Am I going to be sick? she wondered. She walked across the open porch with its sunken couch sodden with rain and past snows, and its milk crates waiting for summer to make them chairs again. She smiled at this, her furniture, propping herself up on it as she unlocked the rickety door and went quickly through her living room. It was furnished with cinderblocks, boards, books and little else. Her roommates had taken most of the other furniture when they went back to Boston after they graduated. She collapsed on the bed, cursing herself for bothering to make it when now she had to struggle to get in it. With one great last effort, holding her breath to prevent nausea, she stripped off her army jacket, jeans, flannel shirt and workboots, wound and set her alarm, and got under the many covers of her damp, cold bed. Finally she took off her cap and laid it beside her head like a beloved teddy bear. She lay still, breathing carefully, hoping she would not have to make the cold trip across the bare linoleum floor to the bathroom, or to the stove to turn on the heater. Thoughts surfaced unexpectedly, but she pushed them down before they were complete and kept her from sleeping. "I never got drunk this much before. Maybe all I need is company. A new way of living. No more wasted days. Tomorrow I'll work more hours. Do something constructive. . . ." Annie Heaphy fell asleep.

∿ ∿ ∿ ∿ ∿

"And shall I get you a cab, Miss Locke?" Dennis asked.

Pleased with herself, Victoria answered, "No, thank you, Dennis, I'm taking the bus." She felt his surprised eyes following her as she left her apartment building. She wore jeans and a pea jacket. Since she got home a week ago she had been busy with Christmas shopping and holiday visits to relatives. Her mother had left her a full social schedule. She was sick of stuffy cabs and stuffy people. Now, in her "freedom garb," she watched the bus approach. She hadn't been on one since high school when she visited her friend Etta in Queens. Victoria's mother had not approved: public transportation was dirty and germy. It was appropriate, Victoria thought, for her to travel this more plebeian way on her first visit to a women's center. Rosemary had called from her Bronxville home where she and Claudia were for the holidays, to invite her to a meeting on lesbians in the women's movement called "Do We Belong?" She and Claudia had been lovers for a month now and Victoria did want to see them, though she had always turned Rosemary down when she wanted to get together in New York before. As the bus came beside her she wondered how Rosemary's parents had reacted to the new twist in her relationship with Claudia. Rosemary felt it was imperative to be open about it with her parents.

"Do you go to 23rd Street?" she asked the driver as she stepped onto the bus.

"Yes, ma'am, but you got to have exact change," he answered, eying her dollar bill.

"Do you mean if I don't have fifty cents I have to get off the bus even though I have a dollar? That's ridiculous!"

The driver shrugged. Angry and embarrassed, Victoria grew desperate. "Here, then, take the whole thing. Will that do?" He took the bill and Victoria turned to walk the length of the bus under the scrutiny of more experienced riders. She scowled, tossed her hair back, and reached for the open flap of her coat to flick it angrily across her legs as she sat, then realized she was no longer wearing the clothing of an indignant rich girl. Shoving her fists into her pockets she turned to look out the window, afraid the other riders would notice she was near tears. If I can't learn the rules of the bus company, she asked herself dejectedly, how will I learn to survive outside the world I know? I can dress like other people, but that doesn't give me their experiences. It's crazy, she thought fearfully. To let Rosemary tempt me out like this, to a part of the city I don't know, to listen to a bunch of women in a converted loft—anything could happen. Perhaps my mother is right. Perhaps I don't belong out here.

Crazy, she repeated, lifitng her hair off the collar of the pea jacket and adjusting her glasses. Dennis must have thought I was in disguise, she laughed softly to herself, forgetting her confusion for a moment. He had never seen her with glasses on. Feeling better, she resolved to go on with her adventure and hope that nothing awful would happen. She concentrated on the paper she would write when she returned to school. She would title it "The Origins of Boccaccio's Anti-Clerical Writing." It would prove that the suppression of human needs began with the individual's inability to deal with those needs. Only later would the suppression become institutionalized by church or state. Victoria withdrew into her subject until she stood on the windy corner where Rosemary and Claudia were to meet her.

She was faintly glad once more to see Rosemary's sallow face and thin, dull brown braid ascending the subway stairs. Behind her, Claudia's full, red-cheeked face beamed at Victoria. She smiled widely back, but when Claudia threw herself, puffing, at Victoria to hug her, Victoria shrugged her off, her hands again in the pockets of the magical pea jacket which, alas, was not magic enough to help her return such an outgoing hug. Victoria attributed Claudia's seeming enthusiasm for everything to her midwestern background. "Have you enjoyed your visit to New York?" she asked politely.

Rosemary answered for Claudia who was bouncing up and down with the cold. "I believe I've managed to show her some of the more interesting parts of the city."

"Here my mom thinks I'm safe and sound in Bronxville and Rosie has me in the evil city every night. I've learned more than I learned in three and a half years at Yale! And I don't stop learning when we get home," she said suggestively. Rosemary lifted her chin and tried to look aloof, but her eyes rested on Claudia warmly. "Tonight," Claudia continued, lowering her voice and glancing around histrionically, "we're going to a gay bar! Why don't you come?"

Victoria looked at Rosemary disapprovingly. Gay bars were not a part of the lifestyle she had envisioned for Yale graduates. "How do you know where to even *find* one? And why would you want to take her there?"

"There is more to life than books, Victoria. Two good friends of my parents are homosexual and were more than glad to shake the foundations of the nuclear family by telling me where to find a women's bar. Just in case our political friends upstairs," she gestured with her pointed little chin to some windows above them with "Women's Center" brightly painted on them, "don't agree that lesbians are an integral part of the women's movement."

Victoria's hair had blown across her face and she lifted it off, wondering if Rosemary was not going too far in her lesbianism. She did not have to become the type that cut their hair and looked like men. Surely she and Claudia could be lovers and still live the lives they had lived before, although, as she thought of it, Victoria wondered why they would want to. But Rosemary was still dressed in her long skirts and braid, and Claudia, though wearing blue jeans, had all that bouncy, curly hair and her awful flowered ski jacket. No, they did not look like lesbians. "Shall we?" Victoria finally asked, indicating a door painted like the loft windows. She was eager to discover what New York lesbians looked like now, but she said, "Though I'm not sure why I'm here."

In answer, Rosemary lifted her chin and adopted her best lecture-hall tone of voice. "Victoria," she began, as they climbed a long flight of stairs, "I don't know what you'll be doing after graduation, but I'm hoping you'll have enough of a commitment to feminism to lend your name, if nothing else, to it."

As they stopped outside a door, Rosemary faced Victoria, her eyes small and intense. "I hope you'll at least consider it," she ended, turning away to open the door. Claudia, smiling encouragingly, followed her lover inside. Victoria weighed once more her option to turn back, to go home before she was stuck and too embarrassed to leave, but she did not want to be alone any longer on this holiday. She went in the door.

The room was small and held about thirty women. Aside from posters on the walls, some cardboard boxes and empty burlap bags, it was bare. One sign read "Women's Food Co-op" and Victoria imagined these women doing their weekly shopping here in front of sacks of flour and crates of vegetables. Folding chairs had been opened and were arranged in loose concentric half-circles around a knot of three women who seemed to be doing most of the talking. Rosemary led them to some chairs in the back by a window.

Victoria was startled to hear that the three central women were raising their voices at one another. She sat aside, drifting in and out of the ideas that passed through her mind. There were a lot of shouts as the argument went on. "Lesbians are women too!" "Straight women won't join the movement if they're afraid to come to meetings here where they know lesbians will be." Victoria decided there was really no such thing as a straight woman. Weren't all people sexual beings and therefore capable of "coming out" as Rosemary would say? That made sense to her. Lesbianism might startle women who had not considered it, but, unless they had some real problems with their own sexuality, they wouldn't run too far. And anyway, how could the straight women in the meeting want to cut so many committed feminists out of their ranks? Victoria listened to the argument that lesbians in the movement forced straight women out, but she could not agree. If straight women did get turned off, how could they be feminists? Aren't women lesbians because they're women first? Surely feminists wouldn't exclude a woman for her sexuality.

Victoria watched a straight woman talk. Her fists pounded the air as she spoke of how her friends would never come to meetings or to consciousness-raising sessions with her because they were afraid of the "bulldykes." Victoria chuckled to herself. She tried without success to picture Rosemary and Claudia menacing the ladies sexually. Then she watched a short woman, a lesbian, go red in the face with rage at being oppressed by her own sisters. "We don't ask you what you do in bed with your men, do we? We don't exclude women who aren't married to men, we don't exclude women who like older or younger men. Why should you exclude women who love women!" Some of the lesbians cheered. A straight woman got up and proclaimed herself to be on the lesbian side. "Sexual expression is another choice women make about their bodies and their lives just as abortion is a choice. How can we embrace the concept of women's choices without also embracing all the choices?" she concluded.

"Do you mean we've got to champion women who like cadavers?" someone yelled out. There was general laughter and Victoria found herself staring at a very attractive woman. She, too, wore a pea jacket and jeans and glasses, though her brown hair was short. With a shock Victoria realized that she was admiring a woman who looked much like herself. Could she be the daughter of that strange woman on the train? The woman lounged, standing, against the wall, hands in her coat pockets. Once in a while she looked toward Victoria who lowered her eyes each time. Avoiding her gaze, she stared at the other woman. Was her twin a gay or a straight? She wanted very much to know, afraid that she was a lesbian, afraid of the implications of that for herself. If someone looked just like her and that person was a lesbian, then she herself might be a lesbian too. Not that she minded. She might like being a lesbian. But the world was already frightening, and so much more frightening for the different.

Rosemary stood and Victoria automatically began to rise with her, until she realized that Rosemary planned to speak. She folded into her seat and sank even lower, embarrassed by her friend's verbosity. What has she to say to these politically sophisticated New Yorkers? They would laugh at her. "A few of us are here from Yale today, expecting to return to New York after graduation next spring." Rosemary paused; there was some giggling and whispering and a low, "Screw Yale," before she went on. "At Yale we have a tender young women's group. Nowhere as large as even this gathering here, but we have been struggling to understand what brings us all together and to gain from it." Victoria looked around to see if the women were bored. Claudia was smiling widely. "We had no lesbians in our group at Yale. No 'bulldykes' as I have heard some of you describe lesbians. No one to frighten away the straight women. Lesbianism was not even an issue for us. Yet I and one other woman came out together. It was a natural evolution, something we politically felt was the right thing to do." The whispering had stopped and Victoria realized that Rosemary did have something important to say. "Now there are two lesbians in the women's group. I urge the straight women here to think about two things. First, that lesbianism is not a disease and is therefore not, as some of you seem to think, contagious. It can happen spontaneously, isolated from any influence but reason and need. Second, that it is a desirable state for some feminists to achieve. It is the ultimate feminism. Women who commit themselves to one another politically, emotionally and sexually are not only pariahs, but are the vanguard of this women's movement." Rosemary sat down, patting her Indian skirt around her and smiling quickly at Claudia. She took Claudia's hand very purposefully and turned to the front of the loft still holding it. The room seemed to exhale all at once.

"Heavy," someone said. Then the straight woman with the fists jumped up out of her seat. "That's the sort of fucked-up thinking that we are trying to avoid." As she spoke her voice rose in pitch. "There will be no women's movement if all women don't feel welcome. Newer women are afraid of lesbians!"

A lesbian cried out, "*We're* afraid of straights who want us to disappear!"

A few other women shouted in agreement.

Fists accelerating, the straight woman went on shrilly. "There has to be a place for us all in the women's liberation movement. We have to welcome more and more women and we won't do that by scaring them off with the threat of changing their lives too radically!"

"Women's lives *must* change!" another lesbian called out.

"You're creating a schism with your radicalism!" yelled another straight woman.

"Then let's stop yelling and start mending the schism," someone suggested quietly.

Victoria felt taut with the tension in the room and the violence of the emotions. Her eyes rested on the woman who looked like her and she remembered again the witch-like woman on the train. Was she her daughter, she wondered. The face not so full as the college picture, but the mother had implied that she had lost weight. Could this woman actually have been married, had children, been beaten by her husband? Now, slouching against the wall, looking strong and experienced, was this the woman who had rejected all that? Victoria realized how much she did find the woman attractive. Not only because she looked like her, but because she looked like she could handle herself, as if she was in control. She smiled toward the woman, glad when she did not see the smile. She was scared that the woman would talk to her and she would be lost to her spell. What if the woman had inherited some of her mother's witch-like qualities and showed Victoria even more of herself than her mother had on the train? She was afraid of this much more dangerous exposure here, as an equal.

The woman, still not aware how Victoria's eyes followed her, reached her hand across the chair of a woman sitting in front of her and laid it on her shoulder. She bent and whispered into her ear. The seated woman rose, took the hand of Victoria's twin, and the two left. Moving to the window, Victoria looked down to see them walk off with their arms around one another.

Victoria sat very still. More women got up to leave. The passion had drained from the discussion. A work group formed to develop recommendations about how to help lesbian and straight women understand each other and work together. She is a lesbian, Victoria thought, stunned despite herself. Is someone marking a trail for me? Did that mother curse or bless me in some way, trying to transfer her daughter's rebellions onto me? "What?" she asked, jumping as Claudia shook her shoulder.

"Wasn't she great? She just floored them!"

"Who?" Victoria asked.

"Rosemary, silly! Weren't you listening?"

Victoria looked at where Rosemary was surrounded by lesbians who were thanking her for what she had said. She still felt stunned by her twin's lesbianism, as if it were a sure sign of her own. "Yes, of course I was listening."

"But you didn't see the light. I can tell. Oh, it was so important that she said it, don't you think? I'm so glad we came. Now they're going to work on it instead of just arguing about it and glaring at each other forever."

"Yes, yes," Victoria said, emerging from her thoughts. "Yes, she spoke well. And I did see the light," she added, but Claudia had turned away to stand proudly with her lover. Victoria was left on the brink of the world of love and women, feeling more alone than she ever had before.

$$\sim \sim \sim \sim \sim$$

Annie Heaphy, Turkey, Peg and Eleanor crowded around the surly bouncer who demanded $3.00 each from them. "Boy, she's tough," Turkey whispered to Annie, admiringly. "Maybe I should forget about college, move to New York and get a job as a bouncer, huh Annie?"

"You got your taste in your ass, Turkey. She's a class A dumb bulldyke who probably makes peanuts here because no one else will hire her she looks so much the part."

"Shh," Turkey answered as she went to pay the bouncer. "Hey, uh," Turkey asked, laughing nervously between each word, "How'd you get this job?"

"Friend a my girl's part owner, why?"

"Oh, thanks," poor Turkey giggled, obviously disappointed. She patted her chest nervously and brushed off her rust-colored, baggy overalls and a voluminous black and light-blue striped shirt.

"So that's why I should get a job as a bouncer," she said as Annie joined them.

"Why?"

"She ain't a bit uglier than me," Turkey laughed loudly.

Annie Heaphy shook her head, rearranging her cap. "But you're nice. Besides, you couldn't stop laughing long enough to throw someone out."

"She's got to throw people *out*?"

"You *turkey*," Eleanor laughed, her light southern accent exaggerated in New York. "Why do you think they call them bouncers?"

Turkey hung her head. "You got a point," she admitted, then looked up and laughed again. "Oh well," she said, "sociology majors probably make lousy bouncers anyway! I'd be too busy lecturing people on why they acted in a way that attracted attention to them in a group of their peers."

"Come on, guys," Peg urged. "There's a table we can grab."

Annie kept her head down as she walked across the half-full dance floor. It was still early, too early to be anonymous, and Annie sensed that she would feel more self-conscious here than at Marcy's. When she had a few drinks she would feel less conspicuous. Even show off a little, probably. She sat with her back to the floor.

"Ain't this a shame," Turkey laughed as she settled her wide bottom on a tiny chair done in ice-cream parlor style.

"I think it's awful cute," Eleanor said. "Whoever decorated this place had good taste." She crossed her legs in their purple denim jeans and slipped her imitation fur jacket onto the back of her chair. She was wearing a silky white blouse splashed with chartreuse and violet and her hair was up in a way that made her look vaguely like a model for shampoo. She kept removing bobby pins and replacing them through the evening. Tapping a long cigarette on the table, she held it out to be lit. As usual, all three of her friends scrambled to light it in the old game of who's butchiest. Eleanor loved it. "You all are getting slow," she laughed after Turkey dropped her lighter on the short cable spool that served as a table. Eleanor sighed with regret, trying to look seductively at both Peg and Annie. "Anybody cute here yet?" she asked as always to start the evening off.

"Just let's get a waitress over here, cute or not, and I'll be happy," Annie said.

"I think you both got your wishes, ladies," Peg said as she waved toward a waitress.

Annie's courage disappeared and she stuttered when she ordered from the good-looking woman in jeans and an Indian shirt open halfway down her chest.

"A Coke," Peg ordered, smiling graciously at the waitress. She shot her light blue cuffs out from under her navy sport jacket and smoothed her cream colored slacks. She met the others' looks when the waitress left. "I'm *driving*. Besides, I'm not in the mood for drinking. I'd like to meet a girl. Hey, El, you like our server?"

"Looked kind of stuck up."

"She can *smell* hicks looking at you guys," Peg teased.

"I'm no hick," Annie protested. "You tell anybody from

Boston, aside from myself who gives you special consideration due to your origins, being from this filthy town—you tell any other Bostonian she's a hick, you'll learn," she threatened.

"Me neither," Turkey added. "New Haven's no small town. Besides, we treat you out-of-towners right, don't we?"

Eleanor patted a bobby pin back into place. "I'd like to issue an invitation to certain big city women to *try* a hick." She smiled up at the waitress who was back with their drinks disinterestedly waiting to be paid. There was a scramble to give her money and she walked away.

"Didn't even say thank you," huffed Eleanor.

Peg hit a fist against the table. "Look what they do to gay women! Did you ever hear such prices?"

"It's New York," Annie explained, taking it for granted.

"Yeah," Peg answered angrily. "So not only do we pay inflated prices to go to a bar not even as nice as one of ours, but we pay more because it's a gay bar. They have us, alright. We've got no place else to go so they know we're going to swarm in here to waste our money. It makes me sick."

"Plus a cover charge." Eleanor, Turkey, Peg and Annie looked as one to the next table. A woman with long braided hair had joined their conversation. She was with two other women. None of them looks as if she's been in a gay bar before, Annie Heaphy thought. She downed her first beer, staring at a woman who looked to her like a thoroughbred, except for her eyes. "They're all alive and warm and excited," Annie thought. "I could fall for those eyes."

Annie almost jumped when the sharp-chinned woman went on. "It's just another way women are oppressed. But obviously you sisters know that."

Eleanor rolled her eyes. Turkey guffawed quietly and Annie glared at both her friends.

"Right you are, sister," Peg answered, toasting their neighbors with her Coke, wondering where she had seen "Sister" before.

"It's good to see you aren't drinking," "Sister" went on, apparently unaware of Turkey's struggle to control her laughter. "The bar trap. How many lesbians fall in it?" she asked rhetorically. "If only lesbians would realize that liquor ambushes them *into* self-destruction to keep them down.''

Annie glanced covertly at the thoroughbred's glass and, relieved, saw a mixed drink before she signalled the waitress for another beer. When she looked back, "Sister" had quieted and the thoroughbred, who met Annie's eyes, looked quickly away. Peg leaned toward Turkey and Eleanor and started talking intently. "Like I was saying, the arm is a magnificent example of the intricacy of the human body. Take the muscles of the upper arm . . .''

"*You* take them,'' Turkey gurgled. "And take your friends too. Is that what you go to your meetings with?''

"Yuk,'' Peg grimaced, almost whispering. "No way. I think I've seen her around somewhere, but I've never been to a meeting with her.''

"Is that how they talk?'' Eleanor wanted to know.

"Listen, guys, she's saying the right things. It's just like she's a cartoon version of a feminist: all politics and no woman.''

"Personally, *I* think she's got something stuck up her ass,'' Turkey nodded seriously, setting Eleanor off into a gale of laughter.

"Cut it out,'' Annie chided them. "Look who she's got with her.'' All three heads turned back to the next table. "Not *now*, you jerks,'' Annie whispered, mortified. All three looked quickly away while Annie hid her face behind her beer mug. She snuck a look toward the thoroughbred who looked uncomfortable.

"All right, Rosemary,'' the thoroughbred was saying, "you persuaded me to come, but not to stay all night. Are you almost ready to leave or shall I call a cab for myself?''

Annie's heart jumped. She wanted to tell the woman to stay. It would take more drinks before she had the nerve to talk to her.

"We just got here a half hour ago. Aren't you having a good time, Victoria?''

Victoria, Victoria, rang in Annie's attentive ears. "Shh,'' she hissed at Turkey who had been trying to get her attention.

"It's not that, Rosemary. I'm just not sure that we belong here.''

"Why not? Claudia and I are lesbians,'' she said, putting an arm awkwardly around Claudia's shoulders, careful not to touch anything but the soft white v-neck sweater across Claudia's fleshy shoulders. "And you're our friend. Why shouldn't we be here?"

Victoria looked at Annie's table just as Annie peeked again from behind her mug at her. "I don't know," Victoria sighed.

"Victoria," Claudia reached her hand across to her. "Please just relax. I'm enjoying it here, but I wouldn't without you. Honest. Pretend I'm observing for a psych class," she smiled. "Help me take notes for another half hour and if you're still uncomfortable we'll go home."

Victoria could not resist Claudia's sincere plea. "All right, but I don't think we belong, whether you're gay or not."

"I'm sure it's the class difference, not sexuality, making you uncomfortable," Rosemary said.

"You may be right."

"There is a definite difference in class, Victoria, but that's no reason not to be here. We need someplace to meet other lesbians and our so-called class just doesn't provide that."

Claudia suggested, "Maybe there are clubs for dykes with Ph.D.'s. Who knows?"

"I wish you wouldn't use that word, Claudia," Rosemary complained. She toyed with the lime in her glass.

"Dyke? What's wrong with it? I kind of like it."

"It implies something bad."

"But, Rosemary," Claudia protested, "so does lesbian and all the other words people use to describe us. It's what they put into the words that does it, not the words themselves, right, Victoria? You're the lit major."

"She's right, Rosemary, you know that," Victoria looked at her puzzled. "Words are used by too many people to control. Dyke is a good old fashioned Celtic word."

"I'd rather be called that than homosexual," Claudia said. "Imagine having to live with the word sexual so close to you all the time. Why, it defines you in purely sexual terms. Dyke is kind of cute."

Victoria stole another look at Annie's table at this, thinking that the word dyke *was* cute and she smiled toward the woman in the hat. Annie Heaphy smiled back at her. "Oh," she said almost aloud, and "I didn't mean to smile," to herself, still smiling, then abruptly frowning at the lesbian. The woman turned away, her shoulders sagging, then shrugged as if to say, "I don't care either." Victoria wanted to correct her signals again, to step over to the lesbian and say, "It isn't that I don't want to smile, I just didn't mean to and then I got confused," but she realized that she wasn't sure that she *would* have wanted to smile in any case because she did not know exactly what she was feeling. She slipped her pea jacket off her shoulders and stretched out the neck of her sweater to let some cooler air touch her body. How warm the bar was!

Annie ordered another drink. "What are *you* looking at," she glowered at Turkey.

"Hey, *I* can't help it if she isn't interested, man. Maybe she's not out yet."

"Then what in the world is she doing here?" wondered Eleanor.

Annie mumbled, "Her friends are gay."

"You really don't think she is?" Turkey asked, staring at the woman again. "You ought to know."

"Me?" asked Annie. "Why me?"

"Cause you see more of the world in that little box of a cab of yours than the rest of us. Me, shut up in classrooms, Peg in a gym."

"And all's I see are truckdrivers devouring hamburgers."

"You're our woman of the world, alright." Turkey leaned back to describe her image of Annie. "Every kind of character there is gets in and out of your cab. ANNIE HEAPHY, STAR CABBIE," she went on, gesturing grandly, "haunting the city to build her collection of Types."

"Cut it out, Turkey," Annie protested.

Turkey only became more involved in her game. She hunched forward and pretended to speak into a microphone. "She starts her day in the subterranean world of a diner. Sharing coffee with the workers of the world who are on their way home from the graveyard shift, indistinguishable from them except for the filth of her cap." Eleanor began to giggle. "Ah, but now she goes into the world to ferry streaming humanity to the places it earns its daily bread. The harried executive,"

Turkey stood surprisingly quickly from her tiny seat and pretended to hold an attache case awkwardly out from her body. "The lady executive. . . ." Here she flipped open an invisible compact and patted her cheeks manically with powder. Peg was chuckling. "The shopper comes in from the suburbs to spend, spend, spend!" She struggled with armloads of packages that fell with each step she took in place. Annie broke into a smile. "The furtive lovers who must part after a sordid night in their dingy hotel room." Gazing adoringly upward, Turkey put her arms around non-existent broad shoulders and smacked wet lips, fishlike, toward the air. Then she turned and bent down as if holding a small woman, all the while sneaking glances out the cab windows to see if they are being observed. Eleanor and Peg were laughing aloud now as Turkey sat and quickly portrayed a frantic racing fan checking a scratch sheet on his way to a bookie's, a pair of nuns clicking rosaries as they began a trip to the airport, and, finally, a mother taking her sick child who is vomiting all over Annie's back seat, to the doctor. At this, even Annie broke into laughter because it had happened to her.

"But wait," Turkey continued, whispering suspensefully into the microphone. "Through all this parade of humanity, our Star Cabbie must see through these facades and play the game we all know so well . . . ," she paused, "the game of—Who's the Dyke?" Laughter came from tables around them. "The sick kid!" called one listener. "The nuns!" cried another. There was more laughter as Turkey became the game show host explaining the game to his studio audience. "It's a well known fact that one out of every ten people is gay. It's the sad fate and the trusted office of the gay cabdriver to penetrate the disguises of every ten people and 'Find the Dyke!' " The women around her broke into a light applause and Turkey stood to bow.

When she sat again she whispered, "Well, Star Cabbie? What's your conclusion about 'Sister's' friend? Is she or isn't she?"

Annie looked thoughtful. "I conclude," and she paused dramatically to place her cap over her heart, catching Turkey's comic spirit, "that if she isn't, she *will* be. And I personally guarantee it."

Peg, Eleanor and Turkey cheered Annie. The waitress

brought more drinks. The four friends sat silently, still smiling over Turkey's performance. Annie was half listening to the conversation at Sister's table. The woman called Claudia was telling stories about the farm where she grew up. "Why don't you ask her to dance?" Eleanor asked. "Even if she isn't as pretty as some."

Annie scowled at her. "I'm not interested."

Eleanor looked at Peg. "Why don't you two dance?" Peg asked.

"Yeah, Annie, won't you dance with me? My feet are getting itchy. Come on, Annie."

"No, you dance with her, Peg."

"Okay."

"Oh, goody!" Eleanor squealed, jumping up from her seat. "Maybe somebody real nice will cut in."

"Ain't I real nice, lady?" Peg asked.

Eleanor took her arm and they stepped into the crowd on the dance floor, squeezing their way through to the center of it. Annie looked over at Victoria again, but she was arguing with "Sister." Claudia tugged on "Sister's" puffed peasant-blouse sleeve, asking her to dance, but it was Victoria who rose to dance with the shorter woman. Annie watched them follow Peg and Eleanor to the floor.

"She your type or what, Annie?" Turkey wanted to know.

"I guess if I have a type, that's it."

"Yeah, you like them educated, don't you?"

"That seems to be who I go for alright, Turkey."

"Then ask 'Sister' to dance."

"Don't make fun."

"Who's making fun?" Turkey straightened her overall straps. "She looks lonely. Probably doesn't know how to dance."

"Then, Turkey, I think it's a good idea for *you* to teach her on account of you being such a good Samaritan and all."

"Oh, Annie, I'm *sure* she prefers blondes. Look at her, so lonely over there, computing her millions."

"Studying weighty matters . . ."

"Her head in the clouds . . ."

"Lusting after your body . . ."

"Annie Heaphy! I'm shocked you could even think such a thing about her."

"Hey, Turkey," Annie whispered conspiratorily, "do you think she *knows* what to do with her little friend?"

Turkey finally bellowed with laughter. "I hope not, 'cause I can't imagine it!"

"We're being mean, now, Turk."

"Yeah, you're right." She paused to giggle. "But it's so much fun."

The couples were leaving the dance floor. Annie spotted Victoria leading Claudia back, a bright flush on their cheeks. Peg and Eleanor were right behind them.

"Come on, Annie, it's your turn. Listen, a slow one," Eleanor invited.

Peg grabbed Annie's collar and playfully pulled her up. "Come on, Heaphy, quit mooning."

Annie glanced over at Victoria as Eleanor found her hand and pulled her onto the dance floor. Victoria was picking up her jacket.

"Hey," Eleanor tugged at her, "You going to dance or not?" Annie silently put her arms around Eleanor, her eyes following Victoria. Was she leaving without her friends? Annie's heart pounded as she thought of herself approaching Victoria and asking her to stay. Eleanor's arms tightened around Annie. "Finally I'm holding you again," she said, nestling her head on Annie's shoulder. Annie felt impatient. She wanted to think, before Victoria went out the door, of a way to stop her and learn who she was so she could find her another time when she had more courage. "I guess you didn't enjoy our night together as much as me," Eleanor was saying.

Annie barely controlled her impatience. "Sure I did, Elly."

"You sound very convincing, let me tell you," Eleanor replied sarcastically.

Annie pulled back from her. "Sorry," she said, feeling bad about her divided attention. She turned Eleanor around on the floor to see the door better. "I enjoyed you," she whispered, pressing her cheek against Eleanor's hair.

Eleanor's body relaxed and she pressed herself against Annie. Victoria was going toward the door. Annie's heart slowed and she exhaled deeply. "Thank you, Annie. I had a good time too," Eleanor breathed back at her as she leaned away to smile at Annie. "Maybe we can do it again."

"Maybe," Annie agreed. They danced in silence for awhile, Annie trying to forget about the woman who had just left, the stranger who had caught her fancy, and think instead of her friend's needs. "I don't know, though," she looked at Eleanor, hoping she would not be hurt. "I like you an awful lot as a friend. I think that's very important to me."

The music stopped and they started back to their table. "I know what you mean, Annie," Eleanor said reflectively, swinging her hand in Annie's. "I'd hate to lose our friendship for some sex."

"Exactly," Annie said as they reached the table. They squeezed hands once more and smiled. "Come on, Turkey. This one sounds just like you, doesn't it?" she asked, directing her question to the whole group.

"This is a lindy, you guys. I'm not a social historian, just a sociologist," Turkey said, struggling up from the tiny low seat.

"Don't sociologists dance?" Annie laughed as they moved to the floor. She secretly wanted Victoria's friends to notice her and led Turkey in that direction, just far enough away not to be obvious. Perhaps they would talk about her to Victoria, perhaps, she daydreamed, Victoria would come back looking for her exactly a year from this night and Annie would pledge to herself to remember the date and come back herself. . . . Annie woke from her daydream suddenly when Victoria returned. Filled with relief, Annie lindied even more frantically and smiled widely at Turkey who did a complicated set of steps in response. Annie's joy overcame her inhibitions. She copied the steps, till Turkey became more inventive. Annie matched her again. When the music stopped they were panting and thirsty and laughingly pushed their way to the table. Peg had ordered more drinks and Annie lifted her beer can, chugging through a smile, spilling the cold stuff on her white shirt and jeans, then laughing and looking at Victoria who was again talking with her friends. Annie was high, finally, and not afraid.

"Would you like to dance?" she found herself asking the woman, intently seeking her eyes through their glasses as if her life depended on Victoria's answer. Victoria looked at Rosemary and Claudia and back to Annie while Annie wiped the sweat of the last dance from her forehead with her sleeve and lifted her cap to run her fingers through her hair in quick, rapid motions. Victoria felt herself warm under her peacoat again and knew she would say yes. Annie looked like a tense, determined dyke-goddess fresh from the heavens as she stood in her white shirt and jeans, her sleeves rolled up to her forearms, her ruby pinky ring making tracks in the air as she moved her arm under the swirling bar light, her short hair messy under the cap, her breasts round and tender-looking just under her shirt. Astonished at herself for thinking of the woman this way, Victoria met her blue eyes and said, "Sure, thank you."

She took off her jacket and followed Annie briskly to the dance floor. "This is a real slow one," Annie said. "I need it after that last dance."

Victoria struggled to keep her eyes open against the warmth that invaded her body at the woman's touch. One hand lay so very gently on the small of her back that only Victoria's suddenly heightened responses made her aware of it guiding her. Just under her own Victoria could feel the woman's breasts against herself and she pulled away slightly each time only to sway back as if seeking their contact again. She was half dizzy by the time she could respond. "Yes," she said, "I saw you. You dance quite well." She was surprised to see the woman redden from the compliment.

"Thanks, but I don't really consider that dancing. More like acrobatics."

"I can see why. Where did you learn?" Victoria asked, pulling herself back again when she wanted to crush the woman to her. What was it about her? She had never felt this compulsion for another being before.

"I just kind of do what I want. I don't really know *how* to dance." Annie had to tilt her arms upward to hold Victoria who was slightly taller than herself. She was aware of her own hands on Victoria's back and waist and of Victoria's hands on her back. "I like the way you dance," she said, needing to talk more before she felt shy again. There was something overpowering about this woman, something that made her want to run, but at the same time kept her dancing with her. She knew that she would be back for more even after she did escape. Victoria felt like the undertow of a larger wave than Annie had ever felt. She wished she could grab a swig of her beer or a shot.

"Thank you," Victoria answered, wishing for some words to end the small talk, for a way to tell this girl how warm she made her feel and to ask her if that made her a lesbian. She was glad she had worn her ceremonial garb. Never before had she so wanted to be acceptable. "My name is Victoria," she said, wondering if one gave out one's last name in a gay bar.

"I'm Annie, Annie Heaphy. I'm from New Haven and I drive a cab." Somehow Annie felt she must make clear her status in the world.

"Hello, Annie Heaphy," Victoria smiled affectionately at her. "It's Victoria Locke and I live in New Haven too. I'm a student." She felt reluctant to tell Annie Heaphy that she went to Yale, afraid it would turn her off.

"Really?" Annie asked, obviously pleased. "I never saw you around."

Knowing Annie meant the gay bars, Victoria felt her way, unsure whether to say that she'd never been in one before.' I don't go out much. I'm afraid I'm not very sociable. This is quite an outing for me."

"To tell the truth," Annie confessed again, "this is the first time I've been here."

"To New York?"

"No. I come down every once in awhile. But I don't get to the New York bars much."

"I've never been in a bar."

"What brings you here?"

"Semester break. My parents live in New York. Rosemary and Claudia," Victoria gestured toward her friends, "took me to a women's movement meeting today. They were coming here so I decided to come along."

Annie felt heavy with the possibility of the next question. It should be so easy to ask for sure if she's gay . . . The music stopped and, frustrated, Annie walked with Victoria to her table. Annie danced again, this time with Eleanor who swept her onto the floor without giving her time to say no.

"Is she nice?" Eleanor wanted to know.

"I hardly talked to her. I think so."

"You don't mind me being jealous, do you?" Eleanor teased.

"Don't be silly," Annie poked her playfully.

"She's pretty," Eleanor mused.

"Not really. Everything is nice to look at, but it doesn't all come together nice, you know?"

"I know what you mean. Like a face that don't know who it belongs to yet."

Annie thought for a moment. "I bet you're right." She stopped dancing. "Wait. She *is* leaving this time."

"What?" Eleanor turned to see. She looked back at Annie. "You scared her off awful fast. Do you want to stop her?" she asked sympathetically.

"Of course I do. But how can I? I just danced with her once. What if I really did scare her away?"

"Maybe she has to get up for work."

"She goes to school."

"She could work too."

Annie looked at Eleanor despairingly. Victoria was gone. The music had stopped. "Well, this is silly," Annie said, shoving her hands into her pockets. "I fell for a dream-woman, that's all. Let her run away with her friends. It's not the end of world, whatever the reason. Maybe Turkey's right. Maybe she's not out yet and she's scared to death. Anyway, she lives in New Haven."

"She does?" Eleanor was surprised.

"Yeah. But she doesn't go to bars. I wonder what school she goes to?"

"If you can get your mind off her for a minute, Annie, why don't you dance this slow one with me since we're standing here anyway. You'll hardly miss her. I promise," Eleanor told Annie seductively.

"Okay, okay," Annie laughed, pulling her cap down over her eyes and taking Eleanor into her arms. Eleanor began to lead Annie in a reserved bump and grind. Annie laughed and said, "Don't try so hard."

"Don't think so hard," Eleanor answered, hugging her more tightly.

CHAPTER FOUR

Annie Heaphy guided the old, heavy cab through the railroad station parking lot and stopped behind two other weary-looking beasts. She checked her watch, noted the next train would not arrive for over ten minutes, and slid down in her seat, hoping the radio would be silent long enough for a nap. She pulled the brim of her cap over her eyes to shield her headache from the glare of the sun on leftover patches of snow, swearing again that tonight she would drink less, hoping she would meet someone and be so taken by her she would not want to get drunk. The radio hissed, crackled a message to someone else and Annie Heaphy drooped beneath the sun to a quick, deep sleep.

Victoria Locke walked briskly ahead of the other passengers and slipped into the first available cab, slamming the door behind her to wake the lazy cabbie sleeping in the front seat. She was anxious to get to the dormitory and start the Boccaccio paper. When the driver merely stirred and did not wake, Victoria was ready to slam her way out of the cab as her mother would have done. But as she reached for her bag she saw the cabbie's hat had fallen off. The hair underneath was the blonde hair of a girl. Victoria stopped breathing and a pain entered her chest. She leaned forward and gently woke Annie Heaphy.

From the touch on her shoulder Annie Heaphy knew it was just a fare; from the gentleness, an older woman with daughters her own age, and she shot up defensively, starting the cab in the same motion and asked, "Yes, ma'am, where to?" The hand had lifted slowly off her shoulder and the fare whispered, "Yale," in a strange, husky voice. Annie could not see her in the rear-view mirror, but her voice sounded young, almost familiar. All business, she set her cap back on her head and began to drive. "What part?" she asked, still trying to see who was in the back. It *is* a student, she decided as the low voice named a college and the street its entrance fronted. She was still puzzled by the touch that was as gentle as a mother's but the accent discouraged her because it belonged to another goddamned rich Yalie. Shit, Annie Heaphy said to herself, no longer trying to see the face, deciding to ride this one through the ghetto, push her face in the mud, maybe curse out another driver to shake her up a little. She rammed her shift through the gears and stepped on the accelerator as she turned into the shortcut through overcrowded streets even Annie didn't care to see.

The wave of strange emotion was ebbing now. Victoria had heard the girl's voice and recognized its gruffness as she recognized the hat. It was the girl with whom she had danced in New York. Victoria still could not forget that night although two months had passed. She had felt awkward and out of place, but more because Rosemary had embarrassed her than because she felt she did not belong. There had been something very exciting in being looked at that way by women. And in looking back. And now her heart had opened again at the sight of the driver. The witch returned to her mind. Was this another sign pointing her toward herself? That she should meet the girl again—and so soon—was too coincidental.

The pale, distant sun was abandoning the sky and small gusts of wind blew trash along the empty streets. Annie drove as if trying to run down some invisible enemy that dodged her with the wind. Victoria sighed when they entered the narrow streets of Yale, not gladdened by this return. Students were double parked, lugging their suitcases into grey stone buildings through heavy black gates. Annie stopped for none of them, weaving in and out and using her horn with what sounded like vengeance.

She stopped short outside the dormitory. She had just remembered to call in her location and got a new destination immediately. "These people don't see past their noses," she thought. "Time is money. Why couldn't this rich bitch count out her goddamned money while I was trying not to run over her stupid friends? Act like they own the streets. Probably do." Finally the girl was pushing the money at her and she turned to take it. Victoria looked slowly from her hands which had touched Annie's to Annie's weary-looking face and noticed the sad slant of her eyes. She told her to keep the change. Annie checked the money as the woman handed it to her, squinting angrily as she glared up from under her cap to mutter thank you. The words stayed inside her mouth when she saw Victoria and she caught her breath and flushed. She zipped her jacket open. She stared and stared as the woman left the cab, then she pushed out of her own door and slammed it behind her. A sports car swerved and honked at her. Victoria stopped to look toward the sound of the car's brakes and Annie called, "Do you have any more luggage?" desperately hoping that she did.

"No, just this," Victoria answered.

Recklessly, Annie asked, "Vickie, wasn't it?" for the woman looked different in the fading daylight and Annie could not believe her luck in finding her again.

"Well, yes. Victoria, actually, but Vickie will do . . ."

"I'm Annie. Annie Heaphy. We met . . ." Victoria turned slowly away and began to mount the steps. "Oh, don't" Annie began to say, but was afraid to scare the woman. She could think of nothing else to keep her there. "Thanks," she finally shouted up the steps. The woman turned again and smiled through the twilight at Annie who was smiling at her, her cap in her hand.

"Damn," Annie said when the woman had disappeared inside the door. "Damn, damn." She walked to her cab with quick, choppy steps, slamming the cap on her head. Muttering to herself, she took off like a teenage boy when she remembered that she was supposed to be several blocks away picking up a fare.

"Forty-seven," hissed the radio.

"Forty-seven," answered Annie.

"Where the hell are you, Heaphy? The party at sixteen Bishop just called again."

"On my way, Mr. G. You know these little old ladies, counting out their pennies," she lied guiltily.

"Don't get lost again," Mr. G. growled before shutting her off.

Annie sped through yellow lights and passed two cars crazily before braking sharply at the address. No one was there.

She honked her horn and slumped in her seat, arms folded, to think about Vicky. How, she wondered, would she get to see her again? Go to the dormitory and knock on her door? The thought sent anxious chills around her body. Lie in wait in a doorway until she went out somewhere? Then what? She would still have to approach her. See if she was in the phone book? Yes! That was perfect. Except, Annie did not remember Vicky's last name. "Crap," she said aloud and looked to see if anyone was coming from the house. She honked again and looked at her watch. Two minutes more, in case it was a slow-moving old person. Whatever she decided, it would have to be cool, she resumed thinking. This was no ordinary woman she was dealing with. This was a Yalie. She would have to be on her toes to win this prize. But she was worth it, Annie thought, full of a glow she had never before experienced so intensely.

She sighed and took another look at the address. Then she radioed Mr. G.

"Nothing right now, forty-seven," he directed.

"Going to the Plaza, then," she replied, deciding as she said it to celebrate finding Vicky. Should she stop for a quick beer? No, it was almost time to go in, she'd get her beer soon. She turned suddenly into an illegal parking space and locked the cab. Not pausing, she ran across a street to a small strip of park in the middle of the road and sat on one of the empty benches. The park, she remembered, was pretty with dogwoods in the spring. Now the trees were empty, but shone eerily with the last of daylight. Annie breathed frost out in front of her mouth and determined to bring Vicky to this park in the spring. "Yalies never know where anything good is," suddenly feeling affectionate toward them, wondering if perhaps the women weren't all that bad. She leaped up and stood on her bench, then leaped from it to the next. She balanced on its edge before getting a running start to the next one.

"Feeling good, huh, Heaphy?" she asked herself as she landed on the third bench, the anxiety of losing her footing all confused with that of seeing Vicky again. "Vicky." she bellowed into the last of the fading winter afternoon. "Vicky!" she cried as she completed each of her leaps to circle the tiny park. Filled with excitement she leaped from the last bench out of the park and ran back to her cab.

~ ~ ~ ~ ~

Victoria's room was cold. She had taken off her coat, but now drew it across her shoulders, rubbing her cheek against its velvet collar. The old radiator had begun to warm with its first heat. She sat directly on it, leaned her head against the window and sighed. Three stories down the confusion of returning students continued, but there were no yellow cabs. Perhaps the next rain, she thought, reaching into her pocket for the schedule. This is foolish, she shook her head slowly at herself. Why would the cab driver want to return? If she did, she would just be doing her job, delivering another passenger like me. And I wouldn't know what to say to her, she mused, withdrawing her hand from her pocket and the schedule. On the other hand, if she did approach me, would that mean she thinks I'm a lesbian? She makes me feel strange, strange.

Turning toward the room she appreciated its tasteful familiarity. With her careful placement of painting and furniture, the tall ceiling and narrow window did not make the room look smaller, but emphasized its height. Her room suggested some part of a cathedral. The bluish winter twilight made this impression even stronger and she bent to the small but heavy-looking dark oak table, which displayed her favorite possessions, to light a candle. If I could just put a skylight in, she thought as she admired the effect of the tiny light up the tall walls to the ceiling where she had tacked a mandala poster. At that distance and in that light it looked like a stained glass window. She slipped off the black heels that made her feel so adult and walked in her stockinged feet to the closet for her floor-length robe. Before she hung up her coat she looked quickly at the train schedule, hardly noticing what she read, and placed it on the dresser. Junk: I should throw it out, she decided, then forgot it as she hung up her city clothes. Pulling the tie of her robe around her and knotting it, she began to pace the room, feeling like a cross between a monk and a late nineteenth century lady troubled with erotic thoughts which horrified her, but gave her no rest.

Would she like me as I look now, Victoria wondered, thinking back to the cab ride. She found Annie attractive with that pale, soft-looking skin, the chopped fine blonde hair, the way she squinted as if she doubted everything, hiding under the brim of her hat. Definitely attractive, Victoria smiled affectionately. If I were going to be a lesbian, it would be easy to fall in love with Annie, Annie Heaphy, just from her looks. She had never much cared about people's looks before this; just what was inside. And what was inside Annie Heaphy? Why did she drive so violently? And then get so shy on her own two feet, stuttering as she talked, afraid to ask Victoria what she so obviously wanted to ask? Why did she take such risks? She drove as she moved: quickly, unthinking, careless of herself, desperate to get where she was going. Victoria had noticed that Annie drank consumingly, too, as if to get herself high fast and keep herself there, at the highest point, as long as possible. She appeared to want life raw, too hungry to wait for it to become more digestible, and this attracted Victoria strongly. She was just the opposite, treating both frightening experience and emotion like untouchables who could serve her at a distance, but never approach her. This intense woman had lodged herself under Victoria's cool facade. Victoria was afraid that Annie had resolved to grab her whole from a life that held her tight and she sensed this resolve roaming outside in the city wild and persistent. And Victoria had run from her twice now.

She jumped at the knock on her door and pulled her robe tighter around her waist. Rosemary came in with a vase of roses. "Welcome back," she said placing them on Victoria's little table.

"They're beautiful," Victoria said in surprise. "What made you do it?"

Rosemary arranged the roses a second time. "I bought a dozen for Claudia, but they looked so much like you I knew I should give them to you too."

"Looked like me?" Victoria asked, fingering the red buds.

"Beautiful, but closed still, just on the verge of straining open."

Victoria looked at her friend, alarmed at such a personal comment. "Would you like to stay for awhile? I brought some cookies back from that bakery you like."

"No, I should go back to the room. Claudia's almost finished with her paper."

"Please stay, Rosemary," Victoria asked, surprised at herself. "I need to talk to you."

Rosemary looked at Victoria for the first time, her small brown eyes elongated by the braid she wore so tightly plaited. "Of course, if you need to," she said and sat down, smoothing her long gray skirt.

Victoria began to pace again. "How did you feel when you first suspected you might be a lesbian?"

"Oh, Victoria, it wasn't a matter of *suspecting* myself," Rosemary said quickly, snapping her head up.

"All right," Victoria said. She didn't really want to know. "What was it then?" she asked despite herself.

"Oh," Rosemary sighed, "it was such a feeling of relief to know I could love women completely!"

"You weren't uncomfortable with it at all?"

"As I said in my poem—and I think you should admit that I won our poetry duel," Rosemary winked at Victoria as she rose to adjust the roses again, " 'Not racked so much by dreams as by/ the aspirations I might fill with you. . . .' How could I be uncomfortable? It's the right thing to do. And already we have a future far beyond what I had imagined. One of the women in the poetry group is an assistant in a lab where they're working on cloning," she looked at Victoria expectantly.

Victoria felt annoyed again. "Yes?" she asked shortly, sitting on the edge of the bed.

"With cloning we don't need men." Her eyes sparkled. "No woman will need a man. We can love each other and reproduce. Men will become vestigial organisms!"

Victoria wondered why she was even flirting with the idea of lesbianism if it had made Rosemary this crazy. "What's wrong with men? For the women who want them I mean."

"I can't understand how anyone could tie herself to an oppressor. *You* don't want a man." Rosemary bore down on Victoria. "Join us! We'll support you."

Victoria looked at the excited eyes, the limp braid hanging in front of Rosemary as she leaned over Victoria. Some kind of crazy rapture seemed to possess Rosemary and Victoria knew that whatever she decided about Annie Heaphy it would bear no resemblance to this politicized love, this sexual exercise of a philosophy. This was not real; it was passion, but not love. As little as Victoria knew about love, she recognized its tenderness, its need to revere the loved one and to be held special by her. Love could not derive from politics, nor could it survive and provide the sustenance humans needed from it if its energy was directed, as Rosemary directed hers, away from the lover. Claudia seemed almost irrelevant for Rosemary, except for the statement their relationship made.

"I don't know if I'm a lesbian, Rosemary, but I will think about it," Victoria concluded. "I really think I'd like to be alone now."

Rosemary straightened. "All women are lesbians, Victoria. There's nothing to be afraid of." She walked toward the door, looking over her shoulder as she opened it and stepped out. "Come out, Victoria!" and was gone.

Victoria sighed in relief wondering why in the world she had asked. The answer, she was sure, was in herself and not in Rosemary. Although Rosemary might be hiding her feelings behind her rhetoric, hers was not the face of love Victoria envisioned. Annie's face assembled between her eyes and the light of the candle. She remembered the hopeful look on her face at the bottom of the steps and her own panic as she turned and fled. The face swam, grew larger in the flame, the yellow of its hair a halo whose light warmed Victoria. She lay carefully, gracefully upon the ice blue spread of her bed. A few moments for myself, she thought as she fell further into a heated fantasy, then I'll start work on that paper.

∿ ∿ ∿ ∿ ∿

The winter sun slipped around the edges of Annie Heaphy's green, cracked window shades to bother her eyes. They hurt somewhere where they attach to my brain, she thought as she picked her head up and forced her feet to the floor. Foghorns sounded distantly, as if in the dreamworld she was leaving. It wasn't as cold as she expected and she went through her morning routine hardly waking until she stepped out of the shower. Then she heard pounding on the door. "She found me," was her first crazy thought and she remembered in a flash the dreams in which she had foolishly indulged yesterday before drowning them. Running to her bed, she pulled on last night's pants and shirt as she yelled, "Be right there!" Her heart beat faster, then her face fell as she opened the door to her landlord. "That time, huh?" she asked, turning from him as he followed her into the living room.

Annie began to search for her checkbook, hoping the rent check would not bounce again, while the landlord sat on the edge of her desk. "Don't forget," he said, chewing his cigar. Annie sat and looked up at the tiny bald man who was so devoted to disturbing his clients that he kept his father's habit of collecting rents himself. "I like to keep an eye on my property," he'd explained once to Annie, peering into her bedroom, bathroom, surreptitiously inspecting the papers on her desk. Annie remembered thinking disgustedly of his property, most of it run down like her own shack. She felt utterly at his mercy, helpless to protest his probing. She remembered to put on her cap and pull it tight over her wet hair.

"Don't forget what?"

"You be ready to leave by June thirty, dear. In case I got summer people starting that weekend."

"Christ, it's only February."

"Just don't give me no trouble. You find someplace else to take your girlfriends," he warned as he slid off the desk, brushed the back of his coat, and tucked Annie's check inside it.

"How much would it cost me to buy this place?" Annie asked on impulse.

The landlord looked at her suspiciously. "Where would *you* get that kind of money?"

"It couldn't be *that* much for a four-room, falling apart shack."

"With a porch facing the Sound," he shot back. "But it might be worth more to me sold than it would keeping it, the way I have to fix it up every year. I'll let you know kid, but meanwhile, don't forget June thirtieth."

"I'll be out," Annie answered nastily."

She slammed the door on his tiny, sauntering back. "Damn your beady rat eyes," she finished and turned to face her home. How much I've given up for this, she thought. How little it is after all. She walked to the window, wondering if it was last night's liquor that made her feel so depressed. The landlord was next door and his long white car obscured her view of the beach. Her hair blended with the heatless light at the window when she took her hat off and flung it to the floor. She gripped the window frame. "Shit," she whispered, breaking out of the light as she shook her head. "You bastard—this is all I have!" she shouted at the house into which he had disappeared. She drew back her fists and pounded the wall with them one heavy, loud time. She felt so attached to the house and let herself remember for a moment the good times she had in it with her roommates. I need to fill it again, she thought, with someone close and with more of myself. She pictured Vicky in the living room, trying to fit her in. Well, she decided, it's all I had, but it ain't all I'm going to have.

Surely it meant something that Annie had found Victoria once more. Fate? No, that sounded too much like the aunts back in Chelsea. But something—perhaps some kind of energy—Peg called it woman energy—drew them to each other. Could it be real? She knew she felt something the first time, that first night, when she looked at Vicky. There was some passion beneath Vicky's reserve, some great desire like her own to reach the depths of experience, the heights of emotion, some burning, burning to have it all, but—Annie felt Vicky's greater discipline, now too much in control. Annie knew she herself lacked the power to shape her energies and that Vicky held such a power. Her own life had become self-destructive, and Annie felt, in the intellect that was so obvious on Vicky's face, in the calm, graceful way she moved her woman's body, in the considered way she spoke, a way to learn control. Annie wanted as desperately to feel productive in what she did as she wanted to live to her limits.

Unlike her attractions to some other women, attractions which had seemed so strong, Annie did not feel an end in this attraction to Vicky. Other relationships had a kernel of self-destruction at their core, a feeling that made Annie want to take what she could and run. From Vicky, Annie felt no ending, but an opening, a doorway to a path. She sat on her desk and looked past where the landlord's car had been at the sand. She pictured Vicky and herself hand in hand on a path in the mountains, barefoot, the grasses and clover tickling their ankles. They climbed higher and higher. At each new elevation they became giddier from the purity of the air and their feelings. They never let go of each other's hands, and they lay down in meadows along the way. For a love like this what would Annie not do! She sighed. Full of peace and passion, she began to assemble her things for work before she walked on the beach. She would look into making this house her own and find a way to make Vicky love her, she determined again. Her own convictions would seduce her if her lesbian body could not. If she could love Annie for herself, so much the better, but Annie did not think of herself as lovable. And when she loves me? Will the circle stop there? Will I really stop going round and round? She returned to lean her forehead against the window and looked sadly again toward the shore. Virginia Woolf had stopped her circle by walking straight into the sea, she thought. Maybe I'm going to drive around in circles all my life just to be safe. Who the hell knows what's straight ahead?

∼ ∼ ∼ ∼ ∼

"Time passes slowly up here on the mountain," Victoria sang to herself. She generally listened to classical music, but she had been restless through the last long weeks of winter, visited with Rosemary and Claudia and some of the other women in the poetry group, listened to the music which they played for her timidly, wanting her approval. She had always moved among them aloof, wearing her scholarship and her talents like a gown she did not want soiled. They knew her by reputation, admired or rejected her from afar, but welcomed her warm charm when she offered it. So Victoria sang a little of their surprisingly moving music as she walked across campus toward the Core restaurant. She was to meet Rosemary and Claudia there and go on to a Women's Poetry Group meeting. Victoria knew they would try again to interest her in joining, in sharing her own poetry. But poetry was such a private thing and she was still frightened of the women's politics in which they were involved. It was not what Victoria was looking for, not what would soothe her unaccustomed restlessness. She looked up as she crossed the street to the Core. No cars were coming, but she felt a faint thud of excitement in her chest as she noticed a yellow cab turning the corner on the next street up. She had not seen the cab driver again, though she still came into Victoria's fantasies irritatingly often. Except for that, Victoria had decided lesbianism and love were passing phases for her and ignored their brief intrusion into her ordered days. Even the constant reminder of Claudia and Rosemary's relationship had faded in importance.

The Core was warm. She moved down the cafeteria-style line to get a mug of coffee, paid, and stood looking for Rosemary and Claudia. They were not along the bare brick walls or by the window which was bright with the late winter sunlight. She carried her mug to a dark corner table and sat on the old wooden chair, glad she had brought a book and hoping no one would approach her while she waited. She did not touch her coffee, wondering again why she was exposing herself to a situation like this when she could just stay in her room or on campus where people did not question her inaccessibility. She heard the door open and looked covertly up to see if Rosemary and Claudia had arrived. Against the bright doorway a dark figure stood peering across the sawdust-covered floor. The cabdriver started walking toward her.

As she walked toward Victoria, Annie's head hurt with the knowledge that what she was doing was real. She was not having a fantasy, but acting it out. A few moments ago she had been grinding her cab and herself through the day, thinking about finding another job, moving to another town, cleaning up her house. Then she had spotted the long-haired figure moving gracefully across the street. She had had to turn the corner because of the traffic, but maneuvered her way through a maze of one way streets until she was on the one Victoria had crossed. Half expecting her to have stopped and waited, Annie went into reverse and labored the bulky cab into a portentously lucky parking spot, beating out another car which had been poised to

take it. She called in to the dispatcher that she was going to
lunch and heard, "Who do you think you are, the Queen of
England?" before she shut off the set and locked the cab.
Sweating in the still cool air she paused at the curb to think.
Victoria could have gone into any shop or around the corner or
into a Yale building she couldn't check! And here was Annie,
marching along the street confident she would find her. With
no clues at all, she decided for once to be methodical and went
to the beginning of the row of businesses.

She could not picture Vicky in The Core, but then she did
not know her at all and here she was again suddenly, mirac-
ulously, as if the curves and angles of her face had always been
near and almost touchable. Now what? Annie asked herself,
but had no time to wonder for suddenly she was shuffling her
scuffed shoes in the sawdust, making patterns with the toes,
painfully aware that she had never since she bought them
polished them. "How have you been?" she was asking as if she
saw this woman every night at the bar.

"Fine, thank you," answered Victoria, with an amused and
haughty expression on her face. Then she leaned forward, offering her limp hand to Annie. "It's Annie Heaphy, isn't it?"

"Yes. Annie. Listen, if you're going to be here for awhile,
let me get a beer and I'll . . . I mean, if you're not waiting for
someone. Or busy. I mean, if you don't mind." Annie was feeling desperate, awkward and out of place, as if she had made a
terrible mistake. All of that first feeling was gone, replaced by
this awful pleading she was doing. "I need," she paused, im-
provising, "I need to talk to you," she finally blurted out,
knowing she was putting a one-sided strain on any conversation
that she could not fulfill, but knowing also that she would not
be turned away.

"Of course," answered the cool Victoria. Victoria, what a
name, thought Annie as she went to the counter for beer. I
would die of embarrassment with a name like that. She tried to
think of a subject she could pretend she needed to talk to Vicky
about. Besides her chances of getting into bed with her immediately. Wouldn't Peg holler at her for being so sexist, but damn
it, wasn't that what this pursuit was all about? Of course I want
to go to bed with her. Annie chuckled and the kid in the dirty

white uniform behind the counter smiled back at her. But, she sighed, the butch in her melting, she wanted so much more than that.

As Annie turned back with her beer she saw that two women were sitting with Victoria. Holy Christ, she thought. What an idiot. Of course she was waiting for someone. Then she recognized "Sister" and her friend. Would Victoria expect her to talk in front of *her*? Annie stopped short and drank half her beer. They had not gotten anything to eat, so they might just be meeting. Then a miracle happened. The women rose and scurried away from Victoria as if they had been dismissed. Annie felt a little less of a fool as "Sister's" friend knocked over a chair on her hurried way across the restaurant.

Laughing softly to cover her embarrassment, Victoria asked herself, "What am I doing?" She watched poor Claudia pick up the chair she had tripped over in her rush to leave Victoria alone with her "dyke." Claudia looked back at Victoria with an embarrassed smile. Then Annie stood above her and Victoria felt her face torn away from Claudia to look directly into the pain-filled eyes that pleaded at her from under Annie's cap. They looked away from each other, trying to hide, and looked at the window. Rosemary and Claudia were passing slowly outside, looking in toward them in a proprietary way. Victoria imagined that Rosemary gave herself full credit for bringing herself and Annie Heaphy together again. When Victoria had said she would join them later, after a beer with the little blonde woman from the bar in New York, nothing would have kept Rosemary there. If she could, Victoria suspected, she would have escorted the two to the nearest bedroom and stood outside the door until Victoria could announce that she had come out. Claudia had tripped when Rosemary swung back to stage whisper to Victoria an urgent message about a woman's dance. Surely she did not expect Victoria to ask a strange woman to go to a dance. But perhaps she would, Victoria smiled to herself, feeling as if Annie's presence made anything possible.

She watched Annie wipe a mustache of beer off her upper lip and smiled more widely, shaking her head.

"Is something wrong, Vicky?" Annie asked as if ready to fight a war to fix it.

"That looks good. What do you ask for, a glass of beer?"

Annie relaxed and smiled back at Victoria, then asked, "You never had a beer?"

Victoria thought she had never seen a smile so light up a person's face. "Yes, but I've never ordered it for myself."

"A draft, then. That's all you have to ask for. Or should I get it for you?"

"No, no. I want to do it myself. How else will I learn?" Victoria asked, laughing as if to mock herself.

"Get two, then, please," Annie said, reaching to her pocket as she drained the other half of her mug.

"Let me pay. You're my guest."

"I am?"

She looks like a little child with the weight of the world on her shoulders, Victoria thought, amazed that this person was in her life. She thought of the child's face, so familiar in her room, hovering over her in bed. The child's lips which she had remembered so accurately from those first meetings. Then she was carrying two overflowing mugs back to the table and they were both laughing at her clumsiness in setting them down.

"Anne, Anne," Victoria marvelled, shaking her head back and forth.

Annie looked up at her puzzled, her soft blue eyes asking for an explanation. "Here," she said, "let me take one of those."

"With anyone else, I'd be cross by now and probably leaving," Victoria confessed. The flood of warmth and the sudden feeling of relaxation she felt had loosened her. She smiled a wide brilliant smile at Annie, looking into her eyes.

Annie felt a blush rise up her neck and into her face. She thought she would be blinded by Victoria's smile. All she could do was smile back, feeling as if she had been hit by a wave. They sat frozen by their smiles too long. Annie felt she had to cover the frankness of her own gaze or tell Vicky she had fallen in love with her. Or touch her. She laid her index finger gently on Victoria's wrist, half expecting her to jump away. "Did you ever feel like the sea opened up and you were the naked wet thing that emerged?" she asked her, wondering at her boldness. "Did you ever feel the earth disassemble around you and then feel the pieces slowly fall back into their new places and know the world would never be the same again? Did you ever wonder if you were real?"

"Yes, to all three," Victoria said, still looking into Annie's eyes.

"When I was a kid," Annie went on, "I used to walk down to the football field and across it to the train tracks. I'd walk along them, full of the big feeling of the field I'd crossed and imagine I could just keep walking forward along the tracks and they'd never, never end." She sighed. "In the summer the grass on the field was so damn green and the tracks stretched into the bluest sky I ever saw. Everything was new and possible. I haven't felt like that in a long time." The blush which had left her face now returned as if she had just realized she was saying these things to a perfect stranger.

Victoria's smile felt strained, frozen. She wanted to respond to Annie, but couldn't think of anything to say. She shook her head again, trying to look sympathetic, wanting to tell Annie to go on. Even her name is delicious, she thought, her faded smile returning to her, Annie, Anne, so regal one way, so common the way Annie used it. And herself as Vicky. She never allowed that, but she couldn't imagine Annie calling her anything else. She wanted to lay her lips on Annie's fine hair. "I used to lie on the grass and try to feel how big the sky was," she said finally, remembering Central Park.

Annie nodded, understanding. She moved to lay her hand again on Victoria's before she realized that it might be too much, too forward of her. She lifted her cap and brushed her hair back from her forehead with her sleeve, studying Victoria's face to fix in her mind what she looked like. Eleanor was right, the face was only partially formed, but Annie yearned to touch the planes and curves of it as they grew, to somehow help mold them. She knew they could not sit and stare at each other any longer, unless she said what was on her mind. Was it too soon? She did not even know if the woman was gay. Annie made an abrupt movement to bring her mug to her lips. Then she swung it out in a toast. "To the sky."

Victoria lifted her mug too. "To the tracks."

"Like it?" Annie asked.

Victoria made a face. "Kind of bitter. What kind is it?"

"Oh, Bud, Miller, Schlitz. Who knows? They all taste the same."

"I've tasted Heineken before, but I remember it being much creamier."

"Maybe you had the dark beer."

"Could be," Victoria agreed. She was thinking of her childhood and of the wonderful feeling she got each time she made a friend and they began to know each other. It was similar to this, but without this sensuality. And each time her parents would uproot her, change her school, or ship her to the relatives on Long Island. After a while she had learned to stop friendships before they mattered. It was just too painful to lose that feeling every time it happened. She had not felt it in years. How could she tell that to Annie, though. Victoria felt the words locked inside her. Against everything she felt, Victoria heard herself say, "I have to join my friends after this, you know. It was rather rude of me to chase them away." Fool! she called herself. Why was she saying this? Annie's smile had fallen.

"I'm sorry to have butted in. I've got to get back to work anyway. All I wanted to talk to you about was, well, I acted kind of mad in the cab that day and I didn't mean to put you off. I didn't know you were you, if you know what I mean."

Victoria remembered Annie's pale, sleeping face as she had seen it in the cab. And who do you think I am, Anne, she wondered as she tried to think of a response. Out loud she said, "I think I do," but she had closed up inside, had felt herself snap shut like a trap, an empty trap, tripped by its innocent prey. She was uncomfortable about having been in a gay bar and the meaning of her presence there to Annie. And her own feelings had begun to frighten her.

Annie felt Victoria's distance. She had started moving; buttoning and unbuttoning her jacket, neatening the table, looking at Victoria and then away. "Do you think," she stuttered, knowing that she was going about it all wrong, scaring Victoria even worse, "do you think you might like to meet me for dinner sometime?" Victoria was silent. "Maybe Wednesday night?" Annie tried to keep the plea out of her voice and sound reassuring. "We could meet at Yale. Go to The Pub."

Victoria was lightheaded with anxiety, but even more afraid of the yawning despair that grew inside her as she began to make an excuse and say no. "All right," she said, "Yes, I'd like that."

"Seven okay? Here and we'll walk over?" Annie asked. When she saw Victoria's nod, her attempt at a smile, that was enough for her. She rushed away, almost upsetting the same chair Claudia had tipped over, escaping like a scared rabbit out the door. Behind her she had left the remains of her own image. She was just Annie Heaphy scurrying away, leaving her fate in the hands of that beautiful woman. She would never be able to see herself as a cool butch again. Her cab, when she reached it, looked huge, too big for her to handle. She slid into the driver's seat and slumped for awhile to recover a fragment of her composure. Behind her also she had left a relieved and apprehensive Victoria. A Victoria who held the promised dinner to herself like a lifebuoy.

CHAPTER FIVE

They paused at The Pub's entrance, adjusting their eyes to its darkness as they waited to be shown to a booth. A young man in sharply creased black pants, a white shirt and black tie walked toward them with quick, tiny steps. "Hiya, Sonny," Annie grinned.

"Annie, sweetheart, aren't you on the wrong side?" Sonny asked, raising his eyebrows to see her in the restaurant and not the gay bar that was its complement.

"Not tonight, Sonny," Annie answered, glancing, embarrassed, toward Victoria.

"Oh, I *see*. Come with me ladies," he winked at Annie, turning to lead them to the last booth. He set wine lists and menus before them as they slid in. "Enjoy your evening—*and* your dinner." Victoria faced the back glass wall of the restaurant and noticed the blueness of the winter twilight fading as it would from her imagined skylight. She ran her hands along her thighs, feeling the softness that had come into her new jeans as she washed them. Annie's face was glowing in the dim light of their table when she turned back to her.

"Sonny's a Yalie, too," Annie said. "But he wants to be a dancer. His father's some bigshot out west and won't hear of it, so Sonny's working, trying to flunk out and save money to go to New York. Poor guy. His father could probably *buy* him a ballet company. But he's got guts. Hey," she smiled mischievously, "want a yard of ale?" She knew that she was rambling out of nervousness, but went on, pointing to a printed card propped under the yellow lamp that barely lit their table.

Victoria looked at Annie as if to decide whether she was joking and laughed. "May I suggest instead that we see if they have any wines we'd like?" and immediately became frightened Annie would feel rejected by her decision.

"Sure," Annie smiled timidly. She set her cap toward the back of her head and admitted, "I don't know much about wine. Outside of the old standbys."

"Well, I'll tell you what I know and you tell me what the old standbys are."

"That's easy: Almaden, Mateus, the popular ones. I used to like Catawba Pink. But that," Annie added emphatically, "was because of Thomas Wolfe."

"Thomas Wolfe?"

"Haven't you read him?" Annie asked, looking surprised and even concerned.

"I read half of one of his books. Last summer. I bought the paperback that was out. But he's so—undisciplined."

Annie saw the look of distaste on Victoria's face. "That's one thing I like about him. I read him in high school and he was like a key to life. He was so full of passion and oh—he made everything sound so beautiful and sad just when I was discovering how beautiful and sad everything is. You know? I mean, I'd go to the Boston Gardens and watch the swanboats go around the pond or ride on one myself when I had the money and everything was lush and bursting, even the boats' colors, people's clothing, and we'd get to that part of the ride where the old oriental lantern is—have you been there? And I'd get such a pang of sadness. Like, it's all been going on so long, over and over, here and in China and a billion adolescents feeling like I felt and a trillion leaves blooming over and over and it was so full, so much, that it hurt." Annie paused, the plea for understanding leaving her face as self-consciousness took over. "Anyway, he wrote about a place called Catawba so the wine always held a lot of promise for me."

Victoria had been watching Annie intently. "I think I understand," she said slowly, rubbing her finger across one cheekbone, in a way Annie wished *she* could. "Or I want to understand and that's why I'm drawn to you. I sensed your fullness, your love of life, when we first met. I want to feel like that." Her eyes, to Annie's surprise, held tears. She was asking Annie to teach her something, just as Annie hoped Vicky would share what she was with her. "Let's see," Victoria continued, composing herself quickly (like she's scared of me, Annie thought), "let's see what the Pub has to offer."

Annie picked up her list and seemed to devote all her attention to it. Worried that she wasn't the way Victoria saw her, she shrugged her shoulders to shake off her intensity and match Victoria's new mood. She lifted her cap and ran her fingers through her hair, then pushed the list toward Victoria. "You pick."

"All right. Here's your Mateus. But do you feel adventurous?" Victoria asked in a tone that sought adventure.

"Sure," Annie responded immediately, meeting Victoria's eyes, ceasing to fidget.

"They have a few German wines. I had a friend once . . . Ah, Zellar Schwarze Katz. Let's try theirs."

"Zellar which cats?"

"Schwarze. It's a Moselle. A white wine. Very dry. Do you think you'd like it?"

"I love Almaden White Mountain."

"Then you may like this," Victoria smiled gently, almost protectively, at Annie.

"Are you ready to order dinner?" a smiling, red-haired waitress asked, suddenly appearing in their small circle of light. She broke into a hum after her question.

"Oh, dinner," Annie smiled, pulling her cap over her eyes. "Forgot all about dinner," she scolded Victoria, shaking her head and wagging her finger playfully.

Victoria laughed. "Why don't you bring us a bottle of Zeller Schwarze Katz and we'll give you our order then."

The waitress hummed in response, smiling broadly, bobbing her head and writing on her pad as she hummed her way to the bar.

"I always eat the same thing here," Annie said. "Is it okay to have steak and kidney pie with *white* wine?" she whispered, leaning close enough to Victoria to smell a faint perfume.

"I don't really know. Kidneys?" Victoria asked, making a face.

"Yeah. They're good. My father used to make my mother cook them although she hated them. Listen, you probably love caviar and junk like that."

"Why do you assume that?"

"Oh, it's a cabbie joke. They call Yalies the Caviar Kids. Anyway, I think that stuff is gross. Fish eggs!"

"All right," Victoria laughed. "I like fish eggs. You win. If you let me taste the kidney."

"Okay. And I'll take my chances on the etiquette."

"To tell you the truth, Anne," Victoria took her turn to whisper and leaned closer to Annie, "I don't really care. I'm not that impressed with the this-enhances-that theory of wine drinking."

"You're not?"

"No. And to prove it, I'll have a steak. Oh, my parents would be shocked. But then, they would order French wine."

"But you like German better?"

"Tonight I do." Victoria answered, glancing quickly at Annie's lips and feeling herself redden.

"You started to say something about a friend and German wine before?"

"Etta. You remind me of her—in spirit." Victoria paused, feeling the flush covering her neck and face. "Her family is German. She introduced me to the wines. Or, I should say, made me appreciate them." She looked up when she heard the waitress humming above them. "Ah. Here's our wine."

The waitress, still humming, tipped the open bottle at Annie and poured a half inch into her glass. Annie turned red and stared at it. She pulled off her cap, shrugged and tasted the wine. Then, not looking up, she nodded toward the waitress. Victoria watched Annie's head come up when the waitress hummed away, sounding like a bee buzzing on to another flower. "I'm sorry," Annie said. "I know I look like a guy. She's new here. I hope it didn't embarrass you."

"Oh, is that why she gave it to you to taste?" Victoria asked.

"That, I guess, plus the goddamned stupid idea that a woman can't tell if the wine is any good herself and has to be allowed to drink it by a goddamned idiot man."

Victoria was shocked by Annie's sudden bitterness. "You don't speak in theories, do you?" Annie looked puzzled. "The women who call themselves feminists at school," Victoria explained, "talk feminist theory till I'm ready to scream. But what you just said and the way you said it, makes feminism more real to me than hours of their talk."

"My only theory," Annie answered, putting her hat back on savagely, "is if you ain't born one, you ain't one."

"Then let me exercise my birthright and pour the wine. Maybe that will balance out your tasting it."

"Perfect. But I ought to learn how to handle that. You know, without getting everybody uptight."

Victoria twirled the bottle expertly as she poured. "Graciously? It wouldn't hurt. Let's see. How about, 'Thank you, we'll finish pouring?' "

"Hey, how come *I* can't think of things like that?" Annie asked, seeking Victoria's eyes behind their glasses.

Victoria smiled. "Probably because you speak from your heart against oppression and I speak from my head to gloss things over. I'm good at that sort of thing."

Annie stopped watching the wine and frowned toward Victoria, as if concerned about her. "Well," she said, raising her glass, "I won't drink to you putting yourself down, but I will drink to something else that's a fact, not theory." She paused while Victoria lifted her glass and raised her eyebrows expectantly. "That every woman has it in her heart to say." Victoria nodded slowly, hating herself for noting the contradiction in Annie's reasoning, and touched her glass to Annie's while Annie's eyes touched hers. They drank. "I feel much less bitter now. Thank you for understanding," Annie said, shivering as she thought that this dinner which seemed to progress so painfully slowly would remain one of the clearest and most detailed of her memories all her life.

"No, thank *you*," Victoria paused. "Thank you for your insights."

"It's good," Annie indicated the wine. "Etta has good taste."

"Or had. I haven't seen her for years. Since I came to Yale." Victoria's eyes wandered back to the now black window.

"Hiya, Annie!" a rough voice growled affectionately as a fist shot out in front of Victoria's line of vision and punched Annie's upper arm.

"Hi, Turkey. What are you doing out so early?"

"Trying to get a head start on you. But you beat me again," the heavy woman laughed loudly while Annie drained her glass as if to fortify herself.

"Turkey, this is Vicky," Annie said slowly, seeming to relish the name. "Vicky, this is Marieanne, but everyone calls her Turkey 'cause it's easier. And true!"

"Hey!" Turkey objected, continuing her banter with Annie while Victoria watched. She recognized Turkey from the bar. Turkey did not stop smiling for a moment and laughed at the end of every sentence. "Join us later if you can," she laughed to Annie, including Victoria with her eyes.

"If you're still on your feet," Annie laughed back.

Victoria waved and called, "Nice to meet you," at the retreating figure that did, with that crest of hair and the heavy-hipped, short-stepped walk, look turkey-like. Annie was watching her face when she looked back.

"She's a lot of fun. Do anything for you," Annie explained as if she were self-conscious about Turkey. "Don't worry. I won't force my crew on you."

"Oh, but I'd like to spend some time with —" she hesitated at the name "—Turkey. After *we* know each other better." They were both silent for a moment under the promise that seemed to have been made with Victoria's words.

Then Annie whispered, "Here comes the Hummer." Victoria pulled her hair back from her ears and made a show of the humming sound becoming too loud to bear as the waitress came toward them. When Annie unobtrusively pretended to cut off the sound as a conductor would, Victoria burst into laughter. Annie joined her.

"Ready to order now?" the Hummer asked cheerfully, rolling on the balls of her feet to the jukebox in the bar.

Annie looked at Victoria. "Yes, yes," Victoria answered and, wiping tears from her eyes, gave their orders. "That wasn't fair," she scolded Annie when the Hummer left.

"But so true," Annie defended herself, leaning around the booth to hear her hum out of sight. "So tell me about your German friend who bathed in wine," she asked, more comfortable now that they had shared something and laughed together.

"No, no," Victoria protested laughingly, suddenly realizing

the barriers she and Annie had broken down. "God, her family was much too staid to allow that! Although, like me, she was brought up on wine. For Etta, though, it was because her family was newly arrived from Europe while mine has been here so long we're in the second generation of returning to European customs."

"A Mayflower person?"

"Not quite. Probably a runaway deported English thief. But an early one who learned how to steal legally over here. He probably never drank anything but stout in his life."

"Maybe he drank with my ancestors. Some of them were Irish stout drinkers. And probably from the same circles."

"Then where did you get such blonde hair?" Victoria gestured toward it, almost touching it, but pulling back when Annie felt that her heart could beat no faster.

"Oh, Indian blood," Annie joked, breathing again. "No, really, it's a wig." She tugged at a tuft of hair as if to slide a wig back and forth.

Vicky laughed again, still shaken by the near touch. "You don't know?"

"I know all too well. My family's from Chelsea. A grungy part of Boston. I grew up in a dark three-story house in rows of dark three-story houses all connected in the back by criss-crossing clotheslines and telephone wires and porchrails. The Irish hated the Italians and if you were Irish you were Irish—no further inquiry needed. If you weren't, you were Italian. However, my mother is Swedish. And pays for it in that family. Now, I don't have any Anglo-Saxon friends. It's hard to in Connecticut."

"Unless you go to Yale," Victoria sighed, pouring more wine.

"You don't like it there?"

"They leave me alone." She was silent, staring at her wine glass, her head bent forward so that her hair fell over her face.

The restaurant was beginning to fill up. Sonny was scurrying around to seat people while the Hummer buzzed from table to table. The jukebox began to be played with more frequency.

Annie looked puzzled. "That's a lot of money to pay to be left alone."

"That, I believe, was their intention."

"Whose?"

"My parents. I spent my first two years at Hunter College. It's a city school and I was finally, slowly, meeting people, making friends, after all those private schools. My friend Etta was a one-of-a-kind in the high school I graduated from and was looked down upon. They've shuttled me from one posh school to another since I was five. But no matter where they enroll me, the girls were always the same well-dusted, personality-deprived mannequins. I would even have settled for transferring to Barnard—at least I could have seen Etta as I did once in a while. She went to school on Long Island." Victoria picked up her wine glass and finished it. Annie split the last wine in the bottle between them. "Its taste reminds me of her, that's all. I guess I'm nostalgic for high school and Hunter and our friendship, its richness, like you are for Thomas Wolfe and *your* discovery of magic in the world."

"Magic?"

"That's how I think of it. Etta was only at our school because her mother was the school nurse. They were from Queens, which, from what I saw of it in Jamaica, must be a lot like your Chelsea." She smiled. "It's only bad when you can't escape. I loved it. Her family was all of it made from the same mold. Short and not fat, but fleshy, heavy. The way I always pictured the family in Mann's *Buddenbrooks*." Victoria paused until Annie nodded familiarity. "I have never seen anyone so mad for opera as that family. Their house was dark, wedged in a block of houses between blocks of new tall pink-brick apartment houses. Their father was one who had refused to sell his house to the developers. The inside usually smelled like a great German restaurant. I was always seated in the parlor and I'd visit with Etta there in the middle of a cluster of heavy dark furniture and spotless ceramic figurines that were never moved. But from all over the house I could hear such a confusion of operas! Everyone must have had a phonograph. Layer on layer of opera: can you imagine it? All that incredible drama just drifting in and out of rooms and up and down stairs and there we sat, like the figurines who couldn't hear. Her brothers would come in to say hello very formally. Her mother and father would sit with us for a minute or two each and Etta would be wild inside her square, stocky body to leave for anyplace. But that, and my parents' apartment, were the only places where we could be alone even a little bit.

"Except the parks. And we walked and walked in them. One day in the spring of that year I remember Etta took me to a new park out in Queens somewhere. It was so woodsy and such a beautiful day. The birds, the flowers, just bursting, as you would say, with song and color and all of a sudden Etta stopped. She put her hands out in front of her and raised her chin so her throat was sharp and clear against the woods and she sang. I never knew she could sing so well, had been trained to sing. She sang a whole segment from *Hansel and Gretel*; did you know it was an opera?

"Then I made her promise to take me to the opera, to share it with me the way she loved it. We went. To her section of it: standing room only. I'd only been in the orchestra where as many people twitched and fell asleep as listened. But in SRO the electricity in the air was amazing." Victoria tossed her head and pulled her hair away from her face. Her eyes, on Annie's, were like knives, and so sharp and intent on making Annie understand or perhaps *be* there with her that Annie looked impaled, she was so still.

"And the people were more amazing. There were old people planning to spend hours standing to hear and see this opera. There were really young kids who barely budged during the performance. There was a 'regular,' Etta called him, wearing a black cape with a red satin lining and dyed black hair with a drawn-on widow's peak and eyebrows penciled into sharp points. He looked like some sort of phantom of the opera. There was a midget who brought a stool to stand on. And there were just as many average, ordinary citizens who looked like Etta's father, like construction workers or like her mother, housewives and nurses. And they all spoke to one another like old friends on a long-awaited outing. Anne, I could see how a child brought up in that atmosphere would not be able to escape being 'an opera nut,' as Etta called herself, no matter what else she was. She and one of her brothers had been saving money since he was ten and she was eight to go to operas in

Europe. That I learned when Etta began to speak with two women next to us. They had been to Salzburg the year before and Etta wanted to know every detail. They told her, too. Then the two women held hands throughout the whole performance."

Victoria's cheeks were flushed. Neither of them had paid any attention when the Hummer, matching her hum to the juke-box, set their dishes before them. "That's when I knew what I was feeling about Etta," Victoria said almost in a whisper. She sat up, pushed her hair back again and picked up her silverware as if to make her words more casual. "I went home that night and told my parents I would be going to Hunter when I gradua-ted. I should have been devious. I should have said I wanted to be near Broadway or some man or the stores in New York. They criticized me and worried me so much about it that when, near the end of my freshman year, Yale announced it would be co-ed in another year, I agreed to transfer. 'That way, at least,' my father said, 'I may get a son-in-law from the old school,' his alma mater. If I had been more like you I suppose I could have withstood their disapproval better, but I'd been too protected and had too few resources of my own." She shook her head slowly and looked down at her plate, her lips tight across her angular face, devoid of all the gloss of sophistication. She cut a piece of beef. "So here I am, pampered product of generations of polishing." She put the meat in her mouth and began to chew.

"I'm glad, Vicky."

Victoria looked up, the lines of her face all drawn down except for her tight jaw.

"I'm glad for me that you're here."

Victoria finished chewing thoughtfully. "Yes," she said with a stiff smile. "Now I feel glad too. But there must have been an easier way." She wondered what had just been said. I *am* glad, she thought in wonder. She looked at Annie's ragged hair and her grubby cap, her army jacket thrown beside her on the seat and laughed a glad laugh, a suddenly loving laugh. "It hasn't been easy for you, either, though, has it? I'm sorry. That's me. Always full of myself."

Annie broke into her meat pie. "I guess growing up is hard for everybody. We're always walking through the woods maybe not even looking for a clearing or a stream or a friend who's going to open up the path for us with a song. We're always getting scratched or catching poison ivy. How come, anyway," she asked, laying down her forkful of meat and sipping some wine, "how come we're allergic to the bad things and they spread so quick? How come we can't be allergic to the good stuff instead so it comes jumping out at us and flares up all over us—joy instead of red itchy patches?"

"You're right. We're constantly avoiding the things we're afraid of. Sometimes so much so that we wander right off the path and miss 'the good stuff.' "

"Wander right off into your isolation?" Annie asked. "Into the stillness that you carry around you? And into the circles I drive around in all day, all night and again the next day, always moving in circles? And you know what they tell us? 'The Lord is my shepherd, I shall not want. He leadeth me to lie down in green pastures.' Bah. We're a bunch of bumbling, half-blind fools almost losing the most important path of our lives. That man they call the lord doesn't do anybody any good at all." Annie had begun to eat, but stopped to watch Vicky. "Not hungry?" she asked when Vicky stopped also.

"Let's order some coffee."

"Sure, but tea for me, not coffee."

"The Irish in you?" Victoria smiled weakly, looking drained.

"I suppose. I remember the women in my family—one aunt lived on the first floor, another on the second, my grandmother on the third, and we were next door—they were always visiting to have a 'cuppa tay.' Or another aunt or a neighbor or a cousin or an in-law would come and it would be tea. I tried to break out of it at school, but couldn't."

"Where did you go to school?" Victoria asked as the waitress hummed away with their plates of cold, uneaten food.

"There wasn't any money, but I lived at home and I got a scholarship to Boston College. So I commuted," Annie shrugged.

"What happened?"

Annie shrugged again and muttered, "I lost my lover." She held her breath, afraid to be bringing up the subject of lesbian lovers.

"And quit school?"

"Just that one."

The Hummer brought apertifs to their table. "Compliments of friends in the bar," she smiled over her shoulder as she left.

"Turkey's trying to get me drunk as usual," Annie said wryly and raised her glass for a toast. "To the woods—and the sky," she added, remembering their toast at the Core.

"And the path—and the tracks!" Victoria answered as they clinked glasses. "Did you flunk out?"

"No. She wanted," Annie could feel her heart stop again, but Vicky still looked into her eyes, "a world more like the one it sounds like you want to leave. She was happy as a Cliffey. I didn't want to be in the same city if I couldn't be with her. And you can see why I couldn't be with her," Annie gestured to herself, her hat, her hair. "I'm a low class bar dyke. Good for a thrill," she went on bitterly, "not to spend her life with. She has ambitions. So I joined some friends who had rented a little shack on the beach and six months later they went back to Boston. With three paying we could afford the place during the summer, but when they left I couldn't. I didn't want to give up my shack so I quit school and started driving full time. I was working already, bartending at night. Now I just put all my hours in driving."

"Did you save your 'shack?' "

"Just barely. I still have it. I asked the landlord how much he'd sell it for, but I haven't seen him since. It means a lot to me to have a home of my own to go to, even if I don't always want to go home. I like having a place to call mine," Annie said, a faraway look on her face.

"And if you lost it?"

"I don't want to think about it."

"How about school?" Victoria asked to shift away from the obviously painful subject. "Did you keep it up?"

"I finished with an Associates. I just couldn't get into it, you know? I'm not aiming for that big pie in the sky stuff. I like driving. I can be myself. I liked bartending until business fell off last summer. We're too close to Provincetown."

The wine was wearing off. They were tired from their intensity. When the Hummer brought coffee and tea and their check, Annie had her chin in her hands and was watching

Victoria pour cream into her coffee so slowly it kept its swirling shape.

"What do you think?" Annie asked. "Do you want to have a drink with Turkey and the gang? I know you said you had to get back to your books," Annie added to protect herself from dashed hopes.

"I do, Anne. I'm just so comfortable. I can't face going out in the cold." And being alone again, Victoria thought. And dealing with having said so *much* to this woman that I will probably hide now, hide for all I'm worth and try never to see her again. She felt guilty when Annie tried to help.

"Maybe it won't be too cold. Spring is coming, you know. Can I give you a ride?"

"No, it's not that far. You'd just have to find another parking space."

"And I have no heater. Can I walk with you?"

Victoria smiled with some relief from the despair that showed briefly in her eyes. "That would be fine. Yes, let's. I don't even really want this coffee, do you?"

"I'm out the door."

They stopped to pay their check and Victoria pulled her gloves on. Annie threw her coat over her shoulders, then jammed her arms into it, knocking off her cap with the coat's hood. She stooped to pick it up and felt Vicky's hand ruffling her hair as she got up. She straightened slowly, Victoria's hand resting on her shoulder. Two gay men pushed in through the door, chattering, unseeing, and separated them. Annie set the cap on her head and led the way out the door. Outside, Victoria shivered. Annie ran her hand heavily across her back saying, "You'll warm up as we walk." Victoria looked at her, nodding, then seemed to pull the cold night like a protective cloak around herself.

So they walked, Victoria slightly taller, moving smoothly with a long measured stride, her arms swinging quietly by her sides; Annie, with shorter, choppier steps, putting her hands in her pockets, then out to turn her collar up, then to her hat, back to her pockets, as if she wanted to be doing something with her body in addition to walking, as if it were not enough to walk down the deserted college street in the frozen night next to this once again cool, stately person. She kept looking up at Victoria, trying to meet her eyes, seeking a smile. Victoria looked straight ahead as if to prepare herself for loneliness. At the gate to her dormitory Victoria turned suddenly and enveloped Annie in her arms, whispering, "Goodnight." Annie got her arms halfway up to return Victoria's embrace when Victoria turned away and, key somehow ready, opened the gate, then locked herself inside. Her back to Annie, she walked under the short archway and turned out of sight into a courtyard. Annie leaned against the ornate black gate, pressing her lips against it, gripping it with her gloveless hands and shook it. "Shit," she said, turning away. "Locked me right out again. Shit."

∿ ∿ ∿ ∿ ∿

Annie Heaphy next saw Victoria at the women's dance. The New Haven Women's Liberation Rock Band was playing feminist songs, intent on an expertise whose absence did not deter the excited crowd of women from wild group dancing. Annie and the rest of the group from the bar, girded for the dance by several rounds in anticipation of a dry or punch-filled evening, made their raucous way into the room only to stand about on the edge of the crowd as if they had reached a cordon. They watched the women dance in threes or more and looked at one another, rolling their eyes at these women who did not have the courage to dance in couples. Peg had told them the political arguments against couples and they still thought what they thought, while willing to participate the "libbers" way because, wow, those were some beautiful women. Annie, like the rest, could not quite believe that these women were gay or would remain gay once the cause was no longer popular. They had never run the risks of being caught or suffered the ostracism of straight peers as the bar women had, and it was as hard not to resent them for the newness of their coming out as it was to resist joining them in this atmosphere of limited acceptance or at least acceptance on their own grounds.

When Annie Heaphy noticed her, Victoria was seated alone in a window seat, wearing a dark turtleneck sweater and jeans and fitting right in. Annie felt like a slob in her army gear and went looking for a bathroom to at least comb her hair. When she found a mirror she saw that her hair was all flat from her cap. She put her whole head under a faucet, hoping her hair was still short enough to dry fast. She found gum in her jacket pocket and tried to mask her beer smell with that. Leaving her jacket off, she returned to the hall and stood with her friends who had barely moved since she left. She stared at Victoria, ruffling her hair to dry it fast, remembering how Vicky had ruffled it the week before. Someone handed her a paper cup of punch and she downed it immediately.

Victoria saw Annie too. She had been sitting and watching, letting Rosemary or Claudia introduce her to women and bring her punch. They wandered off only to return to take care of her, Victoria thought, as if I have not always been alone. Still, she was glad she had come. She did feel the "spirit" they had told her about and she wished she could just abandon herself to it and join in, but it was easier, safer, just to watch.

Now she watched Annie and her friends. They looked like poor relations, uncomfortable in an alien atmosphere. Some wore hats, one had a tie, a couple carried beer bottles. They stood aggressively, almost belligerently, and seemed to be criticizing what they saw. When she saw Annie Heaphy with them she recognized Turkey and two others who had been at the bar in New York. And now Annie was running her hand through that short blonde haircut and looking at her very seriously. Victoria tossed her chin toward her shoulder to get her own hair away from her eyes and gazed back at Annie Heaphy. Maybe it's the punch, she thought; I ought to look away. She was even more frightened than she had been at their dinner.

Finally she saw Annie move when one of the circles of dancers grabbed her and she began to dance with them. She did so awkwardly, studiously, as if afraid to miss a step when all the others were dancing with abandon. Victoria looked away to give Annie more freedom and when she looked back Annie had thrown herself into the dance and was smiling that wonderful smile. Still, Victoria looked away again so that Annie would keep dancing and then suddenly found herself being pulled into the circle. Oh, if it had been anyone but Annie, she would have pulled rudely away. Instead she could not let go and clung to Annie's hand, following her, careful not to lose the women behind her, soon completely involved in this crazy ritual by the warmth of Annie Heaphy's hand.

When the song stopped Annie did not let go. They stood right in front of the band, facing it, still holding hands, while the music began again. Annie had felt more comfortable in motion, but Vicky looked more relaxed like this. Annie felt the heat grow in her body and knew that she had to communicate its intensity to Vicky soon. Then Victoria's eyes closed and she lowered her head. They turned toward one another slowly. Annie waited for Victoria to lift her head and say something, but when she did look up, she said nothing, only looked with glazed eyes at Annie. "Do you want me to let go?" Annie asked hoarsely. Victoria bit her lower lip and shook her head, moving her long hair across her shoulders. The longer they stood, holding hands, the more the crowd seemed to recede. Electrical charges, Annie thought, going up and down our arms, across our hands. Melting, my arm is melting down into her hand, Victoria thought in sudden panic, but kept herself perfectly still, as if the welding were accomplished.

The band went on with a slow, sensuous song. Annie made herself move, move before the wavering light that was Victoria and, never dropping her hand, took Victoria's other hand in hers. Victoria closed her eyes and pulled Annie's arms around her. They began to sway to the music in the cradle their arms made, locked together behind Victoria. Annie tilted her head up so her cheek brushed Victoria's jaw and her lips rested on her thick, sweet-smelling hair. Victoria, seeing through a haze, part of which was actual fog on her glasses, let her face in turn find Annie's soft yellow hair and she rested her lips gently upon it.

Annie whispered, "We better dance," and before Victoria could miss their stillness, Annie had broken the cradle and moved closer, so close their hips, if they were to move them, must move together. Annie's arms settled around Victoria's waist, her hands lightly guiding the movement of Victoria's hips. Victoria pulled her arms back and let them drop across Annie's shoulders, her hands riding, closed, behind Annie. So they danced, Victoria's body beginning to feel as her arms had, as if she were melting into Annie. Her vision blurred and became dark beyond the brightness of Annie's hair. Her hands, clasped behind Annie's back, seemed to be an oasis of discipline for her emotions. So we're dancing, Annie thought, breathless with the feel of Victoria's breasts beneath her sweater, just touching her own. She was stunned by the gentle grinding of their pelvises to the band's slow song. And I'm under control, she thought, forcing all her will into her hands to keep Victoria moving and into her legs to move herself.

The music had to stop. They dropped back from each other, no longer touching, and tried each other's eyes. Victoria was still bent toward Annie and saw such taut excitement in Annie's eyes she felt ready to explode. Annie said, "Let's get some air." Like a horse in blinders, Victoria followed the jeans and flannel shirt and shining head before her as they skirted cleverly the edges of the crowd and reached the door.

These refugees from the collective experience side-stepped quickly out of view of the hall and shared each other's eyes. Victoria broke away, feeling too close to begging for the touch she'd never felt before. Familiar with the building, she headed for the mock trial room. She had been there enough to know the ground even when Annie shut the door behind them and there was only the vague light from two street lamps dimly outlining the room. "Before a jury of my peers," she admonished herself, knowing that if she cared little about her peers before, they might go hang themselves now. Reaching the platform to the side of the jury chairs she gurgled a deep and quiet laugh, turning to Annie and saying very quietly, "The sentence is pronounced."

Annie, not stopping, sat on the edge of the platform. "This is no time for puns," she laughed softly back as Victoria leaned against the short wall that enclosed the chairs.

"Ohhh," Victoria moaned as Annie swiveled to be beside her and moved her index and middle fingers along Victoria's nose and cheeks as if exploring her. Victoria took one finger between her lips, then touched it with her tongue. "Vicky," Annie said as Victoria lightly bit her finger. "Vicky, Vicky, Vicky," she repeated, her hands touching, touching everywhere on Victoria's long, slim body and Victoria's arms coming up to her shoulders, pulling her closer, touching her lips to Annie's lightly over and over until so loudly in the dark Annie heard her say "Please," so deep in her throat it was almost a growl and startled Annie, a growl from this cool perfect woman, but before her thought could get in the way her body responded, her hand slipping between Victoria's pants and her skin, gasping herself as she found the pouring, swollen flesh and began to stroke gently, gently until she found the place that made Victoria groan and stayed there with Victoria's hands fluttering up and down her neck. "Up and down and up and down," Victoria thought over and over until there was nothing but the feel of Annie's babyfine hair in her mouth and then Annie's lips on hers pleading, "Oh, come home with me, come home with me I need to know you naked." Victoria struggled down to consciousness, trying to touch Annie more, while Annie withheld herself with her plea and both of them got up, neatening, touching, stopping, holding each other almost at each step in their slow progress up the aisle of the courtroom.

They went into the hall, separating for their coats. Annie, serious and hurried, grabbed her army jacket, darted to her friends who were still standing, watching, drinking. She made sure they could all fit into the other car they had come in. "Who's your Yalie?" Eleanor teased.

"Vicky, from the bar in New York. Remember?" Annie answered, catching the cap Turkey threw to her.

"Found that on the floor," Turkey laughed. "Say hi—if there's time."

"I'll try," Annie answered with a glare at Turkey's light treatment of Victoria as she skipped, then jogged away.

Victoria meanwhile had glided like a sleepwalker through the women on the other side of the hall, passing Rosemary and Claudia and smiling at their staring faces where they danced in a group. She picked up her coat and swung it across her shoulders as she made her way to them. "I've got a ride home," she smiled, tossing back her hair to cover her excitement. "Thanks for bringing me. It was just what I needed," she said mysteriously to their still speechless stares.

They hurried down the tall old corridor and pushed through

the heavy wooden door into the clear, stinging-cold night. They stretched their arms toward each other and held, then swung around and around, laughing up to the stars through, Victoria thought with her heart pounding in fear and exhilaration, through all the space in the universe.

Later, Victoria lay as close to Annie as she could for warmth in Annie's tiny, cold house. Like a toothpick house, she thought, holding Annie even tighter. Heidi had built her a "toothpick house" one summer. It took a week to make in a careful, patient process. What a wonder it had been to her completed! She was terrified of accidentally breaking it and finally persuaded Heidi to take it with her when she left. Now she'd remembered the toothpick house again and thought, Annie, Annie, what keeps the wind from blowing all this and you away some dark night? She was amazed that Annie found a sense of security in this threatened home.

The little house seemed messy, but more, Victoria thought, because there were neither closets nor adequate drawer space than because things were untidy. She could see Annie had organized her possessions; any disarray gave the impression more of a house no one spent any time in than one uncared for. But there was such a wilderness around it of marsh and beach, with an empty road, another cottage, and a ramshackle bar the nearest neighbors. It did seem just like Annie: delicate, lost in a wilderness, barely keeping herself together, but basically sound and able to offer shelter despite its scarring from the elements. Now, with Annie sleeping, Victoria felt secure enough, warm enough, as if Annie's still, silent presence were stronger than the one that tried to communicate with Victoria. We unsettle each other. We're so uncomfortable. Except laughing and touching. So magic, so simple, the touch. Our real selves do the touching, she thought as she fell asleep curled around Annie Heaphy.

The next night, Sunday, they spent in Victoria's room. They felt some of the joy of Saturday, but as they became more real to each other, it frightened Annie to see the list of their differences grow. She woke at dawn feeling very scared. Her one insistent thought was, "I don't want to be here," but it slept, leaden, in the back of her mind. It weighed her down, paralyzed her, making its silent waves into her tensing body. She remembered the night with Eleanor and other nights in strange beds. Those relationships had come to nothing. Would Vicky become a stranger in a month or a clinging friend like Eleanor? Annie moved slowly away from the curve of the still sleeping Victoria, telling herself it was out of consideration, but really it was because she was afraid to wake the woman she hardly knew. The sight of Victoria's naked back, the lovely soft lines of her shoulders, filled Annie with horror. How could she leave such a woman? How could she stay and face the consequence of such a commitment?

The room was cold, but heat came banging slowly out of the radiator like the disembodied sound in a nightmare. She longed for the softer sounds of her foghorns. The one narrow window allowed in just enough light to make everything grey, to finish taking away all last night's magic from what Annie saw. The room was sterile, not full of Victoria as it had been, but empty of anything familiar or safe for Annie. It did not seem to belong to the Victoria she had begun to know. Yet right now it seemed safer to remember the partial Victoria than to invest more of herself in discovering the unknown. She wished for the closeness and safety of the night at the Pub where they had met in a place comfortable for both of them: Annie's bar in Victoria's community. Where above all, the newness and excitement of getting to know one another had quieted her fears.

Annie sat up on the edge of the bed, surprised to feel warm, and very, very quietly began to dress. Why must she always panic like this, she wondered, regretting the loss of the beautiful woman on the bed. Wasn't Vicky different? Annie had thought so only a few hours ago as she aroused Vicky's warm, responsive flesh with her hands, her mouth. Such intimacy seemed impossible now, absurd. Yet couldn't she, just once, stay and see if it would work? But she felt so naked, so vulnerable. She couldn't, when she finished dressing, look at Victoria. Am I afraid that she'll be someone I don't know, Annie wondered? Afraid then I'll have to admit how alien I feel she is? Tell her, "You're separate and different and strange to me and I've got to get out! You can't hold me here!"

   As the words surfaced, Annie's panic grew. Though part of her longed to stay, her fear was too strong. She tightened her whole body, grabbed her coat and left the room, feeling, as she closed the door with terrified stealth, that she was leaving some sacred place against which she had sinned.

CHAPTER SIX

Bells pealed in Victoria's mind the week after she and Annie Heaphy made love. She didn't understand why Annie had left without saying goodbye, but sensed, in her own fears, that it had something to do with the power of what they felt for each other. She felt, in any case, the ecstasy for which she had longed in her fantasies of a monastic life. She saw bushes filled with fuzzy lavender flowers, just born, blindingly bright in the spring rain that had suddenly come upon the world. She saw the Yale daffodils bellowing all their yellows through the downtown, reflecting themselves in the dozens of yellow cabs she saw every day. Yet now each time she saw a yellow cab, fear and hope fought for a place inside her. The fear went icy into her veins, stabbing its way down her arms, constricting her gut, freezing her legs so she could not move for fear of more fear. The hope warmed her, thawed her frightened tension, bred dizzying dreams in her love-fogged mind. "Anne," she'd cry half aloud, then, "Anne, Anne, Anne. Come to me, call me, hold me." Then, sobbing inside she'd change: "Stay away, don't come near me, I can't bear it, I can't bear your touch, let me stay inside." Embarrassed by her own mental histrionics and confused by the flood of unfamiliar emotion, Victoria would wrap herself in her ice blue bedspread and roll back and forth, sometimes crying, sometimes dreaming of how it would be when Annie came.

She did not answer her telephone, afraid it would be Annie. She did not answer knocks at her door, unable to deal with anything familiar, it would now be so changed. Claudia just walked in before Victoria could lock the door one day when she returned from class. Victoria swung around at the intruder, her face critical of the invasion, while she held her breath that it might be Annie.

"We've been worried about you, Victoria."

"I'd like to be alone, Claudia."

Claudia smiled, not her usual broad-grinned smile, but softly, with concern. Victoria pictured Claudia smiling at a therapy patient like that. "Why are you miserable?"

"I don't want to talk about it."

"Please let me stay," Claudia pleaded, her arms outstretched from her overalls in supplication.

Victoria shrugged, unable to refuse the farm girl side of Claudia she liked so much. She turned to put her books on the desk while Claudia settled herself cross-legged on the bed.

"Why don't you put your jeans on anymore? I like you in them," Claudia said.

Fear flashed through Victoria as she thought of them. "I don't feel comfortable in them," she managed to say.

"Don't they fit your image?" Claudia teased. Victoria was silent as she straightened her room, her back to Claudia. "It must be taking quite a beating," she continued.

"What must be?" Victoria asked wearily.

"Your image. I know mine did at first."

"What are you talking about?" Victoria asked, turning to look through tear-filled eyes at Claudia, who sat alert and straight-faced, a ready well-meaning listener. The pink shirt Claudia wore beneath her overalls brought out the pink of her cheeks, making her seem innocently trustworthy.

"Coming out, silly. Did you think you were hiding anything from us?" Victoria looked defeated. Her shoulders sagged suddenly and she sank onto the bed, facing Claudia. She still had not brushed her hair and the spring breezes had pulled it every which way. "You're a mess, you adorable, unapproachable intellectual," Claudia said, taking Victoria's hand. "Talk to me. You'll feel better."

Victoria looked without hope into her friend's eyes. "You can't help me."

"I know. But you can feel better just talking about it. Maybe it'll all begin to make sense."

"It makes enough sense to me."

"But I want to know what's going on. I'll ask some questions, okay?" Claudia asked without really wanting an answer. "Is it Anne, from the bar in New York?"

"Yes."

"Who is she other than that?"

Victoria watched her friend lean back against the wall, pulling her legs up and hugging them to her chest. "Nobody," she answered. "Everybody. A college dropout cab driver from the wrong part of Boston."

"Why do you like her?"

Victoria paused for a moment. "She's hearty, determined, full of strength and life and not afraid of anything."

"Did you like being with her?"

"Yes," Victoria said, blushing.

"Then what's the problem? When will we meet her officially?"

After another long pause to fight back tears, Victoria said, "One question at a time. Your second one first. *I* may never see her again, so I don't know when *you'll* meet her. As to problems, I don't know where to start." She stood and walked to her dresser, picked up the brush and began to stroke her hair. Claudia stretched out her legs and watched the mirror as Victoria's mouth began to form words and reject them.

"You don't know how to deal with being a lesbian," she suggested as she saw Victoria's eyes redden and her chest begin to move as if she was gasping for air.

Victoria turned to face Claudia, her arms leaning against the dresser behind her. "I don't think I am one. I just love Anne."

"Okay, so you haven't even begun to deal with the fact that this isn't a temporary aberration."

"I'd just like to deal with Anne for now."

"I'll bet you would," Claudia teased. She became serious again when Victoria scowled at her. "Tell me the problem with Anne."

Victoria released the dresser and gestured helplessly toward Claudia. "She's a woman!"

"Have you ever loved a man?"

"No."

"Have you ever loved another woman?"

"Maybe a little, in high school. But one's supposed to be attracted to women at that age."

"Do you want to love a man?"

"Of course not, but I've been thinking about how hard it must be to be gay in this world. Everything I've read talks about one night stands and a lonely old age. Some of Anne's experiences have been so painful and damaging to her."

"Like what?"

"Like never being your real self to most of the world. Always having to hide your emotions. Being humiliated in public with catcalls and obscene jokes."

"I haven't gone through any of that yet, but on the other hand, I've never done anything easier in my life than love Rosemary, even if she does make herself rather difficult to love at times."

"I suppose it might be worth it, but how *does* one face the world then? What do I tell my parents who are hoping for a secure, monied marriage? They might accept me being a single professor, at least that's respectable, but having a woman lover? How do lesbians live? Can they get good jobs? Will I be able to get a teaching job?"

"Hold on, Victoria." Claudia stood, no longer the listener. "I know it affects your whole life, but you can't begin to deal with all that yet. You'd be a frog on a lily pad. There's no way you can keep from losing your balance if you haven't got a hold of yourself." Claudia sat at the edge of the bed, close to Victoria.

"So you think I should decide if I'm a lesbian or not, whatever the consequences."

"It doesn't really bother me, personally, one way or the other, but it would help you to sort things out."

Victoria sat down on the bed and bent her head to her hands. "I don't want to be, Claudia," she cried, rocking herself. "It's too hard. The whole world disapproves of you. It's not safe. I'm too scared."

Claudia's face changed. She looked hurt now, as if she were feeling Victoria's pain. Her hands clasped the straps of her overalls tightly. Finally, she reached over to Victoria and pulled her close, laying her head against her breasts. "Victoria, it is hard, but it's worth it, that's all I can tell you. Oh," she went on, rocking her, "it's so beautiful to love a woman. Let yourself feel it!"

"Every time I do I get scared. I want to scream and run away as if I'd come upon something horrible."

"We've been taught it *is* something horrible. It's not. It's pure and sweet. You'll never feel anything better. People think it's horrible," she soothed Victoria, smoothing her hair, "because they're afraid of it and that goes back a long, long way. Rosemary says it's our responsibility as well-educated lesbians to teach the world there's nothing wrong with lesbianism. In my work, I want to help lesbians adjust to who they are without all the agonizing you're going through. Not that I don't get as scared as you sometimes, too, but I honestly believe it's worth it."

Victoria was still crying, but more gently. "Just hearing the word makes me frightened." Claudia loosened one arm from around Victoria and drew first one, then the other, of Victoria's arms around her waist. She pulled Victoria closer and was quiet. Victoria whimpered for awhile, then found herself relaxing into Claudia's arms. Words disappeared from her mind as a deep comfort invaded her and left her wondering at the magic a woman's body holds. Annie would not be like this, she thought, then decided she'd feel even better. "You should be Anne," she whispered.

"How can it ever be if you won't see her?" Claudia asked gently.

Victoria sobbed once, but her tears did not start again. "I'm too scared."

"What do you think you're risking? Expulsion from the human race? It doesn't happen. I'm living proof," Claudia said as she stroked Victoria's hair.

"I know that. I don't know exactly what I'm afraid of. How *do* I deal with the world?"

"Is that what's worrying you most? I freaked out about how the world would see me, but eventually I realized that I was more concerned with myself. How I would be different in relation to the life I wanted to live. It was hard to see me through *my* eyes and not the world's."

"What are you going to do about your parents?"

"At this point I figure it's going to break their hearts when I tell them I'm not coming home to teach for a few years and then get married and have babies. So even though telling your folks is the in-thing to do right now, I don't want to overburden them. I figure I'll tell them I want to continue school in the East."

"What about Rosemary?"

"Her parents? She told them practically the first day after we made love. She's been such a pain in the ass to them they apparently figured this was just another phase and shrugged it off. She's letting it go for now at that. There's just not enough of her left after our relationship, her writing and all her other activities to be that concerned over her parents."

"Not to mention school," Victoria chuckled, sitting up again and pulling her hair out of her face. "We all have to graduate as well as go through all this."

"We will," Claudia assured her, one arm still around her.

"All this has hardly upset you."

"Us midwesterners are pretty steady on our feet. I know it doesn't seem like it to you, but I think you're making too much of it. Let it happen. The rest will fall into place. You can't solve it all beforehand so it won't hurt later. You're making it so difficult now you can't resolve anything."

"No wonder you want to be a psychologist."

"Do I make sense?"

Victoria nodded sadly. "But it's not easy to live with. Why is it happening? I feel like it came out of the blue."

"No, this isn't coming out of the blue. I thought it was too until I remembered things from my earlier years. Pity's sake, as my mom would say, I made love to a woman before. And I've wanted to again ever since."

"How could you forget that? I feel like such a helpless, naive little girl asking you all this."

"And it's about time you let yourself be helpless and naive. You probably never did before in your life. You know, you can't get anything good unless you open yourself up to it. I didn't open myself up the first time I was with another woman—girl, I guess she was then. That's probably why it was so easy to push into the back of my mind. She was the girl next door and we'd played together all our lives. When we were fourteen we became, like they say, inseparable. One of our favorite things was hanging out in the hayloft of the barn. We could be private there and talk about anything we wanted. But I see now that more than talk we wanted to indulge our feelings for each other. I think you know now the feelings I mean. That warm all over, breathless, blooming feeling? The secret passion that makes being together so painful and exciting?

"So one day we were fooling around and we got physical with each other. We kind of challenged each other to take all our clothes off. I remember the sun was coming in through a little window on the side of the loft and her skin was so golden, like someone had spread it with honey. And my own was milky. We just stared at each other for so long, Victoria. I reached out my hand and touched her breast which was new and untouched. It just sprang to life, the nipple getting firm as if it was glad to see me. Then I touched the other. Then she began touching herself, masturbating, her eyes all glazed, her breathing real shallow. I wanted to be touching her, so I did. But no one ever touched me until Rosemary. And, wow, was that a relief after seven years of waiting!" Claudia laughed.

Victoria rested her head against Claudia's shoulder and gazed up at her, still feeling like a child. "Thank you for telling me. I guess it *is* all right to feel like that."

"You *know* it's all right to feel that good, Victoria love. And I'm so glad Anne does make you feel like that."

"So am I," Victoria said, rising. "I want to see her again. You're right, it's worth it. I'm not sure I'm strong enough. And I have to figure out how. I don't even know if she's called because I haven't been answering the phone all week."

"I know. Maybe you'll have to go and see her."

"That terrifies me."

They smiled at each other. "Ain't life grand?" Claudia asked. "To think that terror could be the door that leads to so much pleasure and fulfillment. And it's yours for the taking, Victoria." She put her plump arms up to Victoria's shoulders. "I'm here if you need me."

Victoria shook her head in amazement. "I never guessed how wonderful you are."

"Aw, shucks," said Claudia, hugging Victoria and quickly leaving her.

∿ ∿ ∿ ∿ ∿

After skulking away from Victoria's room Monday morning, Annie spent the week consumed by conflict. She felt, alternately, victorious at her escape from a difficult and consuming relationship—and crashingly disappointed to have abandoned the woman and relationship she wanted so badly.

She worked long hours without planning to and avoided the bar. At home she crawled into bed dressed and shook, as if with fever, in the damp spring beach air, while the foghorns sang desolate lullabyes. She ate only at the diner where she'd had breakfast the morning after she slept with Eleanor—as if to keep alive in herself the sense of relief she'd felt at that escape.

When she drove it was either in a fog of fantasies about the hours she'd spent with Victoria or hustling as a cab driver must to make good money. She would plan ahead when it was best to be at the Park Plaza, the railroad station, the Doctor's Building, and then dash her fares to their destinations and return for more as fast as she could. Hustling occupied her whole mind as she guessed which passengers would yield the best tips, which routes avoided the most traffic, who would tip her more for special treatment.

For Annie, it was a grey week punctuated by the shy swelling of the buds on the willow trees by her house. Their new light greens brought tears to her eyes as she marched past them on her morning walks. They stirred the part of herself that was like them and she wondered if they were altogether happy that now they were committed to leave their warm winter casings and hang all upside down, exposed to the winds and whatever they might bring.

Friday night Annie drove her VW straight to a bar from the terminal for the first time since before she'd seen Victoria at the dance. The bouncer stamped her hand, she pushed through the chattering men, and anchored herself to the empty side of the bar. As she waited, not making small talk with the bartender on purpose to relish the moment, a vibration, a memory of Victoria, began to wash through her. She stared down at the wooden bar, remembering the wooden tables where they had sat together and Victoria's long fingers on them, and the way those fingers felt on her body. But she'd had those waves of Victoria so many, many times now and she was still without anything but the mirage of her, afraid to make her real again. Unclenching her fists, she took the drink from the bartender and downed it quickly, pushing a bill toward her for another.

Peg drove her home much later, Annie and Turkey reeling with drink. They had spent a dull evening of small talk and gossip, as if her friends suspected Annie was not yet ready to talk about why she'd stayed away from them all week. Turkey was sick and collapsed on Annie's bed while Peg made coffee. She joined Annie at the old kitchen table where Annie was pushing splinters back through the tablecloth into the table.

"What the fuck's the matter with you, Heaphy?" Peg challenged her, standing in a three piece suit at her full height above Annie.

"Nothing," Annie mumbled. "Take your jacket off, you're making me hot."

"Bullshit nothing's wrong. Drink your coffee." Peg brought two mugs back from the stove. "And if you're hot, you're hot from the booze. As usual it's freezing in this hut."

"Aw, Peg, leave my house alone. It's all I've got. And you know damn well what's wrong."

"Well, I figure it's your Yalie, but why? Why are you so hung up?"

"Oh, Peglet, she's so beautiful. She's sensitive and gentle and intelligent and educated and she makes my heart turn over every time I think about her and she turns me on like nothing I've ever felt before. She's just perfect."

"Did you have a fight?"

"No, no, no. No fight. I just love her," and Annie Heaphy started to cry.

Peg glared, unyielding, at Annie, angry that her friend kept throwing love away. "Then why aren't you with her? Where have you been all week? Why'd you get drunk tonight? Doesn't she want to be with you?"

"I think so. I think she's scared of being gay, maybe. I brought her out, for Christ's sake. Besides, we're so different. It wouldn't work."

"You could try."

"It's so hard to talk to her sometimes. It's like we don't need to talk when we're together, but then I don't really know what happened, how it was with her when I left her."

"You mean you snuck out again."

Annie hung her head, wiping the tears off her face. "Yeah. I guess I did."

"I warned you about that, chickenshit," Peg reminded Annie with an affectionate smile.

"It's easier just to get in the cab and drive."

"And then get polluted so you don't have to deal with it?"

"Leave me alone, Peg. You sound like one of those fucking libbers."

Peg got angry again. She brushed invisible dirt from her pants viciously. "And you sound like one of those macho dykes that just want to act like men, running from woman to woman, not caring how you tear *her* up, and being so goddamned stoic about how you're feeling you lose touch with the woman underneath. What *are* you feeling? Never mind all the details of why it can't work. I've never seen you like this over a girl. What are you feeling in one word or less?" she glowered, pushing Annie's mug closer to her. "And drink your coffee while you're thinking."

Annie whispered, "Scared," then drank some coffee.

"Of what, you asshole, she's no different from you."

"She is too. She's smarter and better and has a lot of discipline and comes from a rich family . . ."

"I said no bullshit," Peg demanded.

Annie suddenly saw herself clearly. She saw her own harried, scared self dashing back and forth across the city mindlessly, like a robot. She saw her own rapid, graceless movements like a speeded up film and knew they were signs of her great turmoil and lack of control. It was as if that crazy self were being propelled. And by what? By fear? That's what she'd told Peg. And that's what she saw in the little running vision of herself. She looked at Peg who seemed to sense Annie's need for quiet time to think. Annie felt mad at Peg at the same time that she felt grateful. This was what her friend had done for her time after time: forced her to think about what she was doing.

So, there Annie was, the tiny figure in the city full of tiny figures, running in meaningless circles alone. She could do this forever—or she could stop. It *was* easier to keep running, keep circling like an airplane that never lands. But sooner or later she would crash. She'd be one of those people who have nowhere to go but the diner and the bar. Whose lives revolved around one lonely place after another. Even her house, as much as she loved it, was getting to feel emptier and emptier since Vicky. And Annie would lose it this summer anyway. Was she going to lose Vicky too?

Annie watched Peg wander to the living room where she stared out beyond the porch to the beach as Vicky had done Sunday morning while she waited for Annie to drive her home. Vicky was kind of like Peg and certainly the opposite of Annie: calm and graceful. Annie envied their ways. She smiled drunkenly to think of Vicky. And remembered her words: "I want to understand and that's why I'm drawn to you. I sensed your fullness, your love of life, when we first met. I want to feel like that." Annie remembered thinking Vicky sounded scared.

"Just like I am," she said aloud.

"You talking to me, Heaphy?" Peg asked, as she reentered the kitchen and sat at the table.

"Did you ever wonder if the ways you are and the ways someone else is could just be ways? I mean, that you're basically the same underneath?"

"What do you mean?"

"I'm not sure. I love Vicky for her control, the way she handles things, doesn't just react to them, you know?" Annie asked, passing her hand across her face, tugging at her hair as if to clear her thinking.

"Okay."

"But what if her calm, the way she is, is just how she shows how scared *she* is of everything?"

"So . . . ," Peg encouraged while Annie paused.

"So if I'm scared *and* she's scared, then it's stupid to be scared. Do you think one person's need to be always in motion could be a sign of the same tension that makes another person always need to be still and slow?" Annie beamed at Peg. "Of course," she cried, pulling Peg up, pulling her behind her as she triumphantly dodged her books and shoes and furniture and ran for the porch, Peg following curiously, ready to prevent Annie from driving. "Vicky's just like me!" she yelled back at Peg as she leapt off the steps and ran, hardly stopping to check for cars, across the street, her thighs and arms pumping in unison so that she felt like a running machine turned on full power until she reached the damp sand and the water.

"Vicky's just as scared as me," she thought. "I'm not really scared of her. I'm scared of me and she's scared of herself and we're scared of seeing ourselves in each other. And we're hurting from the awful thing we've both been suffering, the awful experience of being alone in the world." Annie stumbled a little from the liquor as she looked up at the stars. "The whole crazy world's going around and around both of us and I'm standing here like an idiot without her." She stared up at the moon and felt raw with loneliness.

Peg caught up with Annie and stood silently beside her. "Night after night, Peglet, I have stood here looking at the moon in all its shapes and sizes as if it could do something for me. I've been angry, miserable, out of control and I almost just chained myself to the empty old moon because I was so damn afraid of doing the one thing I want: loving a woman. And I've been afraid of *what* she is, not even *who* she is." Annie faced Peg. "And Vicky's done the same thing, I'll bet. She's sitting in her room. She built the damn thing around her so everything she touches is herself and she doesn't have to feel the aloneness. She thinks she can just watch life and not be touched by it."

"Ah, Peg, you son of a bitch," Annie shivered, the sweat turning cool on her back. "Did you know all this? Why didn't you tell me? I think I can tell Vicky now. Thank you, Peg," Annie hugged her silent friend, "thank you. I think I can sit still long enough to tell her. I think I can slow down enough to match her pace if she'll start moving. Oh, Peg, look what you gave me!'' Annie threw her arms toward the sky, swaying a little, and stood smiling at it with Peg, drunk now on wonder too, hurting with the pain of knowing what she knew and crying from the beauty of it all.

∿ ∿ ∿ ∿ ∿

Saturday morning Victoria's phone rang. She was afraid to answer it. She knew it was Annie's call to break the week of long suffering silence. Although she knew now that she wanted Annie, she had not conquered her fear of the relationship. Annie would be in a phone booth in the sun, yellow cab running alongside—she could see her sturdy and bright and hopeful against the empty blue enormous sky. Victoria lay on a small oriental rug, another gift from one of her parents' trips, looking at the ceiling. When she was younger she would pretend to hover just below the ceiling, like an angel, watching her corporeal self perform its crass, worldly functions down below. As she got older she dreamed of becoming a monk or a nun, living a life stripped to its barest essentials, so simple, so close to perfection, so alone. She would share herself with no one.

Later, she dropped the religious trappings and felt enclosed by herself. She planned to look at beautiful things and do her life's work competently, living a simple life without the complications of marriage or a demanding career. She would stay on in school until she had the credentials to teach enough courses to give her life definition. And spend the rest of her time doing—research? writing? Always there would be a place for her in the sheltered academic world. She had planned to go through her life untouched.

The phone rang again as the sun moved more fully through her window and pinned Victoria with its warmth to her rug. She turned onto her stomach, but the sun just brought the brightness of the rug up to her eyes, smashing them with rich red, yellow and blue. It's not true, she screamed silently, clasping her hands together, holding them tight while the phone stopped ringing, holding back the pain. I'm lying Anne, come save me, she cried inside. I'm looking for beauty, sensation, but I can't venture out and enjoy it vicariously through an Etta or through you. You can't give it to me. You don't give it to me. Loving you let it out and now it's out, really out, and I'll never get it back in, and I need someone to share it with. I don't want solitude anymore.

Her fear ebbed and she tried once more to reason her way back to safety. She moved to her bed where the sun never went. All right, she admitted, I want her. I never wanted anybody, but Etta showed me what I might need. And I've let that need lie fallow in me for years. Until Anne.

She let herself think of Annie Heaphy. She almost smiled, but stopped herself. Why couldn't she reach out to her again? She didn't know how. She was frightened. Was she risking too much? Would she be safer ignoring love? Could she ever be strong enough, quick enough to dodge through the traffic of pain and beauty she had seen so briefly? Would Annie teach her? Victoria wondered if she could keep up with Annie. Keep up with her! she laughed. I don't keep up with people, I set the pace. No, she thought wonderingly, sitting upright, looking toward the window. No, the pace was set for me and I hid in it. I can change it.

Victoria sat very still, trying at first to control her panicking heart, then giving in to it, letting it thud. My heart, after all, is part of me. Perhaps it will beat strongly enough to make me move and fast enough for me to keep up with Anne. Perhaps it *is* large enough to hold all I want to feel.

She leapt up toward the telephone across the room full of hot spring sunlight. Maybe Anne had called from her little toothpick house. Victoria's fingers were moving so fast she had to dial three times before she slowed down enough to dial the number right. Then no one was answering and there was a knock on her door. Afraid of missing Annie she did not hang up, but called, "Come in . . ."

Cap in hand, Annie Heaphy stood in the dark doorway to see Victoria, phone in hand, full of the sunlight from her window.

"Hi," said Annie, still as a statue, her voice barely a whisper.

"Hello," Vicky answered, very slowly cradling the phone and standing. The sun made a reddish halo at the top of her head.

"Shall I come back after you finish your phone call?" Annie asked, holding her breath in anticipation.

"I was calling you."

"Oh." Annie's breath rushed out in relief. "Me?" she gulped, suddenly realizing the import of what Victoria had said.

Victoria smiled. "You. Annie. Annie Heaphy. Anne. Your hair was in my eyes."

"My hair," Annie repeated, feeling stupid.

"It's so bright, it glows in my mind even when you're not around."

They looked at each other for a moment. "Vicky," Annie asked, nervous, but obviously somewhat recovered, "can I come into your room?"

"I'm sorry, Anne, of course you can." She stepped across the room toward Annie, her arms outstretched. Annie's hands met hers and Victoria pulled her inside the room. Annie pushed the door shut behind her with her foot. They stood looking into one another's eyes.

"I think I'm in love with you, Vicky."

"I certainly hope you are."

"You do?"

Victoria put her arms around Annie, feeling strong and maternal when she saw Annie's blue eyes lift to her face in disbelief. "Yes." she said, fighting to find words adequate to what she felt. Then she saw nothing, just felt the slightly smaller woman's body tight against her own, the feel again of her soft breasts pushed against her ribcage, the comfort and surprise of her. Annie stared over Victoria's shoulder at her blindingly bright window, its narrow frame aiming all the light of the world at them. She felt the sun on her hands where they reached around Victoria's back and on Victoria's hair where her cheek touched it. The warmth and her own relief made her feel as if she was melting. They stood like that for a long time.

"Can you spend the afternoon with me?" Annie asked.

"Of course. Don't you have to work?"

"I sometimes knock off early on Saturday if I work a lot of hours during the week. And I worked a lot of hours this week. Trying to stay away from you."

"Why?" Victoria asked, hoping Annie would not ask her the same question.

"That's a hard one," Annie said, pulling away from Victoria, still touching her. "You feel so good to touch," she smiled. "I guess I was afraid."

"Of what?" Victoria hoped Annie would answer the question for her too.

Annie shrugged and leaned to kiss the v of Victoria's light blue sweater where it rested just above her breasts. "That you wouldn't be interested, I guess."

"Why would you think that?"

"Didn't think it," Annie answered, shuffling her feet and stepping backwards. "Just afraid of it. You know?"

"Do you think that was all?"

"No." Annie walked over to the window and looking out answered, "I feel something about you I never felt before. I can't even say it's altogether pleasant. I mean," she explained, turning around to face Victoria, "I feel a lot of pleasant things too, but this, it's like you're a magnet and I can't not love you. Like we're supposed to be together. Like you're good for me. An answer. Something I've been looking for. Do you understand?"

"Completely. I've been trying to say that to myself, to explain what I feel about you. Yet for all the incredible things that you make me feel, I'm not sure I'm ready to deal with loving a woman, I'm not sure I would if I didn't feel almost *fated*."

"Do you believe in that, Vicky?"

"In fate?"

They stood now close to each other holding hands. "I didn't," Vicky answered slowly. They looked at each other again a long while. Annie broke the silence.

"Listen, I've got to get the cab back. Want to come with me and pick up my bug and maybe we'll go to the beach by my house?"

Not answering, Victoria asked, "Why didn't you wait to say goodbye?"

Annie hung her head and shook it, her light hair scattering across her head, catching the sun. "That's a long story."

"I need to know," Victoria pressed.

Annie looked at her. "Okay, okay. I don't really know. I always do that if I don't know the woman I'm with very well. I feel uncomfortable."

"I'm just now realizing how much that bothered me and how much a part of my fears about you it is."

Annie watched Victoria's pained face. "*You* didn't make me uncomfortable. *I* did. I was afraid to know you were real. Afraid it wasn't as good as I thought it was. It usually isn't, you know."

"No, I don't have much experience in these things. At first I thought it had been awful for you. Then I convinced myself it hadn't, but the fear was still there."

"Oh, Vicky, no, no," Annie protested, taking her in her arms again. "It was wonderful. I just didn't want it to get shabby in the morning like it always does. I wanted that whole beautiful weekend to be a perfect memory. I didn't want life to go on. People get dull, hurt each other, change. I wanted it to be always like it was. But in all those hours of driving and sitting on the beach, watching the water, I saw there was much more for me with you than a weekend we already had. If you wanted to be with me I felt as if we really would have something to give each other. That's why I'm here."

Victoria confessed, "I've been frightened by reading too much about homosexual one night stands."

"And I've had too many of them. Look, you're never going to believe it unless I show you, unless we live it. Come to my home with me, come let me love you. There's nothing else I want to do," Annie said, still holding Victoria, worrying about the tenuousness of the "home" she offered.

" 'Come live with me and be my love,/ And we will all the pleasures prove/ That hills and valleys, dales and fields,/ Or woods or steepy mountain yields.' " Victoria quoted as she leaned her head on Annie's shoulder. It felt so good to have a woman's shoulder to lean on. She imagined her mother in a swirling cocktail dress and wondered why she'd never felt welcome to lean on her. Because she's so fake, a voice inside her said. Here's a woman who's real. Who wants to stop acting in old ways, painful ways and to find joy with you.

"And that's what I want to do with you, Anne," Victoria said.

"Prove all the pleasures?" Annie put her hat back on, smiling. "Let's go!"

"Shall I pack for the weekend?" Victoria laughed, letting go more of her uncertainties.

"You, lady," Annie pronounced solemnly, "should pack for *life*."

Awhile later they sped over the bridge away from New Haven. "It's only Long Island Sound," Annie shouted over her still mufflerless car, "but it feels like the Atlantic to me!"

Victoria looked at the gulls circling the small harbor and the boats out for their first runs of the season. It reminded her of the lake she had stayed on with her family the summer she fished in New Hampshire. She hadn't thought of that in a long time. Not since that strange encounter on the train with the woman she still thought of as a witch. Well, the witch might have known her future, Victoria marvelled, but that vacation *had* been a happy time. "It's just what the doctor ordered," she shouted back to Annie. "I don't remember this ride at all from last weekend."

"A week ago today," Annie commented as she stopped at a corner and gunned her little motor waiting to turn. "That can be our anniversary. Today we're one week old. Want to celebrate?"

"You silly romantic! We are celebrating!"

"Good, that'll save a lot of planning. This is the road to my house now."

"Over the river and through the woods," Victoria sang, "to Annie's house we go." She stopped when Annie jerked to a halt at the side of the road and threw herself at Victoria.

"You're great!" Annie said, after kissing Victoria with passion. "You're beautiful and sexy and smart and fun too. I can't believe I'm about to embark on a mad passionate love affair with you. And that you haven't shot me down for entertaining hopes that we can have more than an affair."

"You're crazy, little queen. One doesn't go kissing other women in the middle of a public street."

"Oops," Annie said as she began to drive again. "Little queen?"

"Queen Anne. Queen of England and Ireland around seventeen hundred. Noted for her devotion to the Church of England. I looked her up this week. Another thing she is noted for is her great friendship with a woman named Sarah Jennings. They were very close," she winked at Annie.

"Oh, yeah? Do you know something scandalous about this queen?"

"No, but I thought you'd be interested."

"So my original namesake might have been a queer," Annie mused as they rounded a bend in the road. "Look. My willows." She pointed to the three curved willow trees, decorated with light green new leaves. The water sparkled in the sun beyond them.

"They look like they've been through the wars," Victoria commented. "But they're beautiful, like they're flexing their muscles under all that new foliage."

"I think they are. Look how there are no other trees. They're the only ones who have survived the wind and the salt air. They have a different kind of beauty. Usually I think of willows as being sad and delicate. These are strong and hard, yet they still sprout all that beautiful stuff. Like a bulldyke who looks like a truck driver on the outside, but is so gentle making love because she's a woman. She only looks like a bulldyke because life is so hard on her. She keeps the inside tender by hardening the crust."

Victoria reached across to Annie and stroked her cheek. "You love those trees, don't you?"

Embarrassed, Annie said, "Sure do. Here we are."

They pulled into the front yard of what Victoria remembered as the toothpick house and she was struck again by its fragility. Surely it was not strong enough to shelter Anne through the winter months. The porch had no door, the windows were still covered with plastic sheets to keep the winds outside. Ladders and sawhorses lay in the yard of the beach cottage next door.

"The landlord's fixing up my neighbor's shack," Annie said. "I wonder how soon they'll work their way over here. This porch is a mess. But there's no use fixing it until the workmen finish. I don't use it much anyway. Last summer Peg and those guys only came out here a couple of times. They think it's too far to travel. Come on, bring your bag inside, then we'll go over to the beach. Don't look at the mess in here. I tried to fix it up, but what the hell, I'm getting kicked out the end of May anyway."

"Why?" asked Victoria, putting her suitcase on the floor and sitting on a wooden chest.

"The lousy landlord can make more money renting to summer people. Last year nobody would rent it, but this year he found a sucker willing to pay twice as much as me for the summer months."

"Didn't you say you were going to buy it?"

"If he'll sell. Even then I don't know if I could get the money to pay for it. Come on, let's go across the street and talk about happier things. Want a beer to go?"

"No, I don't think so."

"Mind if I bring a couple? Sometimes I like to do this on a Saturday afternoon. Just go across to the beach by my lonesome with a couple of beers, get high and stare at the water. Real relaxing." As she shut the door behind them she realized she was jabbering again in nervousness. To cover her embarrassment she said, "I'll race you."

"Okay," Victoria laughed and began to run in a loose, long-limbed way while Annie shot out, a beer in each hand, like a windmill out of control. But Annie had to wait for a car to go by and Victoria caught up and passed her, her momentum out-distancing Annie's new burst of speed. Annie just followed her, watching her run several yards onto the beach.

"You're amazing!" she breathed at Victoria when they stopped. "Come over here, there's a nice rock to lean on over this way. You don't even look like you could work up a sweat the relaxed way you run, but you cover your distance good."

"And you look like you're running for your life. I'm surprised your hat stays on your head."

"Oh, that's a permanent fixture. I don't want you to find out that I'm bald."

They walked to a group of rocks and collapsed against them. Annie offered Victoria a beer. When Victoria smiled in acceptance, she said, "I suspected you might want it once we were here. Our anniversary party," Annie toasted. She lay her head on Victoria's shoulder. "Vicky," she sighed.

"No one ever calls me that, you know," Victoria said, sliding Annie's hat off her hair and resting her chin on her head.

"And no one takes my hat off and gets away with it," Annie said, pressing herself closer to Victoria.

That night, when the beach was dark and they were in the toothpick house, a little drunk from beer and almost hoarse from talking so much, Victoria said, "I'm no good at people, Anne."

"You're good at me," Annie assured her, putting both of Victoria's hands between her own across the corner of the table.

Victoria smiled sadly. "You're different. You make me be good at you. I can't help myself. You're so easy to be with, easy even for me to touch," and she bent her head to kiss Annie's hand.

"You've never said you love me," Annie replied quietly.

Victoria withdrew her hands. "I know, I know. I wish I could."

"You mean you want to?"

"Oh, Anne, of course I do. At least I think that's what I feel for you. I'm so confused. For years I've wished I could love someone and now I think I finally do and I'm not even sure that's what I feel. Even if it is I can't express it."

Annie had risen and now knelt on the floor, her arms stretched up and around Victoria. "I'm sorry, I'm sorry," she whispered into Victoria's sleeve. "I should never have said that. That's asking too much. Besides, you do say what you feel. You say it in all kinds of ways like when you touch me or when you look at me. I'm just so conventional I think I have to hear it. Next thing you know I'll ask you to put it on a billboard or I won't believe that you even *like* me!"

"It's *not* asking too much. I *do* love you. I do, I do," Victoria half sobbed, getting to her knees also.

"Oh, Vicky, Vicky."

"But I won't put anything on a billboard."

Annie leaned back from Victoria to see that she was smiling, then hugged her even harder. "You'd better get up or you'll develop housemaid's knee like Radcliffe Hall's first love," she laughed.

"Oh, didn't you like that? Wasn't that so English? The 'son' of the manor falling in love with the servant?"

"Wish I'd been brought up in your manor, m'lady," Annie bowed after she had lifted them both to standing positions. They sat at the kitchen table.

"I'm glad you weren't. And that *I* wasn't either. I would have been terribly rich and more of a snob than I am."

"You're not a snob, Vicky," Annie said as they sat at the table again. "And there's nothing wrong with you being rich."

"Except I'm not," Vicky answered.

"Oops, another sensitive spot," Annie said when she heard the defensive tone of Victoria's voice.

"Not being rich can certainly confuse a growing child. When your family lives like it is rich."

"So I see, Vicky. It's okay, really it is. Sit down. Are you really not rich? I'm so glad."

"I am definitely not rich. My parents lost their money, but can't give up the lifestyle. It makes for a lot of lies."

"Come again?"

"They're terrified the family will someday find out how careless they really were. They grew up in the depression. Most of it was lost back then. My father built it up again only to find his investments weren't sound. It left just enough to be able to pretend. They won't let me forget how to *act* privileged. Always lecturing me on how to get more money when I'm trying to deal with it not being there. I suppose I ought to be grateful for what we *do* have, but I've always felt I would have been much happier if I'd been born more middle class or even lower class. Is it very snobbish of me to say that people with less money are more real, live more fully?"

"Probably, but I'll forgive you. Now I've always felt that *everybody* had more fun than me."

"Why, Annie? You have a great sense of fun. We can laugh together. It's one of the things I treasure about you."

Again Annie reached across the table for Victoria's hand. "Because I've been gay so long. I feel like I can't really enjoy life, not that I'd want it any other way. It's kept me so separate from other people, except for my lovers. I hate straights. I can't stand their bigoted, self-centered view of the world, yet I envy them their comfort and freedom to move in it. It *is* theirs, after all."

"Yes, I suppose it is. I have so much to learn."

"Welcome to the gay world. Money may have been your problem before, but now you're despicable."

"What a way to talk to the woman you just seduced!"

"Seduced! *Me* seduce *you*?"

"Well, you don't think an innocent like me could have thought of such a thing?" Victoria asked, bowing her head modestly.

"Of course not, m'lady. I'll take all the blame. But if I'm to be blamed, then I want all the benefits of my foul deeds. Come into my bedroom."

Victoria still hung her head. "You couldn't be meaning me, could you?"

"Come with me or it'll be the floor, Vicky," Annie said into her neck.

"How shocking," Victoria replied, pulling Annie now toward the bedroom.

Later, Annie stirred. "In the dark, you know," she pulled back from the warmth she and Victoria had made, "I can't even tell you're poor."

Victoria sat up, her languorous body luminous in the dark. She tossed her hair over one shoulder and said, low and quietly, "Then we're even. In the dark, I can't tell you're a lesbian."

They laughed and resettled with Victoria's head on Annie's shoulder.

"It's too bad one of us isn't rich," Annie sighed.

"Why?"

"Then we could go buy the house and live here happily ever after." Victoria realized that she too could become attached to this fragile shelter and thought for a moment of her well-to-do relatives. She hoped Annie wasn't counting on her in some way for money.

"Well, we're not," she answered shortly, immediately sorry about her tone.

"Want a beer?" Annie asked, sensing Victoria's disturbance.

Victoria nestled deeper against Annie. "How could you think of leaving me at a time like this?" she murmured.

"Oh, it's not hard. I'm real thirsty."

"You really like to drink, don't you, Annie?"

"No. It's just a habit. Like Turkey says, 'When you put up with as much shit all day as we do, you got to wash it out at night.' "

"I find you much sweeter than any liquor," Victoria growled as she leaned over and bit Annie's breast.

"Umm. Okay. I'll give it up for you."

"No. Go ahead and get one. It'll taste good. But not just yet," she rolled over and pressed her upper body against Annie. "You feel so good. No wonder I didn't like men. They couldn't feel like this."

"My innocent," Annie put her arms around Victoria. "You've never made love with anyone before me?"

"No. And I'm so glad."

"Yeah, I wish I hadn't now too. I wish you were my first."

"Oh, you Romeo. How many women have you been with?"

"Not that many. Just enough to know you've got them all beat."

"You're so diplomatic."

"Not on purpose, Vicky. Hey! You're tickling!"

"I want to have every sensation with you," Victoria said passionately. "I want to experience everything with you for the first time and the hundredth time! No, no! I didn't mean I wanted to be tickled, too!" She broke into giggles, curling in on herself.

"Fair's fair!"

"Go get the beer!"

"You're just saying that to stop me."

"It worked!" Victoria laughed. "Aren't you cold away from the bed?"

Annie ran self-consciously toward the kitchen. "Yes!" she called back. "And damn it, I'll never find the bottle opener."

Victoria lay in the small dark room luxuriating in the sense of being part of someone's life. Why, Annie was actually running around naked in front of her. The intimacy was new to her and felt good. Victoria wanted to sing, just as Etta had joyously in the woods so many years ago. "At last I'm feeling it!" she thought.

Annie came into the room grinning over a tray which she slid onto the bed. Sitting carefully next to it she announced, "Just a snack. Aren't you hungry after all that exercise?" Victoria sat up on her elbow, smiling, her thick hair falling to her belly. "Do you know you're beautiful, Vicky?"

"No, but I know I'm happy," Victoria answered very seriously.

"What is it? What's wrong?" Annie asked, reaching over to touch Victoria.

Victoria tilted her head to catch Annie's hand between it and her shoulder. "I love you. I love you, Anne," she lifted her head to look at Annie, "you make me happy. I know you don't understand how much that means to me." She stopped, took a deep breath and sighed. "Someday I'll explain more, all right? I just want to be with you now. And be happy."

"Okay. I love you, too, you know that." Victoria nodded. "Let's eat then. Look. I got chips and pickles and some pumpernickel bread and bologna and mustard. Oh, I forgot a knife!"

"Don't leave again. We'll use our fingers!" Victoria giggled. They grinned at each other, then began to make their first meal together in Annie's home.

CHAPTER SEVEN

Several weeks later Annie and Victoria sat in the front seats of Annie Heaphy's VW with Peg and Turkey in back. They were all excited to be going to Vermont for the weekend together. By the time they reached the Vermont border even Victoria had been persuaded to join in their singing.

" 'The answer is blowing in the wind,' " Turkey bellowed one last time, opening her window wide so the wind sang with her. It blew her straw hat into Peg's lap and Victoria's hair across Annie's face.

"Hey, close that, you lunatic, I can't see!" Annie shouted.

"It's shut, it's shut, for Christ's sake. You guys don't let me have no fun, do they, Vicky?"

Victoria tried to find a funny answer, but, feeling like a failure, just shook her head and smiled.

"What a diplomat you found, Annie," Turkey went on. "She don't take sides, does she?"

"Doesn't she," Annie corrected. "Open me another beer, will you?"

Peg grabbed the open bottle before Turkey could give it to Annie. "Do you realize, Heaphy, the four of us have finished off close to two six packs and Vicky doesn't drink much?"

"Is that why I got to go to the bathroom so bad?" Annie asked. "But I'm perfectly sober. Don't hardly do me no good at all to drink anymore. I'm high already." She looked quickly at Victoria, then reached across to take her hand. "Would you rather I didn't?" she asked more softly.

Victoria squeezed her hand tightly. "No," she answered softly. "Not if you feel sober."

Annie looked at her again. "Maybe I better not," she admitted, putting her hand back on the wheel.

"Ma, we going to be there soon?" Turkey asked, laughing.

"Ma, I gotta go to the bathroom. Ma, I'm thirsty!"

"Shut up, kid," Peg warned her, then punched her in the arm.

"Yow! She's killing me, Ma!"

"Shut up back there, you two! We're almost there. Speaking of which, do you have the map, Vicky?"

"No. Turkey," Victoria turned around, "I think I gave it to you. May I have it please?"

"So polite, she is," Turkey laughed, rummaging through the junk-filled back seat. "You got to learn to be *crude* with this crowd if you want to survive this trip. 'Specially that Annie. No manners at all. Must have been brought up in the gutter if you want my opinion. Here it is. Sorry, it's a little bit wet."

Victoria laughed as she took the map, now split in two and soaked with beer, into the front seat. "It will be easier to read this way," she said, folding one half away in the glove compartment. "Putney, did you say?"

"Um-huh," Annie answered, looking at Victoria in a way she knew meant Annie was thinking of making love to her. Victoria's body responded to that look as she never imagined it could and her face went red.

"Hey, what are you two doing up there?" Turkey asked as she stuck her head between the front seats. "Are we there or are we there?"

Victoria hid behind the wall of hair she let fall over the map. "Only about two exits away," she answered.

Peg and Turkey cheered. "Bathroom ho! Set course for port, Captain!"

"Ay ay, Peglet, but first we have to find the place!"

"No problem with our trusty navigator, Vicky."

"Oh, I don't know about that," Victoria warned. "I've never navigated before."

Half an hour later Victoria returned to the car, the last out of the bathroom behind the small store of a one pump gas station. They had gotten off the exit and immediately proceeded to get lost. By the time they reached the gas station, Turkey was moaning about the amount of beer in her bladder and Victoria had been assigned to ask directions.

"Did he give you directions?" Annie asked, sitting up from

resting across both their seats.

"Yes. And he said he likes your aunt and uncle a great deal, Turkey. He went up there to deliver some food when they first built their place."

"Great. That means he'll tell them I rolled in here half drunk with a bunch of queers and bought another case of beer!"

"Nobody knows we're gay," Peg said quickly, noticing Victoria had lowered her head. She gestured with her chin towards her.

Turkey nodded. "Only kidding. With Victoria here for our spokesman we're probably all set. I can hear him now. 'Lovely friends your niece has, Mrs. D. Too bad your niece is such a slob!' Thanks for the good impression, Vic. Tell us what he said."

"Apparently we passed it at least three times," Victoria smiled as Turkey moaned over her own needless suffering. "Anne, if you'll take a left out of the supermarket here . . . ," she directed sarcastically.

"Isn't it cute here, though?" Peg asked. "Real New Englandy."

"Ah," Annie sighed loudly, "a weekend in the country."

"With real *hicks*," Turkey laughed.

Victoria looked questioningly at Annie.

"Peg's always saying me and Turkey are hicks because we're not from New York."

"Now she'll see how sophisticated I really am," Turkey said, puffing herself up, turkey-like.

"That's what we were fighting about the first night we met you, Vicky," Annie confessed.

"After this sign coming up we take a left onto a dirt road. Really? You mean we've come full circle back to the same subject? Or is it a recurrent one?"

"Recurrent. They *are* hicks," Peg interjected.

Annie ignored her. "This left?" she asked, turning in. They bounced up a series of hills for two miles until they came to a small unfinished house of weathered wood, a porch with no steps and a mountain behind it. Annie stopped the VW. "This is beautiful country," she said, exhaling a deep breath.

"But I thought my aunt said the house was finished!"

"Looks done enough for me. As long as that roof doesn't leak." Peg squeezed past Victoria's seat into the last of the daylight and Turkey followed her with the key.

Another toothpick house, thought Victoria affectionately, looking at it.

Annie turned to her. "Maybe this wasn't such a hot idea."

"Why?" Victoria asked, taking off her glasses and rubbing her eyes.

Annie put her fingers on Victoria's shoulder and leaned her head on her outstretched arm. "Because I want you so bad. Right now."

"I know. Me too," Victoria answered, leaning to meet Annie's lips.

"I don't want them to think we'll be like this all weekend," Annie breathed, pulling away.

"We won't. We'll get some time alone together. They'll understand, won't they?" Victoria asked, looking hopeful.

"Yes, as long as you can take their teasing."

"I'm not used to it, but I like them. They're part of you. I want so much to fit in. For them to like me. But I can never think of anything to say."

"They like you already. Turkey told me that after we all went to the bar the other night."

They walked around to the trunk of the car and began to carry things to the porch. Peg came to the door. "It'll do," she said. "We have to get firewood before it's completely dark or we'll freeze to death. There's enough big stuff inside for the night. All we need is tinder and kindling."

They spread out around the cabin and began to gather wood. In less than an hour the three friends and Victoria had set up temporary housekeeping and were watching Turkey stir a pot of chili on a grate over the fire. By the time the stars came out, the fire had taken the chill out of the cabin's air and they finished eating.

"If the dishwater's hot I'll start the dishes," Peg volunteered.

"I'll dry," Annie said as she rose and stretched.

"Good, me and Vicky can talk. I have never been so hungry

in my life. If that's not too hard to believe," Turkey said to Victoria, rubbing her stomach as she pushed herself up with her other arm. "What we need now is a joint by the fire," she went on, pulling a small suede bag out of her suitcase.

"You brought marijuana?" Victoria asked.

"Better," Turkey answered, smiling smugly. "Hash!" and she held out a small chunk.

Victoria took it and turned it around in the palm of her hand curiously. "I've never smoked this."

"No? It's great. A lot more potent than grass."

"I never smoked that either," Victoria mumbled.

Turkey looked up. "Oh, I'm sorry. Do you want us not to? I mean, you wouldn't have to anyway. I never thought... Annie, you've been depriving this poor girl of the pleasures of life!"

"*I* have?" Annie called from the fire.

"You never got her stoned." Turkey lowered her voice. "Does Annie know you never smoked?"

"I don't remember it coming up. I just assumed she only drank."

"Usually that's all we do. But a change is nice. You shouldn't feel like you have to. I remember the first time I smoked. It was a riot. I was up here. Not here, but back on the other side of Putney. My aunt stayed at a trailer place. There was a bunch of kids just used to hang out together and one day one of the guys got some real good stuff and laid it on us. I was the only one who never smoked before, but I didn't tell them that. We all walked up the river a ways from the campsite and sat on the rocks. Oh my, was I high. First time in my life I ever shut up. I didn't even laugh. At first. Everything looked so beautiful. The water just flowed on and on. I know sociologists don't talk like this," Turkey said to cover her embarrassment, "But I thought I was experiencing eternity."

"No, Turkey, I think it's wonderful. You said it so beautifully, too. You make me want to try it," Victoria protested, wondering if she was really going to smoke to make Turkey feel more comfortable.

"Good. Just don't think I'm trying to push you. But you won't be sorry." She smiled at the little pipe in her hand.

"Then, after I stopped being all intellectual about it, my friend Maudie came and sat with me and we started fooling around. Everything was so funny. I'll never forget that, how funny the littlest thing was. Maudie had some bubble gum. I swear I never tasted bubble gum so good in all my life. It exploded in my mouth. The pink taste was everywhere. And then it *was* everywhere because I popped a big bubble and it stuck to my nose and cheeks and it just got funnier and funnier that I was sitting there with all this pink stuff on me, you know?"

"Yes, I can imagine," Victoria laughed. "It sounds like the time I took acid."

"I don't believe it. You never smoked, but you did acid?"

Victoria blushed. "Just the one time."

"Tell me about it."

"Do you really want to hear it?"

"Of course I do. I never took acid. You know, I think I got your number lady." Victoria looked alarmed. "You're shy. It's not because you go to Yale or you just came out. You're scared to open your mouth. Are you shy?"

Victoria tried to muster her detachment, to pull away from Turkey and say that she was reticent and introspective, but didn't think she was shy. But while she was struggling with herself, Turkey answered, "Of course you are. And I'm being a klutzy slob again making you admit it. I'm sorry. I'm just glad I feel I know you a little better. You don't have to tell your story. I won't push you. But you know I never kenw a good-looking woman could be shy? I used to be. Shy that is. I was never good-looking," she laughed loudly. "But I overcame it. You know how? I decided the hell with everybody. I'm alright. If they don't like it, that's their loss. So," she ended, toasting Victoria with the tiny hash pipe, "that's sob-sister Marieanne's advice for the night. Hey, would you guys finish up and come help us get stoned?"

Annie was on her way. Her army jacket looked comforting to Victoria against the light of the fire. She sat next to Victoria and hugged her briefly. "What do you mean I deny her pleasures?"

"Because I've never smoked," Victoria admitted.

Annie looked surprised. "Do you want to?"

"Will I like it?" she asked, wondering where in the world her need for independence had gone. She watched Annie take the pipe and draw on it, then hold her breath as she passed it to Victoria who suddenly felt like an awkward child. Soon, though, the four of them were giggling softly and smiling at one another.

"This is really mellow stuff," Peg observed, rolling back onto her sleeping bag which was arranged, like the others, feet toward the fire.

"Knocks you on your ass," Turkey gurgled, rolling over into Peg.

"Watch out, lady, Eleanor would be livid with jealousy if she saw you curling up with me."

"My intentions are so platonic I'm embarrassed. Too bad she couldn't make it, though."

Annie laughed. "Are you kidding? We couldn't pry her away from Dusty. El really wants that to work out. After all, they've been together almost two months now and Dusty's everything she's been looking for. Except you, Peglet."

"And you, Heaphy. Aren't you jealous, Vicky?"

Victoria faced Annie. "Oh, no," she answered very quietly, studying the cut of Annie's face, the pale, pale skin covering her bones like a still-forming baby's face, the blue eyes as gentle and surprised as an infant's. She reached up and played with her fine hair. "Where's your hat?"

"I never wear it when I smoke. Makes me itchy."

"It's nice to see you without it sometimes. It changes you. Makes you softer."

"Why do you think I wear it?" Annie growled.

"Oh, but what's wrong with your softness? I love it."

"I get stepped on too much. You won't step on me. I hope."

"I won't." Victoria said quietly, then mouthed the words, "I promise." She turned away from Annie saying, "Turkey, you were right, I *like* hash." But Turkey was still and silent.

"I'm falling out too," Peg said, moving to roll Turkey inside her bag.

Annie said, "Me and Vicky will go in the bedroom, Peglet. This fire will go out soon."

"Not if I can help it," Peg grunted, zipping Turkey in.

"Can we keep it going all night? Here," Annie offered, "I'll put more wood on. We'll rejoin you later and build it up again then."

"Sounds good to me."

"Vicky, come here," Annie gestured. "Let's tuck Peglet in."

"Now, I'm a big girl. That's not at all necessary."

"No, but it's nice," Victoria admonished her, fluffing up Peg's pillow.

Annie leaned over and kissed Peg on the cheek. "Night, gym teacher."

"Goodnight, Peg," Victoria kissed her on the other cheek and stayed a moment, holding Annie's hand across Peg's covered body, their other hands on Peg's shoulders.

Peg covered both their hands with hers. She looked into Victoria's eyes, gentle looking behind the reflections of the fire in her glasses. "You be good to my woman, here, Vicky. She needs someone to take care of her. She's just a tough kid behind it all, you know."

"I'll do everything I can to help her stay a tough kid, Peg. I like her, too."

"Can it, you two," Annie scowled.

They all laughed softly, careful not to wake Turkey who had begun to snore. Annie and Victoria gathered their sleeping bags and walked hand in hand away from the fire.

∿ ∿ ∿ ∿ ∿

The next morning Annie threw their sleeping bags over an improvised clothesline to get rid of the night's dampness. The sun was beginning to brighten and warm the gentle spring day. Annie leaned against a tree for a moment, staring back over the climbing road that led to the cabin. The main road and general store were hidden, but farther off was a steeple and the interruptions in clusters of trees which indicated a town. She yearned to sneak off there to find a place where she and Vicky could live surrounded by the peace she was finding in the countryside's isolation. Being in Vermont was like drawing a shade upon the real world. No one would be able to see them and they would not have to see anything they did not want to see. Alone and at peace they could continue to explore each other without having to deal with the outer shell that came up when they were exposed to the real world. Annie knew her dream was impossible, even undesirable, since even they could not sustain pure joy forever. Better that unhappiness come from outside themselves than that they find it in each other.

She sighed, feeling the tree's bark rough yet comforting under her hand. A bush full of small red berries drew her eyes. First she had wanted someone to love and now that she had found her it was not enough, she thought, trying to encourage herself to be happy at her good fortune. Now I want a place to protect our love, to make sure it can grow. I want to make it so irresistible for Vicky to stay with me that she'll never have cause to go. The bars are no place for us. My house, she thought heavily, is temporary. And now that part of my life feels better I can't be driving a cab all hours of the day and night. What a trap, she thought. Either you've got nothing to treasure or you're inadequate once you find it. A light touch on her wrist made her worries disappear immediately. She brought her wrist with Vicky's hand still on it to her lips. Vicky's hand turned over sending heat surging into Annie's chest. She caught her breath and began to kiss Vicky's palm, then drew her closer. They both leaned against the tree, Annie marvelling that such a beautiful woman should find her desirable. The smile their closeness brought to Vicky's face, a smile as clear as the water from a spring, as surprised as a child getting a present, as pleased as a woman who's found love, bowled Annie over each time she saw it. That she could make such a woman happy amazed her each time she thought of it.

"Breakfast was just about done when I came to look for you."

"Good. This country air makes me hungry."

"Turkey's really good at cooking on that old fireplace."

"Turkey's good at cooking anywhere."

"Maybe we should all open up a restaurant up here. And a lodge. Just for women."

Annie stopped at the steps to the cabin. "Now there you have it. I've been trying to think of a way to stay up here too.

To buy a little house no one could take from me."

"Have you? Wouldn't it be wonderful?" Victoria beamed. Then she frowned. "But how would we ever . . . ?"

"Oh, it's just fun to imagine. To dream of making a place for us somewhere beautiful, among other women. Safe."

"Anne, we will. I know it's something we can do." Annie watched Victoria draw herself up full of the determination she must have inherited from her pioneer ancestors. "Let's just keep thinking about it until we come up with a way."

Annie laughed, " 'There's a place for us, somewhere a place for us . . .,' " she sang weakly, smiling. "Shall I sing *Maria* too?"

"No, silly duckling, but maybe we can form a gang and call ourselves the Jets—and spell it J-e-t-t-e-s!"

"Duckling!" Annie fussed. "Where did that come from?"

Victoria ran her hand through Annie's hair. "From all this downy stuff on top of your head! Say you'll be my duckling, please!"

"Only if you promise never to say it in public," Annie muttered as they entered the dark cabin. "It's colder in here than outside!"

"Then open the windows and get your ass over here to eat before it gets cold."

"What, Turkey? It's not gone already?"

"Never mind the Turk. *I* was ready to eat it all myself," Peg called. "How are you doing this morning, Vicky? You look like Turkey's snoring didn't keep you awake."

"I didn't even notice it."

"Impossible, girl. Stop being so polite," Turkey said. "Here's your flapjacks."

"*I* heard you, Turkey, and if you weren't such a good cook, we'd have to expel you from the business," Annie threatened as she took a seat.

"What business? Now what are you dreaming about?"

"Fame, fortune, beautiful women," Annie toasted to Victoria with her coffee mug full of tea. "Let's all open a gay ski lodge and restaurant up here."

"Sure."

"I mean it. You can be the recreation director, Peg."

"And Turkey the cook?"

"Yes, and Vicky the manager and I'll drive people to and from the train station."

"What train station?" Turkey laughed.

"We'll persuade them to stop wherever we open up."

Peg cleared her dishes from the table and picked up Turkey's. "And where are we going to find all these rich lesbians who can afford to ski weekends?"

"It won't really be a ski lodge," Victoria joined in to develop the fantasy further. "It'll be a place where women can go with other women for whatever."

"Like a winter women's center?" Turkey laughed again.

"Exactly," said Annie. "Don't do those dishes. Vicky and me will take our turns too."

"And interrupt the honeymoon?"

"Cut it out, Turkey. We could have facilities for meetings and conferences."

"A bar," Peg added.

"A gourmet restaurant," Turkey expanded.

"A showcase for women artists and a stage for performers," said Victoria.

"Courses to keep them during the week," Annie suggested.

"Films," Victoria nodded, "and a women's book and art store."

"An exercise room," Peg clapped, excitedly.

"A honeymoon suite," Turkey laughed, nudging Annie who grabbed the sugar from the table and turned it almost upside down over Turkey's head until Peg took it from her.

"We'll never get this thing together if you two don't stop fooling around," she admonished them.

"Why don't we find the town," Annie proposed, "and check it out for sites."

Turkey leaned back in her chair. "We'll have to make up a flag so we can plant it and claim it in the name of...."

"The New Haven Jettes," Victoria finished, looking at Annie who began to sing, " 'When you're a Jette, you're a Jette all the way ...' "

Peg took up the words in a more tuneful voice. " 'From your first cigarette ...' "

" 'To your last dying day!' " Turkey hollered unmusically. "And we'll call it the Jette Inn! Classy, huh?"

"Maybe too classy," Peg criticized. "For us. What do you think, Vicky?"

Victoria handed the dishes to Annie as she scraped them. "I don't think it's overly classy, but perhaps unrealistic."

"Hitch Inn is more our speed," Annie agreed.

Turkey began to laugh. "With everything that would go wrong if we had a project, that would be a perfect name."

"Let's not jinx ourselves, ladies," Peg laughed too, sweeping pine needles out the front door.

Victoria blushed. "How about, Let's Be Inn?"

It took a moment for everyone to understand the pun. They all stopped working to consider the name.

"Wow," Turkey breathed. "That's it! The name is too good to pass up. Let's go look for it!"

Hiding behind her hair again, Victoria looked pleased. Annie sought out her eyes as Turkey and Peg went to the car. "I told you they like you."

"I was only kidding about that name."

"You didn't want to say it at all, did you?"

"I'm not used to the word yet."

"You will be. Lesbian. You'll hear it as a curse, as a compliment, as pornography, scholastically, and said with love. It's a beautiful word," Annie assured her, cupping Victoria's jaw with her hand, tenderly.

"Kind of erotic."

"Oh, yes. Definitely erotic."

"They're waiting for us."

Annie laughed. "The lesbians?"

Victoria blushed again. "Yes," she stuttered, "the Let's Be Inns."

They descended on the town like four warriors of Boudica seeking food for their hungry people. They rejected the tiny shopping centers on the outskirts for the old brick and stone buildings of the town. High on big plans they invaded all the public buildings, creating excitement in the library, the hardware store and the restaurant. While the others had coffee the straightest looking of them, Victoria, went into the realtor's office to check on commercial properties. By this time, she, too, was disheveled from spending a night almost outdoors and without her accustomed toiletries. Back she came to them, Annie gasping at her new wild beauty, hair streaming behind her in the breeze, jacket over her shoulder under the noon sun, shoes and jeans muddied from wood-gathering.

"Nothing," she said, out of breath and dropping beside Annie in the booth. While a country singer sang tinnily in the jukebox she explained, "I think he must have heard we were coming. Surely there's something in all these acres. But he showed me what he said were all his listings and there were no buildings we could convert and there wasn't a bit of land correctly zoned that was appropriate for building." The waitress brought her a cup of tea and she paused to fix the tea bag. "He suggested we try up in the next county because they're looking for tourist business."

"Did you tell him we were thinking of something private, like a club, membership only deal?" Annie asked.

"Yes. He said he didn't know anything about the Vermont laws on things like that. He also asked where we were getting our capital."

"Did you tell him?"

"I didn't know what to tell him. I figured we'd need loans. I could get a loan on my savings."

"Savings?" Turkey snorted derisively.

"I'm afraid mine wouldn't guarantee a car loan, never mind a property deal," Peg said, resting her chin on her hands.

"What about your family?" Annie ventured softly.

Victoria looked sharply at her. "What about them?"

"Would they help you start a business?"

"Is *that* what you're all hoping?" Victoria asked in an aggrieved tone, looking at all of them. "Suddenly the whole project rests on my financial worth?"

"Well, no," Annie defended herself quickly. "It was just a thought." Turkey and Peg grunted their embarrassed agreement with Annie.

Victoria looked at each of them as if she were about to cry. "I can't get *them* involved in this. They don't even know about you, Anne. Besides, I don't want any help from them."

There was a silence. Then disappointment like a fog settled over them. Victoria noticed that the booth was patched and the men at the counter kept staring their way, especially at her. She jumped when Annie reached to touch her arm. Turkey fell over Peg trying to leave quietly for the bathroom.

"It's not that anybody was expecting you to ask your family, Vic," Peg explained tentatively. "Nobody even mentioned you. I guess we all had the feeling that there was someone among us who knew *how* to get money."

Victoria stared at the cooling tea she was stirring. "I just feel—used."

"Oh, no, you shouldn't, Vicky," Annie protested.

"But I do. It's not your fault. I think it was my expectations. That you saw me as just one of you. I was just letting my guard down, believing that. But I should know better."

"But, Vicky, you've got to understand. We weren't trying to use you or anything. You have to admit that you are different from us," Peg confronted her sympathetically.

"Unfortunately, yes."

"Vicky," the sun was in Peg's eyes, making her face look even more strained that it was, "there's nothing wrong with your difference. We're all different from each other in other ways. It's just that you come on so together and so knowledgeable about the real world. I don't know, I guess I just assumed you'd be able to help get something like this off the ground."

Tears crawled down Victoria's face, doubly embarrassing her. "I'm so sorry I'm carrying on like this. I know you meant no harm. Can we leave?" she asked, turning to Annie.

"Sure, my love," Annie soothed her. "Of course. Here, you go outside and I'll pay."

Victoria stood facing the sun, trying to absorb some of its energy to make herself stronger. How could they, she thought, humiliated and furious. And Anne. Oh, Anne, to treat me like this, like—like what I am, she considered. Her mind was silent as Annie joined her, trying to grasp what was happening. They walked to a bridge and down the embankment next to it. Peg had waited behind for Turkey.

"I love you, Vicky."

Victoria looked out from under her drying tears at Annie's

earnest, pleading face. "I suppose I want to be sure that you do love me and not just my parents' child. Or my grandparents' child, since they're the ones with the money. I don't mean to sound as though I'm fighting off gold diggers. I've never even thought of that, but I hope you don't love me for being things that you're not. Do you know what I mean?"

"I'm not sure. I have to love you at least a little because you're unlike me." Annie was disturbed at this first difference between them. Could it be the beginning of the end? She knew their love was too good to be true.

"Yes, but not because of exterior things like a rich education or what Turkey calls 'classy' clothes."

"God, no. But you do have a fine mind under all that education," Annie tried to smile. She saw that Victoria's lips were trembling toward a smile and she went on despite her own misgivings. "And that beautiful long-legged body didn't get that way on rice and beans." Victoria did smile. "And the incredible teeth," she touched a knuckle to them, "behind your smile did not come from staving off hunger in Ireland with soft potatoes."

"And I have learned so well to be high-strung and sensitive about all sorts of things that are going to make you miserable until you can't stand me anymore."

"Not if I understand them. Shit, there must be stuff your parents taught you to hate about people lower than you on the ladder. And I must personify half of them." Annie wondered if she was trying to reassure herself as well.

"Only the half I grew to love in rebellion."

"Oh, so I'm an act of rebellion against your family now, am I?" Annie teased, tired of trying so hard to patch it up and wanting to just enjoy Victoria. She pulled Victoria's hands to herself, feeling depression sweep over her, even as she comforted Victoria.

"No, no," Victoria laughed. "Let me go, that's Main Street up there! And you're not my rebellion. I'm trying to be real with real people. Actually exposing myself to people who can hurt me like I was hurt just now and learning to survive it."

"Well, then, I'm honored to be part of it, even if I will hurt you sometimes. Because I know I try to give you much more pleasure than pain," Annie assured Victoria while fighting the despair that rose in herself. Could she deal with it? Was it worth it? She wasn't sure.

"And you do give me more pleasure, duckling."

"Here we go again with duckling," Annie teased, still holding out against a nearly overpowering desire to run as far and as fast as she could from their conflict. "Why not just call me ugly duckling and get it over with?"

"Because you're not, you're not. You're lovely. Especially with the sun and the ripples from the water reflected on your face."

Annie smiled, but dropped her eyes. "Do you think we can work it out?"

"I don't want to be alive if we don't. I used to be able to survive alone, but I'm not so sure I'd want to anymore. And I have a very strong desire for survival."

Me too, and I'm not sure I can survive a relationship, Annie thought as she watched the water rush by, running from its winter heights. She felt the chill it brought with it and watched it darken as a cloud passed across the sun.

$$\sim \ \sim \ \sim \ \sim \ \sim$$

Peg and Annie Heaphy were gathering more wood that afternoon.

"I'm going to start laying the fire for tonight," Peg said, kneeling by the circle of rocks they had made for a campfire. "It'll be too dark when we get back from the movies."

"What else do we need?"

"Some kindling."

"Like this?" Annie showed her three long branches she'd been dragging behind her.

"Beautiful. Want my knife?"

"No. I brought my old Girl Scout knife."

"You were a Girl Scout too?"

"Wasn't every dyke?"

Peg laughed. "Probably. It was the first place I ever loved a woman."

"It was?"

"I don't mean I came out in the Girl Scouts. But I sure

loved my camp counselor. I was nine."

"A little early."

"You ain't kidding. But I almost came out when I was a counselor in training. You had to have a buddy. You know, for mountain climbing, swimming, going to the john at night. My buddy and me fell in love. We must have been sixteen. I wish we'd known what was going on. Karen. She'll never know how much I loved her. You know we slept in one another's arms?"

"That must have been tough," Annie panted, finally cutting through the thickest stick. "I'm not sure this one is dry enough."

"Can you snap it?"

"No."

"There's plenty of dry stuff. Chuck that one. Actually, I didn't sleep. Not for hours. We both stayed awake a long time talking. Then we just lay there. I think Karen pretended to fall asleep just so we could stay close. I forget how we got that way." She paused and laid another stick on the foundation she was building. "I remember. We heard something outside the tent in the bushes and were scared. It was one of the last nights at camp. One of us must have been brave enough to grab onto the other. I remember feeling lightheaded with the pleasure of holding her. She was so warm, so soft. She wore her hair long and it smelled of campfire. I remember thinking something like, 'If I were a man I'd probably marry Karen.' What a dummy."

"You're probably lucky."

"Why?"

"That you couldn't marry her. I'm not so sure it's worth getting involved."

"Because of what happened with Vicky this morning?"

"Partly. And because I'm not sure I'm cut out for it." Annie stopped breaking sticks and sat on a log with her head down. "What's the sense if we can't get along already?"

Peg shook her head wearily and thought for a moment. "Remember I told you I started going to a consciousness raising group?" she asked.

"Yeah, why? You're not getting me to one of those," Annie looked up defiantly.

"I'm not trying to. I just want to tell you something somebody said. We were talking about friendship and making the
relationships in the CR group meaningful over a long period of
time and an older woman said, 'That'll take a lot of hard work.'
I asked how you work hard at friendship. We argued back and
forth for awhile, me saying friendships should come naturally
and if you had to work at them maybe they weren't real and
her saying, no, no, no you've got to work for any good things
you get and that women especially had to work real hard at
relationships because we're trained to romanticize things. Like
we're brought up to think that our prince will come and we'll
fall in love and everything will be hunky-dory after that. We're
brought up to think that if we're physically alluring and socially
graceful enough we're going to love and be loved and never even
have to try to make our relationships work. We're brought up
to think that women are catty and bitchy and unreliable and
not worth much so if a friendship gets rocky we should just
dump it because it's not worth working on. We don't have to
work hard at anything except maybe keeping the house or
cooking well.

"She blew my mind, Heaphy. Look what so many lesbians
do. We start a love affair and as soon as a difference comes up
or a problem gets out of hand we want to run, or we 'fall out of
love,' or we develop a passionate attraction for someone else
and are sure it'd be much better if we were with her. Well, we
don't have to. We can stand firm and face it, deal with it,
resolve it. We're worth the effort and our relationships are
worth the effort. My next relationship I'm going to be willing to
lay my life down for. Only after I fight practically to the death
to make it work will I let myself consider whether it's worth it.
I feel like I've got to do that to make sure I don't throw away
something very valuable out of habit. Or culture. And I'll bet
just the process of working hard together to build or keep a relationship makes it even firmer and more valuable to the women
in it." She smiled and walked over to Annie. "Listen, Heaphy, I
feel so strongly about what I'm saying that I feel it not just for
you and Vicky, but for me and Vicky. That's why I didn't leave
with Turkey when things got rough back at the restaurant. I
want you two to make it and because I'm your friend I feel

committed enough to my relationship with Vicky that I want to work it out between her and me, too."

Annie looked up at Peg sullenly. "Maybe you were right. Maybe that libber was wrong. Just because she said it in a 'consciousness raising group,' " Annie sneered, "that makes it right?"

"No, Heaphy. I wasn't sure it was right. And I fought just as hard as you're fighting. But it kept coming back to my mind and ever since this morning, with Vicky, it's all fallen into place. And I feel like I have to tell you because I care about you and Vicky."

Annie stood and walked jerkily around the campfire circle. She yanked her cap off and slammed her fist into it. "Goddammit, Peg, it's not worth it. It's even got you and me fighting." She wheeled to face Peg, her face pleading. "We never fought before."

"I don't mind fighting if it accomplishes something."

"Well, I do," Annie said as she stalked away. She walked down the driveway and around the first curve before she sat down. Calmer, she tried to think through the mess things had become since that morning. What were they all fighting about? She could hardly remember, but certainly it wasn't worth all this aggravation. Obviously she would have to give Victoria up. She'd shot too high. Victoria was out of her league. Too smart, too educated, too upper class, money or not. Why did she ever think she could handle her? Annie's father was a truck driver. Her parents were comfortable, but they owned nothing beyond their four year old car. They couldn't even pay for Annie to go to a local school. She had to get a scholarship and a loan. They went away for a week every year to a cottage in Plymouth which they rented with an aunt and uncle. Their culture was TV and the movies. That was Annie, for all her high-minded reading. Victoria travelled and went to operas and plays and knew how to dress and went to Yale and was brilliant. Annie laughed at herself for thinking that they could ever spend their lives together without conflict. Peg was one of her own. And Turkey. She wasn't losing them for any woman. After you're through with a woman, you got to have good friends to turn to, she thought. Now she just had to decide whether to tell Victoria it was over today or be kind and wait until they got back. She would wake her from her nap and ask her to go for a walk. Maybe she would tell her right away, kind or not. She would see how it went.

She felt afraid and wondered if she was running away. No, damn it, she thought. I'm not running away from anything. I'm going to face her and explain why it can't work. What a shame I love her so much, she thought sadly and felt tears coming. No romantic bullshit, she admonished herself, thinking that Peg had been right to put that down. But not about the other things. How were you supposed to keep a relationship going by fighting about it? Some things you can't change. Or could you? Annie felt confused and didn't like it. She pushed Peg's words away as she resolutely went toward the cabin for her walk with Victoria. She'd trust to her feelings and do what was right. Still, she thought, considering how beautiful and tender Victoria was, if there was a way, maybe it would be worth a try.

"What have you been doing with yourself, duckling?" Victoria asked as they started into the woods.

"Wait," Annie said abruptly, running back to the car and pulling a blanket out of the trunk. "Just in case," she said forgetting for a moment the bad tidings she carried, deciding they needed the blanket because they had to sit when they talked. As she stood before Victoria, out of breath, she relished the woman's wild-looking hair, her brown eyes darkened with intensity and pleasure and the feathers which still clung to her jeans. She plucked one off. "Have a good rest?"

"Yes," Victoria said. "And I love featherbeds. Didn't you just sleep like a child last night?"

"Ummm," Annie replied. "But I didn't think it was feathers that made me sleep good. I thought it had more to do with driving five hours, staying up late and making love pretty energetically."

Victoria laughed. "I know, we never did make it back to the fireplace, did we?"

"I was warm enough. How about you?"

"You know I was." Victoria turned back toward the cabin and, seeing that they were out of its sight, turned to embrace

Annie. Hesitating, Annie allowed herself to be held, rationalizing that it was one of the last times. But Victoria had felt her pull herself away. "What's wrong?" she asked.

"Nothing," Annie tried to say smoothly. "Why?"

"You felt—different."

"I don't think so," Annie lied, wishing she could tell her right then.

They walked on for awhile, quieter. Nothing could dampen their happiness with each other. Victoria kept spotting different types of wildflowers, picking them and running to give them to Annie. Annie took them indulgently, unused to receiving bouquets. "You know you're messing with my image, girl," she told Victoria.

"How?" Victoria asked innocently.

Annie laughed and stopped in the path. "You look like such a little girl! Your hair's a mess, you're all smudged and stained from digging up flowers, your glasses are halfway down your nose—it's great! As for my image, the hell with it. So dykey women aren't supposed to walk around with their arms filled with flowers. You gave them to me and that's all that counts." A look of pain passed over her face.

"There is something wrong," Victoria accused. "Please tell me what it is. Was it because I got upset this morning? I'm sorry. I was suspicious when there was nothing to be suspicious about. I'm just so unused to having friends I don't always know how. Please believe me, Anne. I was afraid you were liking me for being someone I'm not, looking to get out of me what I don't have. I'm not used to being liked for being me. I haven't learned to trust yet. Please give me time."

Annie reached for her hand and they walked again. "You don't know how I wish there were no differences between us and we could just be happy together all the time," she told Victoria, then fell silent. They walked hand in hand awhile longer, soon dropping their confusions again and playing. Victoria picked more flowers and Annie laid hers down to weave a dandelion chain for Victoria's hair. "Wish we had some wine," she said at one point.

"Let's find a stream instead," Victoria suggested. Then their walk became punctuated with brief, quiet stops where they both listened intently for the sound of water. Once they thought they heard it and cut a path of their own through the trees, only to find that they were above the highway. The sound they had heard was traffic, faint and far below.

"Look," Victoria said, pointing up. "A beautiful meadow. Let's go up there!"

"How?" Annie asked, looking around for a path to climb.

"Let's just do it. We'll find a way. I have to feel what it's like to lie on the grass."

Annie smiled indulgently. "Okay, lady." She promised in a low voice, "If that's what you want, we'll do it. Ain't nothing can stop us."

"And when we get there," Victoria suggested, "we'll talk about what's bothering you." She watched Annie frown. "Because we have to, Anne."

Annie nodded a resigned yes, thinking that she would have to tell Victoria today if she was really going to break up with her. She was not sure that she could, but she still felt that she had to. She watched Victoria thread her way through trees and brambles before her, holding branches back so they would not scratch Annie, crawling on her knees through the more tangled places, and making sure Annie found the same firm footholds she found for herself. Annie hurt at the thought of giving up someone who not only wanted to dance and make love and have a good time, but who wanted to take care of her. Annie did not remember ever loving a woman who expressed her love like this. How could she let her go? But it would be better to do it now, before she got used to it, because she would never find another Victoria among her crowd. It just wasn't part of their lifestyle, to take care of each other. Annie saw herself in ten years driving a red convertible with a long-haired blonde in the passenger seat. Walking together into a bar in another city somewhere, sharing a fashionable apartment and having a demanding, important job. Good-looking and smooth and respected: that's how she saw herself, how she had always seen her future self since she came out. She did not want to be a bar dyke forever, or one of Natalie's crowd who could pass for straight. What she wanted was to be somewhere in between, with enough sophistication to impress and room for the things she loved, like walking in the woods and making love in the sun.

Victoria, meanwhile, sensed the conflict in Annie and, for the moment, put her own aside. She knew that she had something special in Annie and that it was not just that she was a woman. Yes, she thought, I'll have to deal with being a lesbian, but I think now I can handle that. Annie had a spirit in her that Victoria wanted to learn and she felt herself become like a mother animal, fierce and possessive of this new thing that had attached itself to her body and soul. Nothing would take her Anne away from her. No preying birds, no hungry animals, and no wandering spirit in Anne herself. Somehow she would make Anne understand that she wanted her above all else and would change in any way that she could to keep her. Was changing already. Annie had said that she looked like a little girl! Just the opposite of how she had wanted to look and feel. So here she was, like a little girl reckless of all risks, tearing through brambles, leaping across gullies, filthy and determined and feeling very good.

"Wait!" Annie called out behind her. "Do you hear it?"

Victoria stopped to listen. Cupping her ears she realized she had been stepping onto softer and softer ground and had led Annie to an overgrown path which opened to a small, clear mountain stream. They smiled broadly at each other, successful explorers, and fell to their knees to scoop handfuls of water to their dry mouths. Annie sat watching Victoria drink. Her hair dragged into the water as she leaned forward and she tossed it back each time she came up before letting the icy cold mountain water run into her throat. The sight of Victoria's throat and chin against the blue sky caught Annie's chest in a vise. She swallowed air as Victoria was swallowing water and found herself gasping.

"What is it?" Victoria asked in alarm, letting a handful of water fall to the swift, shining stream.

"Nothing," Annie answered, shaking her blonde head, her cap already fallen beside the stream. "Nothing is wrong, Vicky. I want to talk. I want to get all this worked out." She was silent a moment, still staring at the wonder that Victoria was to her. "My queen," she said slowly, "you are just too wonderful to lose." Victoria looked solemnly at Annie, feeling that something momentous had just passed. She felt its power beyond her reach, as moved by its strength as Annie seemed immobilized by it. "You are my queen, you know," Annie declared, looking at Victoria.

Victoria felt uncomfortable at being given so much power and sought to equalize it. "How can I be your queen," she asked, "when you're a queen to me?"

"I thought I was your duckling," Annie smiled as they moved toward each other.

"Um," Victoria nuzzled Annie's hair, now warm from the sun, "Queen Anne you are, and I shall be your loyal vassal as long as you require it of me."

"Uh-uh," Annie said, shaking her head. "I'm never going to command nothing from you, my lady. Except love and companionship."

"Then let's pledge," Victoria said ceremoniously, "to command from each other what we need and what we can give or learn to give, Anne."

"Sounds fair," Annie answered. "I command that we get to your meadow and take off all our clothes and roll around on the grass."

"Your command is my wish," Victoria laughed, jumping up, her jeans damp with dark mud. "I'm a mess."

"You're beautiful," Annie called as she ran ahead of Victoria, forgetting the blanket, through the last several yards of clearing woods and onto the field. They met in the middle of the wide, sloping grass and did their dance of joy, their whirling, hand-holding swing, at the apex of the meadow. Dizzy, they fell to the grass and Victoria began to unbutton her flannel shirt. "Not yet," Annie stopped her. "I have to say what's bothering me."

Victoria sat up and pulled her tangled hair back, a serious expression replacing the sensuality of her face. "Vicky," Annie started, "I was feeling like we couldn't be together any more. Like you're too, you know, classy for me. Like I'm just a dumb gutter-dyke and you're this beautiful, gracious woman I can't measure up to. You know?"

"Anne," Victoria answered, shaking her head now. "*You*

are beautiful to *me*. And gracious in a way I'm afraid I'll never master. Gracious and intelligent in ways of life that have eluded me all these years. You give me your spirit and I can—oh, I don't know how to say it to you—I can drink deeply of the stream. You don't know how much that stream meant to me. It was a symbol of all you are to me and all I'm learning with you. Just to dip myself in and drink, drink, drink. Oh," she said, covering her mouth in fear, "to think you were going to stop it, thought you had!"

"Vicky, Vicky, you've got to listen to me. You don't understand. I'm not going away. I was afraid. I'm still afraid." Annie put her arms around Victoria. "Vicky, I didn't think I could handle you. You're so different from me. You were brought up different and I don't know your ways just like you don't know mine. And I was thinking that we're really tying ourselves up in knots together trying to learn not just to love each other, but whole new ways of talking and acting that neither of us have acted like before. It just seemed too hard. Too much to ask of you and beyond me altogether. But I'd rather try. I don't know how to even start, but I can't give you up. You're too special, too much what I want. And I want to learn the new ways, I think. I want us both to learn new ways we can be together. Do you understand?"

Victoria was wiping her tears. "Of course I understand. It's what I've been fighting all my life—the way I am, the way I was brought up. I don't like it, I want to get rid of it. That's something I'm counting on you to help me with."

"But I love you the way you are, Vicky. I don't want you to change."

"I think there are some ways you and I are going to have to change, Anne. In order to be together. And as long as we don't change our —" she groped for words, "our essences, there's no reason that we will change beyond each other's reach."

"Do you really think we can do it?" Annie asked.

"We have to do it, Anne. I'm not rich and there's no reason for me to go on acting like I'm in the upper class. I hate it and it keeps me from being real."

"And I'm not a real bar dyke, I know it. I want too much more out of life."

"So let's learn who we are together. Maybe it'll have something to do with feminism. Maybe I'll never quite get over being a snob and you'll never take off your hat. And maybe we'll step on each other's toes a lot and it'll hurt." She lay three clovers across Annie's hair. "I crown you Queen Duckling," Victoria said smiling tenderly, a deeply solemn look settling in her eyes. "And I pledge myself to you, our life together and our work, whatever it may become."

Annie returned her solemnity, shyly. "Here under the sky, where everything that matters is my witness," she said, pulling Victoria up as she stood, "I also pledge myself to you, in our life and our work." She felt her breath grow shorter with the fear of what she was saying, knowing she would not retract this promise, afraid she was wrong to make it, but unable to stop it, it came from so deep inside herself, back where she couldn't interfere with it. "If I could pull my heart from my body and hand it to you, Vicky," she said half-whispering, "I would do that right now."

They moved along the mountainside feeling the strong tie of their freshly spoken bond and the sensuality it inspired. First they took their shoes off and walked on the spongy grasses. Then they removed their jackets and shirts and left them lying behind with their shoes as they moved together, marvelling at each other's breasts and shoulders in the sunlight. They stopped, touched breasts, looked into one another's eyes, then reached as one for each other's belts and soon were naked, utterly naked in the mountain air.

Annie swallowed hard to see Victoria's beauty so plainly. She moved them to the ground softly.

"It's almost too much," Victoria said. "I'm not sure I can make love." She felt blinded by Annie's brightness, the desire knocked out of her by the enormity of her emotion. So they just touched, ran their hands along the smoothness of each other's bodies for awhile.

Victoria took her glasses off and laid them down. Then they turned away from one another's faces and, laying mouth to vulva, spent another very, very long time lying under the sun touching each other alternately with their mouths and with the sun and air until quietly they came, Victoria starting with a groan and Annie allowing herself to follow so that some of the time they felt what they felt together. They lay still afterward, just like that, breathing each other.

When they were ready, Victoria moved with a long sigh upright alongside Annie. They talked, lips touching, into one another's mouths. "Did you hear the band?" Annie asked.

"You heard it too?" Victoria asked, incredulous.

"Yes," Annie answered, gently surprised, still glowing. "The sound drifted up the mountainside. We must be above a playing field of some sort."

"I thought it was inside my head," Victoria laughed softly.

"You must have been really into making love."

"I was, my duckling."

"Well, you're pretty good for a beginner," Annie laughed.

Victoria sat up and pushed playfully at Annie's still-bare shoulder. "Huh," she said indignantly. "I have a lot of imagination to make up for my inexperience."

"I noticed." They hugged and felt a tension in each other's bodies. "We'd better not," Annie said. "I'm getting nervous about pressing our luck out in the open like this."

"I agree," Victoria answered, bending to kiss Annie's breast as they struggled into their jeans. "Do you remember the way back?"

"No, do you?"

"I scattered bread crumbs," Victoria laughed.

"We're not that far from the stream. Once we find our shirts, my cap and the blanket we just have to guess which way to walk."

"My guess is we should head down," Victoria teased as Annie pulled her up. They kissed again, hungrily, for a long time, pulling back and looking at one another as if to memorize the meaning of their day before turning away from the sun to walk back into the woods.

CHAPTER EIGHT

Annie Heaphy laughed at herself. She was walking down the steps of the Women's Center as if she were entering prison to serve a life sentence. Pulled and prodded there by Peg, she was sulky and hostile. And she was damned if she was going to make it easy for them to convert her. She was as much of a feminist as she wanted to be and probably more of one than they were. You had to be pretty liberated to be queer. She had been thinking more about herself politically, especially in talks with Victoria. Entering the lion's den unnerved her. She followed Peg closely and stood behind her at the door fingering the brim of her cap, peering into the large room from behind her hand. There were a lot of women in the room; they milled about, waiting to hear the poet who would be reading that night.

"What's happening to me," Annie asked herself, "coming to a faggy poetry reading?" Peg had insisted this would not be a "faggy" reading at all. The poet was "a real dyke from California." Annie was still suspicious, but in the face of Peg's determination to save her, Turkey and Eleanor from their apolitical lives, she gave in. Besides, she had found Victoria and now she wanted to be worthy of her. To do that she knew she must break out of or at least widen the circles of her life. She had tried to persuade Victoria to come to the reading too, but Victoria had been adamant about studying that night. She wanted to keep her grades high. Annie realized Victoria had a need for the credentials that came with high grades in order to feel worthwhile.

Rosemary and Claudia were not as concerned about their grades. Annie spotted them through her fingers as she adjusted her cap. Peg paid her own and Annie's way into the Center as Annie tried to hide behind her taller back. When Peg stopped to talk with someone she knew, Annie tried pulling her cap down to her nose and getting further behind Peg, but Rosemary was bearing down on her.

"What a gratifying surprise!" Rosemary called, still halfway across the room. Annie smiled awkwardly and glanced around to see if anyone had noticed. Victoria said Rosemary had some redeeming qualities, but Annie had avoided spending any time with her thus far. Rosemary hugged her and Annie squirmed uncomfortably, making a face at Peg who turned to watch with an amused expression. "I've heard so much about you," Rosemary said, still holding Annie by the shoulders. Annie looked at the sari Rosemary affected and the dull hair coiled tightly in back of her head and wondered what made this woman tick. As Claudia joined them, Annie tried to imagine what the plump-cheeked, cheerful Claudia found physically attractive about this ornery feminist.

"Hiya, Claudia," Annie said, attempting to join in the social graces. She stuck out a hand and shook both of theirs. That's how a dyke says hello, she thought to herself. They ought to learn. "This is my friend Peg."

"The teacher Victoria went to Vermont with?" Claudia asked.

"The same," Peg laughed. "Though I wouldn't think that's how she thinks of me. I have enough problems remembering that's what I am."

"She's told us quite a bit about you, too, Peg," Rosemary added.

Peg answered, "And Vicky has mentioned both of you often."

Rosemary seemed to want to keep the conversation going. "Have you ever heard Judy Grahn before?"

"Never even heard of her till Peg button-holed me into coming tonight," Annie answered.

"You'll like her," Claudia assured her. "She's very real. Not at all intellectual."

Annie wondered how Victoria had described her to her friends. "I don't mind intellectuals," she answered defensively. "I mean, I read poetry and all that."

Claudia still smiled. "I do too, sometimes, though I'm a psych major. But I can't stand these fuddy-duddies who think poetry is pretty words. I like it to *mean* and from what I've read, Judy Grahn means *a lot*."

Comfortable listening to Claudia, Annie almost relaxed. "I think all poets try to mean, but some of them just don't know how to do it, you know? Like they're afraid to get any emotion in there. I'm still not sure that someone like Shelley, even though he's a romantic, really ever feels anything but light-headed. Sometimes I wonder if men poets didn't just hear about emotions from women and want to feel them so bad they spend all their time trying to describe them so they can learn how to have them. I mean, what about all of us back here on earth who've got to drive cabs and can't go floating around mountain-tops?"

"That's just what I mean," Claudia responded excitedly. "Rosemary's never understood what I'm trying to say. Does *that* make sense to you?" She took Rosemary's arm and pressed herself to her side, looking up at her questioningly.

Rosemary squeezed Claudia's arm back and answered, "I think so. You want the raw stuff of life, you two. You don't want puns and philosophy."

"But don't those have a place in poetry too?" Peg asked, joining the discussion.

"Just what I was about to say," Rosemary answered. "I think you need all of it to really speak poetically. Would Judy Grahn have found her poetic voice if she had not read other poets? Could she pack her poetry so full of meaning if she didn't know how to use words every possible way? I can say I love you," she said looking at Claudia, "and I can say I love you many different ways, but that doesn't have the emotional impact of: 'How do I love thee? Let me count the ways . . . ,'" she quoted persuasively.

"By a woman, of course," Annie muttered almost inaudibly.

"Well, anyway," Claudia smiled, not hearing her, "however she does it, Judy Grahn is good."

"Thanks for the reassurance." Annie took off her jacket. "Maybe I'll stay awhile and try her out." She winked at Peg.

"You'd better," Peg punched Annie playfully in the arm. "I didn't fight to get you this far just to lose you. She's afraid she'll be converted," she stage-whispered to Rosemary and Claudia.

"I love it!" Rosemary laughed, a real, deep-throated laugh. "That's just what these women's center people are afraid you and Judy and Peg and now Claudia and I will do: convert them!"

They all laughed together and Annie found herself wondering if Rosemary didn't have some kind of stiff charm that might include a lot of posturing, but was really a desperate attempt to express herself. She must be as shy as I am, Annie thought, amazed, and wanted suddenly to assure her that she could relax with herself and Peg. She smiled up at her and got back a brief shadow of a grin.

"Look!" Claudia whispered. "It's her! I recognize her from her picture!" A thin dyke walked in the door. In her thirties, she looked scarred by time, her face near-exhausted with intensity. To Annie she looked just the way she pictured herself in ten years: marked by the difficulties of gay life.

"She looks so much older than I imagined," Rosemary commented in a shocked voice. The women who escorted her in hovered around her, setting up the room as the poet wanted it, offering her endless refreshments and comforts until Annie felt embarrassed for them and wanted to rescue the trapped poet from their fawning attentions.

"But she's beautiful," Claudia said in an admiring whisper. "She looks like she's felt *everything*."

"Makes me feel like a little kid," Annie commented, no longer absorbed by her social relations with Victoria's friends.

"This calls for a beer. How about it Heaphy?"

"They have beer, Peglet?" Annie's face lit up.

"Rosemary?"

"I don't drink," Rosemary reminded them.

"Oh, yeah," Peg nodded. "Claudia?"

"I'd love one. If it's nice and cold. I can't stand it when beer gets warm. Smells skunky."

"You're right," Annie agreed. "I wondered what it was I didn't like. I'm always so glad to get it I never thought that much about it."

Rosemary took both their arms. "We ought to find seats,"

she said, guiding them to a couch. "Before everybody else thinks of it."

Annie watched for Peg, afraid she would not find them, then realized she was really afraid of being left alone with these two harmless women. Vicky's friends. She grinned.

"What are you smiling at?" Claudia asked.

"You're Vicky's friends," Annie said, watching Claudia's face grow puzzled. "And I like you." Annie's face reddened.

"Here you go, ladies," Peg said as she handed them beer and squeezed in between Annie and Claudia. "Just what I love to do on a spring night: go to a ballgame and pop open a beer." She laughed. "Doesn't this feel strange to you?" she asked Annie. "Drinking a can of beer at a poetry reading?"

"Beer is a male custom—to go with sports. We'll give it a new use," Rosemary answered her, across Claudia. Her voice sounded angry. "They've had too many customs too long. I *will* join you."

"Liberate the beer!" Peg laughed, quickly bringing back another can and watching as Rosemary struggled with the pop top, then tasted the beer. They all laughed at the faces Rosemary made as she drank her first sips.

Annie felt very satisfied with herself, sitting among feminists, ready to hear someone new say something new. She also felt comforted by the beer, a bit of security from her old world. As the poet directed all the lights to be turned off except the one next to her, Annie steadied herself against the fear the darkness brought on, the darkness and the unfamiliar women. Peg was beside her, her good friend Peg. Vicky was near and probably thinking of her. Turkey and Eleanor were at the bar and would be there when Annie arrived. Then the poet spoke into Annie's complacency with raw and violent words about pain and the realities of different women. A lot of the pain was her own. She had never heard another woman speak of it, had never even thought of it in words, had just lived through it. She took her hat off because she was sweating. Someone pushed open the back door that led into an alleyway and she longed to go through it to stand under the lone streetlight she saw outside. She took off her jacket and glanced toward Peg who looked back through the dim light, solemn-faced and obviously as moved as Annie.

The poet read, "Each having tried/ in her own way to over-throw/ the rule of men over women . . ." and Annie Heaphy realized why Judy Grahn was reading in the women's center. Then she read, "She has taken a woman lover/ whatever shall we do . . ." and Annie wished Vicky were there to hear her own experience. She read, "She goes as far/ as woman can go . . ." and Annie felt great excitement and fear inside her-self, wanted to shout out her own ambitions. Finally she read, ". . . the common woman is as common as the best of bread/ and will rise/ and will become strong—I swear it to you on my own head/ I swear it to you on my common / woman's head" and the reading was over.

Annie Heaphy slumped against Peg, still staring at the poet. "Now I know why women scream at their idols in a concert," she whispered.

"She's really great, Heaphy," Peg replied.

"I can't move."

"Do you want to?"

"Not as long as she's here."

"I don't think she'd like us drooling over her, Heaph."

"Why not? She's human."

"Yes, but I think she gives these readings to move us be-yond where we are. To inspire us to do something meaningful ourselves."

"Like what?"

"Building bridges. Killing men. Writing poems. Whatever it takes."

"Making love?"

"With women. Fixing cars. Teaching girls to move with con-fidence and to play with skill."

"I never thought of that, Peg. That's exactly what you do. You teach younger women to be stronger, to do something with their bodies besides have babies." Peg looked proud. "What do I do?"

"Something mostly men do."

"What good is it?"

"Other women see they can."

"Is that enough?"

Peg bent her head to look more closely at Annie. "That's up to you."

"What else can I do?" Annie asked, discouraged at her lack of anything to offer. She became aware of Rosemary and Claudia talking beside her and looked their way.

Rosemary looked up. "We were just wondering how we could ever contribute to the movement as much as that woman has."

Annie and Peg laughed. "That's just what we were feeling."

"We decided not to let her accomplishments discourage us. After all, we're just starting," Rosemary explained.

"Rosie, I want to go meet her," Claudia whispered, tugging at Rosemary's arm.

"Want to come?" Rosemary asked Peg and Annie.

Annie sank deeper into the couch. "No way," she said.

"Come on, Annie," Peg urged. "You're just saying hello."

"Maybe you're just saying hello. *I'm* thinking about getting another beer. Shall I get one for you?"

"Sure."

"Me too," called Claudia as they moved away. Annie suddenly felt herself anchorless once more in the roomful of women. Dungarees and long skirts moved in changing circles around the poet. Annie stood and walked to the room where the beer was kept in a trash barrel filled with ice. She took three as another woman rummaged at the bottom of the barrel for more. "Not much left. We must be heavy drinkers, huh?" she observed to Annie.

Tossing her tab in the trash, Annie answered, "Yeah. More than usual?"

"More people than usual," the woman answered. "We have these gatherings once a month or so and this is the biggest yet."

Annie studied the short, curly-haired woman. She wore wire-rimmed glasses like Victoria's. "I think Judy Grahn brought most of us."

"I never thought we'd get this many women out to hear a lesbian."

"I guess she's pretty well known. Besides, she talks about women, not just lesbians."

"Yes, I identified with a lot of the things she had to say."

Annie was surprised that this woman did not consider herself a lesbian because she looked as if she would fit in at the bar. She smiled to herself. No wonder they're fighting so hard, she thought, they're just on the edge of coming out. "It must be really hard for women to come out in the movement," she said aloud, mischievously. "When I did, it was alone, just me and one other woman, and we kind of didn't have to face it because we were so isolated. We could think it was just us, or just temporary. Then we were able to get used to it and weren't so afraid anymore. We kind of eased into it."

"Do you think women will come out in the movement?" the little feminist asked, obviously concerned.

"I hope so," Annie answered, knowing she was probably upsetting her but feeling almost as if the woman was asking to be pushed. She retreated with her beers saying that her friends were waiting. "So did you meet her?" Annie asked when she rejoined her group.

"Yes," Claudia answered. "She's really comfortable." She winked at Annie, "And sexy."

"Claudia!" Rosemary chided her.

"Well she is!"

Peg put her hand on top of Claudia's head. "She's right, Rosemary," she laughed. "Can't poets be sexy?"

"It's not that she's a poet, but that she's a woman," Rosemary answered, looking concerned. "If we start responding to women on a sexual basis only, aren't we acting like men? The next thing is to ask her out for a drink and then take her home with you."

Claudia looked ashamed of herself, but Peg defended her still. "Look, Rosemary, I'm not much of a thinker, but you're being too narrow here. Surely what we want is to see women as more than sexual, not to erase that part of ourselves altogether."

"Maybe that's the difference between old gay and new," Annie contributed. "That we're so used to seeing each other sexually, those of us who have been living in the bars for years."

"Seeing each other sexually and in many other ways aping the male," Rosemary accused.

"Whoa," Peg said, stooping as if to stop a fight on the gym floor, laying her hands on Rosemary and Annie's shoulders. "I think you're both right. Yes, Rosemary, we do still do a lot of stuff the way we learned it from men. We sleep around irresponsibly sometimes, we drink a lot, we only want 'attractive' women, and we talk about women's bodies sometimes in a sexist way. We need to change a lot. At the same time sexuality is part of our lives and we don't want to lose it, or lose our ability to identify the sexual aspects of each other. Old gay women do that all too well while new lesbians are exploring new ways to relate to women. And here we are talking about it. Isn't this exciting?"

Rosemary and Annie still would not meet one another's eyes, but Rosemary turned to Claudia. "I'm sorry, Claudia, it's something I'm still very confused about. I criticized you because I don't *know* how to respond to attractive women."

Claudia's cheeks took back their color and she watched Peg pull Rosemary toward Annie. "Hey, you two. We have a movement to build. Let's not lose each other in the first round," Peg cautioned laughingly.

"Okay, okay," Annie said and reached to shake Rosemary's hand.

"No. This way," Rosemary demonstrated, wrapping her thumb around Annie's.

"Hey, that's neat," Annie said. "How did you do it? What does it mean?"

"This is the revolutionary handshake," Rosemary showed her, her hostility leaving.

"Almost as good as a pinky ring," laughed Peg.

Claudia asked, "A pinky ring?"

"Sure," Peg answered, holding hers up and gesturing to include Annie. "Gay people have worn them for years to communicate to each other that we're gay. The first school where I student-taught there was this older teacher named Gert. Wow did she look like an old-fashioned diesel dyke."

"Diesel dyke?" asked Claudia and Rosemary together.

"You know," Peg said, pretending to slick back her hair and bowing her legs.

"Goodness," said Rosemary. "I didn't know such types really existed."

"Well, they do," Annie answered in a hostile voice.

"I'm not criticizing, just ignorant, Annie."

Annie grinned and pulled her cap lower over her face.

"Anyway, you two," Peg chided them, "this Gert was something else and of course I worshipped the ground she walked on. I attached myself to her. Wanted to learn everything she had to teach, shot baskets like her, set up her equipment—you name it, I did it for that woman. But all that time I couldn't figure for the life of me if she was out or not, you know? She looked it and acted it, but she never talked about it. So one day almost the last day of my assignment I went into the office to ask what equipment we'd need for that day. No one was there but Gert and she was standing leaning against a desk in a way that looked to me like a butch coming on to a femme. 'Shit,' I said to myself, 'this is it.'

" 'Morning, Gert,' I said.

" 'Hi, kid,' she answered. That's what she called me. I stood there grinning, foolish, not knowing what to do. She wasn't in her gym clothes, I finally noticed, but wearing street casual clothes, chinos, a plaid, short-sleeved shirt. And then I saw it: bold and beautiful, a ruby pinky ring in a lot of gold. She saw me look at it and grinned back.

" 'Just stopping to get some papers,' she said. She had the day off. Had it off and came in, I know, only to show me her real self, to answer my question, but to do it in a way that made it clear she wanted to keep her two lives separate." Peg looked at Rosemary and Claudia. "That's one way we used to communicate. And still do, a lot of us."

"You're still wearing your ring," Claudia noted. She turned to Rosemary excitedly. "I want one!"

"To me, this ring," Peg made a fist and displayed it again, "is a symbol of who I really am. I don't think I'll ever stop wearing a pinky ring. I'm proud of it and I like having underground connections, a symbol that speaks to other people who may not be out themselves." The others were silent while Peg went on thoughtfully. "I'm really glad there's a woman's movement and that now I can move more freely more places and with more women. But I'm not going to forget how they kept us down because I think it can happen again, just like that." She snapped her fingers. "And I'm going to be ready by keeping our symbols alive. A lot of these women can just bow right out when it gets tough. Hide their real selves behind men. I'm never going to do that."

Rosemary looked awed. "So you feel a big difference between new and old gay women."

"Not a *big* difference. And not one that I want to separate us. But, damn, you can see for yourself that I sure feel a lot different than most of the women in the movement. A few of you came out here. In New York there's a lot more, but still, I don't hear any of you being gay first and feminists second."

"I'm not sure I want to be," Rosemary said.

"And I'm not saying you should. Or even that I should. I'm just telling you how strong it is in me."

"I see."

"Sorry to get all heavy on you."

"That's fine, Peg, it really is," Rosemary assured her. "I want to learn all this and to understand how our parts can construct a whole."

"It ain't fine with me," Annie joked. "The beer's all gone and the women are starting to leave. Not that one necessarily precedes the other."

"So you want to go, Heaphy?"

"You're reading my mind, Peglet."

"Want to come to the bar with us, Rose? Claudia?"

Annie glared at her, but Rosemary answered, "Of course. We thought you'd never ask."

"Wait, then," Annie said. "Is there a phone here I can use?"

"Over there."

"I'm going to call Vicky. See if I can tempt her away from her books by telling her you guys are coming."

"Good!" Claudia said as Annie picked up the phone. Her head was spinning from the night's excitement. She wanted the comfort of her lover. "I need you," she whispered when she heard Victoria's voice. "The poet is beautiful, but the politics are over my head. I'm losing ground fast. And Rosemary and Claudia are coming to the bar with us."

"Anne, you're so strong you'll never lose ground," Victoria soothed her. "However, I'm awfully bored."

"Does that mean you'll come?"

"It means I've been waiting here hoping that you'd call."

"Hallelujah!" Annie yelled.

Claudia ran up to Annie and grabbed her arm. "Tell her Judy Grahn's going to the bar too!"

"With us?" Annie asked, star-struck.

"Well, to the same bar."

"Vicky, you there? Okay, you can still get to feast your eyes on this marvelous dyke. *If* you promise not to run off with her."

"Silly, I haven't even run off with you yet. I'm certainly not thinking of doing it with anyone else."

"That's good. Because her lover's here too and I hear she knows karate. Shall I pick you up on the way?"

"Are we going to Marcy's?"

"Yes, ma'am. Put on your dancing shoes."

"I can't wait. I love you."

"I love you, Vicky. And I miss you."

"I'm so glad. I missed you too. Now stop talking and come get me."

Annie hung up, hitched up her jeans and tried to stop grinning before turning to face Peg and Annie's friends. "Guess she's coming," Peg said.

"You know me too well."

"Rosemary and Claude are waiting upstairs. They wanted to escort the poet out."

"Claude, huh? Got your eyes on her?"

"Isn't she cute?"

"Not hardly your type."

"I'm getting a lot less picky," Peg laughed. "And a lot more needy. But I wouldn't mess up Rosemary's head. She needs Claudia too badly. Anybody who could love Rosemary must be a saint. And I wouldn't know what to do with a saint."

"You sure wouldn't," Annie joked, watching the sadness in Peg's face. "You'll meet your girl soon, Peg. But what are we going to talk to these women about tonight? And how will Turkey and Eleanor and Dusty fit in?"

"We'll dance them to death if things get too bad."

"Oh, man, can you see it? Rosemary dancing?"

"Now don't be cruel."

Annie flashed a weary look at Peg as they went through the door to find Rosemary and Claudia.

"Over here," Rosemary called. She and Claudia were speaking with two other women.

"Listen," Claudia motioned to them excitedly. "Can I tell them?" she asked the other women. They looked at each other and nodded, then took each other's hands. "They just came out last night!"

The women looked at the ground, embarrassed. One shrugged. In the dark they glowed in the light jackets and jeans, their long hair touching between them. Peg and Annie exchanged glances. "Welcome," said Peg, bowing.

Annie shifted her weight from one foot to the other and tipped her cap to them. "That's great," she smiled.

"They're going to come, okay? They have a car. They want to celebrate."

"Actually, Judy Grahn's reading was our celebration," said one. "I'm Jean."

"And I'm Faye."

"Oh, I'm sorry," Claudia apologized. "This is Peg and this is Annie Heaphy."

"Sure," said Peg. "Please join us. We'd like to share your celebration."

"We've got to get moving," Annie prompted them. "Vicky's waiting."

"Victoria?" asked Faye.

"Victoria Locke?" Jean said at the same time. The new lovers looked at each other.

"Isn't it a small world?" laughed Peg.

Faye looked pleased. "I knew she'd changed, but I didn't realize that this was why."

"How did she change?" Annie asked.

Faye and Jean looked at one another again. "She's gotten friendlier," Jean said. "More open, more relaxed. She smiles, walks down the hall in pajamas. Little things like that. We liked her before, of course, but she was so unapproachable, so wrapped up in her poetry and studying."

Annie smiled proudly. Peg tapped her in the arm with her fist. "You've changed, too, Heaphy. She's been a softening agent for you as much as you have for her."

"Let's go," Annie said, scowling in embarrassment.

Rosemary and Claudia climbed into Annie's back seat and they drove a few blocks to pick up Victoria. She squeezed in the back with them. There was no parking near Marcy's so Annie dropped everyone but Victoria outside. The others went in to get a booth while Annie parked. Victoria stayed in the back seat and sprawled as much as she could across it.

"What are you doing back there, Queen?"

"Feeling sexy."

Annie had stopped to parallel park and looked over her shoulder into the back seat. "So you are," she agreed when she saw Victoria lying, hands under her head, shirt open halfway down her chest. She felt a rush of desire. "How the hell do you expect me to concentrate on parking this damn car?"

"Oh, Anne, I couldn't concentrate tonight," Victoria complained, sitting up. "All I could think about was making love. Is that because it's new to me? Or am I abnormal?"

Annie smiled gently as she got into the back seat with Victoria. She did not stop smiling as she opened two more buttons of Victoria's shirt to brush a breast with her lips. "You are a perfectly normal, healthy woman. A little kooky maybe, luring me into the back seat like this in a nice, quiet neighborhood where we could get arrested, but otherwise normal." She ran her cool hands up and down Victoria's back until Victoria laid her head on Annie's shoulder. "And you're powerfully sexy, woman."

"I wrote you a poem," Victoria interrupted, leaning against the back of the seat, her long hair covering her breasts. She put her glasses back on and pulled it from her jeans pocket. "It's not finished," she apologized, handing it to Annie. "But I thought since you were listening to poetry tonight you might like to read some about you."

Annie lifted her cap off her head. "Thank you," she said, impressed. "I've been waiting to see your poetry a long time now."

"It isn't that I didn't want you to see it, Anne. It's just not that terribly good and it didn't have anything to do with us. I tried to put us in this one. It's a whole new style for me."

Victoria laughed. "Are you just going to stare at me or are you going to read it?"

Annie switched on the overhead light and settled against Victoria to read. When she finished Annie sat silently staring at the sheet of paper. After a while she turned to Victoria. "That's beautiful. Thank you. I need to read it more slowly. I think it's like a good wine that needs to be rolled around my tongue, having someone write me a poem."

Victoria buttoned her shirt. Annie looked down at it. "I wish we could make love right here," she said.

"Yes," agreed Victoria, touching Annie's face. "But you're right. We could get arrested."

"Let's compromise and wait until later. I'll be more comfortable anyway. Shit," Annie said, suddenly pushing Victoria toward her door.

"What's wrong?" asked Victoria, rigid with unexpected fear.

"Cops, damn it. Get out before they want to know what's going on." Annie slipped quickly out of the car, cap in hand and looked the driver full in the face. "We stopped just in time," she sighed in relief as she joined Victoria on the sidewalk.

"What would he have done?"

"I don't know, my beauty. Maybe nothing, but I don't want to be in any man's power long enough to find out. Hope he's not headed for Marcy's. Wouldn't that be a kick in the teeth, busting Judy Grahn in New Haven."

"I never thought of that," Victoria said, pulling her pea jacket tighter across her chest. "And what if a bar we were in got raided and my parents found out that way. My goodness, that would be unpleasant."

"I thought you wanted them to know."

"When I tell them. All I need is a scandal to contend with. As much as I can't depend on them for money, I don't want to be cut off from any that may someday come from the other relatives. My picture in the paper would be a shame."

"I see your point," Annie said, stopping just short of the bar and running her fingers through her hair.

"You look wonderful," Victoria approved, leaning to kiss

Annie, then quickly straightening up as she remembered about the cop.

"You know," Annie said thoughtfully, "I'd hate to see you paralyzed by this money over your head."

"It's not the money, Anne. It's what I'd have to go through if they found out. The emotional punishment including withholding money would be more than I want to deal with."

"What are you going to do about your poetry then? It's going to be dyke poetry like Judy Grahn's. Are you not going to publish it so your family won't find out?"

"I don't think we have to worry about my poetry getting published just yet, Anne, though you're right, it's becoming more and more about women. Let's go meet this famous person."

"Lesbian," Anne challenged.

"Lesbian," Victoria repeated, shyly but proudly. "I like rolling it around on my tongue," she teased, "like a good wine." Then she winked, "Or a good woman."

Annie raised her eyebrows. "I'm shocked," she smiled. "And very pleased." She replaced her cap and held the door open for Victoria. "After you—good woman."

They were stopped inside the door by an unusually heavy wave of smoke and noise. "It's very crowded tonight," Victoria observed.

"Come on," Annie said, taking her hand and leading her to a group of tables bunched together around a booth. Peg stood and waved at them and Claudia jumped up to hug Victoria.

"It's so exciting," said Claudia. "Judy," she called across to a booth. "This is the poet we were telling you about." She held Victoria's hand up as if announcing a winner. "Victoria Locke, meet Judy Grahn," she said guiding Victoria toward her.

Peg reached Annie through the throng and Annie lost sight of Victoria. "They're really pushing your girl, Heaphy."

"She is good," Annie said proudly. "She just gave me a poem tonight."

"May I see it?"

"You'd have to ask her. But where's Turkey? And Elly? And that mammoth, Dusty?"

"Playing the jukebox, where else?"

Annie heard the first notes of *Help Me Make It Through the Night* and groaned. "Elly's depressed."

"You know how it is," Peg shouted although she was standing next to Annie, "she and Turkey feel really out of it because they didn't go to the reading. Turkey can't believe Judy is one of those 'faggy poets.' She claims I didn't tell them she was a bar dyke. I told them I don't even know if she really is. But she sure fits in, doesn't she, Heaphy?"

"I expected she would, Peglet. But take a look at Rosie the Revolutionary and Claudia and Vicky. Don't they look just fine here?"

"Yeah, like the women's band says, 'So fine. . . . !' "

"Hey, big shots, can you spare me a dance?" Eleanor weaved her way over to them.

"You can't dance in that condition. Where's Dusty?" Peg asked.

"Waiting to use the john. Where else? All your libber friends got weak kidneys. Along with weak everything else. So which one is the hotshot from California, the land of fruit and nuts?" She hiccoughed.

"Judy's the one talking to Vicky."

"Should have figured your Yalie would be part of all this," Eleanor said resentfully.

"Hey, Elly," Annie said with some anger, "Vicky didn't even go to the reading. She just came down here to be with us."

"Fine job she's doing of being with the lowlifes."

"Let's sit down," Peg suggested, putting her arm around Eleanor and guiding her toward their table.

"I want to dance. Don't neither of you want to be seen dancing with me?"

"Of course we do, Elly," Annie said. "Come on, let's dance."

"Oh, no, I don't want none of your charity," she said bitterly. "You ain't even drinking. Are you going to give *that* up along with your friends?"

"Elly, Elly, I'm not giving anybody up, I swear. All I did is go to the Women's Center. Once. What's wrong with that?"

"You two are shouting. Sit down," Peg ordered. "What's wrong Elly? What's upsetting you?"

Eleanor put her head in her hands. "Everybody's leaving me. You two want to go away and be libbers and you know I don't want to be like them. I can't. I'm not smart enough. I'm only a waitress with no bucks or education. I can't fit in. You two can and you're going to leave me alone with all these dumb fags and I need you." She looked at them through her tears and reached across the table to hold their hands. "Don't leave me. They're not like you. I am." Peg and Annie looked in helpless puzzlement at each other and at Eleanor.

"All I can tell you, El . . . ," Peg began.

"Don't tell me nothing," Eleanor said shrilly as she stood up and hurried from the booth. Dusty came out of the bathroom and caught her in her arms, then led her to dance.

"Shit," Annie said, removing her hat. "What was that all about?"

"I don't know," Peg admitted, shaking her head. "I just don't know. The women's movement wants us to be less gay because they say we're acting heterosexual and male and don't see we're just acting naturally for us. And the dykes don't want us to act so much like libbers when that's part of our world now too. I can't stop thinking politically. Nor do I want to stop wearing my pinky ring."

"No, Peglet, I really can't see you in long hair and a workshirt. Well, maybe if it was ironed," Annie smiled crookedly under the lowered brim of her hat as she looked at Peg's burgundy corduroy pantsuit.

"Iron my hair?" Peg teased.

"No, your thinking. Whoops. I just missed meeting the celebrity again."

Peg turned her head to see Judy Grahn slip into her jacket. "She's staying with that collective."

"What collective?"

"A bunch of lesbians who live together."

"Libbers?"

"Rabid. Some of them even look gay, though. Over there, leaving with Judy. That little yacky one drives me up a wall. Look at her talk Judy's ear off."

"Some of them do look alright. Shit, I hope Vicky doesn't fall for any of them. They look more her type than me."

"I wouldn't worry. I hear they're so busy sleeping with each other they wouldn't look twice at anyone outside."

"You think it's true?"

"I don't know. They say it's a new way of loving or something. They don't think women should be in couples."

"You're really giving me an education, Peg. You believe in any of this stuff?"

"Some of it makes sense, as long as they don't try to ram it down my throat. I know what I want and I'm going to look for the women I can have it with, libber or not."

"We've got to make Elly feel better, though. Persuade her we're not going to abandon her."

"Maybe we are, I don't know. How much longer can we be comfortable with her if she won't learn at least to understand the changes we're going through? Just listen to us, you know?" Peg asked sadly.

"I guess it's really messed up of her to be chasing after a butch like Dusty. What does she want, to be possessed? To have her heart broken?"

"Dusty looks like the type who walks right over women. Maybe even hits them on the way by. But that's what Elly wants."

"Maybe all we can do," Annie said resignedly, "is to let her know we're here if she needs us."

Victoria came to their booth, her hair as wild as it was in Vermont and a similar glow on her face. "I'm going to send her some of my work."

"Well, that calls for a drink," Peg announced.

"Yeah," said Annie, "I can't believe we've been here an hour and haven't had a drink yet."

"That's great!" Victoria approved.

"Oh, you think everything is great tonight," Annie replied, nuzzling Victoria's cheek. "I'm glad Judy is interested. What do you want to drink?"

"A big cold mug of beer."

"Sounds good. You think you can get some cold beer out of Marcy, Peg?"

"I doubt it, but I'll try. I'll see you at Rosie the Revolutionary's table," Peg smiled, striding toward the bar with her smooth gait, straightening the lapels of her sports jacket.

"Rosie the Revolutionary?" Victoria asked.

Annie looked shame-faced, but her blue eyes twinkled. "She does come on kind of strong."

"I guess I have to laugh. Her grimness has annoyed me a lot," Victoria said, pulling her hair back into a leather barrette.

"No," Annie said, putting her hand on Victoria's. "Leave it like that. I love it."

"It'll take hours to unsnarl."

"I'll help."

"I'll bet. You'll make it worse. Maybe I'll get it all cut off like yours."

Horrified, Annie began to protest. "You wouldn't be you!"

"But I'm really thinking about it. Not until after graduation, of course. So don't worry yet. You have plenty of time to get used to the idea."

"Not sure I can," Annie said, leading her over to Claudia and Rosemary. "Hi, Rosie," she said.

"Rosie?" Claudia giggled.

"Rosie the Revolutionary. Because you're so serious, Rosemary," Annie explained, fingering her hat ready to retract it all should Rosemary be offended.

"I like it," Rosemary said. "It's like Rosie the Riveter."

"Figures you'd have a comparison. Who's that?"

"In World War Two she was used to represent the women who left their homes and children to go into the factories and contribute to the war effort."

"You mean make bombs?" Claudia asked innocently.

"And all the other destructive toys that men wanted to play with."

"Where are they now?" Victoria wanted to know.

"Where most women are, back in their homes, powerless to earn substantial money, valueless to society other than as child bearers. As soon as the men returned they said, 'Go home, girls, we don't need you any more.' But we're their daughters."

"Let's drink to that," Annie toasted with the beer she had just set down.

Claudia drank, but said, "You mean they just fired them? Sent them home? And they went? Think where they'd be today if they had refused to leave."

"I'm sure it was a little more complex than that, but in effect that was it. Claudia, would you like another drink?"

"How many have we had?"

"I think this is our third."

"We're not used to all this liquor, Rose, do you think we ought to?"

"It's not every day that Judy Grahn comes to see us, is it?"

"No, but I think I'll nurse mine anyway."

Rosemary went off to the bar while Claudia worried about her. "This is only the second time she's drunk liquor in her life," she whispered.

"I can't believe she's doing it," Victoria said, shaking her head.

"Ah, it's good for her once in a while," Annie decided. "It'll make her feel more accepted. And it'll loosen her up so she'll *be* more accepted. We'll drive her home. Hey, Turkey," she called, waving to her friend, "join us?"

Turkey approached them slowly, not smiling. "Sit down, Turkus Major," Peg said, patting the space she made at the edge of the booth. "What's up with Elly?"

"She's not up, you dumb shit, she's real down."

"You don't sound much better."

"I'm kind of confused. And not sure why. I've never fit in at school with all those straight people so I come here to feel good. Now all your feminists are taking the bar over and I don't fit in here either."

"We love you a lot, Turkey, and don't you forget it," said Peg firmly. "Nobody will kick you out. This is Claudia, Rosie the Revolutionary's girl." She paused while Claudia burst into laughter. Turkey could not suppress a smile. "And here comes Rosie herself."

"I brought two in case you change your mind, Claudia. And if you don't, *I'll* help you out. Hello," she reponded to the introduction to Turkey. "We've heard about you. You're the sociology major with the wonderful sense of humor."

"I am? Not the fat one who looks like a turkey?"

"No."

"Not the dumb one who can't find a girl?"

"No."

"Not the one with the birthday everyone forgets?"

"No! Surely it can't be that bad!"

"Did you ever lose your tail?"

"I beg your pardon?"

"I didn't think so. I never did either. But Eeyore did and I know just how he felt."

"Oh, Eeyore! Of course, the melancholy Eeyore. That's who you sound like," Rosemary realized. "You do him well."

"Thank you," Turkey said, still subdued. She looked with sad eyes at Claudia, Peg, Annie and Victoria, then suddenly began to laugh. "I love it! I made you guys all sad!"

"That's mean," Victoria laughed also. "You did that on purpose."

"I had to know if you cared."

Peg scolded her. "You could have asked, you ass."

"No, no. I stopped playing Eeyore. He's the ass."

"Did you ever think of going on the stage?" Rosemary wanted to know, finishing the first drink.

"Well, I'll tell you. Once, when I worked in an anti-poverty program summer job, I had to sweep up the stage in the high school auditorium. I went backstage, center stage, upstage and down. It was an excellent experience. So I'll tell you, Rosie, I've *been* on stage. I'm a real pro." Rosemary laughed. "Why do you ask?" Turkey questioned her, cocking her head to one side, turkey-like.

"Because you can affect people with your face and manner. That's what the stage is all about isn't it?"

"Except how many fat dykes do you see up there doing routines? And I only would do it for dykes, you know."

"Then do a show here. For the bars in New Haven. Women would love it."

Turkey looked seriously at Annie. "Where'd you find this one, Cabbie?" she joked finally.

"Hey," Annie protested, "it's a good idea. I'd love you to be a stand-up comic. You could really do it."

Claudia put her hand out to stop Rosemary from drinking more of the second drink. "It's okay. Rosie the Revolutionary can get drunk once in her life," Rosemary said, beginning to slur her words. "Damn it."

"So what do you think of Judy?" Peg asked Victoria.

"She was wonderful. I'm so glad to know that there's a poet out there doing what she says she's trying to do. I can't wait to read her poetry. And to use some of her ideas myself. It will help to loosen *me* up."

"When are you going to show us some of your stuff?"

"When there's something worth showing you, Peg."

"You're being modest."

"Perhaps. But I'm also just realizing what a silly fantasist I've been. I want to write poetry that means something to us. Not just write pretty pictures."

"All this time," Rosemary said, her braid half undone and her hands clumsily rebraiding it, "I've been trying to get you to go to the women's poetry group so you would turn your words into weapons for the movement. Now I learn that all you needed was to meet a lesbian poet to see that you are one too."

"Seeing her I think made all of us feel that we may just be able to live the lives we want to live," Annie said.

"That's called validation," said Turkey. "Judy Grahn sounds like she must be a role model."

Claudia helped Rosemary with the last of the braid. She smiled winningly at Turkey. "What are your plans?"

Turkey flushed. "Well, when I figure which end is up," and she laughed loudly, "not that that's not obvious to anyone but me, I guess I'll do some kind of social work."

"But what's your dream?" Claudia persisted.

"If I have one," Turkey said, licking her lips and drawing an index finger through a puddle of moisture on the table, "I guess it'd be teaching people that it's okay to be different. Showing them how society is made up of all of us, not just one privileged group who gets to shit on everyone else."

"What a great thing to teach," Peg said, shaking her head in admiration. "I never knew you wanted to do something like that."

"I never really said it out loud till now. In so many words. When Claudia asked, it just popped into my head, so I guess it's been there for awhile."

"Nothing can survive for long in your head, Turk," Annie

teased as she set down a pitcher.

"Speak for yourself, Heaphy," Turkey said, grabbing the pitcher and pouring a glass for herself. "Anyone want what this chick is offering?" There was silence. "Whoops," Turkey corrected herself. "What this here *woman* is offering?"

Rosemary held out her empty glass. "One of the hardest words there is to say," she commented, spilling part of what Turkey poured. "Used to be ashamed of it myself. Woman isn't a title to be proud of in this world."

"Or lesbian, either," Victoria added. "Remember how I just couldn't say that at first, Anne?" She reached for Annie's hand and smiled at her.

"Yes. You had a rough time. I practically had to give you lessons." Annie set her cap on Victoria's head. They gazed at each other, their smiles getting broader.

"Why don't you ever do things like that to me, Claudie?" Rosemary asked, laying her head on Claudia's shoulder.

"You don't like it, Rose. Especially not in public."

"Well, I like it now," Rosemary said, pulling Claudia's arm around her shoulders. "A little romance won't compromise feminism."

Turkey groaned in memory of first meeting Rosemary in New York and met Annie's eyes. "You sure have changed since we first met you, Rosemary."

"Have I?" asked Rosemary, taking her head from Claudia's shoulder and sitting up. "Ohhh," she moaned. "Moved too fast. Guess this is called being drunk. Call me Rosie, Turkey. Claudia, I think I'm going to be sick."

"Come on, Rosie, then," Turkey soothed, pulling Rosemary out of the booth. "I've done this enough times." She and Claudia got Rosemary between them and walked to the door through the crowd of lesbians and gay men. Victoria and Annie and Peg laughed when the door shut behind them.

"Poor Rosemary. She'll never be the same," Victoria said, and laughed harder. "I love it. That stiff, sour woman is turning into a dyke."

Annie took her hat back from Victoria. "Boy, is she going to be sick in the morning."

"And embarrassed."

"But maybe she'll stay changed. She won't have to get drunk next time to relax."

"Or else she'll get drunk every time."

"Oh, Anne, you're such a pessimist."

"Yeah, Heaphy. Let's have high hopes. I still have hopes of finding a woman to love."

"You blew your best chance," accused a glazed-eyed Eleanor who slumped into the booth next to Peg. "Just like my Annie. 'Scuse me, lady. Your Annie," she said, looking at Victoria.

"Elly," Annie warned.

"Oh, so I can't sit at your booth and talk to your lady?"

Annie looked to Peg for help, her blue eyes hurt.

"Elly," Victoria asked, "were you and Annie lovers before I came along?"

The boothful of women went still.

Elly looked like a child who had been reprimanded. "Not hardly to speak of, I guess," she answered, her head hanging.

"We spent one night together awhile back," Annie explained, looking directly into Victoria's eyes with concern. "Before you," she added gently.

"I don't care, Anne. I just want to stop Elly from feeling so bad and left out."

"Annie, I hope I didn't screw things up for you," Eleanor cried in alarm, her hand over her mouth. "I just couldn't live with myself."

"El, nobody's going to mess up this relationship," Annie said, still looking into Victoria's eyes.

"I really do wish you well. It's just that I'm going to miss you."

"We miss you too, Elly," Peg chided her. "Ever since you met Dusty you have no time for us."

"But at least I'm not running around with a whole new crowd. That's different! Besides, I can't help it if you all don't like my Dusty."

"Well, damn it, we've never been able to spend enough time with her to find out. Why don't you tell her to come sit with us?"

"She has a mind of her own. Doesn't like libbers. I tried to tell her you all aren't really libbers. That you were gay first. But she don't believe me."

"Maybe we can all do something sometime. Spend time together. You think she'd like that?" Peg asked.

"Maybe if you ask her."

"I will," Peg promised. "Can't you get her over here?"

"Into the enemy camp? What if you *don't* like her? Or she don't like you?" Eleanor asked, suddenly losing her drunken aspect.

Annie shrugged. "We'll never know till we try."

As Eleanor waved Dusty to the booth Annie measured the woman apprehensively. She was big and butch and, from what Elly said, not very educated, a perfect stereotype of a bulldyke right down to the pointy black boots. Would Dusty's rough ways scare Vicky off? She was watching Dusty approach too, and Annie thought she saw fear widen Vicky's eyes. But then Victoria rose.

"Hi, Dusty. I'm glad to meet you. Elly's been raving about you every chance she gets."

Annie was proud of the way her lover's few words and welcoming manner put Dusty at her ease. Vicky might have learned this social ease in the sophisticated world Annie despised, but it looked like it might come in handy right here in the bar, with these very different people. Perhaps she should stop protecting Vicky from the gay world and let her find her own place in it.

Dusty was shifting shyly from one foot to the other, obviously pleased to hear of Eleanor's pride in her. "I don't know what she finds to say about me."

Peg smiled warmly. "Sit down and let us find out if it's all true!"

A silence fell. Shyness seemed to take hold of the group. Again Victoria came to the rescue. "We came down here to talk to that gay poet who just left. I didn't hear her, but from what everybody says, she writes about people like us, about real people."

"I'll believe it when I see it," Eleanor said.

Peg took the book she'd bought from the seat next to her. "How's that for a title," she said, displaying *Edward the Dyke*.

Dusty said, "I never could understand all that fancy stuff

they made us memorize in school. This looks like a different matter."

"We probably wouldn't *have* to memorize these," Victoria offered. "We'll *want* to know them."

"What kind of things does she say?" Dusty asked curiously.

As the conversation went on Annie smiled to see a bunch of dykes sitting in a bar talking about poetry. Dusty seemed to warm to the group perhaps because they were all so different: Victoria the Yalie, Turkey the first in her family to go to college, Peg the professional, Eleanor the Southern waitress, Dusty the Northern factory worker, herself most like Turkey, but a dropout. She felt a warmth for this crazy mixed-up group of women that felt like hope. Hope that they'd all stay together somehow and make each others' lives a little easier. And maybe leave something of themselves behind for other kids like them.

"I guess it's time to clear out of the enemy camp," Eleanor said after awhile. "Goodnight everybody. I hope I'm forgiven for getting mad before."

"Of course you are," Peg called after her. She shook her head when they were gone. "So she was really just worried that Dusty wouldn't like us. It wasn't our fault at all. How do you like that?"

"Maybe there is hope that things will work out," Annie agreed.

"Well, I'm too tired to work on it any more tonight," Peg said, standing.

"Want a ride?" Annie joked.

"I think I can make it across the street. Unless Vicky here wants to help me."

"Now, no girl-stealing. I mean, woman-stealing."

"Nobody can steal me," Victoria said, yawning.

"You're just too tired to fool around," Annie teased as they got outside into the warm spring night. She looked up at the stars.

"If I can't steal a warm body, then I'll have to find a big one," said Peg as Turkey and Claudia came back towards the bar.

"We put Rosemary in Jean and Faye's car," Claudia said. "You won't have to drive us home."

"I wouldn't have anyway. I thought it would do her good to walk," Annie teased. "How is she?"

Turkey sighed. "Sick as a dog. I think she threw up everything she ever had inside her."

"Then maybe her metamorphosis will be easier," Victoria suggested. When Claudia looked puzzled she went to her side and took her arm. "We were talking about the changes in Rosemary before," she explained.

"I know," Claudia said, turning and putting her arms around Victoria. "I don't know if I can handle it. I feel as though I'm learning to love a new woman. Or reinvent one."

"Is that bad?" asked Victoria, holding Claudia.

"I don't know yet," Claudia said. "That's what's so frightening. What if I can't keep loving her? After all, I've been encouraging the changes."

"Somehow," Victoria said, running her hand up and down Claudia's back, "I think you'll come out okay. I really do." She hugged Claudia tightly, then pushed her toward Jean and Faye's car. "You'd better get 'Rosie' home before she completely metamorphoses—into a pumpkin!" she laughed.

CHAPTER NINE

Annie Heaphy felt an unfamiliar anxiety as the train entered New York City. She wasn't going to a gay bar for an evening. She was visiting her own New York City lover. Victoria had preceded her to talk to her parents. She would definitely tell them she would not be living the life they had planned for her. She might tell them she was a lesbian. Annie half hoped she would not get that far as it would make meeting the Lockes that much harder on her. Poor Vicky, she thought. If I'm scared, imagine what she's feeling.

The buildings grew taller as she penetrated deeper into the city. And her fear grew too. What if they had changed Victoria's mind? What if all the years of training had proven too strong for Victoria to overthrow? Annie could be left waiting for her at the station. Victoria might meet her only to say that it had all been a mistake—that her parents were right. She drew her jean jacket closer around herself.

The man next to her snored once loudly and woke up. "Hundred twenty-fifth Street," he muttered as they slowed for the station. Annie felt frightened of him, vulnerable. He blocked her way to the aisle. She would have felt better if she had brought her car, but Victoria was right, the parking would be too difficult. The strange man reminded Annie of the old woman Victoria had met on the train who foretold Victoria's future. When the man shifted again she rose, climbing over him to pull her knapsack down from the luggage rack. She was too excited to sit anymore and her fears diminished when the train went underground, into the romance of the dark tunnel to New York City and Victoria.

Annie was the first off the train. She started to run up the platform, but calmed herself and slowed to a long, rapid stride. At an arched opening to the huge hall of Grand Central Station she paused to seek Victoria in the crowd, her anxiety high again. Victoria came to her side and was touching her before Annie saw her. Smiling widely, they drew each other out of the crowd of people coming from Annie's train and hugged. "How are you?" Annie asked.

"It's been hellish," Victoria blurted. She stood straight but willowy, ready to bend back to Annie's arms. "I told them everything, Anne. I decided I didn't want the fear of their finding out looming over me all my life. How are you?"

"My house was so empty. And I was so scared. And you're so brave."

"Scared of what?"

"That they'd take you away from me," Annie said chokingly, tears of relief escaping with her tensions.

"How in the world could they do that? I've been waiting all my life for you to help me get away from them, silly duckling."

Annie pressed her head to Victoria's shoulder. "Let's leave," Victoria said. "There's so much I want to do with you before we have to go meet them."

"Okay, okay," Annie said, wiping her eyes with her hat. "I just needed to break down a little, I guess."

"Why didn't you go stay with Peg and Turkey? They would have comforted you."

"I don't want to lose my ability to be alone, to take care of myself. I would have been okay if I hadn't known how difficult this was going to be for you. It was being without you *and* worrying that did me in."

They were moving across the shining floors toward another dark arch. "I'm stronger now, Annie, much stronger after just a few months of being with you, learning that it's possible to be me and having you appreciate me for who I am, not for a role you want me to play."

"Were they awful?"

"Yes. Very formal and stiff and cold. They kept coming to me with propositions. For example, they would send me to Oxford if I would give up my 'bohemian attitudes.' " Laughing, Victoria leaned into the dark wood and glass door out of the station. "As if there was not really a *me* talking to them, but an entity which could still be molded to their use." She pushed the door open forcefully.

"You're angry at them."

"You're damn straight, as Turkey would say."

Annie laughed. "It's funny to hear you say that." She stood and looked at Victoria in wonder. At her jeans, at her loose, heavy hair, at her round glasses glinting in the city's afternoon sunlight, at the white tennis sweater over a yellow shirt. "You look like a million dollars. Sorry, I forgot about the money phobia. You look like a beautiful dyke. Where are we?"

"First of all, I'm not sure I want to look like a dyke, beautiful or not. But to answer your question, this is Forty-second Street. You haven't been in New York much have you?"

"Not in the daytime," Annie admitted, drawing a deep breath and looking up at the towering buildings. "Sure is bigger than Boston."

"Sure is," Victoria agreed, taking Annie's hand and leading her toward Fifth Avenue.

"Where are we going?"

"I haven't planned it. I just want to be with you, to see you in New York. Like I want to see you against a background of Paris and London and everywhere else in the world I've been without you. You'd fill them with color and life, I just know it. My whole past seems so drab and spiritless since I've loved you, Anne. Loving you is like carrying a candle which sheds light on everything I see and warmth over everything I feel. Oh, Anne, I could embrace the Empire State Building I'm so excited!" They grinned at each other and Annie hopped into the air in happiness.

Holding hands, they crossed Fifth Avenue. Victoria led Annie to the front of the 42nd Street Library. It was the end of lunch hour and people were leaving the spaces in the sun where they had eaten. Annie jumped onto a newly vacated lion and rode it, horse-style, hitting its flank with her cap. They ran hand in hand up the rest of the steps and into the lobby. Annie wanted to see the library, but didn't want to have her knapsack inspected, so they left and followed the stairs around into Bryant Park. Between lunch hours it was empty of all but stragglers: a couple of gay men, a wino, a man selling joints, two women who talked intently and kept glancing at their watches and at the strange men. Annie and Victoria looked at each other, then smiled and shrugged away the bad vibrations of the park. The city was theirs today and they would allow no one to interfere. They walked slowly to a bench and sat admiring the old building.

"If I'd grown up in New York would I have met you at this library and come out with you?" Annie asked.

"Only if our story can have a different ending."

"I wonder how she wants it to end?" Annie questioned a nearby statue.

A cloud moved and the sun beat down on them. Victoria squinted from its brightness. "I don't want the story to end at all, Anne."

"I know. Listen, why don't you get a pair of sunglasses made? You'd look great in them." She held her hand over Victoria's eyes to shade them.

"I can't stand them."

"That's too bad. I remember when sunglasses were so cool. All the dykes in Boston wore them. The coolest ones wore them at night, too, in the bars."

"Did they wear the reflective type?"

"You had to be a tough butch to get away with those."

"And were you tough enough?" Victoria asked, hugging Annie's arm to herself.

Annie shook her head regretfully. "That took a lot more arrogance than I had. Besides, I didn't spend much time in the bars. Natalie didn't like them. She didn't want me to look like a bar-dyke because she wasn't one. She didn't like me acting dykey. She said bar-dykes were too obvious and we'd be left alone more if their kind would drop their affectations and act like women. As a matter of fact, that's what our first fight was about. Acting like a woman. I said she was talking about acting like women who want men to like them and asked why we shouldn't act differently. She thought the older women with real short hair slicked back who wore men's pants were repulsive. I couldn't fall in love with someone like Eleanor's Dusty, but there was something about them I liked. Their style. They looked like they wouldn't take anybody's shit. And those were the women who wore sunglasses. No, I wasn't tough enough."

"Those were the women who liked to look like men."

"You say that like they're some foreign breed. A lot of people think I'm a man."

Victoria shook her head in disbelief. "You've told me that, but you don't look like a man at all!"

"To you. You know better. You're not scared off by my appearance, thank goodness. A lot of poeple, something clicks in their heads if they can't immediately identify where someone's coming from. It makes them not so sure who they are. You've never heard the comments. Either they won't make them in front of two people, one of whom looks normal, or they think I *am* a guy. It mostly happens when I'm alone and occasionally with Turkey or Peg."

"Do I look that straight?"

"Pretty much—to them. I see the dyke in you."

"I'm confused about that. I'd like to look like who I am." Victoria thought for a moment. "Maybe I *will* cut my hair."

"I thought you didn't want to look dykey."

"I'm frightened of being so identifiable. And I still feel as if it's no one's business but ours. Yet I'm proud of being a lesbian and I don't want to hide it."

"Don't you dare cut your hair, though," Annie said, whirling on Victoria. "I love it."

Victoria giggled. "I know, but it *is* awfully hot." She jumped up from the bench and skipped away from it while Annie pretended to drag her back.

"That's only the sun. It'll get cooler," she pleaded, laughing as she tried to grab Victoria's arm.

"It's *my* hair. Don't you want me to be comfortable?" Victoria called back as she ran through the now half-full park and onto the street.

Annie was right behind her. "I'll buy you reflective sunglasses and a pinky ring! You won't have to cut your hair!"

Victoria leaned against the fence. "Perfect solution," she said, catching her breath. "But I have an even better idea." She took Annie's hand again and pulled her across 42nd Street. A bus honked loudly at them. They walked past a few stores and stopped at a tiny shop that sold ties.

"You don't want a tie, do you?" Annie asked Victoria.

"I've *always* wanted a tie. Women used to wear ties. Why shouldn't I?"

"The day I meet your parents? Give me a break!"

"I'd only wear it if we go out later. I think I'd look good in one. I used to pick out all of my father's."

Annie shook her head. "Let's go in," she sighed.

They had fun trying on ties and upsetting the shop manager who never offered to help them, only stared. When they left Victoria had three ties, one to match her eyes, one to match Annie's eyes and one for her father. Annie bought a wide orange tie with blue elephants staggered across it. She proudly held it up to Victoria on the corner of 6th and 42nd.

"Why in the world did you buy it?" Victoria asked.

"To show that man that dykes aren't all bad. He's probably been trying to unload it for years. Besides, it was only a dollar."

"Can't resist a bargain? Where will you wear it?"

Annie looked victorious. "Wherever you wear yours!"

"Oh, no! Is that a threat?"

"Well, you wouldn't want me to go anywhere inappropriately dressed, would you? And if ties are called for, I'll have one."

"But, Anne, I think that one should be declared illegal. I'm not sure you can bring it across state lines." She watched Annie trying to knot it around her neck. "And it clashes horribly with your hat."

Annie looked crushed. "I never thought of that."

Victoria sensed that she might win yet. "You'll just have to buy a new hat."

"No way. Uh-uh. Not me," Annie declared, shaking her head. "It'll just have to look bad."

"Don't you want a hat from New York?"

Annie thought a minute. She folded the tie neatly and put it in its bag.

"Some of the greatest haberdashers in the world work in this city," Victoria went on. "It would be a present."

Annie looked suspiciously at Victoria. "You don't like my hat?" She removed it and fingered its edges.

"Of course I like your hat. But it doesn't match your tie."

She drew her hair back from her face. "And I wouldn't mind some variety," she added gently.

"I knew you didn't like my hat," Annie said in the same tone she would use to say that someone did not like *her*. Her face was full of hurt. The traffic forged by them crosstown and uptown, like herded cattle. The horns lowed, while brakes, wheels and engines bellowed and roared at various levels. Victoria began to think that she had hurt Annie beyond repair when she felt Annie's hand tuck her arm under her own. "Which way to the hats, ma'am?" Annie asked her.

"I'm not sure," Victoria hesitated. "This wasn't planned, you know. I suppose uptown might mean quality, though I'm not sure of finding any of that on Sixth Avenue."

"Let's try. Remember, I'm not rich either."

"I said it would be a gift if you recall." There was still a slight edge of uneasiness between them as they walked through the crowds on 6th Avenue.

"Is this Broadway?" Annie asked.

"It's a block over."

"I want to buy a hat on Broadway."

"I have a feeling quality will be sacrificed for sentiment there."

Annie smiled. "I feel tacky today."

"I noticed."

Annie stopped and hugged Victoria fiercely. "I really don't mind you wanting me to have a new hat. I've been thinking about it myself. I guess I was just feeling like the hat was a part of me you didn't like. And I need for you to like all of me, Vicky."

"Poor Anne," Victoria soothed her. "My wonderful woman. Maybe I am rejecting a part of you. Maybe I want to put my own stamp on you more completely. I don't think it would change you essentially. Do you?"

"No. And we're bound to change from being with each other. Can you imagine ten years from now?" she joked, leaning back from Victoria to share her vision. "You won't hardly be able to tell us apart!"

Victoria laughed too as she stepped away and took Annie's hand. "I hope we won't get like that," she said, "I don't think I could love me anywhere near as much as I love you. We have to find out how to be together and change together without becoming indistinguishable from each other or inseparable. As you said, we have to learn how 'not to lose our ability to be alone.' And speaking of being alone—what have you heard about your house?"

"Nothing," Annie answered sadly. "The workers are just about finished next door. I guess they'll start painting and hammering on my place next. I better start looking for someplace else to rent." She shrugged as if it didn't matter and Victoria felt helpless to see her so defeated.

"Wait," commanded Annie, stopping in her tracks as they turned onto Broadway. "I love it."

"What?" Victoria looked all around her at the people and cars and shops until her eyes came to rest on the white cowboy hat in the window of a souvenir store. "You like it?" Victoria asked, looking doubtfully at it.

"No," said Annie finally. "It's not me."

Victoria sighed in relief, suddenly hearing the new sounds that signalled Broadway, the raucous speakers blasting bad rock music and come-on speeches out the doors. "I didn't think so. As little as I want to be a repressed uptowner, that was a little flamboyant."

"I might like to be flamboyant once in a while, you know."

"Once in a while, Anne. But you wear your hats all the time everywhere."

"So it's hats in the plural already, huh?"

"We *are* looking for one . . ."

"True. Very true. If we can find it." They trudged on up into the theatre district and Victoria pointed out the sights to Annie. They were both very hot and thirsty. Annie kept lifting the knapsack away from her back to dry off the sweat. "Let's find a nice air-conditioned shop to look in."

"How about that shop?" They went in and Annie bought a lightweight navy Greek sailor's cap.

"Now, that was easy," Annie said, stuffing her green cap into her knapsack as they emerged into the heat.

"And I love it. It does suit you. Kind of dignified, but kind of fun. It looks great with your light hair."

"You're just pleased as hell you've left your mark on my head."

"I'd rather be leaving it on your body," Victoria whispered and ran her tongue around the rim of Annie's ear. "Let's go up to my parent's apartment. It'll be cooler and they won't be home for hours yet."

Annie took off her sailor's hat and bent the brim to a peak in her hand. "Got to train this hat to fit me right. Yes, let's go. It's too damn hot out here for June. Somebody ought to adjust the thermostat."

∿ ∿ ∿ ∿ ∿

"Sometimes it seems as if we spend all our time in bed," Annie noted as she pulled on her jeans.

Victoria giggled deep in her throat. "I wish we could."

"We might never have stopped if your parents weren't due soon."

"Not if I had anything to do with it, Anne." Victoria nuzzled Annie's neck before she went, naked, to the dresser to brush her hair. "Do you have any idea how liberating it is to make love with a woman in one's parents' home?"

Annie brushed the top of her new hat clean, and set it on her head. "Some," she said shyly.

"So you're not innocent of this rebellion yourself?"

"Where else did me and Natalie have to go? My problem was that my house was never empty."

"The aunts?"

"And my grandmother. When I think of that house it's a nightmare of faceless women floating, like ghosts, in and out of rooms, constantly searching for me."

"And where were you?"

"On the narrow hard bed under a window in my room. Lying on a white bedspread, feeling its fuzzy little bumps under our asses as we made love, scared and tense, tense, tense. I don't know how we ever had orgasms."

"Quietly, I'll bet."

Annie bent over Victoria from behind and hugged her. "Quieter than you, anyway," she teased, cupping her hands around Victoria's still-uncovered breasts.

"Anne!"

"Did I embarrass you?" Annie asked as she knelt at Victoria's side and spoke against a breast, touching it as she spoke with her mouth. "I love to hear you. Every time you come I hear you coming on the mountainside in Vermont again. You open up the sky for me, wherever we are. Suddenly I'm outdoors with you in open space."

Victoria leaned her head back, knowing that she wanted to make love again, but anxious about her parents arrival. The fact that they knew she and Annie were lovers did not make Victoria feel any more comfortable about making love in their home. Still, she let her legs go slack as Annie reached between them. "No, Anne," she whispered, letting the hairbrush rest on Annie's hat. Then she swept the hat off Annie's head. Annie sat between Victoria's legs and began to explore her with her tongue. Victoria, shaken with tenderness by the intimacy of what Annie was doing, half-dropped, half-placed her brush on the floor and softly ran her hands over and over Annie's hair. "I feel so connected to you," she breathed at Annie who leaned back and looked up toward Victoria, her lips glistening above her naked shoulders. "You're making a circle with me," Victoria explained softly. "It's like a halo, or a rainbow. I can see all this light curving into you and out of me and out of you and into me. I feel its warmth." She played with Annie's hair, astonished again by its blondeness.

"I feel it," replied Annie, bending once more and kissing Victoria's exposed outer lips lightly until Victoria found herself moving her pelvis closer to Annie's mouth, pushing against her. Overwhelmed, she stopped worrying about her parents. Annie circled Victoria's ankles with her fingers and steadied herself until with a half-loud cry Victoria came. Victoria bent to kiss Annie's still-wet lips, her hair falling between them and making a fine grinding sound as it rubbed between their lips. "I have never met anyone as sensual as you," Annie said, her eyes still bright with pleasure.

Victoria stared at their blueness, unable to talk yet, her hands resting lightly to either side of Annie's jaw. "This isn't sex," she finally said, closing her eyes and shaking her head slowly. "It's bliss." Her smile disappeared as she heard the key in the front door. She looked at Annie in panic and Annie stood, slowly, pulling Victoria up with her. She bent to hand Victoria her jeans and looked for her pullover as Mrs. Locke called, "Victoria, are you and your friend home?" Victoria rolled her eyes at Annie before she disappeared into her sweater. Annie was fumbling with the buttons of her own shirt.

"We'll be right there, mother," she called, hoping she would wait for them. Her heart raced when she heard her mother's footsteps approaching. Annie pushed her shirttails into her jeans still unbuttoned. Victoria quickly ran a brush through her hair. Her mother would think it odd she wore no shirt under her sweater, but there was no time for proprieties. Almost simultaneously she thought of her mother's perfunctory kiss. Her mouth and hair smelled like herself from kissing Annie. She looked quickly around to Annie who was sitting, composed, legs crossed, hat on her lap, almost daintly on the desk chair. For a moment she wished that Annie had long hair, looked more straight, but then she was flooded with love for her short yellow hair, her lesbian ways. It gave her courage and she remembered to slip her glasses off just as Mrs. Locke rounded the door.

"Hello girls," Mrs. Locke said, hesitating in the doorway to Victoria's relief. "You must be Anne." She did not walk in to shake Annie's hand.

"Yes," Annie replied, smiling nervously. "Thanks for giving me a place to stay in the city."

"We welcome Victoria's friends," Mrs. Locke said, her face expressionless. She looked as if, had she seen Annie at Victoria's feet, she would not have given any sign, thought Annie. She knew the type: frozen women, so far from their feelings they seem to have none. And the thought chilled her as she realized in fear how much of that coldness might be in Victoria. The thawing that had come with loving Annie might be temporary— or partial. Annie considered her ability to love a half-frozen woman. She would try to keep her melted by helping her feel safe and loved. What a consuming job it could be. But there, she thought as Mrs. Locke advised them to dress and meet her and Mr. Locke in the parlor for cocktails, there is the difference. Mrs. Locke turned regally and swept out of the room with her skirt and matching high heels. Victoria is a lesbian. In her own world she doesn't have to protect herself quite so much as her mother who must wear clothes to please men, move to please them and think to please them. In learning Annie's pleasures, Victoria learned her own, just as in learning Annie's needs and how to meet them, she found how to meet her own. The battle's half won, thought Annie: remove her from this world. In the new world, help her to find and to meet her own real needs.

Victoria watched Annie's eyes follow her mother out of the room. She felt torn away from Annie. The intimacy of their lovemaking had been so moving that the intrusion of her straight, judgemental mother was almost an act of violence. In order to regain that intimacy she felt she must do something violent in turn, but she was paralyzed.

"Do you like your mother?" asked Annie, hoping Victoria did not.

"No. Not at all. I've tried to find something in her I could like or love," Victoria whispered, "but she's not reclaimable. She's lost."

"I'm sorry."

"It makes me freer in a way. I know what I don't want."

"You mean I might never have had you if it hadn't been for her failure?"

"Exactly. And if my father hadn't thought that my mind was as important as my body so that I was allowed to develop it. Of course, that was in lieu of training a son, but the end result is the same for me."

They sat on the bed next to each other, not touching. "We came to each other such different ways," said Annie.

"I hardly know anything about your background. Except that you had a household of aunts and not much money. Why do you think you didn't want to be like your family?"

"That's easy. As earthy as my aunts seem next to your mother, they had their airs and pretenses. They thought their husbands should be strapped to their jobs to earn more and more money so they could spend their lives prettying up their flats and serving each other tea. They would not have admired your mother, but they would have emulated her lifestyle. And my mother, though she was different from them, more purposeful, still relegated herself to second place at home. The men cursed and got loud, but the aunts made them stop brawling, demanded that they treat them like ladies. I suppose it was their way of getting away from the ugliness of life, from the poverty their parents knew in Ireland and then here, but it made them such damned fakes.

"There wasn't one person in my family I wanted to be like. My mother a little bit, because at least she kept her integrity by staying aloof from my father's family and working part-time. But she was still part of it all because my father was. It was her spirit, maybe, that I admired. I think without my father she might have gone and built herself a farm out west like her brother did. Instead, she invited my father's relatives to our gloomy flat, cooked turkey for all of them when it was her turn and settled family tiffs. I didn't want to get buried like that." Annie paused, looking toward Victoria from the window where she had wandered. "Sorry, that was quite a speech."

Victoria joined her at the window. "You're right, it was quite a speech. But I want to hear your speeches. We really know each other so little, don't we?"

Annie smiled and replaced her hat. "I was thinking of that myself. I probably know more about your body than your personality."

"Then no matter how awful this is I think it's been worth it to let us get to know each other better."

"Agreed. Now I see that it's really important to take you home to Chelsea so you can see from whence I sprung," Annie laughed. "Although you won't have to deal with my family as my lover. I'd rather disappear from their lives than come out to them. I'd feel so entangled by their responses."

"I can see you as a little girl."

"A spindly-legged little kid with long blonde hair and a poodle skirt?"

Victoria looked shocked. "Poodle skirts?"

"Can you imagine?"

"Not at all, but I love the idea. Wouldn't my mother have a fit if you appeared for dinner in one of those."

"Speaking of which, what am I supposed to change to? I only brought my dungarees."

"They'll do. I, however, will change into some 'slacks' that will look more familiar to mater and pater and something a bit frillier on top. They may look at you funny, but don't let it worry you. I hope you'll never have occasion to be scrutinized by them again. My sun-shot love."

"Huh?"

"You're so bright that sometimes when I close my eyes I confuse you with the sun."

"I'm not feeling very bright right now. I'm feeling more like a drink," Annie said in a strained voice from the window where Victoria had left her to change.

"That you'll have soon enough."

"But not in the quantity I'm craving, my love."

"You mean you want to get drunk?"

"You got it."

"Why?" Victoria asked, returning to the window as she buttoned her blouse, a pale yellow one of light, soft material. She felt as if she were wearing Annie's hair.

"I don't know. I just get in the mood."

"When things are going bad?"

"Or good. It's good for despairing or celebrating."

Victoria peered with concern at Annie who was averting her eyes. "Do you want to get drunk or go to a bar where you can be with our own people?"

"Good question," Annie mused and fell silent. She looked up at Victoria's glasses. "Why are you holding those instead of wearing them?"

"My mother gets upset when she sees me in glasses. I'm not sure my father ever has."

"But you're so nearsighted."

"I'm used to it," Victoria shrugged as she turned to finish her preparations. "People who aren't half-blind don't understand what the world looks like without these."

"What about contacts?"

"Can't wear them. Something about my eyes, they would be bad for them."

"So you feel your way around in front of your parents

rather than upset them." When Victoria looked sharply at Annie she apologized. "Sorry, I'm feeling ornery. I'm not really criticizing you."

"Yes you are, just as I'm criticizing you for drinking when you have a perfect right to want to run from these people."

"Oh," said Annie. They stared at each other.

"I'm not ready to wear my glasses in front of them."

"And I want a drink, whatever the reason."

Suddenly they both smiled and walked to each other, then hugged tightly. "It's going to be hard," Victoria whispered, her voice low with emotion.

"We'll probably end up hating each other sometimes," Annie said, running her fingers along Victoria's soft blouse.

"But it will only deepen our love, these differences and adjustments."

"Do you think so?"

"If we want it to."

Annie set her jaw as she pulled away. "I think it will if we don't direct it all inside our relationship." Victoria looked puzzled. "I'm scared that we'll spend every waking minute taking care of each other and our pet poodle and never do anything beyond ourselves."

"Do you mean that you want a focus outside ourselves?"

"Yes. Or focuses. Hell, I don't care if we just volunteer for something, if our lives leave some mark somewhere besides on each other."

"And that comes from your family being so inward."

Annie raised her eyebrows and tipped her cap forward. "I guess it does, Vicky. I never thought of that."

"But it's a fine commitment and I want to share it with you."

"We need to talk about it more. Not just fooling around with Peg and those guys, but seriously, you and me."

Annie looked so intent that Victoria wanted to smile out of love for her, but she knew how serious she was. "On the train tomorrow, Anne, if not before. We'll come up with some ideas. We'll really start to plan."

Satisfied, Annie smiled and began to pace. "Is it time to approach the colosseum yet?"

"Are you feeling like a lion or a slave?"

"I'm feeling like the meat they use to lure the lion out of its cage."

"Okay," smiled Victoria as she put her glasses into their case. "Let's get this over with."

~ ~ ~ ~ ~

"A lady on the train told me," Victoria answered her mother after dinner when they had settled in the parlor.

"What lady, what train, darling? I'm afraid I don't quite understand you," Mrs. Locke said, glancing minutely at Annie. "She told you that you were a—homosexual person—so you became one?"

"No, Mother, I was only joking," Victoria said patiently, "but it was part of the whole sequence. You asked me when it happened, when I came out. It wasn't a sudden thing. I love women because of everything that ever happened to me." Mrs. Locke visibly shuddered while her husband looked puzzled.

"You see, dear?" she turned to her husband. "I knew it would have been worth the expense to have a coming out party for her."

"That wouldn't have changed anything, Mother. In fact, it might have pushed me to find out about myself sooner. I would have been so disgusted with parties I would have looked even harder for a way out."

"These women," Mrs. Locke asked, pointing her chin slightly toward Annie, "these women don't go to parties?"

"That's not the point."

Annie had watched Victoria's patience run out. She tried to picture herself talking to her own parents in order to find a way to help Victoria. "I think, Mrs. Locke," she said, "that Victoria's trying to say she felt she had no choices when you arranged her life for her. They never fit her, she never fit them. And the more plans you made for her, the more she would have wanted to get out of them."

"If you've always been like this," Mrs. Locke replied after nodding abstractedly toward Annie, "what do you mean about that woman who told you to be like this."

"She didn't tell me what to do. And she wasn't all that important. I just mentioned her because she was one of the ways I began to see myself. She seemed able to see into me and my future, like a witch would do. Because of her my mind opened up to possibilities for myself I'd never considered." Victoria's father straightened his new tie and looked skeptical. "Then other things began to happen which opened my eyes further. For example, I met lesbians."

"I can't think that's anything but a silly way to make such a decision."

Annie started to speak, but Victoria went ahead. "Mother, I feel like we're not communicating. I'm trying to explain only because you're my parents, but maybe you'll never fully understand, or maybe it'll take time."

"I appreciate it, dear. It's all so foreign to me," Mrs. Locke said.

"And I know how hard it is. Our whole society teaches us not to accept or understand or even *see* gay people. That's why it took so much to wake me up, too." Victoria paused and looked defiantly at her mother, ready for another challenge.

"Then you don't think you'll ever get married?"

Victoria looked toward Annie as if to ask, "Did she miss the whole point?" Annie shook her head sympathetically. Victoria answered quietly, "No."

"It's not as if she's an only son turned pansy, you know," Mr. Locke comforted his wife. "And I'm sure you'll be discreet, Victoria."

She doesn't count for him at all, Annie thought. Mrs. Locke, meanwhile, seemed to take her husband's pronouncements as a signal to end the discussion. She turned back to Victoria. "Won't you tell us about your friend?"

"We've only known each other a few months, but it feels like a lifetime," Victoria smiled at Annie.

"I remember what a rebel I was at school. I defied all the rules when I went to a local roadhouse with your father," Mrs. Locke said. "I suppose my daughter cares for you in much the same way, to defy convention for your sake," she continued as if to compliment Annie.

Annie squirmed under her gaze, trying to respond to her

without showing hostility. She felt uncomfortably drowsy from cocktails and dinner wine. The room was full of summer heat under its air conditioning. She wished Mrs. Locke would get tired of being polite. The woman was not interested in understanding Victoria, only in fitting her into the stereotypes she already had. Annie saw her as a manipulator who loses interest in anything which doesn't suit her purposes. She wanted to say, sarcastically, "I hope you'll find me worthy of your daughter," and in desperation was about to, when Mrs. Locke asked her to talk about herself. "I'm from Boston," was all she could think of to say.

"What was your last name?"

"Heaphy."

"What an Irish name. Yet you don't look particularly Irish."

I don't believe this genealogical inspection, thought Annie. She looked at Victoria who seemed to be still recovering from her own ordeal. Annie decided to shock Mrs. Locke in revenge. "I'm Swedish or Norwegian. I always forget which," she lied recklessly, and saw the shock pass briefly across Mrs. Locke's face. "That's where the blonde comes from," Annie went on. "And how come I'm so quiet even if I am Irish."

"You've lovely manners. You know, we had a Scandinavian girl for Victoria when she was small. I hope you don't mind me saying so," she tittered, "but I can never remember which one of those little countries she came from either." Annie watched the woman relax a bit, less on her guard now that she had placed Annie in a category.

"She was Swiss, mother."

"Nevertheless, I wonder whether some of this," she paused to find a word, "fascination you feel for Anne, might not be connected to that little blonde governess. A parent never knows what's right or wrong. Did you go to college?"

"To a local college. Then I went to the state school down here and dropped out."

"Why?"

"Money."

Mrs. Locke made a sympathetic face, but dropped the subject. It was too close to home. "Perhaps we should have coffee and dessert now," she suggested, leaving for the kitchen.

Mr. Locke straightened, apparently ready to take over as host. "Which school did you go to in Boston?"

"Boston College."

"That's a pretty good school," he approved. "What's your father do?" He smiled for the first time.

"He drives a truck," Annie offered humbly. She was too afraid of men to confront them. "In season mostly, for a construction firm."

Mr. Locke nodded again, trying to figure out how to make that information last. "Know the name of the company? Fellow I went to Yale with is in construction up there."

"I'm afraid not. It's a small company. Someone from the neighborhood owns it. He does some building himself."

"A contractor?"

"Could be. They grew up together."

"Not too close to your family, are you?"

"No, I've been away for awhile." Annie began to warm to Victoria's father. His manner was not as hard as Mrs. Locke's though he seemed to hide this in her presence. "I'm the first one to go to college. It makes me different from the rest of them. None of my cousins went. Except little Johnny who's considering the priesthood."

Mr. Locke brightened. "Have you visited St. Patrick's Cathedral?"

"No, sir. I hear it's beautiful."

"A classic. I love to go there and sit on a hot day. Seems like their God keeps the coolness in there for His worshippers. Lovely place. Say, it's Saturday night. They may keep the doors open late enough for you girls to see the place. I don't believe my daughter ever saw the inside of an American cathedral. Perhaps she'll take an interest now."

"My father's been trying to get me to visit St. Patrick's since I was a child," Victoria explained. "Religious architecture is a hobby of his."

"Want to go see it after coffee?" Annie hinted to Victoria.

"Wonderful idea," Victoria agreed, glad of the excuse to escape.

"What's a good idea?" Mrs. Locke wanted to know as she carried in the coffee.

"Going to church," Victoria laughed. Annie couldn't help but join in and Mr. Locke smiled again. When they had explained their plan to the humorless Mrs. Locke and she laughed briefly.

"You *will* take a cab?" she advised. "The element in this city at night would make your skin crawl."

Victoria, communicating to Annie in a smile their membership in the element her mother warned against, assured her they would take a cab. As the visit wound down with more silences and small talk, Annie wondered if she would ever have a discussion like this with her own parents. She couldn't imagine it or their reaction. Lesbianism would be so alien to their world Annie suspected they wouldn't be able to take in the information. Life was hard enough for them without visiting this upon them. Nor did Annie feel any need to tell them, although she understood that for Vicky it was a necessary part of her separation from her family.

Annie looked at the Lockes. They seemed more comfortable now that they were ignoring the issue. Finally, they rose and Annie went to Victoria's room for her hat. Everyone said goodnight at the parlor entrance. "We may go downtown for a drink after church, Mother," Victoria said as they left.

"Even *my* mother would be shocked at that combination," Annie laughed as they waited for the elevator.

"I couldn't help it, duckling. One parting blow. I was enjoying rubbing it in after the way they were questioning you. I hope you didn't mind too much?"

"Their behavior? I was angry, but I know they don't know any better and I certainly didn't want to mess things up for you by confronting them," Annie said as the elevator closed behind them. Wordlessly they embraced one another. Toward the first floor they let go and looked at each other as if they had been apart for years. As soon as they were out of sight of the night doorman they began to run, hand in hand, downtown, exhilarated by the freedom of the night air and release. They ran past doormen fanning themselves with their hats, old people strolling to catch the cooler breezes that were descending with darkness, singles walking their well-groomed, panting dogs. Like magic, they skipped over crosstown streets without traffic, running down and down toward the display of winking red and green traffic lights that lined the avenue. At the bottom of Central Park they stopped and leaned on one another to catch their breath. "Are we really going to St. Patrick's?" Annie asked.

"Would I disobey my father?"

"Only in bed," Annie teased. They walked on. At the corner of 59th and 5th, they kissed, Victoria unheeding of the night strollers who stared as they went past.

"Oh, Anne, Anne, will it always be this delicious?"

"No, but pretty often," Annie answered, her eyes slanting with silent laughter. "You're a lesbian now. That means, to me anyway, that we can be whatever else or however else we want to be—except maybe in good shape," she laughed, still tired out by their run.

"You know, the sweat is streaming down my sides and I don't mind? It feels good! I don't ever remember sweating like this. Only politely into my anti-perspirant."

"A little damp around the armpits?" Annie mocked, folding her hands in prayer. "We'll take care of that in a jiff. A special little prayer will do it, don't you know. Come with me to the little church on the corner and we'll pray for dry armpits. Pray to God!" she raised her voice like a preacher, "for dryness of the flesh and coolness of the passions. God," she whispered in Victoria's ear as they resumed walking, "will dry you up. Dry you up," she began to shout to Victoria's delight on another street corner, "and blow you away in a little puff of breeze. Dust to dust."

"Amen."

"Ah woman," Annie was back at Victoria's side gazing salaciously at her breasts. "I covet you, woman."

"My daddy wouldn't like that."

"Your daddy isn't here, little girl."

"Thank goodness."

"Oh, he isn't that bad," Annie said, slowing. "At least he tried to be pleasant. Unless he forgot to be unpleasant."

"I think the latter is more the case. Even though I'm not a son and therefore haven't broken the line, I'm still bringing disgrace onto the family's head. Especially if I write lesbian things.

He'll be humiliated."

"Good," Annie said, suddenly sounding bitter. "Let's humiliate them all. They've done it to us long enough."

"Wow. Where is all that anger coming from?"

"The last time I was humiliated by a man."

"My father?"

"No, he didn't have it together enough to humiliate me. Although I'm sure he could, given the chance. It was my landlord coming to collect the rent and reminding me that I have to leave his property when he wants me to. They're so arrogant about their territory. And everything is their territory. They won it all and only let us use it when it's to their advantage. Then we pay, one way or another. We've got to get something of our own."

"I never thought about it that much. They almost own us, don't they?" Victoria concluded quietly.

"Not us, not lesbians. We're probably the biggest threat there is against them. We don't need them for anything. We're free of them in our heads."

"But they pay us to work for them. And rent us apartments. My father's still supporting me. And as long as he does I owe him something. I see what you mean, Anne. It's great to feel free and run through the streets, but we don't really escape their power over us."

They stopped in front of St. Patrick's. "Look at that monstrosity," Annie snarled. "So huge and ugly. And all built to honor their mythological father. Look at the money they poured into that building. All for the purpose of worship, damn it, Vicky. Wasting all that space to mutter meaningless words under their breath and expect life to get easier or better for them because they're doing it."

At the top of the steps Annie hesitated. "I feel as though I'm stepping into their net going in here. I was brought up to believe this crap. I want to desecrate it. Look at the woman praying, Vicky. It makes me sick. They're praying to the male master for their husbands to stop beating them or for better places to live when it's the male landlords who are ripping them off, letting their homes rot rather than spare the money."

"Or praying that their sons survive the wars that men insist on waging," Victoria whispered. "You're right. It's ludicrous. Just think of people praying to end a war when it's the worship of that god that makes them feel righteous about killing. In *his* name. Remember the holy wars? Fighting over which way to worship their figurehead best?"

Along the side of the church they paused by the candles. "It's creepy in here, isn't it?" Annie asked. "Want to light a candle?"

"Yes. Let's light a candle for the speedy overthrow of men by women," Victoria giggled. "Wouldn't Rosemary be proud of our conversation?"

"And Peg," Annie agreed. A woman who stood with them said, "Shh," and moved on.

"She doesn't know any better, Anne," Victoria observed to calm Annie's anger.

"You're right. Come here." Annie took Victoria's arms roughly and kissed her hard. Victoria pushed her lips and hips back at Annie. They kissed with determination, not for the pleasure of it, but to make their point to themselves and the church. "Let's get the fuck out of here."

"Wait," Victoria said as she pulled her tie out of her pocket. She put it around her neck and stood tying it in the chapel defiantly. "*Now* let's leave."

They took a bus downtown and wandered, feeling depressed, but liberated, and somewhat among their own, on the Village streets. They decided to go to the bar where they had met, but found the bitter taste of the church's incense was stronger in their mouths at the thought of paying cover to the men who owned it. They stood outside, holding hands, feeling let down after their earlier exhilaration. Women came and went into the bar while Annie and Victoria looked at the buildings or at each other, desultorily finding things to say to each other. They were about to leave when a particularly rowdy group emerged drunkenly from the bar and moved off in a body. "Let's follow them," Annie suggested.

Victoria's eyes lit up. "Sounds great. Where do you think they're going?"

"Somewhere to have fun. If it's not private, we'll just blend with them." Conspiratorily, the two followed the crowd several blocks to the sound of music falling to the street from open windows. Figures lounged on the fire escape.

"Don't they look like dykes?" Annie asked, excited.

The sign on the building read "Firehouse." "I've heard of a firehouse," Victoria said. "I think Rosemary may have been here. I don't think it's a bar. More like a women's center."

"Sounds like a party to me," Annie said before preceding Victoria through a knot of women at the top of the stairs. "Who does it go to?" she asked the woman taking the cover money. "Tonight's a benefit for the women's center," she answered as Annie noted the difference between this slight, short-haired woman with a pleasant manner and the bouncer at the bar. Either she hadn't been out long, Annie thought, or there's a whole new breed of lesbian coming down the road.

Inside, Annie and Victoria walked around a makeshift dance floor and through clusters of lesbians who were shouting and clapping and talking intently. One woman was painting the naked torso of another while several more waited their turns. Marijuana smoke drifted through the huge room. They could see the fire escape across the room where several women still lounged. Victoria spotted a counter where beer was being sold. "Are you sure you don't want cider instead?" she yelled at Annie jokingly as they opened their cans and drifted again, looking for a space of their own.

"What a great atmosphere," Annie shouted, leaning against a pole to watch the dancers. "It's like New Haven. Look at the group dancing."

"Yes, I don't feel as though I'm in the big bad city at all. Or just a cab drive away from my parents."

"Look, there's Faye and Jean from Yale!" Annie said. They saw Victoria and Annie at the same time and drew them into their group. Soon they found themselves whirling around the room in separate dances of liberation. Annie wondered if they would ever feel this high again and worried lest their relationship was starting out too intense to sustain normal life. She resolved to renew their discussion of goals on the train tomorrow no matter how tired they were from tonight. They would certainly need a commitment beyond themselves to survive. She imagined, as she spun around the room, running a printing press with Victoria or opening a women's bar. She saw them playing together in a band, or giving lectures about lesbianism to straight women. None of it felt real, but as she caught Victoria's eye across the room she knew that there was something very real waiting for their combined energy. Their relationship would be a strength to sustain them, a haven from which they would go into the world, expose themselves to accomplish something, and to which they could return for nurturing and binding up of wounds. While they healed themselves they would find the strength that they would need to go out again and again until they began to make a mark upon the world, until all the women were strong and loud, until women began to be heard and felt as a power in the world to change it from the warring, hateful, hungry place that it was into, simply, a better place to be. Annie realized that she was getting drunk and stepped out of the dancing circle to stop from getting dizzy. For the first time in a long time, she did not want to be drunk. She wanted to be at her best, ready for anything.

Suddenly there were several uniformed men at the door and Annie felt herself go cold with fear. She looked for Victoria in the crowd of equally paralyzed women and began to make her way to her. Were they shooting? Would they arrest them? Were they here to beat and rape? These were the terrified thoughts that went through Annie's mind until she found Victoria. They took one another's hands and stared until it became clear that this was the fire department. "A complaint," was the skeptical murmur that went through the crowd. Someone had complained about something and they were here to investigate. The women without shirts had hurriedly put them on. "We can't even be naked among ourselves because of their damn law," Victoria whispered. The woman at the door would not let the firemen in without papers.

"I'm glad these women know what they're doing," Annie whispered. "How many of them are there?"

"There's more on the stairs," another woman whispered back, her eyes wide with fright.

"I think it's okay," Annie heard someone say, aloud. She saw the woman at the door nod affirmatively and the men begin to back away. The crowd stood still and silent. Annie could feel the women, like herself, fighting their own weakness and paralyzing fear. She could sense them all tensing and retreating, ready to spring or to fall back. She looked around for support and saw both strength and fear in the faces. Annie wondered, as the firemen left and the women drifted back to what they had been doing, which would have been the dominant force had the enemy shown their weapons and a belligerent intent. She hoped she would have had the strength to fight. And that Victoria would have joined her.

"Tense, huh?" she said to Victoria.

Victoria visibly relaxed. She took her glasses off and wiped sweat from around her eyes. "I didn't like that at all."

"Me neither. I've never been in a bar when one was raided."

"What time is it?"

"Late, my love, but I hate to go back."

"Me too, but I think we ought to. I'd like to go to the park in the morning to show you where I really grew up when I was in New York."

"I'd like that too. You're right. We have a lot more to do than just party," said Annie, remembering her resolve.

They said goodbye to Faye and Jean, then slipped through the women, through the bodies painted bright colors, through the hair long and cropped, through the touching, loud women, and made their way to the street. It was after midnight and cool. They walked toward the subway arm-in-arm looking up at the stars. The walls of the buildings seemed to meet over their heads. "It feels as if we're at the bottom of a well, tonight," Victoria said.

The music grew fainter behind them and for one whole block all they could hear was distantly passing cars. Two men went by arm-in-arm. The four smiled at one another. "Maybe we should live in New York," Annie suggested.

"Maybe we should live in Iowa," Victoria laughed softly.

"Do you have a preference?"

"I want to live with you."

Annie lifted her cap and spun it on her index finger. "I feel as if I've just been asked for my hand."

"Except I want your whole body," Victoria squeezed Annie closer to her.

"Do you really want to live with me?"

"I never want to be away from you." Victoria watched Annie lower her head. "What is it, Anne? Did I upset you? We don't have to. We could just be lovers," she said, afraid once again that she had scared Annie by wanting too much.

"I'm sorry Vic. Of course I want to live with you. I want nothing more than that. You just said it like Natalie did. And I got scared that we'd end up the same way."

"I can't predict," Victoria told Annie as they went down the subway steps. "But I promise you I'll never just take off. I'll work on staying together."

They had stopped outside the turnstile. "Will you? I'd feel much more hopeful if I felt like you were as committed to making us work as I am."

"Remember how you said when you're making love to me it sounds as if I'm opening the world for you?" Annie nodded. "Well, Anne, that's you. Over and over you open up the world for me. You unlocked it for me. I can walk into it and around in it now. I'm not just hiding inside anymore. Do you think I would ever throw away my key?" She gently tugged Annie's arm.

"Someday you won't need a key any more."

"But I'll always know you made it possible. And when I am as free and open and brave as you all the time, I hope that you'll still want to be all those things *with* me and not just a teacher for someone else. How can I know that you won't leave me when the excitement of watching me come out farther and farther wears off?"

Horrified, Annie shook her head until her hat almost fell off. "Then we'll have the excitement of accomplishing things together, Vicky, or of watching each other succeed at what we want to do. Of sharing our victories or just of being together. I want to be *old* with you, Vicky. I want to love the lines on your beautiful face and admire your grey hair. I want to have memories with you." There was a rumbling in the station. Victoria gestured toward the arriving train and handed Annie a token which she fished out of her jean pockets.

"No," she decided when Annie went to insert her token. She reached over and put her token into Annie's turnstile while Annie did the same for her. Their eyes met as they moved together slowly through the turnstiles each had unlocked for the other and they broke through at the end into a run which took them down the stairs together and into a car. The nearly empty train slid away from the station carrying two lesbians hugging just inside the door.

CHAPTER TEN

Annie and Victoria boarded the train the next night and sat, not touching, collapsed into themselves from the strain of visiting the Lockes. As they pulled out of Grand Central Station and rushed up past 125th Street and into the suburbs, they were nearly silent, beginning to recover. Annie giggled unexpectedly.

"What is it, Anne?" Victoria asked softly, laying a hand on Annie's thigh.

"Just remembering the ducks in the Children's Zoo at Central Park."

"How they waddle?"

Annie giggled again, "Yes, it tickled me somehow."

"I like the goats. They seem to have such sweet dispositions. Like you." Victoria kissed her cheek.

"Silly," Annie teased, ducking her kiss.

"Bar car at the rear of the train," a uniformed man sang through their car. Annie looked at Victoria. "Want a drink?" she asked.

"I'll join you if you do, but I have no desire for one."

Annie squirmed in her seat. "I guess I don't want one either. It's just habit. When somebody offers a drink I want it," she shrugged. Victoria smiled at her. "You know, I'd really rather not drink," Annie confessed. "It just seems to go with everything I do. It's an easy way to relax from the tension of hustling in the cab all day, an easy way to have fun in what isn't such a fun place: a gay bar; and an easy way to loosen up enough to socialize with people like your parents or new lesbians."

"As you said, it's habit," Victoria agreed, cleaning her glasses with the tail of Annie's shirt.

"I think of drinking when I think of the high points of my

227

life. I drink to celebrate, to party, to make love."

"My parents do the same thing."

"That's a kick in the teeth. I really have something in common with your parents?"

Victoria laughed warmly and ran her fingertips through Annie's hair. "Just what you share in a bottle."

"I'll try not having a drink now and see what happens. After all, we'll be in New Haven in an hour. If I need a fix I can get one then. Are you coming home with me?"

"Let's see how we feel in town. I have to get ready for graduation, you know. It'll be here in just a couple of days."

"You're not going to do anything productive tonight, though," Annie suggested temptingly, leaning to lay her lips on Victoria's bare arm.

"I'm certainly not if you're going to be in that kind of mood."

"What other kind is there around your lovely body?"

They held hands, each losing herself in her own thoughts. Soon, Victoria noticed Annie's hand become slack. Her head had rolled toward Victoria's shoulder and Victoria settled it there, kissing her blonde hair after she removed the hat. She fingered the brim in her lap, loving it and loving Annie Heaphy, so trustingly asleep on her shoulder.

When Victoria had time to think, which did not seem to be often anymore, she was overwhelmed by two things. One was her enormous love for Annie where there had been no amount of love for anyone before. Included with that were the sexual feelings she now found in herself. The excitement Annie had unleashed in her had become a need. When she thought of Annie's mouth between her legs or even of touching Annie's breasts through a flannel shirt, she felt warm and sensual and had to close her eyes to handle the flood of feeling in herself. Her underwear was always damp. Annie teased her about it. About having grown so passionate that even when Annie wasn't around, Victoria could keep herself turned on with thoughts of them together. Victoria admitted it gladly to Annie, but wondered what would ever happen should she lose her. Could she feel this way about another woman? Would she always feel this way about Annie and forever be unsatisfied without her?

Victoria remembered Annie's head on her shoulder when Annie stirred. No need to worry about losing her. She wouldn't let it happen. They would learn how to give each other what they could and how to let each other meet their other needs elsewhere.

Smiling into the deep darkness outside the window, Victoria thought of the other thing by which she was overwhelmed: herself. How quickly she had blossomed, not just into love, but into a fuller person. It was as if, in responding to Annie's kisses, she learned to respond to the rest of the world around her. As if, in learning what mattered to her, what was meaningful to her in love, the rest of the world had finally been revealed to her in a way that made sense. All the pieces of the puzzle had fallen into place when she opened herself to another woman. The academic world which had consumed almost all of her, while still important, was receding a bit and she saw it in a new perspective. She would use it, use her background, training and literacy for herself. Rather than be buried by it, she would use it to stand on when she learned what her next step would be. Perhaps the best thing for her to do would be to go on, to teach literature from a female perspective or to study women's literature. Perhaps it would be more important for her to write clearly about what was happening to women and to show women themselves where they were going. Or she could go on a search for women's poetry and put it in a volume to inspire other women with their own achievements. There was no end to her options and she continued, as she thought of new ones, to smile into the window.

Outside it had become totally dark. All she had been able to see for awhile were lampposts, highway lights and occasional partially lit towns. Connecticut closed early on a Saturday night. The window was double glass and Victoria could see her own faint blurred reflection in it. There were two of her, one inside the other, the edge of neither self sharp and clear. Her image disappeared now and then as the outside lights became brighter. It was this ghostly reflection that made her think of Louise, the witch-like woman on the train at Thanksgiving. It seemed as if Louise had started it all. Victoria saw Louise's now lesbian daughter in the window—or was it her own lesbian self?

The images of her past and her future selves, the witch's daughter, merged, but were not yet one. For a long while there was only darkness outside and Victoria stared at this glowing woman in the glass, wondering and wondering what would happen to her. She was a trick of the light thrown on darkness, an impression of the deep unknown dark of her future. She could almost see the image speak to her, to herself, or to her other. She let herself imagine what she was saying. The sound in her head merged with the noise of the train, a long rushing sound. Victoria had to slow it to make any words distinct. Then, rather than actually hearing them, she seemed to feel them as, with eyes closed, she experienced their message.

Victoria was a small round being, almost fetal, being shot into space. She floated, allowing herself the weightlessness of imagination. Soon she tired of floating, though, and wanted a way to attach herself somewhere. Arms detached from her round form, stretched to objects hurtling by. She winced at the pain she felt at attachment, before her body accustomed itself to the greater speed. Then she was straddling the amorphous object, entering it, walking in it, part of it. It felt familiar enough to her to be her own self, then became her own form. She began to turn, to look for a direction, and felt the ecstasy of choice, the confused excitement of options. She felt drawn to one path and walked it, her vision suddenly disintegrating into Dorothy on the yellow brick road. When she opened her eyes she was laughing quietly, amused by the last image, still full of the empowering feelings of the earlier ones. There she was again in the window. A woman crazed with happiness, inside another woman smiling back at her, beside another woman whose yellow head rose next to her own and smiled too.

"What are you laughing about?" Annie asked sleepily.

"It just came out."

"Did I say something funny in my sleep?"

"Not that I heard. I might have been a little asleep myself."

Annie sat all the way up. "Oh—I didn't mean to nod off. We were going to talk about our futures. But what a dream I had," she said, beginning to remember it. "Wow."

"Tell me," Victoria said, leaning back, interested. Perhaps

their dreams were connected.

Annie yawned and shook her head, taking back her hat. "Everyone was there. In my house. You and me, our families. Peg and Turkey, Eleanor and Dusty, Rosemary and Claudia, all our other friends and women I haven't seen for years. Even Natalie was there." Victoria felt a pang of jealousy. "It seems to me they were there for a party. Funny, I never gave a party there. But there was all this noise and a lot of lights, a roar which could have been the water and could have been the train I guess. But in the dream it was a combination of the ocean and foghorns and the noise of all these people having a good time.

"You and I are standing outside, holding hands, proud of the party we made because everyone was happy. As we stand there the wind gets stronger and I watch your hair flying around your face. But we're too happy to go inside, just want to stand there and enjoy what we've done. We were so awfully happy that we'd made all of them so happy. And that we were so content with each other. That happiness and the feeling of giving something to all those people was so much a part of our love. It seemed to make us love each other more as well as love all of them more. We felt like we were on top of the world."

Annie took Victoria's hand and squeezed it progressively tighter as she talked. "But the wind was getting really strong. Without talking to each other we somehow agreed that we should go back to the house and blow out the candles and shut some windows or the party would turn to chaos with everything blowing around." Annie was quiet for a moment, shaking her head again in concern. Victoria felt anxious about the outcome of the dream. The train, hurtling through the darkness toward their future, seemed suddenly fragile and vulnerable. Anything could happen: a trainwreck, some crazy hijacker, a gang of toughs with guns. They were so unprotected in the world.

Annie went on, finally. "We tried to make it back to the house. We're walking against the wind, really struggling against it to walk even a step forward. Your hair is everywhere. My hat blows off. I start to go back for it, but you stop me, afraid I'll be blown right into the water. You tell me it's more important to get to our friends before they're hurt. We made so little progress." Annie seemed too moved to speak for a moment, then continued. "The wind got so strong we could barely hold our ground, much less go on. The foghorns sounded over and over as if in warning. Then the tide came up in a great swirling wave off to our right. It curled around us and swept over the house, as if it was really the toothpick house you call it. All the toothpicks and all the people were carried away by it. The noise of the party was now screams. And you and I just stood there, rooted to the ground, watching, listening to the foghorns' mourning wail. It was awful.

"Then, from behind us, comes this other wave. I know we are doomed and I turn to say goodbye to you, but you just smile and take both my hands in yours. When the wave comes we hold tight to each other and I realize that the others had not been screaming, but shouting with joy. This wave was not destructive, but a transporter, taking us somewhere we wanted and needed to go. We were so pleased. You seemed then to have known it all the time. We went with the flow of the water and swirled in it, facing each other, spinning, still holding hands, like we did after that first time we made love. We went around and around and I felt an incredible transcendent joy like nothing I've ever experienced before. Like an orgasm, only an emotional orgasm that just opened my mind. I felt like everything could come in and all that went out would be calm, peaceful and good. You were still smiling and not talking. See, if I look at you now," Annie said, turning to Victoria, "you'll look the same way."

They gazed at each other for a long time. "Where did we land?" Victoria finally asked.

"I don't remember. I think I dreamed it, too, but I don't remember where it was. Damn," Annie said, annoyed. "But the important thing is what I felt. And how you felt too. What do you think it all means?"

"I don't know much about dreams. Maybe Claudia would be able to explain it. I think it was at least partially sexual, but sexual in a way that has to do with overall fulfillment. You felt very good about what was going on in your life. I'm happy about the dream whatever it meant."

"Why?"

"Because I was with you when you were so happy."

Annie leaned over to kiss Victoria. "Won't you come home with me tonight and we'll see what kind of wave we can create ourselves?" she whispered.

"How can I resist?" Victoria replied, kissing Annie again and slipping one hand between her legs.

"Station stop New Haven," the conductor bawled in the aisle. Victoria moved away from Annie, but they allowed their eyes to remain connected. As if words would say no more, they stayed like that until the train stopped, then rose as one to go home.

∿ ∿ ∿ ∿ ∿

Graduation was over. Victoria's parents took her to dinner and left immediately for New York. After a quick call to Annie, who'd left the ceremony to wait for her at Peg and Turkey's apartment, Victoria changed and rushed downstairs. Annie pulled up as she reached the street and they sped off to the bar.

Victoria and Annie walked into Marcy's and saw Turkey before them resplendent in a white tuxedo. She hoisted a mug of beer in the air and everyone in the bar began to sing. *For She's a Jolly Good Woman.* Victoria pretended to leave in embarrassment before she turned back, blushing, and let Annie lead her to the several tables where their friends had assembled. Congratulations descended on Victoria from everywhere. A few moments later Rosemary entered with Claudia bouncing by her side. Turkey climbed on a chair to get the bar's attention and they sang again. Marcy kissed all three of them with her glossy lipstick. "This is the first time we graduated Yalies in here!" she boasted. Rudy scurried to kiss them all.

"This is a great improvement over celebrating with my parents," Victoria exclaimed, turning to Rosemary. She gasped. "You cut your hair off!" Rosemary beamed proudly.

"Isn't it great?" asked Claudia.

"My goodness. It does alter you." Rosemary pulled her glasses off and modeled the cut which had been simply a cropping of the braid so that her brown hair fell lankly to her neck instead of her hips. The front was parted in the middle as it had always been. Most significant was the way it seemed to alter

Rosemary's stance and face. Her features were not pulled back by tight braiding. Her chin seemed to have risen upward on its own rather than be thrust forward. Her shirt did not so much fall down her thin body as sit loosely on it, emphasizing her squared shoulders. She stood tall and, putting her glasses back on, seemed to have become more self-assured than belligerent. Everyone was staring at her.

Turkey called for drinks for all of them and held one of Rosemary's arms up when they came. "To the true graduate. Welcome to the gay world," she shouted with a sweep of her white top hat. "Now I'm gonna present the first annual Marcy's Awards!" The group cheered her. As the drinks arrived, she motioned for them to be brought to her and arranged them neatly, by size places, on the table in front of her. She looked up, waving a small crumpled napkin in front of her.

"Our first is called the Avis award. It's for the woman-in-love who tried hardest to get her girl!" Her friends were quiet while Turkey ripped the napkin as if she were opening an envelope. "I could have called *this* one," she winked. "And the winner is, Elly!"

They all cheered and laughed, while Eleanor, enjoying the attention, threw her arms around Dusty and then proudly presented herself to Turkey who handed her a drink. "This ain't my drink!" Eleanor protested.

"Shut up and take it, kid. This is a once in a lifetime honor!"

The group laughed, then quieted for the next prize. "This one," Turkey announced, holding up what was left of the napkin, "is for Most Promising Intellectual! We call it that because the winner has to promise to stop being an intellectual and come down to earth!"

They were all looking at Rosemary and Victoria who were in turn looking down at the floor. "The winner," and Turkey ripped the napkin in half again, "is Rosie-baby!" Claudia had to push the embarrassed Rosemary toward Turkey.

"Speech! Speech!" cried Peg.

Rosemary couldn't pass up such a chance. She held up her drink as if it actually was a trophy. "I was brought up by intellectuals, to be an intellectual, so I don't know how easily I can change.... But I *can* promise you that as a dyke, I'm not going to be like any intellectual you ever saw before!" Victoria led the applause for Rosemary's speech.

Turkey raised her arms for silence. She took off her hat and pressed it to her heart. Her face grew serious. "Now for the highest honor Marcy's bar can bestow. It's our Escape Award, for the Greatest Escape of the year." She paused to build suspense and replace her hat. "This year's award," she went on in a voice quivering with emotion, "goes to the kid who escaped the worst prison of all: the prison of a cowardly heart." She wiped an imaginary tear with her napkin. "This woman has stopped running from what scared her, has stopped playing the fickle Casanova, has found the lady of her dreams and given her heart away. This woman . . . ," and Turkey lifted the last shred of napkin in the air, tore its corner the best she could, and announced, "is our own improper Bostonian, our beach-squatter, our reformed drunk and beloved: Annie Heaphy!"

Annie was bright red and shoved her hat practically to her nose, but the group pushed her forward. Turkey handed her a drink, shook her hand and raised their arms, saying, "The champ!" Annie, half smiling, hurried back to Victoria's side, began to drink, but remembered what Turkey had said about her and set it down. Victoria hugged her.

"The rest of these here awards go to the losers!" Turkey yelled, grabbing one for herself.

"To the losers!" Peg toasted and they all, except Annie, joined her as she drank.

Someone played the juke box then and the group moved to the dance floor.

Eleanor grabbed Annie and led her to the floor. Annie looked around and found Dusty, big and awkward, dancing with the newly shorn Rosemary. Claudia looked dreamily toward Annie as she danced in Peg's arms. Victoria was with Turkey, allowing her once dignified self to play at dancing a minuet. "What a night, huh, Annie?" Eleanor called her attention back to herself.

"We won't forget it for a long time," Annie smiled. "How are you doing, Elly?"

"Dusty and me are about to get married," Eleanor

whispered proudly.

"Married! Why?" Annie asked, realizing too late that she was criticizing her old friend. "I'm glad for you. I hope you're going to be really happy. When are you going to do it?"

"As soon as she leaves the woman she's still living with."

"You mean she's been seeing you while she's been living with someone else?"

"Yeah. That's where she used to disappear to. But she really loves *me*. And that woman is a bitch."

"Does the other woman know what's going on?" Annie asked, unable to stop from feeling horrified that Eleanor would participate in treachery like this.

"Yes and no. She knows something is up, but they haven't had it out." Eleanor frowned, hurt. "You've gone all moral on me now with your new friends."

"I'm sorry," Annie said as the music stopped. She was disturbed and sad and felt a need, which she held in check, to get back to her drink. "I'm so involved now in seeing how women are getting hurt every minute of the day: financially, physically, in every possible way by men, that I hate to see women hurt each other. But I shouldn't put you down."

"She is a real bitch."

"Did Dusty always think that way?"

"Of course not, but the dame has changed. They used to have a good time. In the last three years she doesn't even want to go out."

"The last three years! How long have they been together?"

"Seventeen years."

Annie felt Eleanor's answer like a blow in the pit of her stomach. Was there no safety in life? Would she leave Vicky after seventeen years? Annie pledged never to let herself drift so far from Victoria that their separation could sneak up on them like this poor woman's would. "Do the others know yet?"

"We're going to announce it after tonight. The wedding will be in about a month. Will you stand up for me?"

"Do I get to kiss the bride?" Annie teased, running her hand across Eleanor's cheek.

Eleanor smiled tenderly at her friend. "If I'm still alive.

Dusty's going to tell *her* when she gets home tonight. I'll wait in the car in case there's any trouble."

"If there is, Elly, and you need help, please call."

"Okay, Annie, thanks. I appreciate that. And don't worry about me. Dusty will never do that to me. I'll never give her cause to."

"I hope not, El. And I hope I'm not capable of it either. I guess that's what affects me so much, knowing how careless I used to be of other women's feelings."

"I know," Eleanor said significantly.

Annie looked properly ashamed. "Hey," she reminded Eleanor, "we never stopped being friends."

"What are you two looking so serious about?" Turkey asked, pushing them back toward the group.

"I just wanted you to be the first to know," Eleanor whispered before she rejoined Dusty with a passionate kiss.

"What did she want you to know first?" Victoria asked Annie, slipping an arm under hers.

"Don't ask. It's too sad." But Victoria was concerned and Annie told her about Dusty and Eleanor and how upset it made her.

"Anne, Anne, it's not us," Victoria comforted her. "I'll never leave you." She stepped closer to Annie and held her tightly. When a slow dance began they moved slightly to it.

"I tried to tell Elly about women hurting each other. Like we've got better things to do with our energy."

"But we can't always control the circumstances," Victoria said.

"I know that, Vicky, but that's a man's game, using women and abandoning them, whatever petty rationalizations you give."

"Do you think if Dusty and Eleanor had been in the women's movement they would have decided differently?"

"I don't know. Maybe there's a good reason. But at least the 'other woman' would know what was happening to her. That's enough of that, though," Annie said abruptly. "This is your night and I'm not going to upset you anymore. I hope we'll always know what we want from each other, even if we can't figure out what we want to do with our lives."

Victoria nodded. "Let's talk to everyone now and get their ideas about plans for the future."

"I brought the list of ideas we wrote," Annie said, searching her pockets. "Want to share that?"

"It can't hurt, my handsome prince."

"I couldn't help but overhear that," said Rosemary, disengaging herself from a conversation with Faye as Annie and Victoria sat beside them. "I'm thinking of doing a paper called, *Patriarchy in Our Language: Calling Each Other Names*. We really don't have good female endearments. What should we call a woman who is princelike?"

"I see you've started drinking," Victoria teased her wordy friend.

"No, I'm drinking club soda. I'm not all that impressed with alcohol. I don't want to get my highs confused and I'm very high on life right now. And I'm very serious about our endearments."

"That sounds like a paper I'd do," Victoria said.

"I got the impression you didn't want to do any more papers."

Victoria looked at Annie. "That's something we want to talk about."

"What do you want to talk about?" Turkey asked, reappearing to put her arms around Rosemary and kiss her loudly on the cheek. "Your hair is really neat, Rosie," she said. "Unlike mine, which has never known a neat day in its life." She stopped to think. "No, I take it back. Once I stole my dad's Vitalis and tried it out on my hair." She ran her hand down its sloped back. "It didn't help much," she admitted sheepishly. "It just sort of dripped smelly, greasy stuff and took a week to go away." They joined her infectious laughter.

"We want to talk about our future, Turk. What do you want to be when you grow up?"

"Skinny," Turkey laughed again.

"Come on, you Turkey, get serious," Eleanor prodded her with a fist as she sat down. "*I've* decided I want my own little place where I can be the cook and the boss. Let somebody else waitress," she said, leaning back onto Dusty's broad shoulder.

"Okay guys," Turkey gave in, "you want it straight? I'm getting my doctorate in sociology and teach in a big name school. I'll be a famous sociologist. Never mind the liberation. I'll *prove* a woman can make it in the academic world."

"Who ever heard of a sociologist getting famous?" Peg scoffed.

"You are about to, dear gym teacher. What is your claim to fame?"

Peg leaned against the side of a booth, hands in her pockets, legs crossed in loose cream-colored slacks. "Don't know as I'd want to *be* famous, Turkey. It might cramp my style. I'll settle for teaching gym. I don't like being on the front lines or being in trouble."

"When I was a kid, I always wanted to be a railroad engineer," Dusty volunteered unexpectedly. "You libbers going to do anything about getting women into the railroad?"

There was a short silence which Peg gracefully broke. "The women's movement ought to make a dent in just about every profession that's out there. What do you do now?"

Still sober-faced, Dusty answered. "Run a machine. Let me tell you, it makes as much noise as an engine. I know how to set up and everything. Course, they won't pay me for set-up because they got a man they already pay for it, but I do my own anyway. I enjoy it." The shadow of a smile crossed her face.

"It's a real hard job," Eleanor added proudly.

"I wouldn't mind doing hard work like that," Annie said earnestly. "But I want what I do to have some meaning for women."

"It does, damn it," Dusty defended herself.

Annie jumped. "I'm sorry."

"You let me talk to some of those liberationists. *I'll* tell them what a woman can really do. One of the girls I work with, she raised six kids by herself, works second shift at the plant, then cooks all night in a little joint."

"That's who's going to teach me to cook," Eleanor added, combing her hair.

Rosemary broke in. "That's great, women teaching other women their skills."

"Makes me feel useless, not having a skill," Annie said.

"You're a good cab driver," Victoria reminded her.

"But what good does it do anybody beyond getting them from one place to the next?"

"What she's really trying to say," Victoria explained, "is that we've got to make some decisions. And we need your help. I'm supposed to go on at Yale, but I'm not at all sure I want to do that. I used to think of graduate school and teaching as the perfect place for me: sheltered and totally unreal. But I don't need that anymore."

"And I've got to get out of my shack by the end of the month. When I left tonight there were paint cans and ladders lined up outside my porch like an invading army. We don't even know whether to look for a new place around here or go off to California," Annie added.

"California!" Claudia approved. "I've always wanted to live there. It's supposed to be so easy-going."

"But we're not surfers or student revolutionaries. And we don't necessarily want to settle where it's easier," Annie said. "Maybe we should go to Alaska where we could practically import feminism and certainly could build a women's community from scratch."

"Can you organize?" Turkey asked, serious for once. "You're not loudmouths like me. You're kind of quiet, booky people. And Annie, look how you fall apart when you get shit on in the street. Organizers have to take that all the time. You might not be able to do anything but hold yourselves together. And Victoria, it's taken you so long to be with people in the first place, I wonder if you're ready to take that kind of life at all."

"But remember," Claudia argued, "women have to realize their potential. It's been buried for so long under our quietness. Annie's and Victoria's weaknesses may just be hiding their strengths. You know," she went on, her firm, round body leaning intently forward, "they might have been so outgoing when they were kids that they learned to cover it up because it wasn't ladylike and that's why they're quiet now."

"You've got me more confused than ever," Annie said, presenting a battered piece of paper. "Here's a list we thought up. See what you think of these ideas."

After a pause Eleanor exclaimed, "I like this one: 'Starting a fleet of volunteer cabs for senior citizens and women.' Think how that would cut down on rapes and muggings."

"Where would you get the money?" Peg asked.

Clucking in disgust, Turkey said, "Such a realist!"

"You might get a bus," the serious Dusty volunteered. "And run it around town certain times of the day so's old people could get rides free and know you'd be there." She blushed up to her slicked-back hair.

"That would be a lot cheaper," Annie agreed. She looked toward Victoria, eyebrows raised.

"What about some of the other ideas?" Victoria pursued.

Eleanor read slowly. "Start a magazine, it says, for articles about the women's movement. Discussions of politics and practical matters like how to contribute to the movement. Hey, it's too bad somebody didn't already write that. It'd be a big help for you all. But I've got another idea. Let's start a restaurant, all of us. I'll still be the cook. You guys can hire Turkey to entertain, Dusty to build things, one of you can keep the books, and somebody else will do the dishes."

"You may have hit on something there, Eleanor," Rosemary said. She smiled at Annie who was looking skeptically toward her. "When so many people get involved in a project we should start talking about doing it collectively."

"What's that? Like communism?" Eleanor asked.

"It's a distant relation. It would mean that we would all put ourselves into this equally and we'd all learn to do everything so that we could share the responsibilities."

"You mean I'd have to waitress?" Eleanor asked, disappointed.

"I mean we'd have to think so hard and so differently," Rosemary said slowly, obviously beginning to do what she was describing, "that we would have to rethink the very structure of a restaurant." The group was silent, waiting for her idea to grow. "We could do away with waitresses. Some sort of personalized cafeteria. With no men allowed."

"Sounds great to me!" said Eleanor. "No more . . ."

"Ouch!" Turkey yelled, jumping from Eleanor's pinch.

"Just demonstrating," Eleanor explained as she smiled graciously into Turkey's smile.

"But the point is well taken," Rosemary continued. "No more waiting on men! No more serving anybody in that sense."

"I like the magazine idea," Victoria said, "but I'd have no idea how to do it."

Claudia had the list. "I still like the idea of travelling. Maybe you ought to just take off and *see* if something's happening in Alaska and watch what they're doing in California. And bring it all back here when you decide what to do."

"I love it!" Rosemary interrupted. "Listen to this! Buy a boat and run a fishing business. You'd be poor and smell bad, but I bet being on the water all the time would toughen you up! Imagine facing the sea alone every day and then coming ashore and some mere male trying to intimidate you."

"I'd beat the shit out of him," Dusty threatened.

"I think that's the least practical suggestion yet," Peg said decisively.

"Then maybe it's the one most worth looking toward, you old spoil sport. Just because you're all settled in your niche don't mean everybody is. *You* suggest something," Turkey urged.

"I'm thinking on it. I admit I like having a job I can always fall back on. I have great hours. The job changes with the kids. I'm active. It suits me fine. But I knew what I wanted to do since I was a kid," she said, adjusting the crease in her slacks. "I think you two know what you want, but you haven't seen it in yourselves yet. Maybe Claudia's idea is good about taking time to look for what you want."

"Ooh. I want to go too," Claudia said, excited. Rosemary looked stricken. "Not without you, Rosie."

"I've travelled so much," Victoria said. "I never got to stay in one place long enough to make friends. To feel secure. I don't know if I could handle a nomadic life."

Annie asked, "Do we have to travel to discover what we want? Like Peg says, I feel it in me. The answer's just not ready to come out." Annie slipped an arm around Victoria's waist and a hand under the waistband.

"So when do you have to decide by, lovebirds?"

"Two weeks," Annie answered. "That's when I have to be out."

"You living there in the meantime, Vic?" Peg asked.

"I'm moving in tomorrow."

Turkey stood. "Step right up and sign up for the moving party. I hear there's going to be plenty of free beer and eats for everybody that helps Vicky move in!"

"Hey, you," protested Annie, laughing as she tugged Turkey down into her seat.

"We do need help," Victoria interceded.

"Then come on and help. We'll all go swimming afterwards," Annie gave in. "Bring your bathing suits!"

"And innertubes!" Turkey added.

"Party, party," Claudia sang, a little tipsy on one beer. She knocked her chair over getting up to lead Rosemary to the dance floor.

Suddenly Dusty and Eleanor were alone at the table with Victoria and Annie. "So you all think you're going to travel?" Eleanor asked.

Annie looked into Victoria's sparkling eyes. "Now that I've found the woman I was looking for, there isn't much reason to travel, if you ask me."

"And we'd miss our friends," Victoria said. "We haven't even had a chance to get to know Dusty. Would you still be around when we got back?"

"Yes," said Dusty shyly, looking at Eleanor. "If she still wants me."

"And why wouldn't I, you old butch?"

"Because I'm so old. And you're such a Southern belle."

"You can still back out, honey," Eleanor told her, moving her hand along Dusty's upper arm. Dusty was silent. Annie looked at Victoria.

"I think I'm doing right," Dusty finally said, slowly and thoughtfully. "I haven't been happy for a lot of years and I thought I ought to stay for her sake. I like my job, the house. Who can have everything? But she's been seeing this man for a couple of years now—did El here tell you that? I told her not to say nothing, but it's almost over now. I don't want to hurt her, but I feel so bad when she goes with him. If I truly loved her then I think I could put up with anything. But she just took me in when I was drinking a lot and I've been beholden to her all these years, but I never felt about her like I thought I ought to. You can't really know with your first woman unless you're lucky, I guess."

"She was your first lover?"

Dusty hung her head at Victoria's question. "I know I come on like an old bulldyke, but I wasn't really nothing till I met her. I mean, I didn't know who I was. And now I do. But it's not fair for her to go away to a man and expect me to be waiting is it? Elly, here, treats me with respect. I know I'm doing right. I think she just likes to take care of people and I don't need her like that no more and he does. No, El. I won't back out on you. We'll make a better life. Maybe I can help other little dykes find their way better than I did. What do you think?"

"I think I want to dance with you. So's I can hold you, you old bear."

Annie Heaphy and Victoria looked after the couple with tears in their eyes. "Wow," said Annie.

"This is really hard for her."

"I should've known Elly wouldn't be all that rotten. I wonder why she didn't tell me the whole story?"

"To protect Dusty, silly."

They looked at each other in silence. "You're not Dusty, Anne."

"We won't break up after seventeen years, will we Vicky?"

"Remember," Victoria said after a short silence, "when we promised not to give up without a fight?"

"Yes."

"Let's not forget that."

"Okay. You're right. I'm leaving it all in the hands of the gods, or goddesses. I'll take some responsibility too."

"You'd better," Victoria said playfully. "*And* be responsible for taking me home."

"So soon?"

"Soon? It's after midnight."

"You're right. After all, we've got to make love on your graduation day. Your place or mine?" Annie asked for the last time, running her hands over Victoria's hair.

"My room is all packed. Let's officially move into your house."

As they crossed the dance floor to say goodnight, their friends came toward them dancing until the moving mass was all together. Rosemary took the hands of the women around her and soon Annie and Victoria were pulled into a circle dance. "Marcy's will never be the same!" shouted Turkey. The other bar regulars fell back to watch this phenomenon. Even Dusty was coaxed into the circle by Eleanor. When the music ended the group pressed together in a giant hug, parting, finally, to let Annie and Victoria go home.

∿ ∿ ∿ ∿ ∿

Nearly summer, Annie Heaphy's toothpick house bloomed. It was June, and the porch furniture was newly dry after the spring rains. The porch itself still sagged, doorless, but the bushes before it thrust themselves up its sides, camouflaging some of its scars and festooning it with themselves. Even the bare front yard sported a few whiskers of green—crabgrass mostly, and a sparse growth of assertive weeds.

Annie and Victoria sat on the porch. They had thrown the workmen's materials behind the house out of sight. The moving party had been the day before and they had slept almost until noon afterwards. The rest of the day they spent putting the house in order without making their arrangements too perma-nent. They were waiting for Rosemary and Claudia who had called that morning to say they wanted to talk. It was not as hot as it had been, but the porch was still cooler than the house.

"It's a good thing we moved you yesterday," Annie said.

"The heat?"

"It's nice after winter, but enough is enough."

"It would have helped the beach party."

Annie grunted. "We could have done without that. Those women sure do like to drink. I can't believe I ever kept up with them."

"It's mostly Turkey and Ellie and Dusty and a few others. Peg drinks slowly, I noticed. But she hides it, like she doesn't want anyone to know she's not keeping up."

"Saving face."

"Why is it so important to them to be hard drinkers?"

Annie was quiet for a minute. "I've been thinking more about that and I think I can tell you why it was important to me. First off, there's the macho element. Downing a big hearty beer with gusto makes an image I liked. Made me feel strong. And the higher I got, the more invincible I felt. I was no longer the hard-working cab driver saying yes ma'am and no ma'am and thank you sir, but me, among my own kind, with the advantage of being super-me."

"So the bar was a kind of refuge for you. A place where you could let down your hair—or take off your hat," Victoria giggled, "and be yourself while other people approved of who you were."

"Yes. And the liquor made it possible for me to shut out the world I'd just come from and knew I had to return to. It was like drawing a curtain, only the curtain was made of liquid."

"Like the liquid out there." Victoria pointed to Long Island Sound lying almost still in the windless evening. "Doesn't it make you wish you could lie on it?"

"Only if we had every last stitch of our clothes off and could make love on it," Annie said, sliding her chair closer to Victoria's. She put her lips to Victoria's hand and kissed each finger, then turned the hand over and traced a spiral with her tongue on the palm. Victoria squirmed in her tattered white wicker chair.

"The things you make me feel in broad daylight, Anne Heaphy," Victoria chided.

"You enjoy every minute of it, girl."

"You're right. Now tell me why else you had to be such a hard drinker."

"That was it, mostly," Annie sighed. "You went to the bar because you needed to be there and then you learned this whole way of life that went with it. Hard drinking is part of it. For me, too, once I got high, I'd do anything to stay high. I was scared to come down. If I could have sustained it, I would've drank twenty-four hours a day."

"Yet you've stopped so quickly and easily."

"I get the yen now and then, like at the party yesterday. But when I get it, I've been trying to figure out what it really is that I want. Confidence? Relaxation? Strength? A good time? Then usually I can figure out another way of getting what I want. Besides, I've spent very little time in bars since we met and if I don't get high on liquor in the first place I don't have to sustain the high."

Victoria smiled. "You mean I've been good for you?"

"You know you have," Annie smiled back.

"What's going to happen to the women who are still going to the bars?"

"If they're lucky they'll meet their Victorias."

"That's not everyone's solution, silly. Look at Eleanor and Dusty. They'll go to the bar together."

"You're probably right. I'm so glad Dusty's friend took it well."

"She was probably frightened half to death about having to tell Dusty she wanted out."

"Too bad it was for a man," Annie sighed, making a distasteful face.

"The woman just couldn't deal with being a lesbian, Anne. I understand that. I'll bet she started going out with him to make herself feel normal."

"But all those years with Dusty. Especially someone as butchy-looking as Dusty."

"You heard what Dusty said about how they never went out and didn't have any friends. If you hide well enough, you can pretend you're like everyone else. As long as she could keep Dusty home with her she felt safe. But when Dusty got itchy, met those lesbians at work and realized she'd been wanting to be with other lesbians, then it didn't work any more. Dusty brought reality home to her."

"Damn shame," Annie said. "Don't you wish we could somehow reach out to women like that? Like you were before Rosie and Claudia told you about themselves and you met me? Like I was before Natalie? Dusty said the other night she'd like to help the little dykes. Educate them, so they wouldn't be afraid to come out or to stay out."

"I can't think of a greater life work."

"Or one where you could earn less money," Annie laughed. "I'm going to make a cup of tea. Want some?"

"You've been reading my mind."

Annie went inside and admired the way Victoria's possessions fit into her living room. The items that had made Victoria seem so inaccessible before—the candles and wall hangings—added class to her home. She was beginning to understand Victoria's attachment to them and to feel their pull herself. There was something deep and mysterious about the light of her colored candles. And the pattern of her mandala poster. They stirred something very deep in Annie. Something that lived in the same place that got stirred by Victoria. That woman reached inside her and shook up her core. They had some profound and wordless tie, Annie thought. Almost as if they'd known each other for centuries and been wandering the earth searching for each other again. Often they did read one another's minds.

If they could just know their own minds about the future they could really make something powerful of themselves. Annie straightened her sturdy body and moved to the window where one day, months ago, she'd seen the mourning dove. How lonely she'd been then. And now? Maybe she, Annie, wasn't listening hard enough to what Victoria was really saying. She tried to tune in more clearly to her mind as she took teabags from the cabinet. Victoria had brought her favorite mug from the dormitory and now their two mugs sat side by side on a counter. It gave Annie a little thrill when she saw them.

"They are officially late," Victoria said as Annie rejoined her.

"That's okay. I feel like I can wait forever if I've got you by my side." They held hands across their chairs. Very few cars went by the beach at dinner hour and they felt isolated from the whole world.

"Were they borrowing a car to get here?" Annie asked.

"I don't know, why?"

"Because that looks like them in that red car about to pull into our driveway."

It was a long red convertible with tail fins. Rosemary patted it as she got out. Claudia bent to polish the insignia on its hood with a kerchief. Annie and Victoria tried not to laugh.

"Well, what do you think?" called Rosemary, still at the car.

"Come see it," Claudia waved excitedly toward them.

Annie groaned. "How much?" she asked as she got near the car.

"Five hundred," Rosemary replied proudly. "My graduation money from my grandparents."

"It's only got a hundred-thirty thousand miles on it," Claudia boasted.

"We've named it Sojourner Truth. We'll use it to give out pamphlets, take women to rallies, go to meetings in other cities."

Victoria regained her composure first. "It'll certainly be a trademark. I guess that means you've decided to stay with your graduate school plans."

"We've made a lot of decisions which we'll share with you. And," Rosemary continued, "we have a proposition for you. But first, I need Annie's opinion on Sojourner."

"Striking," Annie said evasively. "Red, even." She looked up at Rosemary. "A hundred-thirty thousand miles?"

"That's not too bad, is it?" Rosemary asked, looking like a kid who's done something wrong. "My parents' Volvo has a hundred-fifty thousand miles on it and it runs great."

"Maybe they rolled the odometer forward to impress you," Annie teased. "I don't know a lot about cars, Rosemary. Maybe it's okay. But I don't think you can expect it to last a long time."

"Then I just have one more favor to ask you." Annie found herself thinking that she hadn't known Rosemary knew how to look coy. "We can't figure how to put the top up."

"I'll take a look at it," Annie sighed patiently. "You go ahead in, I won't be long, I hope," Annie mumbled to Victoria.

The three graduates went inside. Rosemary fell despondently into a chair. "We'll never be able to survive in the real world," she concluded.

"Sure you will," Victoria assured her, moving to Rosemary and gingerly patting her arm.

"No we won't. I don't understand anything about it. I don't know the rules about fixing a car or buying a car. I wouldn't know how to look for an apartment without the University's help. I can't even think about someday looking for a job. What if one of us gets sick? How will the other ever take care of her and organize survival?"

"You're still hung over, Rose," Claudia suggested.

"I think you're right. One thing I've learned from Annie's friends is not to drink. Makes me depressed and sick. Yesterday was my last attempt to be part of the gang," Rosemary told them.

Claudia had been walking around the house. "I see you've already made your mark here, Vicky."

"I couldn't help it. I feel so at home here. In Anne's little toothpick house."

"Toothpick house?" Rosemary asked.

"You remember," Claudia said. "When you were little, didn't you ever try to build a house out of toothpicks? With Elmer's Glue all over your hands and probably a soggy mess of sticks after two hours? My mother could do it. She showed me one she built as a girl. Out of rough toothpicks my grandfather whittled as he carved a cane. Such little tiny breakable parts and it lasted, then, about thirty years. She still has it."

Victoria smiled. "When I first came here I thought, 'How can she live like this? Why don't the winds blow her away?' I guess she's the glue that held it together. I like to think with two of us it'll be even stronger."

"It sounds," Rosemary observed, "as if you'd like to stay here."

"If everything works out that way, yes, I would. I'd even like to take *my* graduation money and see if that would make a down payment on it. We could fix it up." The three smiled at one another, their eyes full of the promise of the future. "Shall we celebrate? Want a cup of tea?"

"What are we celebrating now?" Annie asked as she slammed in the back door.

"Our new car!" Claudia and Rosemary said together.

"I'm not sure why you're celebrating the damned thing."

"What's wrong with it?" Rosemary asked in a panicked voice.

"Nothing new that I know of. Except that the electric

button that's supposed to put the top up and down doesn't. I did it manually."

"Oh, no." Rosemary watched, horrified, as Annie cleaned blood and grease from her hands.

"Poor Anne," Victoria said, moving toward Annie at the sink. "Are you badly cut?"

"No. I'll recover. It's just a cut."

"Can't I help?" Victoria asked, looking helpless.

Annie's irritation seemed to disappear and she laughed. "If you really need to, my love. You can get me a bandaid and some antiseptic."

But Claudia was already coming from the bathroom with both. She'd quietly disappeared and now firmly rewashed Annie's hand and bandaged it. "Hey, you guys always leave your mail in the bathroom?" she said, handing two envelopes to Annie.

"Turkey told me at some point yesterday she'd brought the mail in and couldn't remember what she'd done with it," Annie said, slightly annoyed. "This is from the landlord, Vicky." They stood together reading the letter.

Claudia had moved to Rosemary who sat with her head in her hands at the kitchen table. "It'll be okay, Rosie. Honest it will."

"How? What will we ever do if it rains when we're using the car to get people—or worse, written material—anyplace?"

"Rosie, you wanted a convertible, but if I could offer a suggestion . . ." Rosemary looked pleadingly to Claudia. "Now that Annie's got the top up, we could keep it there."

Rosemary looked at Claudia in wonder. "What a great idea. What a soldier you'll make in the revolution." Greatly cheered, Rosemary went to Claudia and proudly placed her hands on her shoulders. "What a team we'll be. Me, the theoretician. Claudia the practician. I love you, my stolid, midwestern woman." She put her arms around the blushing Claudia.

Victoria and Annie looked at one another. "I wish he'd told me the price he wanted months ago. I'll never be able to afford this," Annie said, dejectedly. Victoria said nothing. But her eyes sparkled with hope as she comforted Annie. The teakettle whistled.

"Tea's ready, ladies," Victoria announced and soon led them all to the living room. When they were all settled she proposed a toast to Sojourner.

"And that's why we're here, women," Rosemary announced. "Buying a car was all part of it. We have a suggestion for your future. And ours."

"Leave it to Rosemary to plan our future," Annie said, only half-joking, still disheartened.

"You asked for help," Rosemary reminded her.

Annie surrendered on the legless couch, her legs spread, leaning forward. "Let's have it."

"Claudia and I were thinking about how hard it is for someone like Dusty or Turkey or me or any of us, to understand what's happening as we come out. It's as if no one has ever done it before. Claudia has studied every phase of heterosexual development, but not one word about lesbian growth. There are some books out there, but not many. We know nothing about what *we're* going through as lesbians. We don't even understand what we've *been* through when it's over. And we can't tell anyone else about it, because of our own ignorance and because it's not talked about. So the next woman who comes out is as much in the dark as we were.

"And we're coming out in the more sophisticated places in the world. Can you imagine what it's like for a kid in the midwest like Claudia, having those feelings like she had for her friend, and knowing no better than to deny them? Or being a poor woman who just doesn't *know* that she has a choice, that she can say no to men and babies?"

Victoria was pouring from the teapot again. Annie had leaned back and was listening intently.

"I'll get to the point," Rosemary said. "We'd like to develop some way to show other women that they're not the first ones this is happening to and that they do have some positive choices. It could take the form of a magazine, but nothing slick. Or maybe a newsletter. Or pictures—like the slides parents show when they get back from another country. Because we're *in* another country now. And our country has a history and a literature and even a language all its own. We have heroines and leaders we'll never even discover unless more of us begin to research like the women at *The Ladder* do. And we have to learn how to tell the people what we've learned. Then we'll know we are a country and a people and we'll be less lonely, we'll understand more, we'll be stronger."

The others sat in silence, staring at Rosemary. Finally, Annie said, "You ought to give speeches, lady."

"That was quite impressive, Rosemary," Victoria agreed.

Claudia grinned and bounced up. "What do you think? Want to work on a project like that with us?"

Annie and Victoria looked at one another. "Sure," said Annie.

"In fact," Victoria explained, "that's exactly what we want to do, too. We were talking, before you came, about how we wished we could reach out to women who are making a mess of their lives because they don't know what to do about their feelings about women. And how we wanted to educate them—and ourselves."

"And," Annie added, "Vicky couldn't think of a better life work."

"We'll be educators," Rosemary concluded, "however we decide to do it."

"What about money?" Annie asked.

"We talked a little about that," Claudia answered. "Rosemary and I will be in school and can still count on our parents. We can get part-time jobs if we need to. The project itself shouldn't take much money. But you two will still have to work to support yourselves."

"I could keep driving," Annie said. "It's not that bad a job if it's not your whole life. Though someday I will want something better."

"This is getting into the land of dreams," Rosemary interjected, "but if the Project becomes a success in some way—a book we can sell or a movie that earns us money—we might be able to make some sort of career of it, though that is almost beyond my imagination now. I'm thinking of changing my graduate major to business in case that should happen."

Victoria seemed about to burst. "I have some ideas too, Anne. I wanted to wait until I was more sure, but I think, with my graduation money, we might begin to look into buying the toothpick house. I'm certain a mortgage would be lower than what that man is charging you for rent and we wouldn't have to leave." She watched as Annie's face got pink and her eyes lit up. "If we could get our expenses down that way we could both work part-time to make ends meet. I saw a poster recruiting adult education teachers. I'm sure I could do that."

"You'd feel okay about using your money to buy the house?"

"Yes! It's what I've wanted!" Victoria answered.

Claudia bounced out of her chair again. "I'm so excited about all this opening up for us. And I feel so very lucky that we have the advantages we have so we're able to do it."

"We have a responsibility to use those advantages," Rosemary reminded them, "for the good of lesbians everywhere."

Annie looked suddenly disconsolate. "I wish Peg and Turkey would get turned on to this stuff."

"They may yet," Victoria soothed Annie.

Annie shook her head, pulling her hat over her eyes. "No," she mumbled, "I don't think so. Even Peg, who introduced me to feminism, she's scared of it. She'd rather just be a gym teacher. I think she'll keep going to meetings and readings and maybe someday marches too, but I don't see her sticking her neck out any farther than that. She wants to be comfortable. And I don't blame her. It's so damn uncomfortable being gay, that you take your comforts where you can get them. But, now, I'd sure like to expand the gay world beyond bars, so we *could* take our comfort a lot of places. And, Rosemary, I'd like to do it for all women, like you said, not just lesbians. Because then more women could see their choices and more women who want to come out could if they were freer to be themselves."

"We're agreed on the project, then," Rosemary concluded. "When do you want to start talking about what we're going to do and what the structure will be?"

"Want us to come to your rooms tomorrow evening?"

When Claudia nodded eagerly, Rosemary looked suspiciously at her. "Don't you trust Sojourner to get us out here again?"

Everyone laughed and got up to say goodbye. It was an excited, hopeful group that hugged goodnight. Annie stood leaning against the porch rail looking tiredly after the retreating Sojourner. Then she turned toward Victoria coming up the steps. "I get to keep you here with me, now, don't I, lady?" Annie said, pulling Victoria up to her and kissing her neck. "Got enough energy to walk to the beach?" she said into her neck, still kissing her.

"Annie, please stop," Victoria said weakly, "or we'll go straight to bed."

"Okay, okay. I really need the beach first to clear my head, you sexy woman."

$$\sim \ \sim \ \sim \ \sim \ \sim$$

The moon was large and round in the sky and they walked under it, hand in hand. At the water's edge they stopped.

"That was really nice of you, Vicky, to offer a down payment on the house."

"Would it be okay? I wouldn't want it to be all mine. We'd both be the owners and we could work it out financially in the long run."

"How did you know what I was thinking again, you witch?" Annie asked affectionately, turning to hold Victoria. "That would be important for me. To really know it belonged to both of us."

"I get excited every time I realize how well I do know you, Anne. And toothpick house could never not belong to you. It wouldn't be the same house."

They walked in silence for awhile, their arms around each other. It was clear enough for the sky to look crowded with stars.

"How do you think it will work out, this project?" Annie asked.

"I think it *will* become a life work. Maybe not always with Rosemary and Claudia, but always for me, and I hope for us."

"I think you're right. I've been waiting for something like this for a long time."

"I know, you've been a lost spirit, looking for a cause. Full of energy and talent and nowhere to use it."

Annie nodded in agreement, then turned back to look at

their home. "Do you still think it's a toothpick house?" she asked Victoria.

"It'll always be a toothpick house for me, Anne. But that doesn't mean I think it can be swept away, like in your dream. Listen. I can't even hear the foghorns. There's nothing for them to warn us about."

"To tell you the truth, except for that dream, I find the foghorns kind of comforting. They sound like home to me. I hope you're right."

"I know I'm right."

"How, my wise woman?" Annie teased, falling to her knees in jest before Victoria. She looked up and saw her lover's head half-crowned by the moon. The sight was strangely moving for Annie who stayed where she was, as if entranced.

"Come up here with me, silly."

Annie rose and stood touching Victoria, her eyes still on the moon. Victoria continued. "The house won't be swept away because we won't let it be. We'll take our four strong hands," and Victoria drew Annie around so they faced each other, taking her hands, "and we'll do what we must to make it solid. And then we'll bring our work into it. I can't think of a stronger cement, can you?"

"I guess it was my old house that was carried off by the tides. Toothpick house is yours too. You're what it needed all along."

"*We're* what it needed. Two women who found with each other what they want. And part of what we wanted was a home. We're rebuilding it around us."

Annie felt she ought to seal the important things they were saying somehow. Shyly, she put her arms around Victoria. Their bodies touched full length. As they kissed Annie drew as much of herself as she could summon into her lips and gave it all to Victoria, while Victoria poured as much of herself back into Annie. They felt so open to each other they ached and the flow from one to the other went on even as they moved apart. When they turned back toward their house, the moon sat directly on top of it, like a big pot of glue.

A few of the publications of
THE NAIAD PRESS, INC.
P.O. Box 10543 • Tallahassee, Florida 32302
Mail orders welcome. Please include 15% postage.

The Long Trail by Penny Hayes. A western novel. 248 pp.
ISBN 0-930044-76-2 — $8.95

Horizon of the Heart by Shelley Smith. A novel. 192 pp.
ISBN 0-930044-75-4 — $7.95

An Emergence of Green by Katherine V. Forrest. A novel.
288 pp. ISBN 0-930044-69-X — $8.95

The Lesbian Periodical Index edited by Clare Potter. 432 pp.
ISBN 0-930044-74-6 — $29.95

Desert of the Heart by Jane Rule. A novel. 224 pp.
ISBN 0-930044-73-8 — $7.95

Spring Forward/Fall Back by Sheila Ortiz Taylor. A novel.
288 pp. ISBN 0-930044-70-3 — $7.95

For Keeps by Elisabeth C. Nonas. A novel. 144 pp.
ISBN 0-930044-71-1 — $7.95

Torchlight to Valhalla by Gail Wilhelm. A novel. 128 pp.
ISBN 0-930044-68-1 — $7.95

Lesbian Nuns: Breaking Silence edited by Rosemary Curb and
Nancy Manahan. Autobiographies. 432 pp.
ISBN 0-930044-62-2 — $9.95
ISBN 0-930044-63-0 — $16.95

The Swashbuckler by Lee Lynch. A novel. 288 pp.
ISBN 0-930044-66-5 — $7.95

Misfortune's Friend by Sarah Aldridge. A novel. 320 pp.
ISBN 0-930044-67-3 — $7.95

A Studio of One's Own by Ann Stokes. Edited by Dolores
Klaich. Autobiography. 128 pp. ISBN 0-930044-64-9 — $7.95

Sex Variant Women in Literature by Jeannette Howard Foster.
Literary history. 448 pp. ISBN 0-930044-65-7 — $8.95

A Hot-Eyed Moderate by Jane Rule. Essays. 252 pp.
ISBN 0-930044-57-6 — $7.95
ISBN 0-930044-59-2 — $13.95

Inland Passage and Other Stories by Jane Rule. 288 pp.
ISBN 0-930044-56-8 — $7.95
ISBN 0-930044-58-4 — $13.95

We Too Are Drifting by Gale Wilhelm. A novel. 128 pp.
ISBN 0-930044-61-4 — $6.95

Amateur City by Katherine V. Forrest. A mystery novel. 224 pp.
ISBN 0-930044-55-X — $7.95

The Sophie Horowitz Story by Sarah Schulman. A novel. 176 pp.
ISBN 0-930044-54-1 — $7.95

The Young in One Another's Arms by Jane Rule. A novel.
224 pp. ISBN 0-930044-53-3 — $7.95

The Burnton Widows by Vicki P. McConnell. A mystery novel.
272 pp. ISBN 0-930044-52-5 — $7.95

Old Dyke Tales by Lee Lynch. Short stories. 224 pp.
ISBN 0-930044-51-7 — $7.95

Daughters of a Coral Dawn by Katherine V. Forrest. Science
fiction. 240 pp. ISBN 0-930044-50-9 — $7.95

The Price of Salt by Claire Morgan. A novel. 288 pp.
ISBN 0-930044-49-5 — $8.95

Against the Season by Jane Rule. A novel. 224 pp.
ISBN 0-930044-48-7 — $7.95

Lovers in the Present Afternoon by Kathleen Fleming. A novel.
288 pp. ISBN 0-930044-46-0 — $8.50

Toothpick House by Lee Lynch. A novel. 264 pp.
ISBN 0-930044-45-2 — $7.95

Madame Aurora by Sarah Aldridge. A novel. 256 pp.
ISBN 0-930044-44-4 ... $7.95

Curious Wine by Katherine V. Forrest. A novel. 176 pp.
ISBN 0-930044-43-6 ... $7.95

Black Lesbian in White America by Anita Cornwell. Short stories, essays, autobiography. 144 pp. ISBN 0-930044-41-X ... $7.50

Contract with the World by Jane Rule. A novel. 340 pp.
ISBN 0-930044-28-2 ... $7.95

Yantras of Womanlove by Tee A. Corinne. Photographs. 64 pp. ISBN 0-930044-30-4 ... $6.95

Mrs. Porter's Letter by Vicki P. McConnell. A mystery novel. 224 pp. ISBN 0-930044-29-0 ... $6.95

To the Cleveland Station by Carol Anne Douglas. A novel. 192 pp. ISBN 0-930044-27-4 ... $6.95

The Nesting Place by Sarah Aldridge. A novel. 224 pp.
ISBN 0-930044-26-6 ... $6.95

This Is Not for You by Jane Rule. A novel. 284 pp.
ISBN 0-930044-25-8 ... $7.95

Faultline by Sheila Ortiz Taylor. A novel. 140 pp.
ISBN 0-930044-24-X ... $6.95

The Lesbian in Literature by Barbara Grier. 3d ed. Foreword by Maida Tilchen. A comprehensive bibliography. 240 pp.
ISBN 0-930044-23-1 ... $7.95

Anna's Country by Elizabeth Lang. A novel. 208 pp.
ISBN 0-930044-19-3 ... $6.95

Prism by Valerie Taylor. A novel. 158 pp.
ISBN 0-930044-18-5 ... $6.95

Black Lesbians: An Annotated Bibliography compiled by J. R. Roberts. Foreword by Barbara Smith. 112 pp.
ISBN 0-930044-21-5 ... $5.95

The Marquise and the Novice by Victoria Ramstetter. A novel. 108 pp. ISBN 0-930044-16-9 ... $4.95

Labiaflowers by Tee A. Corinne. 40 pp.
ISBN 0-930044-20-7 ... $3.95

Outlander by Jane Rule. Short stories, essays. 207 pp.
ISBN 0-930044-17-7 ... $6.95

Sapphistry: The Book of Lesbian Sexuality by Pat Califia. 2nd edition, revised. 195 pp. ISBN 0-930044-47-9 ... $7.95

All True Lovers by Sarah Aldridge. A novel. 292 pp.
ISBN 0-930044-10-X ... $6.95

A Woman Appeared to Me by Renee Vivien. Translated by Jeannette H. Foster. A novel. xxxi, 65 pp.
ISBN 0-930044-06-1 ... $5.00

Cytherea's Breath by Sarah Aldridge. A novel. 240 pp.
ISBN 0-930044-02-9 ... $6.95

Tottie by Sarah Aldridge. A novel. 181 pp.
ISBN 0-930044-01-0 ... $6.95

The Latecomer by Sarah Aldridge. A novel. 107 pp.
ISBN 0-930044-00-2 ... $5.00

VOLUTE BOOKS

Journey to Fulfillment	by Valerie Taylor	$3.95
A World without Men	by Valerie Taylor	$3.95
Return to Lesbos	by Valerie Taylor	$3.95
Odd Girl Out	by Ann Bannon	$3.95
I Am a Woman	by Ann Bannon	$3.95
Women in the Shadows	by Ann Bannon	$3.95
Journey to a Woman	by Ann Bannon	$3.95
Beebo Brinker	by Ann Bannon	$3.95

These are just a few of the many Naiad Press titles. Please request a complete catalog! We encourage and welcome direct mail orders from individuals who have limited access to bookstores carrying our publications.